Praise for *Travelers Rest*

'A fine addition to the creepy hotel thriller genre . . . It says much of Morris's skill that he's able to keep us bewitched and beguiled in a topsy-turvy world with endless corridors, twisting stairs and Escher-like surroundings. The novel culminates in an almost operatic grand finale where past and present meet in a satisfying conclusion' *Independent*

'The writing is persuasive, the characters are rich, and there are moments of great emotional resonance. Should you choose to stay a while in Good Night, Idaho, then – unlike the Addisons – you won't regret it' *Guardian*

'A subtle, meticulous examination of strained relationships, the effects of isolation on the mind, and the persistent hold memory has over us . . . it exerts a powerful hold'
Financial Times

'Keith Lee Morris's prose has a hypnotic rhythm that perfectly captures the uncanny ambience' *SFX*

'The children's characters are well-sketched, the supernatural element is unsettling and the action has pace . . . he is certainly a rising star in the genre and one to watch for. So, if you like Stephen King-esque stories, don't bypass *Travelers Rest*!' *Fantasy Book Review*

'There's no ghouls here, no rotting women reaching out of bathtubs – just the town, the snow and an inexplicable evil leaking up from beneath the hotel's foundations. The prose is appropriately disorienting. His sentences are long and labyrinthine; they seem to reach up off the page, trying to drag the reader down into their depths . . . it's a stunning read – just not for reading late at night' *Sci-Fi Now*

'In *Travelers Rest* [Keith Lee Morris] creates an intriguing world, poses big questions, and gives us sentences that by themselves are worth the read. What happens, he asks, when the person who goes missing is yourself?'

Charlotte Rogan, author of the *New York Times* bestseller *The Lifeboat*

'Echoing the fantastic work of Shirley Jackson and Stephen King, *Travelers Rest* is both fiercely gripping and deeply unsettling, a perfect mixture of horror and fairy tale . . . a novel that pulls you in immediately and refuses to let you go'

Kevin Wilson, author of the *New York Times* bestseller *The Family Fang*

'It won't take long – a page, maybe two – before you feel wondrously disquieted by Keith Lee Morris's *Travelers Rest*. The novel traps its characters in the town of Good Night, Idaho, and the reader in its shaken snow globe of a world. The language dazzles and the circumstances chill and put this story in the good company of Stephen King's *The Shining*, Shirley Jackson's *The Haunting of Hill House*, and David Lynch's *Twin Peaks*. This book will earn Morris the wide readership he richly deserves'

Benjamin Percy, author of *The Dead Lands* and *Red Moon*

Keith Lee Morris is a professor of English and Creative Writing at Clemson University, South Carolina. His previous book, *The Dart League King*, was selected for the Barnes & Noble Discover Great New Writers programme. His work has appeared in numerous publications including *Tin House*, the *Southern Review* and *New England Review*.

TRAVELERS REST

KEITH LEE MORRIS

WEIDENFELD & NICOLSON

First published in Great Britain in 2016
by Weidenfeld & Nicolson

This paperback edition first published in 2016
by Weidenfeld & Nicolson
an imprint of the Orion Publishing Group Ltd
Carmelite House, 50 Victoria Embankment
London EC4Y 0DZ
An Hachette UK Company

1 3 5 7 9 10 8 6 4 2

A CIP catalogue record for this book is
available from the British Library.

ISBN (Mass Market Paperback) 978 1 780 22885 3
ISBN (eBook) 978 0 297 60896 7

Printed in Great Britain by Clays Ltd, St Ives plc

www.orionbooks.co.uk

For my mother and father, about whom
I find something new to appreciate every day

A moment of the past, did I say? Was it not perhaps very much more: something that, common both to the past and to the present, is much more essential than either of them?

—Marcel Proust, *Remembrance of Things Past*

PART I

MOVABLE THINGS

Perhaps the immobility of the things that surround us is forced upon them by our conviction that they are themselves, and not anything else, and by the immobility of our conceptions of them. For it always happened that when I awoke like this, and my mind struggled in an unsuccessful attempt to discover where I was, everything would be moving round me through the darkness: things, places, years.

—Marcel Proust, *Remembrance of Things Past*

1

It was snowing. The storm had started as soon as they crossed the Cascades from Seattle, and now, here in what his dad called the Idaho panhandle, Dewey looked out from the backseat at the snow sweeping over the interstate in huge white gusts, covering everything in sight. His dad held on to the steering wheel at ten and two, which meant the weather was bad. His dad had grown up in this part of the country—well, Seattle, anyway—but now they lived in South Carolina and he wasn't used to driving in the snow. And it would be getting dark soon.

Uncle Robbie, who sat with Dewey in back, tried to ease the tension by showing how to play the armpit trombone, an instrument he claimed he could use to perform the song "Camptown Races" in its entirety, verses and chorus, and which he proceeded to demonstrate, sort of. It sounded like a long series of farts, and Dewey, age ten, found this highly amusing. His mother, smiling just slightly in the front seat as she looked dreamily out the window, seemed to find it somewhat amusing. His father not at all. His father never found much of anything about Uncle Robbie—who was more than a decade younger than Dewey's father and who was coming to stay with them in Charleston for a while as part of his court-ordered rehabilitation program—amusing at all. His dad probably wished now that they'd decided to fly instead of taking the car. The plan had been to travel at a leisurely pace, get a good look at the country.

No one said anything for a while and Dewey gazed out the window. It was a pretty area, with a river running along the highway and evergreens, white with snow, covering the hills. They passed a sign, exit 70, for a town called Good Night. It seemed like a funny name for a town in Idaho. Or anyplace, for that matter.

His mother had also noticed the sign. She quit staring out the window and looked over at his dad. "Might as well be here as anywhere," she said.

His dad opened his mouth and squinted his eyes up tight. "We're thinking of stopping?" he said. He fumbled around the console for his glasses, which he wore only when he needed to see something clearly, which he claimed wasn't often. He put the glasses on and leaned in toward the windshield and looked at the sky. "I don't guess this is going to get better anytime soon," he said.

"It's fine with me if we stop," his mother said. She was the sort of person who was usually fine with things. "In fact the snow makes me nervous—I'd *rather* stop."

Dewey knew his father well enough to understand that he was probably trying to decide whether to argue. He wouldn't want to admit to himself that he'd been forced off the road by the snow, especially after all the times he'd made fun of drivers back home who, he said, couldn't even drive in the rain. A few moments passed. A huge pickup truck roared by them in the left lane, snow spinning up from the tires. His father sighed. "All right," he said.

They pulled off at the exit, the car sliding a little bit on the ramp, his father's knuckles ridged on the steering wheel. They turned onto a quiet, winding road with no traffic. His mom used her cell phone to find the town on the Internet. "This place sounds familiar," she said. "Good Night, Idaho. I've heard of this place. It's not the kind of name you forget."

His father smiled but didn't take his eyes off the road. "You always say that. You always think you've heard of someplace."

His mother ignored him and held out her phone for Dewey and Uncle Robbie in the backseat. "Here, see? It's an old mining town," she said. "It seems like a nice place. Look, they have a beautiful old hotel." On the screen was the small image of an old brick building taller than any other building in the town, though that wasn't saying much, even Dewey knew. His mother showed it to his dad.

"That does seem nice," he said.

"I'm glad we're staying," she said. "This can be like a little adventure along the way. It'll be a good way to start off the new year." It was January 2. Dewey had to be back at school in four days.

His father adjusted his glasses and leaned forward to squint out the windshield at the falling snow, which seemed to be coming down harder every minute. "Exactly what I was thinking," he said, in that flat tone where you couldn't tell if he was being sarcastic.

"That's what I hate about the interstate," his mother said. "You just drive and drive and pass right by interesting places like this one." She turned and smiled brightly at Dewey and Robbie. "You'd never even know they were here."

2

The sign on the outside of the old hotel identified it as the Travelers Rest. Julia Addison, advancing carefully in her slick shoes on the snowy sidewalk, holding on to her son Dewey's hand to keep from falling, paused for a moment and considered—something wasn't right about the name. As punctuated, it amounted to a bland statement of fact—yes, travelers rested. All people did, eventually. Maybe they had forgotten a comma and exclamation point—it was intended to be a command: Travelers, rest! Or maybe just an apostrophe—Travelers' Rest—which she decided was the nicest way to think about it: this place *belonged* to the travelers, and offered them rest.

Dewey pulled on her hand and they went up the marble steps to the hotel entrance and she held open the door for her brother-in-law, Robbie, and her husband, Tonio, who were lugging the suitcases. She was the last to step inside the door and she was busy brushing snow off her coat sleeves and her hair when she heard a voice that brought her up sharply, made her heart beat fast. Maybe she was still out of breath—they'd had to park the car at the bottom of a hill and walk up the town's main street to the hotel. But she heard the voice again—"Welcome to Travelers Rest"—and again her pulse quickened.

The voice belonged to an odd-looking man with a large nose and a thick mustache who stood behind a desk to the left of the entrance, and she couldn't figure out why his voice would affect her that way—if anything, his appearance was much more startling. His nose was so large and his mustache was so bushy that he almost had no eyes, no chin, and he wore a dusty black hat with a wide brim that seemed designed to trap the chaotic mass of brown hair curling around his ears and neckline. His clothes—a striped, tight-fitting vest over a heavy shirt worn thin at the elbows, pants of a loose, shiny material with rolled cuffs, boots that appeared to be covered in soot or ash—and his stiff gait as he moved across the room made him look as if he'd been stored in a crate of mothballs and tipped up onto his feet just moments before their arrival. She felt, more than anything, a temptation to sneeze.

While Tonio asked about a room, she got her bearings and surveyed the hotel's interior. The first impression was one of disorder. In the dim and rather dusty light of the lobby she saw ladders and toolboxes and paint cans and drop cloths and sawhorses—clearly the place was under renovation. Maybe the hotel wasn't even open, and they wouldn't be staying here after all. That would be disappointing. Why? She studied the room more closely. An enormous fireplace that, if it had contained a roaring fire, would have dispelled every shred of the hotel's gloom. Beautiful old gas lamps on the walls, tasteful (although awfully faded) wallpaper, elaborate moldings in the corners of the room, a high ceiling with a breathtaking chandelier that spanned almost half the lobby, a grand wooden staircase ascending to a second-floor landing, solid overstuffed chairs (Dewey was sitting in one of them and wiping dust from the arm), a huge circular ottoman directly beneath the chandelier. It must have been a stunningly opulent place at one time—what could it possibly be doing in this little town? Who would have built a hotel like this here? She hadn't spent much time in fancy hotels, but she had a sharply tuned aesthetic sense, and that sense told her now that she was in a remarkable place, or at least a place that had once been remarkable.

She stood gazing out the front windows at the snow flying past outside. Tonio was still talking, going on in the slightly nasal voice that he used when he lectured his anthropology students. She didn't pay any attention to what he was saying. Robbie had discovered, of all things, a monocle lying around somewhere. He placed it over his right eye and marched around the room with a military air, his hands clasped behind his back, a stern expression on his face, as if he were considering weighty matters. He bumped into the furniture, staged pratfalls over the armchairs and end tables. Dewey, of course, found this wildly entertaining. She stood looking out the windows.

And then she had a funny feeling. Her mind felt white with snow, cold and pleasantly numb, and something began to form behind her vision—not exactly a memory, not exactly a dream. From somewhere she heard voices and music, lilting strings, a waltz rhythm. She had the feeling that if she turned around she would have already known exactly what was behind her, the ballroom, the dancers, the string quartet, the strange man peering out of his little eyes at the proceedings, twirling the ends of his mustache. The hotel must be hosting some gala event, some elaborate banquet from bygone days, something she never could have expected when she chose to stop here, but which she seemed somehow to have anticipated, and which now she couldn't wait to see. She could almost feel herself dancing, flowing across some huge open space. She began to say something to Tonio over her shoulder and as she turned…there it was. Through a pair of stately French doors with old, warped glass panes, a massive room with a parquet floor and curtainless floor-to-ceiling windows facing onto a snowy street. It was a ballroom, it had to be. But there were no people, nobody there, as if they'd all vanished in a heartbeat. It must have been a recording, music they played over speakers hidden somewhere, but whatever it was, it had stopped. She stepped lightly toward the doors, imagined them swinging open before her, allowing her entry, and again it was as if she heard something, saw something. Was it some movie she was remembering?

Suddenly Tonio was next to her, ready to make his report. "That's the owner," he said. "He's nuts."

She glanced over Tonio's shoulder. There the owner stood, firm and upright, hands behind his back, a welcoming smile creasing his cheeks behind the mustache. His smile seemed intended only for her, as if the two of them understood something no one else could.

"Why?" she said. "Is the room too expensive?"

Tonio grunted. "Too *expensive*? No, the rate's plenty cheap. In fact, he seems reluctant to let me pay him at all. He won't take a credit card."

"Then what's the problem?" she said.

"What's the *problem*? Look at this place."

"It's amazing," she said.

"Yeah," he said, "as, like, an archaeological specimen, maybe. He says the storm knocked out the electricity. He can't promise there'll be any heat. The place looks like it was hit by a fucking tornado."

She walked slowly back across the room, toward Dewey and Robbie at the front entrance. Old photographs lined the walls, one of them an image straight from her thoughts, from the vision in the back of her head—it was the lobby full of people, dressed for the ball, coat and tails, satin dresses, all smiling, all toasting the camera with glasses of champagne. In faded ink, under the photograph, it said "January, 1886, Travelers Rest." Next to that picture was another one, an exterior shot of the burned-out husk of a hotel, and underneath it had the same caption, "January, 1886, Travelers Rest." One of them must have been wrong.

"But he'll let us have a room," she said.

"He'll give us a *suite,*" Tonio said. "But get this—we're the only guests. It's pretty weird. Don't you think Dewey would be happier if we drove on and found—I don't know—a Comfort Inn? There's always a Comfort Inn."

The light in the lobby had grown even fainter. Dewey was quiet, slumped down in one of the oversized chairs. Robbie stood at the window, still wearing the monocle over his right eye. It almost looked like it belonged there.

"You go on to the Comfort Inn if you want to," she said. "I'm staying here."

3

Robbie Addison had been awake for hours, had not gone to sleep the whole time, not at all, that buzzing or crinkling in his fingers, that spot at the base of his spine where it felt like something clutched or clawed, some creature trapped in the mattress... looking up through the gap in the ancient curtains he could see the twirling flakes of snow, dazzling and hypnotic, yet even they could not induce sleep.

There were no clocks in the hotel room, but his internal clock, which was pretty finely tuned to closing time, suggested that it was about 1 a.m. He lay on his back and stared at the snow and concentrated on what he could hear. High in the air there seemed to be a ringing, but it was true that that might have been in his head. There was another sound, like a vacuum, like something taking *away* sound, sucking sound out of the room, converting it to negative space—that had to be, what, the wind? The heating vents? Did this old barn of a hotel even have central heat? He could hear also, now that he concentrated, the sound of Tonio's snoring, and he tried hard to tell, straining his senses outward, whether the door to Tonio and Julia's room was closed. Could you tell, if you tried to picture it hard enough, whether Julia's eyes were open, whether she too was awake and hearing Tonio snore? No, you couldn't.

After a minute he set aside the covers, the heavy quilt, and swung his legs over the side of the bed. His arms, propped on the mattress, began to shake. He ran one hand through his unruly hair and he squinted and bared his teeth and very cautiously stood up with no noise but the cracking of one knee, the one with the cartilage damage from his old basketball days. He took two steps across the hardwood floor—gingerly, but he could see right away that it was no use. The floor groaning, creaking—they would hear him or they wouldn't. He didn't know much about the sleeping habits of his brother's family. Was Dewey likely to wake up?

He slipped into his jeans and he felt around on the cold floor until he located his wool socks and he eased back down onto the bed and got the socks pulled on and he grabbed his boots to carry.

He had no idea where to find his coat. Standing in the doorway to his room in the suite, he could make out the entryway that led to the hall and the stairs, but there was a myriad of closet doors and he couldn't go around opening them all to find his coat. He'd have to make do with the T-shirt and long johns undershirt he'd worn to bed.

He stepped out into the area between his room and Tonio's, the goddamn floor groaning at every step. If someone—Julia, not Tonio, he could still hear Tonio snoring—called out to him now, said *Robbie?* He could say he was using the bathroom, but no, he had the boots in his hand. Going outside for a smoke. But his cigarettes were in his coat. He could say he'd thought they were in his pants pocket. So he walked toward the door quickly, no sense in being secretive, and he took in the fact that Dewey was asleep there on the large sofa in the main room, and he was within maybe three steps of the door when he made out in the faint light, on top of a small end table, what appeared to be Tonio's wallet and keys. He hadn't thought—really, he would never have suspected—that Tonio could be that dumb.

Certainly, of course, there was a second where he asked himself, where he talked to himself like this—*Now Robbie, Tonio is your brother and he came all the way out here to "help" you, and you like Julia, don't you, and what about Dewey, great kid, and what about their disappointment, think about Julia and how she'll have to try to make excuses for you again*—but he'd already spent half his life disappointing people so now it didn't stop him long. He stepped over as lightly as possible and carefully, very carefully separated the wallet from the keys—the keys were of no use to him—and unfolded the wallet and took out a few—no, all—of the bills. Tonio had credit cards. Tonio would be fine.

He walked out of the room and down the creaky stairs and still no one interrupted him. At the bottom of the stairs he paused with his hand on the banister and surveyed the old, ghostly hotel lobby. Ladders, sawhorses, band saws, planks, bags of nails, God knew what all, you couldn't see it very well in the dark—had to be a violation of every safety code imaginable. But the lobby itself—you could see how this must have been a pretty impressive place back in the day. Not that it interested him much. He exhaled slowly, and he told himself to consider the things they'd talked about in rehab, and he did consider them, but not in the way they would have wanted him to. What he'd heard them say over and over was that an addict could never get better until he wanted to get better, and that to want to get better you had to hit bottom, you had to see yourself as the lowest of the low. That was a comforting thought for Robbie, because he wasn't anywhere near the bottom yet. There were a whole lot of depths left to sink to.

The heavy front door to the hotel was unlocked, and that was a good thing, he could get back in if he wanted to. But he knew he wouldn't. He struggled into his boots and went outside and shut the door behind him. The air was sharp, intense, the wind a bit more bracing than he had allowed for. But there across the street was the oasis he'd spotted right from the first, when they were walking up the hill with the suitcases. It was a bar called the Miner's Hat, lit in the circle of a yellow streetlight, neon signs buzzing in the window, the snow flying round it in waves that accompanied the thump of a bass guitar coming from inside the door.

The street was deserted except for a couple of cars parked near the entrance. Robbie crossed slowly, still aware that Tonio or Julia or Dewey could be watching from the window—wouldn't do to be in a hurry. The snow in the street was already more than a foot deep. They'd have to call out the plows. Everything was utterly quiet. Pine trees stabbed the white sky on the tightly bunched hills. As he made his way across the street, he heard the click of the town's one traffic light, and it switched from red to green. Go. There was the oasis, the bar, the bad music, the awful cover band. He tipped his head back, opened his mouth, closed his eyes, tasted the snow on his tongue and felt it on his eyelids. Then he opened his eyes and went across the street and blew on his stinging hands and reached for the door. Inside were the drunks and the losers and the beautiful loud noise—he could find every comfort he wanted here.

4

For the longest time after she saw the door across the street shut behind him she sat very still on some cushions in a little bay window, looking out at the snow.

She had never seen it snow so hard in her life. She and Tonio and Dewey lived now in Charleston, South Carolina, or just outside Charleston, South Carolina, in a community called Mount Pleasant, and she had grown up mostly in California, in a succession of sunny beachside towns, so her knowledge and experience of snow were by no means extensive. Still, she had never seen it snow so hard in her life.

The snow fell rapidly, flakes spinning down in the light, and if she stared hard enough she felt as if she were in a boat moving on waves. Down and down it came, more and more, the wind whisking it along in what seemed like prearranged patterns, as if it were a show prepared just for her. In fact it all felt that way, everything, from the time they'd turned off the interstate. The discovery of the quaint hotel, the snow flying down while they trudged up the walk, the sign on the door, the dusty, dim light of the lobby, the strangely arresting voice of the proprietor, the voices and music she had heard and almost felt she remembered—all of it seemed as if it were a story being told to her and her alone, in a high whisper.

She loved this old hotel. She wouldn't mind staying another night, and another, if the storm continued.

It would be better, maybe, if Tonio weren't here, because Tonio had a way of interfering. But definitely not if Robbie weren't here, in which case it would feel like nothing important was happening. This was a horrible way to think, a horrible thing to realize, downright awful in a karmic sense, a feeling for which you'd have to do a lot of atoning, but she knew that and was prepared for it. She had a peculiar ability to be honest with herself.

The feeling about Robbie wasn't sexual, or not so much, or at least it wasn't the main thing. She wasn't afraid of it, and she knew that, if it ever surfaced, that feeling, in a sexual way, it wouldn't necessarily be better than what she had with Tonio, which was at least comfortable and uninhibited. And the sex thing with Robbie didn't matter because she wouldn't let it happen anyway.

So it wasn't that, not really. So what was it? What made her want to defend him?

The first time she met Robbie was after she'd already married Tonio. They'd driven up the coast to visit Tonio's parents in Seattle. And it wasn't that Tonio's parents weren't nice and gracious and hospitable, etc., because they were, and it wasn't that Tonio was boring, because he wasn't, he was one of the smartest people she'd ever known, and she'd known a lot of people, and a whole lot of them thought they were pretty smart. No, it was just the color and movement that caught her eye, there through the window, out past the garden with all the pretty rosebushes.

She had known somehow that he was the brother, even though no one had said a word about him or paid any attention to him out there. She excused herself to go roam around—they were talking about politics, probably, it was an election year, Bush versus Gore. Tonio's father was an appellate court judge. She walked out past the rosebushes, beyond the unruly dandelions and clover that cropped up by the property's edge. The Addisons lived in one of the more desirable areas of Madison Park, and off behind the house you could look across Lake Union toward Mount Rainier. Robbie was busy building a fence, carefully hammering one slat at a time, standing and hammering, kneeling and hammering, grab a new slat, stand and hammer, kneel and hammer, the movements rapid and graceful in a way she'd never seen Tonio move, with his dangling arms and hunched shoulders.

"Why would you put a fence here?" she asked. Each new slat further obstructed the view across the water.

He wore a red T-shirt and a pair of long khaki shorts frayed at the ends and he was working barefoot. He stopped and examined her for a second. "Why?" he said. He turned around and swept his hair away from his eyes and looked down the hill and hitched up his shorts. "I guess because they care more about the stray dogs that come in the garden than they do about the view." He stood there with his mouth open looking at her until she started wondering if he was stupid, if Tonio had gotten whatever brains there were to be had in the gene pool and poor Robbie had just gotten handyman skills. And then she realized what was happening—he had no idea who she was or why she was there in the yard talking to him.

It made her laugh. "I'm your sister-in-law," she said. "I'm Julia."

And she could go back to that one moment. Until that one moment there really wasn't anything all that unusual. She had looked out the window. She had seen him in his red shirt working on the fence. He had long brown hair then, so thick that it looked like some kind of pelt he had to keep displacing to the side of his head—but it hadn't mattered how he looked. She had been aware of how she looked herself, a tiny thing there in the grass, all of five foot two, weighing in at about a hundred pounds, no breasts no hips no curves to speak of. What she understood then, for maybe the first time, was that it was her *eyes* that held men's attention. She could feel them there in her head, staring out at him, warm and big and brown. Robbie was seventeen then. She was twenty-five.

She had always believed strongly in a spirit world, in the idea that nature was animated in a way she could never quite understand or see, but never very strongly in God, who, if he existed, didn't seem to be much good for anything. And she had always believed in fate, that there was some place she was destined to end up, and from the beginning, she had felt that Robbie had something to do with that place. But why? Because she and Robbie were alike? Her mother had been a late-blooming flower child, and she had raised her daughters around people who claimed to be enlightened, to have tapped into some higher consciousness, but who were really just losers and hypocrites and fools. At times, when things went sour at a moment's notice, they'd had to live in abandoned cabins or tents or vans or even other people's garages—she was used to that. She was used to screwups like Robbie. And there was something she didn't trust about people who did everything right, or something she didn't trust, when in the presence of people who did everything right, about herself.

But if there was such a thing as fate, if there was some place, some moment she was destined to travel toward, she believed strongly that it was her job to get herself there. Robbie could and should take care of himself. A grown man, a thirty-year-old man, who'd never had a steady job, who had dropped out of college *four times*. She had never had the chance to go to college *once*.

She could just picture him over there in the bar. He'd be everyone's best friend in about five minutes. Good God, you'd think he'd learn. That's why they were out here, collecting Robbie after yet another stay in rehab with a bunch of other spoiled rich kid degenerates, privileged people who couldn't control the one thing in the world you had the capacity to control—yourself. She'd had a difficult childhood and didn't feel much sympathy.

The thing to do right now was wake up Tonio. He would be over there in no time hustling Robbie back out into the snow, bringing him back to bed, and they could get on the road in the morning. But then he would see that they had power across the street, and she'd never hear the end of it. And also she wanted to believe—against all evidence—that Robbie could manage on his own. Maybe he was over there having a cheeseburger. Maybe he'd have a beer for a nightcap and then she'd see him wander leisurely back across the road.

Everything was dark and quiet behind her in the hotel room—Tonio was done with his snoring, even—and the snow beyond the window fell so steadily that she couldn't imagine it stopping. She tried to think of their house in Mount Pleasant, the row of azaleas to the side of the front door, the oak tree in the yard, Dewey bouncing a basketball in the driveway. She tried to think of the places where she'd spent her childhood, in California, the house with the pool where they'd crashed for a while, the bus she used to take to the boardwalk in Santa Cruz. None of it was there, not anywhere in her head, just this window framing the snow, her place tucked right here inside it, as if she were wound into a snow cocoon. Then something in her loosened, and she felt very sleepy suddenly, and she leaned her head against the cold damp windowpane, and with her ear against the glass she heard the tiny hiss of snow, like faint radio static, sticking to the windowsill.

5

A re you going to finish that?" he asked Dewey, pointing at a half-eaten strip of bacon.

Dewey considered it, wanted to eat it, of course, to *claim* it at least—*my bacon*—but he had stuffed himself silly with pancakes, Tonio knew.

"All right?" Tonio said, reaching over to Dewey's plate, and Dewey nodded reluctantly.

He ate the cold, gristly bacon, sipped his weak coffee, the waitress brought the bill. He looked out the window through the falling snow—*Jesus* what a storm—and tried to figure out which window on the hotel's face was his. It was an extraordinary old place, really. Check out the window lattices, the cornices, the marble steps. It was like an old, sepia-toned photograph, a reminder of bygone days. Maybe Julia was right: Good Night, Idaho—it had a familiar ring to it.

"Dad," Dewey said, "are you a degenerate?"

Tonio wiped his mouth with a napkin and reached for his wallet. "Dooze," he said, "you don't know what that word means."

"Do too."

"Nope. Do not. Do you need to go to the restroom before we leave?"

They could leave real quick, provided Julia was up and ready. Hopefully Robbie was back in the room by now—where else would he be, for Christ's sake, except there in the room with Julia alone, which was exactly the situation he'd probably been trying to create from the outset, the asshole. When Robbie wasn't in the room in the morning, Tonio had figured that he'd be at the diner, but obviously not, he had probably gone out for a walk in the snow and was now there in the room chitchatting with good old Julia, shooting the breeze, ha ha ha Robbie you're so funny, such a card.

It would be rough out there on the interstate, but Tonio was ready to give it a try in the daylight, even though they'd be driving east, moving in the same direction as the storm. And the snow had to let up sometime.

"I know what it means," Dewey said.

"Dooze Man, you don't. You're ten years old. Let's go." He stood up first and waited for Dewey to follow suit and they walked up to the cash register near the front.

"I'll go," Dewey said, "but I do know."

"You might know the *definition* of the word," he said, "but you don't know what it *means*."

The cook was over at the grill and the waitress was who knew where. He searched around for a bell to ding. Dewey had his eye on the pie behind the glass counter, but Tonio could see the wheels were still turning. "That's what you call one of those other things you told me about. That other word."

"A paradox."

"Right. That's a paradox."

Tonio reached in his coat pocket for his glasses. "Okay," he said, "but not really."

"Anyway, I heard you talking about it before," Dewey said. "I just don't know if Uncle Robbie is one."

"Yeah, well, that's the sixty-four-thousand-dollar question." He put on the glasses and opened his wallet and…something not right. His wallet. His money. Wallet empty. "Son of a bitch," he said quietly.

"Don't kill the magic, Dad," Dewey said. This was just one of their funny little expressions. There were others.

"Not killing the magic here, Dooze, not killing the magic." He put his hand up to his forehead and squeezed hard, closing his eyes. When he opened them, he saw that Dewey had wandered over to the gumball machine. "You didn't happen to take any money out of Dad's wallet, did you, bud?"

"Nope," Dewey said. "Can I have a quarter?"

He fished in his pocket and found one and tossed it and Dewey caught it. He had excellent coordination for a ten-year-old. People were always remarking on it.

"Sure about that, Dooze?"

"Yep."

The guy behind the counter stared at them. He had stubbly hair and bloodshot eyes and he appeared to be clenching a guitar pick between his teeth. Tonio smiled and handed over a credit card.

So he hadn't left this morning at all. It had been last night. He had gotten up during the night and stolen all the money, and if he hadn't reappeared by now it was likely he wasn't going to. Tonio was relieved, actually. He pictured Robbie on a bus back to Portland, where he supposedly lived now when he wasn't mooching off their parents or drying out in detox. He would have spent most of the money on booze and drugs, but Tonio would bet that Robbie had just enough of his wits about him to slide out of whatever situation he'd gotten himself into with enough money left for bus fare.

Dewey asked him for another quarter.

"You don't need another quarter," he said.

"I do, Dad," Dewey said. "See? It's a game. The quarter makes the gumball go around…what would you call this thing?"

He looked over. "It's like a maze, or a labyrinth," he said.

"The quarter makes the gumball go around the maze or labyrinth."

Tonio reached in his pocket and tossed over another quarter. He shook his head and peered out at the snow falling, settling into drifts along the street. Well, he could just about kiss the idea of getting out of town today goodbye. Julia wasn't going to let him leave without at least trying to find out where Robbie had gone.

"You from out of town?" the guy behind the counter said.

Tonio looked at the buzz cut, the bloodshot eyes, the greasy T-shirt. "Wow," he said. "How'd you know?"

The guy gave him a twisted smile. "Lucky guess," he said. He looked at Dewey and at Tonio and back to Dewey again, and then handed Tonio his credit card. "We don't take these." Tonio stared at him for a second and then started to thumb through his wallet for another card. The guy held a hand up to stop him. "It's on me," he said.

6

The snow was two feet deep at least and piling up by the second and still no plow in sight. The world was absolutely silent when you observed it through the window, the silent wind blowing hard through the treetops, the snow cascading from the branches in a thick swirl that funneled into town. The entirety of heaven seemed bent on dumping snow on this little street.

"You guys in the market for a snowplow operator? Seriously," he said.

Some guy at the table laughed. "Kids aren't in school today," he said. "Nobody gives a shit."

Robbie took a sip from the beer can on the table. Warm and nasty. There was a keg around somewhere with cold beer. He was sure of it. And somebody had a bottle of something. He could tell by the thick taste on his tongue.

Near as he could figure he was in the back room of a bar or store or restaurant. The place was obviously closed right now, so one of the people at the table must have had a key. Again he looked out the window and took a deep breath and watched the snow fly in great buzzing sheets. His teeth hurt. Why? No telling. All right all right all right. Where were we, he wondered, where were we now? We were in a town off the interstate in Idaho. It was snowing like a motherfucker, and the wind was blowing like a motherfucker, too. He was with Tonio and Julia and Dewey, on the way to South Carolina, where they would all have a cheery family visit. And that crazy hotel, where the owner had given them a fistful of candles and sent them to their room. Jesus. He remembered showing the Dooze Man card tricks by candlelight—I, the amazing Fartamundo, hold the very card you selected right here in my hand. Then he'd been lying in bed and he'd been thinking or dreaming of Julia and then he'd started wanting a drink so bad it made him itch and hurt. And then, right, the money. Damn. And they were supposed to be on the road again now and they would be looking for him, that unreliable irresponsible son of a bitching Robbie, who'd gone and fucked everything up again. Should have known. Should have planned ahead for it. He could see Tonio seething, fuming, apoplectic, blood exploding from his eyeballs. That's what you got for being the levelheaded sibling, the college professor, the professional douche bag.

Well.

"Did I sleep here?" he said. "Where'd I sleep?"

One of the guys at the table pointed to a booth against the wall.

"Ooof," Robbie said. More laughter.

Okay, now—what was the situation, what were the possibilities. Around the table sat six guys—all younger than Robbie except maybe the one guy who talked about the snowplow—and two women, the brunette clearly with the big blond guy with the buck teeth and the tiny ears—was he slightly mongoloid? The dude over there with the long hair, the glasses, he was the bass player in that god-awful band, good God how long would it take to get the sound of that shit out of his head. The blonde sitting next to Robbie was the bartender. She had nice tits, which was why he'd wandered over here with these people in the first place. It was all coming back to him. They weren't much of a bunch, but sometimes you had to work with what you had. Goodbye Tonio, goodbye Doozer, good-bye sweet Julia.

He pointed at the guy to his left, dude wearing a black cowboy hat, sideburns, jean jacket. "Glenn," he said. Glenn raised his beer can. Robbie went on around, pointing. "Tyler. Rusty. Cheryl. Ray. You," he said, "you call yourself Double Dog, for some reason. You," he said, "are Lance."

"Fuck, dude, that's awesome," Lance said. "How did you remember all that?"

"I'm a smart motherfucker," Robbie said. Someone opened him a beer and set the can in front of him. "What's on the agenda for today?"

"What about me?" the blonde said. "What's my name?"

"You're," he said, and pointed at her, not actually knowing her name while he pointed but trusting it would come to him when he opened his mouth, "Stephanie."

She smiled.

"Stephanie," he said, "scoot over here."

7

"Are you sure you've got all your things together?" she asked Dewey.

"How many times have you asked me?" Dewey said.

"Don't answer me like that," she said.

"Because that's how many times I'm sure," Dewey told her. "However many times you asked me."

She made one more dab with her lip gloss and dropped it and the hand mirror into the makeup bag and dropped the makeup bag into the suitcase and zipped the suitcase closed, pressing down vigorously on a pair of knee boots to get the zipper around.

"I don't even know why you're bothering," Tonio said. He looked out the window, scanning the street in either direction. It was still snowing. "It's almost ten already. Obviously we're not going anywhere today."

"Don't blame me," she said. "I tried to call him. It's not my fault my cell phone doesn't want to work here. Besides, he could show up any minute." She sat at the foot of the bed with her hands on her knees, as if she were ready to spring up, suitcase in hand, at a second's notice if Robbie suddenly materialized there in the doorway. By assuming that pose she could almost convince herself this was an actual possibility.

"That's ridiculous," Tonio said. "Where would he be if he were just going to show up all of a sudden?"

"Taking a walk," she said. "Getting something to eat."

"Oh, of course. How many diners do you see open out there, Dewey?" Dewey had gone over and joined Tonio at the window, examining the street the same as his father.

"I see one," Dewey said.

Tonio nodded. "That's the only one I see, too, big guy. Grand total of one diner. At least it has electricity. And who was not at that diner when we were there half an hour ago eating breakfast?"

"There were a *lot* of people not at that diner," Dewey said.

Tonio nodded. "Yeah, and one of them was Robbie," he said.

"You're right," Dewey said. "Robbie's a degenerate."

"Where does he get this stuff?" she asked. "You're *ten,*" she told him.

"But I have ears," he said. "I hear things."

Tonio moved away from the window and started pacing back and forth. "So clearly he stole my fucking money and went to that bar across the road." He put his hands in his jeans pockets and shrugged his shoulders and scowled at her, as if he was daring her to refute this. She felt perfectly calm.

"Excuse me?" she said, nodding toward Dewey, who now sat on the window ledge where she'd watched Robbie cross the street.

"Oh, right," Tonio said. "He stole my *frigging* money. He stole my *frigging* money, Dewey."

"I hear you, Dad," Dewey said.

"He stole my *frigging* money, the asshole, and he went to that bar and spent it, and from the looks of the few people who *were* at that diner, I'll bet one or two of them probably *helped* him spend it, but naturally they'd be on Robbie's side, everyone's always on Robbie's side, including you, because if you weren't you would just admit that what we ought to do is pack up and leave him." Tonio rocked on his heels, his mouth pooched up. "*If* he's still around here, which I doubt."

"Please," she said. "He's your brother. You're not just going to run off and leave him."

"Right," Tonio said. "Like he'd wait around for me."

"How are you so sure that's what happened to him?"

"Why? Do you know something I don't?"

"No," she said.

"Are you sure you don't know something I don't?" he said. "Because if it turns out you're covering up for him or making excuses for him in some way…" He tilted his head back subtly, and then he glanced over at Dewey to let her know what he wasn't saying, that this was it, the last straw, the one that broke the camel's back, blah blah, etc.

"Why would I do that?" she asked. She stared at him from the foot of the bed.

He kept his eyes locked on her for a second or two, then he looked down and away. "Come on, Dooze," he said. "Let's go see what the deal is with staying another night."

"Okay," Dewey said.

"Maybe if this town has a frigging store of some kind we can buy a frigging sled while we're at it."

"That'll be fun," Dewey said. "I bet they've got one. A store. There must be one somewhere."

They walked out and she heard them talking on the stairs. She unzipped the suitcase and started to unpack.

8

There was a bell on the desk and he held up Dewey by his armpits so he could ding it. No one came. There were no lights on anywhere and no noise of any kind. Outside the bank of windows at the front of the hotel, the snow flew as steadily as it had all night long.

Dewey pulled his bag of jacks out of his pocket and spread them on the floor in the lobby and bounced the red ball up and down.

"Don't do that here, Dooze," he said.

"Really?" Dewey said. There was no one around, nothing happening.

"No," he said, "not really. Go ahead."

"Cool," Dewey said. He appeared to be on his threes already.

He stood quietly at the desk and listened but he didn't hear anything and he peered through the doors behind the desk area and he walked over and looked into the huge empty room off the lobby. There was no one to be found anywhere. He walked back over to where his son sat on the floor.

"Hey," he said, "I'm going to walk outside for a second and see if I see anyone. Just stay right there."

"Okay," Dewey said.

He walked to the front entrance and turned back around. His

son was still sitting there, scooping up the jacks in his small hand. "Just stay there," he said again.

"Okay," Dewey said, without glancing up.

He opened the heavy front door and stepped into a swarm of snowflakes and turned to the right and headed up the sidewalk. The snow was two feet deep, easily, maybe more, and there were no prints in it. What the hell went on in this town, anyway? Who exactly lived here? He made it around the corner of the hotel into a narrow street or alleyway, still seeing nothing and nobody. There was only more snow and some wind. Moving up the alley, along the seemingly endless brick wall of the hotel, he spotted far ahead what appeared to be a doorway. The farther he went, the more the wind died down, and the snow fell in slow, lazy spirals, settling on his hair and the back of his neck inside his shirt collar. It seemed to him the alley grew narrower as it went along, the buildings slightly taller on either side, leaning in.

How far did it stretch? It began to seem impossibly long. On the way into town, he hadn't seen a street that this alley could belong to. Worse, he hadn't worn his boots, and his feet were getting cold. He knew from the sign at the city limits that there were close to a thousand residents. Where were they all, and why did they need a street this long anyway? Some distance ahead, dimly visible through the screen of snow, there seemed to be an opening. Was it the doorway he'd seen earlier?

He lowered his head against the falling snow and examined the alley from side to side to find the answer to a question he had in his mind suddenly, which was, he was a little scared to admit, *Why did I come out here?* He honestly couldn't remember. He couldn't say just right this moment. Dewey was on the floor playing jacks, they had been in a hotel lobby, and he had come out here…he had come out here searching for someone or something. What? That was going to take a moment. Meanwhile the snow kept falling. A white blur, the bricks of the buildings obscured on either side, so that the world appeared to be an ice tunnel. And still he found his feet moving him ahead. He wondered how long he'd been outside. He thought, *Hypothermia.* He had on just a thin jacket, and his arms were numb, and he had not worn a hat, and his face was frozen, and he had not worn his boots, so he slipped along ungracefully in his jogging shoes while the snow soaked through his socks.

It occurred to him to return to the hotel. He could see in his mind the hotel facade, as if it were a photograph. There were the marble steps, there the hanging sign above the wide doors: Travelers Rest. It would be right there if he turned around. He stopped and faced in the direction he had come. Looking back, he saw nothing but snow. How to describe this snow? It needed some investigating. He put on his glasses. *Columns* of snow, *pillars* of snow, *infinite rising whirlwinds* of snow that reached all the way to outer space. He'd never seen anything like it. And now he was just standing out here in it, and there had been Dewey…and he had come…he had…it was very cold. Something about the hotel. He knew of a place like this, a lost place, a place of lost time and people. He'd read about it somewhere—a journal article, maybe something a colleague had asked him to proof. A ghost town, a legend, a place of ceaseless snow, searing heat, inundating rains, all manner of extremes. He had laughed at it, the flimsy research, the fairy-tale nature of the whole proposition, like something written by a child. Now he was here in the middle of it, a fantasy, a dream, nothing but the cold wind and the dull clouds and the emptiness.

Up ahead, a door opened. The only sounds were his own feet squeaking in the snow and that vague hissing, the sound the snow brought down from the far reaches of the universe. A face appeared in the open doorway. Quickly the face was averted from him, and he saw a figure, a woman, wrapped in a long coat and a scarf, her blonde hair pinned up, hunching her shoulders and moving away.

A blonde woman in a long, dark coat, rather stunning there in the middle of the snowy street. He remembered the hotel now—Julia, Dewey, Robbie. Back in that direction he could see very faintly, like the barest outline in watercolor, the corner he'd come around from the hotel entrance. He took off his glasses and wiped the wet lenses on his shirt and put the glasses on again.

He followed the woman and caught her by the arm. She turned and he thought at first that he recognized her, that she was someone he knew.

She smiled at him, a little wearily. "I didn't expect to see you here," she said. Her breath was an icy, crystal swirl, her words almost settling on him physically. He felt heavy, weighed down by something in her face that seemed terribly sad. "I'll go on," she said, "but I don't think it's any use."

He wanted to say something to her, to console her, to offer her a smile and perhaps pat her shoulder gently, and at the thought of it something moved deep within him, something he almost couldn't trace, it seemed so many miles away, and he was so *tired* suddenly.

The woman's blue eyes stayed on him as she moved up the alley, so delicate and light that the little silver shoes on her feet sifted through the snow without making any impression. He watched her move away until she dissolved in the thick veil of snow and he turned to go in the door from which she had come. He swept away the snow at its base but then discovered that it opened inward. For a frantic moment, when he first pushed on it, the door appeared to be locked, but when he shoved harder it gave way, and as he stepped forward he felt he was moving into nothing, a vast hollow space both light and dark, like a world of snow that you watched with your eyes closed.

9

As far as she could tell, everything in the room was antique. All the furniture had a heavy, brooding feel. The deep chest of drawers seemed filled with darkness, and there was a label in it that showed it had been made in Philadelphia, Olson Brothers, 1885. The mirror on the dresser was cloudy like mother-of-pearl, the light in the room a hard, waxy yellow. It was a sober and serious room, and sometimes she loved things that were sober and serious, which was probably how she got mixed up with Tonio in the first place. The room was sober and serious like the tree-lined hills out the window in the falling snow and the black mine shafts she knew tunneled down into those hills from a long time ago. If she tried hard she could almost feel herself going down into them, feel herself bottoming out, as if someone had scraped her empty. Some elusive connection to this place, something she couldn't put her finger on just yet. She hoped they would stay a few days, that the heaps of snow in the street would turn truly mountainous, that the wind would blow unceasingly. Who knew? Robbie might even turn up again.

She hung her clothes back in the closet and put Dewey's things in a drawer and left Tonio's clothes for him to put away himself. She lay down on the bed. It had been almost an hour since Tonio and Dewey left for the lobby. For the first half hour she hadn't been concerned at all, probably because they'd mentioned buying a sled, although she hoped Tonio would have enough common sense to come back to the room and put on their boots and warm coats before they went out to find a sledding hill. There was no sound at all, anywhere, except for the creaking of the old hotel. After a while it was too much for her. In what she guessed you'd call the sitting room, there was a TV, an old wooden console, and though she seriously doubted it would work, she turned the knob anyway. And something did come on. It was like the old days with the rabbit ears, like when she was a girl in San Diego, Lompoc, Modesto, Mount Shasta, Eureka, Monterey, Santa Cruz—so many places. The picture was obscured by snow and there was no sound, and whatever was on didn't look like a show from any regular broadcast or station. It consisted primarily of hazy figures moving in vague, languid patterns, as if they were slow dancing, or sleepwalking, she couldn't tell. It occurred to her that it would probably be a good idea to go find Tonio and Dewey.

Something passed by in the hallway and she turned and saw Robbie there—Robbie, plain as day. By the time she got to the doorway she could see only his feet—she felt certain those were his boots—going up the stairs. Without saying anything she followed.

When she reached the third-floor landing Robbie was nowhere in sight. It didn't seem to matter much for some reason. It was just like Robbie to saunter past when everyone was looking for him and then disappear again. The Addisons were a peculiar bunch. Inarguably, being part of the family conferred privileges; when you wanted to buy a car, a house, a small tropical island, maybe, there were the Addisons, checkbook at the ready—any amount of money was fine, just so long as you didn't ask them for an emotional response to anything. But they were definitely eccentric, possibly a little bit insane, and certainly exasperating, every last one of them, Robbie included. She didn't really believe in God, but she did believe in the idea of penance, and she was ready to accept the Addison family as an elaborate form of it, but still—they were getting on her nerves. She'd take one good look around for Robbie, but that was it.

Obviously the third floor had not been renovated—there were holes in the walls and holes in the planks of the ceiling and in one place she could see all the way up through the fourth floor and the roof. Only one door in the hall stood open, and she found herself in the doorway, room 306. She stood there in the half-light from the window and her hand stretched forward into the space of the open room, as if she were trying to push aside a screen. But there was no screen.

Room 306. A room of light and air, so different from room 202, where they were staying. This room let in the whiteness of the snow through every window; it had a pure, crisp whiteness. Everything smelled of...what...jasmine? Jasmine, with a hint of oil and smoke. The furnishings too were white, like an embodied form of air. She sat down on the edge of the bed and stared out at the world of snow and whiteness. She picked up a snow globe from the nightstand. She swirled the fake snow and it came down thick, so thick she could barely make out that in the globe was a hotel, a hotel just like this one. She lay down on the bed and watched the whiteness out the window spread and spread, and she determined she would not go anywhere until she could sleep. As she drifted, she noticed one last thing—the door had shut behind her.

10

Dewey sat there on the floor and played more jacks than he would have guessed he'd ever play in a lifetime. He was getting so good at jacks that he wished jacks were an activity he cared about getting good at, like archery.

No one came around. The lobby was pretty dark, even in the daylight with the white snow flying by the windows. There were a lot of windows, and Dewey had a good view of the street, which almost nobody ever came down, and he had a good view of the door his father had gone out and the path he'd taken around the corner, and every minute or so Dewey would look out at the path in hopes of his father's return but his father was never there. It seemed like it might be getting time for lunch, and if they didn't manage to start something soon, it was going to be too late for sledding.

His father had told him to wait in the lobby, but he felt pretty certain he hadn't been expected to wait this long, although it could be one of those deals where he lost track of time again, which he did frequently, and not in the usual sense, but where he would get so absorbed in some line of thought that almost entire days could pass without him recalling them in any way. This had happened once recently when he went to his friend Avery's house for the first time and found out that Avery's dad had a two-hundred-gallon aquarium with some of the most awesome tropical fish Dewey had ever seen, and not only that but all the stuff in the tank, like the coral and rocks and plants, was *real,* Avery's dad had shown him. Dewey loved tropical fish, and the sight of this awe-inspiring tank, so ocean-like in every way, had sent him into a reverie that lasted the entire night he spent at Avery's house, so that when Avery talked at school later about how they'd stayed up until 3 a.m. and played the new Grand Theft Auto and snuck into the TV room and watched movies with actual female nudity, these events were absolutely nowhere in Dewey's memory. He believed Avery that they'd taken place, but he'd been thinking about the fish tank, and he could remember only the things he thought, not the things he did, unless the things he thought and the things he did were the same. It was kind of scary, really, and not something he liked to talk about, or think about for that matter.

But the losing track of time thing, at least up to now, had always worked in the other direction, meaning that the actual amount of time elapsed was always *greater* than it had felt like to Dewey, so that it would be really strange now if the amount of time was *less,* meaning that Dewey's father hadn't really been gone all that long and that he was still expected to be waiting in the lobby, plus the fact that Dewey hadn't been particularly stimulated by anything that would make him lose time in the usual way.

So after taking one last look around the lobby and one last look out the windows and not noticing anything other than the ladders and buckets of paint and toolboxes and stuff he'd seen already the night before, and of course the snow, which kept on falling just as hard, so that Dewey had to stop and think for just a second, just to make sure he remembered, what it was like when it *didn't* snow, he decided to go upstairs to his mother. He gathered his jacks and put them in the little pouch and put the pouch in his pocket and headed up the stairs.

The hotel seemed to be getting colder. He had on a long-sleeve shirt over a T-shirt, so his arms were pretty warm, and his legs were fine, but his hands were cold, and when he blew on them it seemed as though he could almost see his breath. Maybe that's why his father had been gone so long, because he was still trying to find the hotel owner or any of the people who were supposed to be working at the hotel and was going to keep looking until they came, because Dewey was only ten but he knew some things, his test scores were off the charts, and one of the things he knew was that part of what you paid for when you rented a hotel room was heat, and another part of what you paid for was some people there to complain to if you weren't getting any heat.

His mother almost never complained. For instance, if they were at a restaurant and let's say the waiter made a mistake, let's say he brought out a baked potato with Dewey's father's prime rib instead of French fries or mashed potatoes or vegetables—his father hated baked potatoes and would order whatever else was available with his meal, no matter what—his father would stop the waiter in the middle of putting the plates and stuff on the table, and he would say in this complaining tone, "Hold on, I asked for fries and you brought me a baked potato. This is a baked potato." Whereas his mother would sit there with no expression on her face at all and wait calmly until all the plates of food were out, and everybody's water had been refilled, and then she'd say, "Excuse me, I'm sorry, this looks like an orange–poppy seed dressing and I think I ordered the vinaigrette." He could remember that sentence so distinctly and his mother's utterance of it so vividly that he said it now under his breath while he walked down the hall: "I ordered the vinaigrette. Excuse me, I ordered the vinaigrette." And it wasn't a complaint, and the waiter or the waitress always knew the difference, you could tell. "Excuse me," Dewey said softly, "you brought me a baked potato."

His father wasn't a mean person, he was really very nice, and he loved Dewey so much that it was sometimes hard for Dewey to understand. His father would say things like, "Dooze Man, if it weren't for you, I don't know what I'd do." And he would shake his head slowly and study the air, as if everything were so far away that there was nothing to see.

Sometimes Dewey thought his father's problem was just that he got impatient about having to live in a world where almost no one was as smart as him. He liked his father best, most of the time, because they thought the same things were funny (with the exception of Uncle Robbie) and they knew what each other meant without really having to say what they meant or sometimes by saying just the opposite or sometimes by saying nothing at all. But it was his mother he most "respected." His mother was what they meant when they called somebody "a good person."

"This looks like a baked potato," Dewey said aloud, approaching the doorway.

Something didn't feel right. The door was wide open. Dewey stopped in the hall. He was only ten years old, but he sometimes thought pretty complicated things in pretty complicated ways, and what he thought right now was that he could hear himself saying, many years in the future, maybe when he was an adult himself, "I could tell before I walked in the door that something was desperately wrong."

Something was desperately wrong. An odd, chalky light seeped from the room, and there were whispering sounds, or buzzing sounds, like when you put the edge of a piece of paper in your mouth and blow. From where he stood in the hall he could see through the door and into the room where Uncle Robbie had slept and on past the bed in Uncle Robbie's room he could see the snow in the air at the window, which gave him the peculiar feeling that no one was going to be in the hotel room unless, maybe, it was Uncle Robbie.

But when he entered room 202, he found nobody there, only the television. He checked the bathroom and the room where Robbie had slept and his parents' room but there was no mother and no Robbie.

This was not the time to panic. Actually, he told himself, a typical ten-year-old would probably be oblivious to the situation, to the fact that there was anything a little scary and strange going on. At least for a while. A typical ten-year-old would probably just sit down and watch TV. So that's what he did.

Only the TV wasn't showing anything a typical ten-year-old would want to watch—meaning of course that Dewey was soon fascinated, fascinated by the murky, snowy screen that showed figures drifting back and forth in a slow, silent procession with what looked like lights dancing around their heads, disappearing into or emerging from a mouth.

Dewey discovered a wire that ran from the back of the TV and culminated in what he suspected was an antenna, a little box with two stretchable rods, which he set on top of the TV. The antenna didn't do much except make different images fade in and out, the long lines of men with the lights giving way to someone running endlessly up and down stairs and through passageways, and then to a room in which no one did anything, nothing was even there, it was just a room, and then the image would change to one of a lot of people holding drinks by a fireplace.

Dewey sat in front of the TV deciphering the images as best he could, and he thought about how his mother would watch old movies late at night sitting by herself on the couch, and how he would sometimes, half asleep, sneak into the hallway and watch her there, and he would feel just like this, snowy and dim and sleepy in the same way the images were.

Finally he felt hungry and he looked around the room to find that there was still no one there and it was dark outside the windows and the snow still fell. He would not say yet that he was panicked. Panic, as when his mother would tell his father not to panic because he'd misplaced his car keys and claimed he would miss his flight at the airport, involved a lot of frantic running around and cursing, while Dewey was just sitting quietly on the floor in front of the TV. But he was growing concerned, yes he was. This had never happened before. It was dark outside and he was alone.

He began to check the room for clues. The floorboards creaked as he moved around. There was nothing to suggest that his father had been back to the room—his suitcase was sitting right there on the bed where Dewey had seen it earlier. His mother's suitcase, though, which had also been used to pack Dewey's clothes, lay open on a kind of rack in the corner, and the clothes had been taken out except for Dewey's underwear and his socks. In the closet were most of his mother's clothes, it turned out upon inspection, but in one of the dresser drawers he discovered something useful—the thick wool sweater he always refused to wear. He pulled it over his head quickly and almost right away felt not quite as bad. At least he quit shivering.

His mother's purse was on a table next to the bed, and its presence there made Dewey feel even a bit better. He stopped for a second to consider why that was, staring at his own reflection in the window, beyond which he could see the floating snow, so that he himself, Dewey, very much resembled one of the figures on the strange TV screen, obscured by dots and shadows.

The reason the purse made him feel good was that he knew his mother wouldn't go somewhere without it for long. If the purse—a soft, massive purple thing that she insisted on referring to as "lavender"—was still here, then his mother would have to come back soon. She hadn't left him here alone on purpose. Once, Dewey had threatened to run away from home (even though it was really only a joke between him and his father, who responded to Dewey's threat by making him a sandwich and chips and putting them in a handkerchief and tying the handkerchief to an old broomstick and handing the broomstick to Dewey and saying, "Well, son, I reckon this is all the stake we can spot you in this hard world," after which Dewey went to the other side of the backyard fence and ate the sandwich and chips and watched squirrels run along the telephone lines), and he was relieved now to know that his *mother* had not run away from *him*. And there was no question about his father having run away—this was maybe the first time Dewey had missed his father's odd clinginess.

He did begin to panic now, a little bit, because he was all alone in a cold, dark hotel a gazillion miles from anyplace or anyone he knew, and he didn't understand what had happened to everyone, and this would be enough to make *anyone* panic, Dewey knew, so he didn't feel so bad about panicking just this slight amount. He went back down the stairs into the lobby, which was just like before only totally dark now, and he shouted out, "Hel-*lo!,*" but there was no one, not anyone, there. The snow flew by the windows, leaving the hotel in its wake, and the dark was broken only by the streetlight and the neon sign of the bar across the street and beyond it the yellow windows of the diner his father had taken him to for breakfast.

Dewey yelled as loud as he could a word his father had told him it would not be a good idea to use around his mother and felt pretty confident he could explain his reasons for using it now if he was called upon to do so. He would be more than happy for someone to hear him but no one heard.

He marched glumly back up the stairs, and he thought of the things a normal ten-year-old boy would think of or do in this situation. One of them was cry, and Dewey had not done that and did not intend to, but when he thought about how he was ten years old and his mother and father had disappeared and left him in a *situation,* one in which a normal ten-year-old would no doubt cry, he did begin to cry, just a tiny bit.

He went inside the quiet hotel room and shut the door behind him and he thought of turning on the TV again just to hear some noise but in truth the TV was a little creepy. And it was a little creepy, too, how he was the only person in the hotel, and how you could probably see him from the street, standing alone there at the window thinking about his mom and dad.

He thought about his mom and dad. For the first time he could remember, he thought of them as only themselves, who they actually were, and not as the mother and father of him, Dewey, and how the two of them, each of them separately, had to actually be out there in the world somewhere, out there in a separate place from him doing a separate thing, and thinking of them this way—as living creatures out there somewhere, who could be touched and felt and heard if they could only be gotten to—helped him to calm down and quit sniffling. Because if they were out there and they weren't with him and they weren't dead or severely injured—and he couldn't think they were—then there was only one explanation: it had something to do with Uncle Robbie. As his father would say, *It figures.*

He felt so sure suddenly that Uncle Robbie lay at the bottom of this, that it would all be cleared up somehow in a way that left Uncle Robbie in trouble as usual and not anyone else, that he started to feel hungry again. He went into the bathroom and wiped his nose and he went through his mom's big purse and found her small purse there and took twenty dollars without thinking of it as stealing and he grabbed her cell phone, too—it was only 5 p.m., he was relieved to see—and he walked back downstairs into the dark lobby and to the front door and out into the street and the falling snow. He saw that his mother's cell phone was still charged so he started to call someone but then realized that the person he was starting to call was his mother. His father had left his cell phone at home because he didn't want anyone from the college to call him. Dewey didn't know Uncle Robbie's number, or his grandparents', or, frustratingly, anybody's. He thought he could find a number in his mom's contacts, but when he was searching for the right icon the screen suddenly started moving in wavy rainbow colors and then it went black.

The only place he knew where he could find human beings was the diner across the street. What he thought about all of a sudden was a patty melt. He was going to order one at the diner. He'd checked it out when he and his dad were there that morning. He knew for a fact they had it on the menu.

11

He had spent the better part of the day at the house of his new friend, a guy named Ruby, who lived in a ramshackle place boarded up in various spots, one whole side covered in Visqueen. Robbie hadn't worn any of his warm clothes when he left the hotel room, of course, so he'd had to borrow a jacket from said Ruby, who was apparently not the only local resident with the name of a precious stone—Robbie had been told there was also a man named Diamond.

The keg they'd bought around lunchtime was drained now, or maybe it was just the pump had gone bad. Robbie could remember standing out by the back porch in the snow where they'd placed the keg trying to get the beer to flow again, but he couldn't remember the verdict as to why it wouldn't.

It had gotten dark outside and he was in Ruby's house watching the snow—twenty-four hours straight now—the *snow* still coming down outside and he was lying in bed with Stephanie, who had fallen asleep. He was somewhere between the stage of first drunkenness and initial hangover, teetering on the edge of a binge, and theoretically at this point he could still pick up his chips and vacate the table. See you later, nice to meet all of you, let's do it again next time I'm in town. It was the hour of damage assessment. It was the time of leave or stay put. Actually it depended to some extent on which of two courses Tonio had adopted.

Robbie hoped with what was left of his heart that Tonio had packed up and hit the road. It would be easier all around that way, and it would shift the burden of guilt from his own shoulders to Tonio's. Let Tonio explain to Julia, driving along I-90 in the teeth of a raging blizzard, why he had felt it necessary to leave his brother, his *only* brother, behind, particularly when Tonio had to have known from the outset that this wasn't going to be easy, that Robbie wouldn't exactly be in a mood to cooperate with the plan. If Tonio had pulled out of town, Robbie could pretty much go ahead carte blanche and ruin himself to whatever degree he pleased. It would leave him feeling a little bad that he hadn't spent more time with Dewey, the Dooze Man, but hey, the time he *had* spent with him had been quality time, as the good Uncle Robbie, in the role he liked to call Regular Guy...a little manic, maybe, a little bit skating along the edge of physical and psychological neediness, trying to stay on the right side of all the annoyance without even so much as a fucking beer to blunt the edges, but a good time nonetheless, time on best behavior. Regular Guy. And then of course there was the fact that he wouldn't be able to spend more time with Julia, but honestly, when it came right down to it, he didn't want to spend time with Julia, it was just the idea of this imaginary thing he might have with her that was interesting. When he was actually *with* Julia it just felt like an act he was putting on, an act he was *attempting* to put on, since he didn't even feel like he was very good at it.

One of the few times Tonio—who had never been a horrible brother, just a largely indifferent and rather mythical big brother figure who was always *out there,* always somewhere else, even when he was with the family physically, which was mostly for short stints of time during breaks in his academic career—had done something with Robbie alone was once when he came home for Christmas and took Robbie, maybe ten at the time, to the circus. Robbie's impression of the circus had been that there was a lot of frantic and unnecessary business—it had made him tired. There was Tonio, buying Robbie peanuts and a gigantic Coke, sitting there with his gloomy stare and his hunched shoulders and his bony elbows and his pathetic box of popcorn. Jesus. *Tonio,* thinking he could take a kid to the circus. And the performers. What struck him most about the performers—the trapeze artists, the lion tamers, the sword throwers and swallowers, the goddamn midgets on motorcycles—was how, with all the energy they could muster, they accomplished more and more difficult feats until...well, until they didn't. It became clear to Robbie with the juggling clown—there he was, riding his unicycle on a tightrope, juggling balls then bowling pins then flaming batons until there was simply nothing harder he could do. When there were no more balls to be juggled, only two things could happen—he could keep going till he dropped one of them, or he could quit. That was how things felt with Julia, Robbie had decided a long time ago. He was the circus clown who'd already performed his best tricks. And then there was another simple reason he hoped they'd left town without him, which was just that he knew he had nothing to offer any one of them—what good, for instance, could possibly come of his hanging around with Dewey?

The other possibility: for whatever reason, due to whoever's influence, Tonio had decided to stick it out for at least another day, wait out the storm and try to find the wayward brother. In this version of the story—and even thinking about it right at this moment while he checked out the plump upper arm of Stephanie, touched his finger lightly to a dark brown penny-sized birthmark on her bicep, then shifted his gaze to the snow out the window in the back porch light, he disliked this version intensely—all the guilt rested squarely with Robbie and in fact increased with every passing moment. He could picture the family at the crappy little diner across the street from the hotel, Dewey gnawing on a stale French fry, Julia absently running her painted fingernail around the rim of her water glass, Tonio red-faced, steam puffing out of his ears. Then the family back in the hotel room, tiring out Dewey properly with a game of crazy eights, so that they could tuck him into bed and sit up and argue till the wee hours.

This was an awful scenario, and it was one in which Robbie was expected to do something—namely, swallow his pride, go back to the hotel, apologize, man up the best he could to Tonio and try to look Dewey and Julia in the eye, so they could get on out of this town and over to Charleston as planned. At which point there would be, for him, good old Uncle Robbie, a long, dried-out, spectral time of nothingness.

He considered this possibility. What would the spectral time of nothingness actually entail? Doddering strolls around some sunbleached lane with a name like Sea Oats Drive, populated by Volvos and Volkswagens and one or two palm trees, tossing a plastic football back and forth with Dewey. Hours spent staring at Tonio's bookshelves, trying to find something to read that he could convince himself was more entertaining than getting drunk or high. Awkward silences around the dinner table, staring at plates of grits or chicken livers or whatever they ate in Charleston. Awkward silences especially with Julia, watching her pull dirty clothes from the laundry hamper while Tonio rushed to get ready for work, keeping a nervous and critical eye on the proceedings. Boredom. Boredom more than anything else. Not the DTs or any kind of hallucinations or paranoid fantasies or whatever people like Tonio imagined—boredom was the chief problem with all attempts at sobriety. The physical symptoms of withdrawal one could deal with. Boredom and the prospect of further boredom, boredom forevermore, was the killer.

So, but, say he was ready to give up the cheap keg beer and

the bad whiskey and the company of Stephanie and all his new white trash friends, call it quits right now, give himself up peaceably to Tonio and his superior silent anger. Then what? It was all too exhausting to think about. The easy thing would be just to plow ahead on the route he'd chosen. There'd be a good week or two of steady drunkenness before these new friends got sick of him and figured out that he had no more money and no desire to work for it and no real attachment to anyone or anything here. Stephanie would be the last to turn on him. He'd manage to negotiate a bus ticket out of town, either from Stephanie or someone who had an interest in seeing him removed from the situation with Stephanie, or from his mother and father if it came to that. Then he could either go back to Portland or go back to rehab. It was by far the easier and therefore the preferable and therefore the inevitable plan. All this other stuff, this back and forth in his head while he rubbed this sleeping girl's shoulder and sat awake and slightly buzzing in the quiet and watched, as he'd seemingly been watching forever, the snow fall—all of this was just parsing, just sifting, the broken mumbling of the remnants of himself.

He got dressed and went out on the covered porch to smoke a cigarette. He hunched against the cold and blew streams of smoke into the air and hopped up and down in his sock feet. There was hardly any noise from the house. Had they all gone to sleep already? Robbie himself was ready to head out to the bar, although he'd have to put some thought into that, have to figure out a way to avoid Tonio and/or Julia, probably Tonio, who could certainly be out on a scouting mission.

When he thought about it, though, he was nearly as miserable out here on the porch steps as he would be back in the hotel. Could these people really be as tame as they seemed? Weren't the small towns of America supposed to be rife with meth these days? Where was someone to hand him a crack pipe, for Christ's sake, if he was going to be stuck here for a while? So far all he'd seen was flat beer and a little bit of skank weed.

There was a lot of noise and a couple of beefy guys burst out onto the porch. "Let's go," the one named Ray said.

"Where to?" Robbie asked him.

"'Where to?' he says. 'Where to?'" the one who wasn't Ray said.

"Where to?" Robbie asked again.

The one named Ray burped up something under his breath, the last part of which sounded like "key to the city, giving you key to the city."

"I'm kind of keeping a low profile, guys," Robbie said. "I don't want to meet the mayor."

"You already met the mayor," the one not named Ray said.

Robbie watched them for a second to see if he could locate a joke. "Okay, even so," he said, "there are certain people in this town with whom I do not want to make visual contact."

The one named Ray and the one not named Ray nodded to each other and laughed. The one named Ray punched Robbie on the shoulder, almost apologetically, Robbie felt.

12

She liked her new room about as well as she'd ever liked any place. Possibly this was the result of having had a nice nap away from Tonio's snoring. It might have been a *long* nap—she couldn't tell because there were no clocks in the room and no TV and she didn't have her cell phone. It was still light outside, though—it must have been late afternoon.

The double bed was small, with a cast-iron frame, but it wasn't rickety or clangy. She'd slept deeply, which wasn't usually easy for her, God knows, what with being Tonio's wife, a condition that carried with it a variety of problems of various dimensions, and Dewey's mother, another condition that carried with it a variety of problems of various dimensions, although not the same ones, so that the problems were constantly overlapping one another and becoming new, subtly morphed problems that often kept her awake at night. One was always snoring or needing something and the other was always needing something or wanting to go somewhere…God, how *sleepy* she was right now. She felt like Cleopatra, the family cat back home in Mount Pleasant (must call the graduate student they'd left with the key, make sure he was checking on Cleo regularly).

High ceilings with antique fixtures hanging from them, a beautiful little—what was it, cherrywood?—yes, a cherrywood end table, along with other extravagant furniture arrayed around the room, velvet-upholstered chairs and a delicately carved nightstand and a massive old armoire, stern-looking, positively and properly Victorian in its solidity and breadth and height and weight, its stained and polished enormity, staring at her out of its dual-mirrored face, a face that presented a scene so lifelike, so perfectly real, somehow, exceeding the capacities of mere reflection, that it suggested immense depths beyond the actual measurements of the room. Oak dresser, deep claw-foot bathtub in the bathroom with its black-and-white tile floor.

At some point she was going to have to eat.

There had been a little surprise in that regard, a little potential difficulty. She had tried to open the door, but it was definitely, certainly, beyond a shadow of a doubt locked from the outside. And in case anyone there on the other side of the door was wondering, she *had* looked around for a key, but had so far been unable to find one. There was maybe the chance of sliding a nail file or a bobby pin into the keyhole, but she had neither of those items in her possession, since she'd left her purse downstairs. The purse, or the absence of the purse, would be a problem eventually, if she stayed here long enough. But she wasn't worried yet. She wasn't *worried* yet—how remarkable a thing was that? List the things that didn't worry her: it didn't worry her that she hadn't seen Dewey the entire afternoon, it didn't worry her that she hadn't seen Tonio the entire afternoon, it didn't worry her that she had no idea where they were and that they apparently had no idea where she was either, it didn't worry her that Robbie still might not have reappeared, it didn't worry her that they were not going to get back home when they were supposed to, it didn't worry her that she was, well, *stuck* in this perfectly pleasant room, it didn't worry her that she was so sleepy, that she was beginning to get hungry. She was still prepared to see it as an adventure—remember the time she got locked in that hotel room in that odd little town and *nobody* came looking for her, not *anyone*? She wasn't even worried about how little she was worried about these things. Might as well go ahead and admit to herself that she didn't want anyone to find her. At least not yet, not now. In theory, Tonio and Dewey could be looking for her frantically, but if so they were doing a really pathetic job. Good. Let them have fun with their sledding.

Here was the thing about Tonio and Robbie, now that she had a good chance to sit down and ruminate on the subject: Tonio (he of the drooping shoulders and the dry stare and the monotone speech patterns, the infuriating imaginary superiority and the factual near helplessness) was hard to like in a superficial way, while he was, at the same time, with his steadfastness and his seriousness and his honesty and his intense love for his family, etc., etc., impossible not to love on a deeper level, whereas Robbie was almost universally liked but not really available for or capable of being loved. And yet she always found herself *accepting* Robbie easily, as if the things she saw in him and felt about him were true—with Tonio she always thought there was something she was missing, as if there were another version of Tonio and of her and even of Dewey that didn't live somewhat happily on a quiet street in Mount Pleasant, South Carolina, and that at any minute it would all just slip down, like a poorly hung stage backdrop, to reveal something else.

If only the room had a vaseful of flowers. There was the smell of jasmine in the air, but no flowers. There was also the issue of food—room service would be welcome. Her stomach, at the moment, was capable of grinding and polishing stones. Aside from that, the possibility of staying in here overnight did not seem distressing at all. There was just this craving for…*pesto tortellini*…a sudden and intense craving for pesto tortellini. Otherwise all was well. Except how would she take off her makeup? When it was bedtime, that is. She didn't wear that much, her skin was naturally olive and quite smooth, but still. There was nothing but a bar of soap in the bathroom. She'd already checked.

From her spot on the bed she watched the snow fall. It was like being inside a snow globe. The room was very quiet, that was one thing you noticed for sure. The room was intensely quiet. You might even go so far as to say the room was very, very intensely and almost *oppressively quiet,* if you were going to comment on the quiet in that room, which she didn't intend to, liking it so much the way she did. But *wow* — talk about quiet. Whew.

The thing about Tonio was. The thing about Tonio.

Hadn't she initially gotten into this mess because she thought she saw Robbie going up the stairs?

She went over to the door and she knocked on it tentatively (strange to be on the inside of the door knocking to see if someone was on the outside) and called out, "Robbie?" Just once. Then she went back and sat on the side of the bed and gazed out the window again.

There was something strange about the snow, about the light outside. It looked brighter. It was getting brighter instead of darker. My God, no wonder she was hungry. She'd slept all night. It was tomorrow.

13

The Dooze Man was feeling a little low this particular morning, he had to admit. First, there was no one there to call him the Dooze Man, no one to pour him a bowl of cereal, show him what clothes to wear. As it turned out, parents came in handy in all sorts of ways—for instance if his mother were here he wouldn't be wiping his nose on his sleeve and he would know where the toothpaste was.

Last night it hadn't seemed so bad. The people at the diner, Hugh and Lorraine, had been really nice. When they found out he was here all by himself and he wasn't exactly sure when his parents were coming back for him, they gave him his dessert, a piece of chocolate pie, for free. Then when he was leaving, Lorraine helped him with his coat because the zipper was stuck. He played the gumball maze eight times, not so much because the game was all that fun—it was pretty fun—or because he wanted that much gum—he did want quite a bit of gum—but because the idea of going back across the street to the dark hotel—when he looked out the window of the diner, he couldn't see a light on anywhere—was kind of depressing and scary.

The interesting thing for the Dooze Man to consider, here in the cold hard light of morning, was that he hadn't really even thought too much last night about what it all *meant,* he just had this vague idea, like, get some food, come back and go to sleep. He had fallen asleep on the couch watching the weird patterns on the TV, and he had dreamed of his dad and his mom coming back during the night, waking him up there on the couch and telling him to be quiet and go to his own bed, *Shhh, don't wake Dewey,* which didn't make any sense, of course, because Dewey was himself.

But now it was the next day and they still weren't here, no Dad, no Mom, no Uncle Robbie, so this whole experience had now gone beyond being strange and was getting closer to the territory that his dad would refer to as "unique." Not many things were unique—it was an even more restricted category than "special," which was a word his dad also used a lot, and which was related to the scientific word "species," but which in everyday usage meant something that gave something a specific or particular designation apart from other less distinct designations. Certainly this occasion was special, this being abandoned here in this town where he knew no one, where everyone was a stranger, where he had no way to communicate with anyone he knew, his teachers, his grandparents, his friends (and in fact it was difficult to find *anyone* to communicate with here—where *was* that guy who owned the hotel, for instance?), and where he had no place to stay other than this very cold and very lonely and pretty creepy hotel, and nobody to make him meals other than Hugh and Lorraine at the diner across the street, and not a whole lot of money, by Dewey's reckoning, with which to pay them to keep cooking for him. Whether the situation was *unique,* meaning whether it had never happened before in the history of the world and would likely never happen again, remained to be seen. It was definitely unique to the Dooze Man's experience, he could say that much for sure.

He sat at the foot of the bed wearing his coat and his warm hat and his boots, his hands folded in his lap, as if he were waiting patiently for someone or something. He had grown so used to the snow now, the sight of the flakes falling one by one, starting from the upper-left-hand corner of the window and twirling softly downward toward the right, or, if the wind was gusting, blowing almost straight across, or, at times, even upward in a gravity-defying dance, that it would only feel worth thinking anything about if he were to turn toward the window and *not* see snow, not in the air, not on the buildings, not in the street, not on the hills, not in the neon light of the diner sign. A snow town, a town of snow, of snow women and snow men.

Dewey had been told various things about what to do in emergency situations, and, since he was peculiarly smart and even moderately diligent, he had listened to and understood and now even remembered several of these things: Never go anywhere with strangers, even if they say your mother and father told you to. When lost, go to the last place you were before you got separated. Apply vinegar to jellyfish stings. Do not touch electrical wiring. Always wash your hands before you eat. Not many of these rules seemed to apply, except maybe the one about going to the last place before you were separated, but he was *doing* that, right *now,* and it wasn't *helping.* None of the usual things seemed to work in this place. For instance, his mother's cell phone. When he first found it, he had been relieved to see that it was still charged, and then when he had tried to use it, there was the weird rainbow pattern, and then nothing. Like, nothing. No voice mail, no texts, not even any kind of message telling him that he had no service here. By the time he had woken up this morning, the thing was completely, totally, *irrefutably* (another of his father's favorite words) dead. So he had literally been cut off from every single thing he'd ever been used to having pretty much every day of his entire life.

But overall the Dooze Man thought he was doing pretty well, and that when this whole thing had been cleared up somehow, he was going to be getting some pretty serious rewards not only of the guilt-trip variety but also due to his extreme levels of maturity and responsibility. There had been only a few moments, a few fleeting moments at intervals through the night, when he had really been scared…moments when he thought his parents might have abandoned him, but then he would remember all the truly nice things his mother did for him — basically fix him snacks whenever he wanted, unless it was right before dinner, and also how she would practically stop whatever she was doing almost anytime to give him a ride to one of his friends' houses, or if there was a certain movie he wanted to see she would take him to it, whereas his dad would say, "Dooze, can't you wait until that comes out on Netflix?" And then there was his dad, of course, and, well, he couldn't get his dad to abandon him for five seconds if he paid him to. So it couldn't be that.

And he didn't think they'd wandered off into the woods and frozen to death. And he didn't think they'd been in a car wreck. And he didn't think they'd been kidnapped. And he didn't think they'd been arrested.

He still thought it had something to do with Uncle Robbie, and it was unfortunate, Dewey thought, that at ten years old you didn't have enough experience of the world to determine how a person like Uncle Robbie, a degenerate if you agreed with the use of the term that you most certainly *did* understand and which you'd heard tossed around, could cause the disappearance of two adult human beings who were specifically enlisted in the ongoing effort to offer him assistance. Could Uncle Robbie have gotten himself arrested — Dewey knew he'd done that a couple of times before — in such a way that his parents had been detained as witnesses? And not allowed to contact their one and only son?

His father had this saying he used on certain occasions, like when the chair of the anthropology department did something he didn't like, or when the guy at the car repair place explained something to him as if he were a child, or almost anytime he had to talk on the phone: "Human beings are easier to like in theory than in fact." It was just the opposite with Uncle Robbie as far as Dewey was concerned—he was much easier to like in fact than in theory. When he was sitting with you in the backseat showing you card tricks, or making you laugh in a restaurant until you shot Coke out of your nose, he was a pretty great guy. But when you had to sit around and think about how much trouble he was always causing for pretty much everyone in the entire universe who ever talked to him or had anything to do with him, then not so much.

If there was one thing Dewey knew, or at least suspected strongly, it was that he wasn't going to learn his parents' whereabouts by staying in this hotel room. And he did like the diner across the street, and he did *especially* like the hash browns and the biscuits and gravy, which he could order at the same time if his parents weren't there. Which was what you called a small consolation.

So to the diner he would go, and he would keep acting like everything was normal. At least it was really quiet here, which when you thought about it actually *was* kind of more normal than the way things were at home. He closed his eyes and pictured his mother frantically running around from this place to that place, this project to that one, one errand to another, so that she was always flying in and out of the bathroom, flashing through the kitchen or the living room with a jangle of keys, zipping up and down the driveway, Dewey never knowing from one minute to the next whether he would be whisked along or no, and his father sometimes there in the house giving him a hug or a pat on the back and asking him all these goofy questions, and then the next thing you knew you'd turn around to answer him and Mom would say, "He's off to Arizona," or "He flew out this morning to Saskatchewan."

At the diner he asked Hugh and Lorraine where to find the police station and they told him there wasn't one and then they glanced at each other. They didn't seem too surprised to find him alone again. In the Dooze Man's experience, adults were generally more helpful, or at least they thought they were, or at least they tried to make it appear that way. Hugh and Lorraine just looked at each other and Lorraine frowned and narrowed her eyes and shook her head a little. But they did give him quarters for the gumball maze. Dewey put the quarters in and stared out the window, wondering how many more hours of daylight before it started to get dark again.

14

He sat thoughtfully stirring a cup of tea, the same thing he'd been doing off and on for several minutes without actually drinking any. Tea held little interest for him. Head lowered, he took a guarded look at "Tiffany, A., Tiffany, initial A," as the hotel owner, who sat in an armchair to his left, wanted to be called. He could have passed for a character from a Zola novel, or one of Cézanne's card-playing peasants, a human being presented in that post-Darwinian wave when the emphasis was all on the animalistic properties, the dangling arms, the large hands and feet, the scraping knuckles, the cranial asymmetry. Tonio shared a few of those characteristics himself—"You're so *gangly,*" his mother always told him, disapprovingly, that furrow in her brow—but the effect with him was smoothed by a rather babyish face, soft round cheeks, a mildly pug nose.

"Amenities can make all the difference," this Tiffany, the hotel owner, said. "For instance, the lighted fire. Our guests expect luxury, and rightfully so, but they're always surprised when they see that our lobby, while built on a grand scale, is at the same time quite cheerful." His large hands were as rough as bark, the fingers thick and long like cigars, with a heavy silver ring on his left index finger, and yet he held his teacup delicately, the pinkie extended.

He was long and gaunt and a little stooped in the shoulders, concave in the chest, and today he wore a dark blazer over a colorful wool sweater of the sort favored by Tonio's hipster students and somewhat threadbare corduroy pants. His hair was a shaggy brown mass tinged with gray around the ears, and his face, or what could be seen of it through his bushy mustache, was absolutely bland and nondescript except for a large, crooked nose that made him resemble both a boxer and a Frenchman. His voice had a strangely nasal twang that seemed at once overarticulated and mumbled. He was, Tonio decided, unlikely, in all respects.

"The fire is nice," Tonio said. "Thank you for the tea."

He had been sitting on this sofa in the lobby for ten minutes, he estimated, and he was busily keeping it a secret from the hotel owner that he had no clear idea how he'd gotten here or what he'd been doing prior to sitting on the sofa. He was certain now that this was the place he'd read about, an article attempting to verify a string of disappearances, a mystery at the root of some Old West town's foundations, so unscientific that he had been offended by its mere presence in the journal, one to which he himself had submitted articles unsuccessfully on several occasions. But it was more than that, more than the journal article, and more than what he'd learned from Mr. A. Tiffany in the few minutes he'd been sitting here, trying to manipulate the teacup with his shaking hand: that construction on the hotel had been completed in 1886 under the supervision of another A. Tiffany, Alfred Tiffany, whom this newer Tiffany mentioned with a boastful air; that it had burned nearly to the ground soon afterward and had then been restored; that it had originally contained 105 rooms, a four-star restaurant (according to a reviewer from a paper in San Francisco), a saloon, a Turkish bath, and a barbershop; that it was the first hotel in the territory to feature gas lighting in all the rooms; that at the time the town of Good Night had a much larger population, more than two thousand inhabitants; and that this hotel, as Tiffany pointed out with pride, in fact formed the centerpiece of a mining town that was once the largest in the western states. It was more than any of that—it was a growing awareness that he knew these things already, that he knew this place himself, maybe through some dim memory of early childhood. And it was that time somehow seemed to have disappeared, that the hours had begun to slip away without his noticing. He was terrified.

Mr. A. Tiffany smiled crookedly and placed his big, gnarled hands on his knees. "Mr. Addison," he said, "I'm very glad you'll stay another night. Honestly, it can get rather lonely."

Tonio didn't say anything. He was wondering why it was nearly dark outside and he was trying to recall having spoken to the owner earlier about the possibility of extending their stay, and he seemed to remember being outside in the snow, even though he was perfectly dry and warm now, lingering over a cup of tea. He had been outside in the snow on a narrow street and there was a woman, wasn't there, a woman he'd known before, and there was a door she'd come out of and he'd tried to enter, and most of all now he wanted to know why Dewey wasn't in the lobby and how long ago he'd left Dewey here and whether Dewey was upstairs safe in the room with Julia, and he also wanted to know what was wrong with him and why he didn't know all these things.

"I'm sorry," he said to Tiffany, and he held his hand open with the tip of his thumb placed lightly against his forehead and he shook his head slowly from side to side.

The hotel owner chuckled, low and throaty. He sounded foreign somehow, as if he belonged somewhere else. "You've had a bit of a scare, haven't you?" he said. "That's okay. You're okay."

Tonio tapped his thumb against his forehead. "Am I?" he said. "Because, well…"

Tiffany's smiling face hovered there, the strangely crooked nose pointing toward a horseshoe that decorated the fireplace mantel. It occurred to Tonio that he'd somehow been gone long enough for the workers to complete the renovations in the lobby, the ladders and buckets and sawhorses all gone, electrical work all done, paint all dry, furnishings all arranged, fire in the fireplace. He'd thought the job would take weeks.

The owner leaned in to Tonio and whispered confidentially. "Naturally, you'll want to go see for yourself how things are upstairs." He settled back and then abruptly leaned in again. "Let me ask you, though, before you begin…"

But Tonio was already halfway up the first flight of stairs. He had been walking or running endlessly all day, it seemed, and his breathing was shallow and his head felt light, and when he reached the second-floor landing, he was suddenly so tired that only the most outsize act of will kept him from curling up in the corner right there and going to sleep. He went on to the room instead, and he stumbled in, and found nothing. A light slanted into the room from the big bay windows but he couldn't tell if it was day or night, and there was nothing but stillness, although a certain animal feeling lingered in the air. The suitcases were gone. He remembered the spot where the big one had lain on the bed that morning, with all of Dewey's socks tumbling out. The closet was empty, but so narrowly altered by time that he could almost see Julia's things, her blouses and skirts and cold-weather sweaters, the way they had hung there this morning. He thought of going into the closet and reaching at the empty air where his wife's clothes had been, as if he were a grieving husband in a movie. But he didn't. It wasn't logical that anything bad had happened. Maybe they had moved into a different suite. It was odd, though—everything in the room looked perfectly new, and in fact so undisturbed that you would have guessed no one had stayed here in a long time. He experienced a brief moment of duality, as if he were standing, at the same time, in both this bare room and the same room as it had been this morning, before he'd gone out into the snow. He closed his eyes and saw Julia seated on the bed, Dewey looking out the window, and he opened his eyes to the empty room again. He scanned it one last time, with his glasses on, but nothing seemed any clearer, so he put the glasses away and went wearily back down the stairs.

Tiffany sat there in his chair, waiting for Tonio contentedly, as if he had never left. Tonio lowered himself onto the sofa and said, as carefully as he could, "Do you know where my wife and my son are?"

"Well," Tiffany said, adjusting his pants leg. "Well, no. Not exactly. I haven't seen your wife and son since yesterday evening. And you have not seen them. And you've looked in the room and you've found they aren't there. But I'm going to suggest to you that no one has vacated the room. If anything, the room has vacated them. The room has *moved,* Mr. Addison. In your perception. For you."

Not once in his entire life had Tonio wondered, while he was awake, if he were in fact dreaming. Until this point he would have doubted that any waking person, ever, had *actually* confused the two states—he understood claims to the contrary to be simply a manner of speaking. But the past day had all the qualities of a dream—first of all the presence of Robbie and the trouble he always represented, then the driving, then the blinding snowstorm, then how the blinding snowstorm wouldn't *stop,* how it *had no end,* how even now, there it was, *snow,* still falling out the window, and the strange hotel that had seemed to transform itself, the disappearance of the paint cans and the drop cloths and the sawhorses and the planks and the appearance of the overstuffed chairs and the sofas and the fireplace, and before that the walk in the snow down the long, lonely alley and the vision of the strange and yet familiar woman, the sense of something forgotten, missing, displaced, and then his own displacement, and the disappearance of Dewey, the disappearance of Julia, and now this odd conversation while he looked out the window at the falling snow, that *snow*... it couldn't be real. But it was. You could mistake a dream for reality, but not the other way around.

"You're saying something is wrong with me," Tonio said quietly. "Something wrong with me physically, or in my mind, my perception of things. You're right. I can feel it. I feel strange." He turned to Tiffany, who now leaned so far back in his chair that he seemed to have tipped already, his chin pointing at Tonio where his nose should have been. "You're saying that because of whatever's wrong with me I couldn't find my way to the right room."

"No, I'm saying the room is no longer where you left it. Or vice versa, really."

Tonio put his hands in his pockets and squeezed his fists tight, tried to make sure his blood was pumping, that he was awake and hearing this. "That's..." he said. "That's..." He discovered he was almost crying.

Tiffany rubbed his mustache. He shook his head rather sadly. "Mr. Addison," he said. "Is it harder to imagine that certain places in the world"—he looked down at his hands—"are different from other places, or that all places are the same?"

"I'll ask you again," Tonio said. His breath came up short in his throat, he could feel his heart beating there. "Do you know where my wife and my son are?"

Tiffany sipped his tea. He put a finger in the air, then withdrew it, and rested his hand on his knee. "Not exactly."

"That's what I thought," Tonio said, and he walked to the door and opened it and went back out into the snow.

He started off walking in the opposite direction from the hotel this time, because he had a vague notion that the car was parked that way. It was essential to find the car, make sure it was still there and still running properly, capable of getting them the hell out of here at the first available opportunity. He was sure he had started off in the opposite direction, but when he turned the corner everything began to feel familiar—the same alleyway with the same snow flying down, the same brick walls of the same two-story buildings, the same tunneled effect to the walls and to his vision.

Soon it was just the same as it had been before, staggering along in the cold, the snow, half petrified, nobody in sight, not anywhere. There was a frozen moment, a kind of existential breakdown, an acquiescence to biological commands—seek warmth, go to sleep. He had hoped to avoid this sort of thinking in this sort of situation, when the time came, because dying was always, he imagined, under any circumstances, like this, in one form or another. Here he was out in the snow, slipping along in his jogging shoes, his arms spread to keep from falling, and he desperately regretted leaving the lobby and his cup of tea. "Dewey! Dewey! Dewey!" he yelled. He cupped his icy hands to his mouth—"Help!"—and then he fell. He lay on his back watching the snow come down, feeling it land on his cheeks, his eyelashes, and it came to him suddenly—the *woman,* the *door*—and he leaned up on one elbow and peered through the snow, and sure enough there the door was, no woman, but the door. There was the door, but he knew what had happened the last time he tried to go in there, that was when he'd lost track, somehow lost track of something—the time, the place, himself—and hadn't been able to get it back again.

But what else was there to do now? He rolled over onto his hands and his knees, then stood rather gingerly and straightened himself, and he went to the door. This time he was aware enough of what had happened before that he managed, as the door yielded to his weight, to keep a little better hold of himself inside his own head, where things were becoming soft and sleepy again, and white, maybe not white like snow so much as absent, blank, void, but also peaceful, and there was just the bare edge of panic that held him to his usual world, asking him where was Dewey, what was happening here, and then without any particular sensation of walking, in fact he was fairly certain that he was not in any way using his feet for the purpose of transportation, he found himself moving through a tight space, a vein, something that worked with a kind of capillary action, and time flowed the way it did in dreams, he saw Julia and Dewey each in the hotel, in their room, but not together, and there were people who seemed to have been here long ago, and there was a place with trees and water and something was burning—he was often in this place in his dreams—and his body felt as if he'd slept on it, like an arm that has lost circulation, and then his eyes opened, and there he was again in the hotel lobby in front of the fireplace. Next to him sat a woman he recognized, although he couldn't recall her name, and looking down he saw that she wore a delicate silver shoe.

15

She dreamed that she was walking past storefronts swaddled in snow. The snow was everywhere, so thick it formed a screen between her and the tangible world, and yet it fell so lightly that it registered as nothing more than a slight coldness on her face and hands. The brick facades of the buildings were perfectly new, the masonry perfectly intact, and the painted signs in the windows and on the storefronts were sharp and colorful—Jameson's Hardware, Good Night General Store, J & F Grocers, Tolley's Haberdashery. But there were no people in the stores and there was no merchandise in the windows. She was all alone.

She moved through the world of snow and shimmering glass and up ahead, far away, a faint patch of color loomed in a window. She drew closer and found that it was a single page of yellowed paper, taped to the glass from inside, covered with elaborate script. It was a letter, and the salutation read, *To Julia.*

The letter said, *Passing the storefronts in the snow, gliding by in the middle of a dream, you have the advantage of solitude, of time for contemplation. You have perhaps been waiting for an opportunity just like this one. You have not been able, really, ever (wouldn't you agree?) to come to grips with the final questions, the last extensions of the half-*

thought thoughts, the half-remembered memories, the things you have half known in secret all your life.

These whole truths, these entire revelations are available now to you, here on the street, here in your little room, here in the dream from which you either cannot or will not wake yourself. Wake yourself! Come to the threshold of the door that leads to the knowledge of your life, use the key you have obtained, the one in the pocket of your dress, the dress you wear in this dream of old times and places. Use the key! Use the key to cross worlds, cross dreams, cross lives, to arrive at the moment of decision. Use this time only for yourself, for only in this solitude and this great sleep and this abiding hunger will you be able to approach the moment for which you have prepared yourself, the one to which all things come, again and again and again, the one you have kept hidden close to your heart—now is the time for unlocking.

When she had finished reading the letter, she found herself still in the dream, if it really was a dream, which she was beginning to doubt, as the cold on her hands and her face felt real, more piercing now, approaching numbness. It was hard to move her lips, and her stomach gnawed at her in a way it never had before in dreams. Across the street, the glow of a lamp in an upstairs window caught her attention. She saw a woman approach a door, stand motionless for a moment, then reach into her dress and produce a key. In the air somewhere above her head (whose head? The woman in the window? The woman on the street?), the steady sound of footsteps could be heard.

16

Near as Dewey could figure, he had just woken up in the early hours of his second morning alone in the strange hotel. There was really nothing to tell time by other than his understanding of the earth's passage through the solar system. He was old enough and wise enough to know that the earth went around the sun, that it spun on its axis while it did so, and that a complete spin took twenty-four hours, which was a day, and he was even smart enough to know that in the winter the earth was tilted away from the sun, which meant the days were shorter, that the sun went down earlier in the evening and came up later in the morning, so that in a winter month like this one less than half the day was spent in daylight, and believe it or not (this was the kind of thing adults always doubted until his dad got him to answer questions or make some demonstration), he even knew that being farther north, as in, say, the northern part of Idaho rather than South Carolina, added to the reduced sunlight effect because...because why? Because of the increased angle of the tilt away from the sun if you were farther from the equator, that was it, all of which actually meant that, right now, it could possibly be as late as, say, 6 a.m. And 6 a.m. was one hour before the diner opened across the street. The

Dooze Man had really come to count on that diner, he wouldn't hesitate to tell you.

It wasn't much to brag about, the diner. It was basically a big rectangle with booths up front against the window, the kitchen off to one side, and small tables stretching to the back where the restrooms were. The "decor," as his mother would call it, was pretty much nonexistent, just some crookedly hung pictures of the town, old brownish-tinted photographs of buildings (but not the hotel, he noticed) and men on horses and women in long dresses standing on a balcony and canvas tents pitched along a river and a couple of Indians holding rifles and some miners leaving a pit, looking like they'd had a hard day. But the place was warm and Dewey felt comfortable there. First, you had the fact that there were actual people at the diner, specifically Hugh and Lorraine, who were very nice and seemed quite concerned about his welfare and showed it in ways Dewey could appreciate, such as extra French fries and free dessert and quarters for the highly entertaining gumball machine. Some of the other people who went to the diner—and there didn't seem to be very many of them—were kind of creepy, like the men were big and hairy and quiet, and the women were either really fat or really skinny with tons of lines on their faces and dirty hair that wasn't a real color you'd find anywhere on earth. And they never talked to you or acted like you were smart or cute, the way people did back home in South Carolina, and they mostly looked at you out of the corners of their eyes as if either you or they were doing something wrong. In short, none of the citizens of Good Night seemed to want him to have a good anything. Even so, they weren't as scary, all things considered, as being alone at the hotel.

Then there was the matter of food, which the diner had in abundance, whereas the amount of food available in the hotel was, Dewey had determined, zero. Zero food. Zero tasty beverages, not even running water. This was strange. Dewey was sure that on the first night they came to the hotel he had brushed his teeth at the sink. He was thoroughly exhausted, but his mother had insisted on it, and he could remember quite clearly watching himself in the oval mirror while he scrubbed back and forth enough times to satisfy her, and although he couldn't actually remember the running water or putting any on his toothbrush, if there hadn't been water, that was something he would definitely remember, wouldn't he? And yet after that first night there had been no more running water. Or maybe once, the next morning, he couldn't exactly recall. But there was no water now. And no Coke machines. And no snack machines. He had scoured the place yesterday, so he knew. It was a spooky journey, one that he had been willing to make only during daylight hours, because at night the hotel, other than his room, where the streetlight shined, was pretty dark, only a sliver of light illuminating the corridor and the stairs.

So the food and beverage expedition had by necessity taken place during the day, and even then it had been really weird. All traces of life had vanished, except for the room in which Dewey was staying. There was no sign of the hotel owner, the crazy-looking dude who had greeted them. The deserted lobby seemed like it hadn't been touched by anyone in years. The same layer of dust covering everything, spiderwebs up in the corners of the ceiling, basically all the stuff you saw on TV whenever they wanted to get across the idea that someplace was abandoned and scary. But there was something else, too, something you couldn't sense from being shown a place like this on TV, which was the feeling Dewey got when he stood in the middle of the lobby, a feeling of being so completely alone that you were sure there were no other people within a hundred miles and that no one else had been alive on earth for a hundred years. Dewey blinked his eyes against the dust and listened to his own breathing and, after a minute, worked up the courage to venture through the door on the other side of the lobby.

There he found a large room with a fireplace and tall thin windows on both sides. It was the kind of room in which you could imagine people waltzing—if not for the dust, the cobwebs, the broken windowpane through which the snow filtered quietly. He imagined a man in a tuxedo rising from a long table and making a toast.

He moved on. At the back of the room he encountered two more doors, and behind them another large room, but one that seemed more promising in terms of food and drink opportunities. This room was obviously a kitchen, or used to be a kitchen. There were massive ovens embedded in the walls and long wooden tables with knife scars and long wooden shelves in something like a closet and another area with a door that swung open to expose hooks hung from the ceiling. A kitchen, no doubt, but no food in it anywhere.

He went back upstairs to the room, empty-handed, and turned on the scary TV, and glanced every once in a while at the ghostly images, the people moving in lines in a dark place, a man walking up some stairs, a woman in a room, lights that danced up and down, smoke pouring into a twilit sky. He finally fell asleep.

And now it was morning but it was still mostly dark. And he was freezing. And then he saw someone walk right by the room, plain as day, nonchalantly as you please. It was his mother.

Oh, the flood of relief. The flood of love, if you wanted to call it by its real name, though Dewey would normally have been uncomfortable calling it that. The flood of love and relief that surged up through him as if he had suddenly come across a warm fire, some life-sustaining place. The flood that pushed him out of the room and out into the hall where he could dimly see his mother's form receding from him, so that his voice rose automatically, shouting the word he had always been able to shout in the past when he wanted to feel safe, to be comforted, to be rescued from boredom or a momentary bout of sadness: "Mom, Mom, Mom!" It was terrifying that his mother didn't seem to hear him, just marched calmly up the stairs. Dewey shot forward in pursuit, up to the third-floor landing and down the hallway, and just as he came close to her his mother paused and turned, standing in the doorway to a room. In the gray early-morning light, snow streamed through a broken window at the end of the passageway. Her eyes seemed to flit over him briefly, like an unconscious acknowledgment of memory, a half recollection of something that had once been known. Then she turned her head and slipped into the room, and Dewey's breath left him at the suddenness of it.

He lurched ahead, yelling again—"Mom Mom Mom, it's me"—afraid that in the next split second she would shut the door and, this time, disappear forever. But she didn't shut the door, merely drifted in, her hand lingering for a moment on the frame. Dewey stopped, started forward again, stopped again, opened his mouth, closed it. He stood there, mere feet from his mother, mere feet from the angled light in the doorway. Everything was quiet. He could not hear any noise from the room his mother had just entered—no rustling of clothes, no creaking of floorboards, no displacement of objects, not a single thing that could normally be associated with the activity of a person, even a sometimes sneakily quiet person such as Dewey's mother, in a room. Or possibly there was a faint kind of shushing sound, like the noise of the ocean in a seashell. But this could be the snow falling outside, or his own breathing, or the blood pumping rapidly through his veins from his racing heart. So he listened as carefully as he could. And then, though it made him afraid for some reason, he moved forward and stood in the doorway.

There on the bed, just as you would logically expect her to be, if the laws of the universe were in fact "immutable," as his father always explained that they were, sat his mother, her hands folded in her lap, a slight smile playing across her features—Dewey would have described the scene as *peaceful*. There was his mother, normally a bundle of energy, gazing peacefully at her hands. And in the moment before Dewey spoke to her he had time to recognize that the dress she wore—an old-fashioned kind of dress that was wide at the hips and had a high collar and long sleeves, and which came down all the way to her feet—was new, or at least one he'd never seen before, and that, curiously, the decorative wall lamps on either end of the room were now bursting with light, little flames flickering inside their glass domes.

"Mom?" he said, and stepped through the doorway. And stepping through the doorway was like nothing he'd ever done before—it was as if he passed through the thinnest, coldest waterfall, a sheer veil of water and ice that poured slowly over everything, and for a moment he lost all sensation. And then he was in the room, empty and dark. Sagging old bed with a water-stained mattress. Cobwebs and dust bunnies. Chunks of plaster fallen from the ceiling. His mother nowhere to be found.

Then it seemed to Dewey that a long time had passed, as if he were having one of his "episodes," though he couldn't say for sure because no one was there to tell him all the things he'd done and said and subsequently forgotten. He was very sleepy, and after he guided his feet, in a sort of floating way, back out of the room and into the hall, he turned around to see exactly what he had first seen—there was the bed with the flowered sheets, there was his mother sitting on it, there were the lights in the room. There was an end table and a snow globe and a large chest of drawers and a colorful rug and some wispy curtains and, of course, the snow falling outside. How much it hurt to see his mother sitting there without being able to reach her. He hadn't known it would hurt so much. "Mom?" he said again, though he didn't hold out much hope. And his mother, not answering, went on sitting and smiling and gazing downward.

PART II

ECHOES FROM WITHIN

For even if we have the sensation of being always enveloped in, surrounded by our own soul, still it does not seem a fixed and immovable prison; rather do we seem to be borne away with it, and perpetually struggling to pass beyond it, to break out into the world, with a perpetual discouragement as we hear endlessly, all around us, that unvarying sound which is no echo from without, but the resonance of a vibration from within.

—Marcel Proust, *Remembrance of Things Past*

17

It was the third consecutive day of snow, as lengthy and heavy a snow as the residents of Good Night could remember in the town's short history, and it was gumming up Tiffany's plans for the hotel's grand opening. The train had arrived at the depot all right, but it was impossible for the hired carriages to make their way up the street, which meant the senator and his wife and staff and the musicians from San Francisco with their instruments and the reporter from the magazine in Chicago and the mine owner from down in Colorado and heaven knew who else Tiffany had invited were having a disastrous time plunging through the snowdrifts in their best shoes or, in at least one case, that of the Broadway actress who was coming from Seattle, being carried to the hotel piggyback by one of the local miscreants, reportedly that Harrington boy, who didn't have the sense of a mule. Tiffany himself was a proper fool, thought Anthony Addison, seated on the sofa next to his wife, Julia (who looked handsome in the new dress she'd purchased in Spokane Falls). He, Addison, had told Tiffany that the hotel would never be completed by October, when Tiffany had first tried to entice the high and mighty for the unveiling. Tiffany was incredulous at the suggestion—the raw materials were all in place, damn it, what could possibly hold up the works? And when Addison had successfully predicted that it wasn't a question of materials but of labor—namely that Tiffany wouldn't be able to find enough steady workers among the miners, who were earning considerably better wages in the booming industry underground than they could make by waiting for Tiffany to dig the gold from his pockets—Tiffany began referring to him around town as an "obstruction to progress."

It had all worked out in the end. Tiffany had his grand hotel with its finely appointed rooms and its internationally renowned chef and its thousand-piece glass chandelier. He now employed a staff of nearly fifty workers, including, if one believed the rumors, a half dozen of the nicer variety of prostitutes, whose services he had purchased outright from a wealthy madam in San Francisco. Yes, it had all worked out fine…just a few months behind schedule, as Addison had guessed. So he laughed to himself sitting in front of the fire, admiring his wife (what a marvelous find she had been for him, it was a pleasure just to watch her sitting there), basking in the lobby's warm glow while Tiffany bumbled back and forth behind the desk, nervously knocking over the candles he tried to place in the candelabra, cursing the snow in an audible whisper, fussing anxiously with the ends of his mustache.

"I wonder what she said to the president," mused Mrs. Addison, referring to the actress, Miss Rose Blanchard, who had been the primary subject of discussion among most of the women for the past month, and who, if the telegraph Tiffany had received from the depot could be taken as the literal truth, was right now en route to the hotel on the back of young Harrington. Miss Blanchard had been a guest at the White House in the fall, and Mrs. Addison wanted to believe of her that she had something interesting to say. It was the principal failing of the few proper female residents of Good Night, according to Mrs. Addison, that they rarely said anything interesting. Mr. Addison tried to oblige by being interesting himself, but he was not always sure he succeeded, at least in the eyes of his wife, who had met many interesting people in her day. "I would have said to him…" Mrs. Addison continued, staring at the orange flames dancing in the fireplace. "I would have said…What would I have said to him?" she asked no one in particular, and she ran her thumbnail across her bottom teeth in a way she often had when concentrating fiercely on a troublesome idea. Addison looked at her perched there on the ottoman—her head held forward, her back as straight as a plumb line, her whole figure leaning eagerly toward something in the middle distance, perhaps there in the vicinity of the fire tongs, expressive of an energy to which he did not feel equal. This was one of those moments when he felt decidedly that he should not have brought her to this town. "That's the trouble with this place," Mrs. Addison said, to herself more than to her husband. "After one has been here for a while, one no longer knows what to say."

Mr. Addison sighed. Out the window nothing could be seen but the snow. If only the guests would start arriving, he could quit thinking of Mrs. Addison's evident dissatisfactions. This hotel of Tiffany's really was spectacular, no getting around it, and it was a day to be enjoyed despite the weather, a banner day for the town in this year of 1886. "Would you like to take a little turn about the place, dear?" he asked his wife.

She took his arm—why weren't the guests here already, to see how neatly she did that? "Mr. Tiffany?" she asked. "Could we take a stroll through the rooms?" And Tiffany hopped to. Mrs. Addison commanded that sort of attention, even from a man as nervous and busy as Tiffany was today. So he gave them the tour, starting with the kitchen, where he had employed a small army of help—some of them miners Addison recognized from La Mine de Rêve, the silver mining operation that had drawn him out here in the hope of earning his living and had in fact made him a fortune in a few short years, at least in his own estimation of what a fortune entailed: one of the few stately homes that had taken its place outside the mining camps and the clapboard houses of the town, a respectable two-story Queen Anne style designed by an architect from Boston; a rather princely salary negotiated with Mr. Tillbrook, the president of the operation, and a share in the company's ownership that would increase over time; the esteem and deference of his fellow citizens, people like Tiffany, who despite the little disagreement over the construction schedule of the hotel was a man with whom you could enjoy a mutual respect; and the finest wife in the Idaho territory, with her dark hair piled high on her head easily the most striking, with her East Coast education and her aristocratic pedigree easily the most admirable. Despite her petite form and delicate features, she scared Mr. Addison half to death.

Tiffany took them strolling through the kitchen and into the spacious dining hall, where there would be dancing and revelry later on this evening, and where, undoubtedly, some of the miners would burst in and break something expensive. But it couldn't be helped, and Addison wasn't the sort to look down his nose at people anyway, having come from common stock himself.

They were led up a back stairway to the third floor, where Tiffany said the finest rooms were, and Mrs. Addison asked questions in the silky voice she saved for such occasions, and Mr. Addison soon grew bored. Tiffany showed them the room where they would be staying, room 306, and Addison lingered at the window staring at the snow, turning a snow globe around and around in his hand. And then he saw something very curious—out in the street was a small boy, lifting his legs as high as he could to wade through the drifts of snow, which were almost up to his hips by now. The boy had apparently just come out the front door of the hotel, as he was now making his way straight across the street to the other side, but Addison had certainly not seen him downstairs. First, the boy wore an unusual-looking sweater that Addison would have noticed, never having come across one of that sort before. Second, the boy's head of tousled blond hair was of the type that Addison had always imagined his own son might have, were he ever to have a son. Something about the boy and his bare head of golden hair and the cloud of his breath and the vigorous effort with which he lifted his feet, grimly determined to surmount the ever-growing hills of snow, clutched at Addison's heart, and he found himself, inexplicably, overcome with strong emotion. He stepped toward the window and, loudly enough that it must have been heard by Tiffany and Mrs. Addison, he rapped on the glass. But the boy did not hear.

18

Could you believe a town this size had so many stairs? They ran from building to building, hidden from the street, a world of ruined planks and crumbling masonry and musty smells. The stairs never seemed to empty out anywhere, never led outside, just wended through forgotten corridors above or below or in between the stores and bars and restaurants, occasionally revealing glimpses of the public spaces—a kitchen where a white-hatted, dirty-aproned cook stood flipping an omelet in a greasy pan, a furniture store where a lone employee sat in a recliner reading a magazine and pulling the lever on the chair up and down—that lay between the stairways and the street. Occasionally, as the troop led Robbie racing up and down and around, they would pass a window through which he could see again the endless snowfall and the grayish-white sky.

"How can a town this size have all these fucking stairs?" he asked Rusty, the guy in front of him.

"Everything's connected," Rusty said, racing up another flight, huffing and puffing his way down a narrow passage scattered with paint cans and an assortment of discarded power tools. There were other people above them—he could hear the clunking footsteps, the occasional laughter—but they'd passed out of sight, and he was tired of following Rusty's back.

A window appeared just up ahead, and instead of chasing the group to the next floor, Robbie stepped toward the little landing that contained the rectangle of dim light. A massive spiderweb drooped from the corner of the ceiling, and the remains of a potted plant, long dead, hung in the window frame. He pushed aside the plant with one hand and held his other hand in front of the windowpane, where a thin line of cold air crept through a jagged crack in the glass. Outside the streetlamps winked on and there was a half-light over the hills and he didn't know whether it was dawn or dusk. There had been many, many times in the past when he hadn't known whether it was dawn or dusk, and generally he hadn't cared. Right now, though, releasing the plant so that it swayed back and forth on its creaky chain, staring out the window at the line of pencil-thin fir trees that formed the outline of the hills, everything beyond enveloped in a blanket of snowy white, he had a gnawing feeling that he should know the time of day, as if the time of day were of vital importance to him somehow, and a kind of irritation grew in his brain, the irritation that almost always came from some distant connection to the world of times and schedules and responsibilities, came whenever he felt it incumbent upon him to do a thing in the way that other people did it.

Why he should feel that particular form of irritation right now was a bit of a mystery—he had just been hanging out with some people over at a house, and there had been a young woman of malleable temperament and soft breasts and hardly any scruples, right? And then those guys had come outside and they had carted him off and they had gone in a door somewhere and run up and down a lot of stairs and…that had been less than a minute ago. And yet he could barely remember it, as if it were something he'd done yesterday or last week. And hadn't the light out the window changed rather abruptly? The hills had sunk into darkness, so that it was almost impossible for him to make out their silhouettes against the backdrop of cold, gray clouds. Could he have gone into some weird trance? Of course—after all, that too had happened before. But he hadn't really had a whole lot to drink, comparatively, and he felt pretty goddamn sober, if you wanted to know the truth, and in fact a little bored, and now maybe even a little bit alarmed because...huh.

He heard something, and hearing something brought to mind the fact that he had been hearing almost nothing for quite some time, just the whistling of wind through the windowpane and the steady sting of snowflakes on the glass. It had been a long time since he'd heard voices or footsteps, for instance, and yet now he was hearing both, only he couldn't tell whether the footsteps were above or below, or what the voice was saying in the air around his head, except that it was one distinct word being repeated over and over. Then someone was breathing in his ear. "Robbie?" a familiar voice said.

It was Julia. His eyes closed, though he didn't mean for them to, and inside his head there was a whirl of light and sound, and the air turned bitter cold, and then he was again in one of the long corridors, one of the infinite passages that you came across every minute or two in this insane place, came to after running up and down more flights of broken stairs, finding yet another locked doorway, and he couldn't tell if he was physically passing through this haunted landscape or merely dreaming it.

There was Julia's voice again, coming to him from somewhere else, a place far away or a time in the past, as if the voice had been suspended in the air forever, floating on a breeze, waiting to reach him. He seemed to be floating, traveling through some unknown dimension, some space between who he was and once was, an in-between place in which he still heard Julia's voice, but different now, muted and wispy, coming from someplace he recognized. Tangled white sheets, an open window, twirling curtains, brisk air with a watery feel. The ceiling turning, turning, turning above him. And Julia laughing. She was in his parents' kitchen, it was morning, and he was in his room upstairs. He listened to the voices—his father's carefully modulated tone, his mother's brightly false chatter, Julia's voice, appealingly straightforward and calm. He put his leg over the edge of the bed and his foot touched the cold floor and the room slowed down and stopped spinning. Julia's laughter again, disturbing to him on some level, disruptive to his basic assumptions about the world. Tonio had just brought her home for the first time. Robbie was seventeen, already a fuckup, already written off in some subtle, unstated way by everyone, or at least everyone who *counted,* like his high school teachers who'd endured his years of underachievement and his lackadaisical attitude and his failure at this and his inability to see that, etc. He had long since quit imagining Tonio as anyone he wanted to emulate. It puzzled him, observing his brother when he came home for Christmas, or vacations, or breaks in the academic year—what had he ever seen to admire? In fact he had almost quit noticing his brother until he showed up at home with Julia. Now *there* was a puzzle to consider. How had Tonio, he of the apishly long arms and the heavy shuffling footsteps and the outsize cranium, the collared shirts with coffee stains, the boat-size running shoes and huarache sandals, the cowlick wetted down carelessly and unsuccessfully, the nose always in a book or a set of field notes—how had *that* guy convinced this woman to marry him?

Julia's voice again, floating up from the kitchen. He could hear everyone but Tonio, who he guessed wasn't there, which made it worthwhile to go downstairs, maybe. He descended quietly, his head throbbing, balancing himself against the wall, to find all the major characters (excepting Tonio) in the family drama assembled.

Addison mater and pater were in their usual morning gowns and pajamas, and Julia had apparently made them breakfast, a weird rite of passage, when everything was interrupted by the sudden appearance of Robbie, stumbling down the last two stairs in an obvious state of post-drunken dishevelment, attempting to procure a box of cereal from the pantry without dislodging the pantry door, trying to pour the milk without spilling it all over the table. "Aaah," he said as he sat on the vinyl-covered chair in the breakfast nook, the chair making that sound like a polite fart.

His parents' immediate situation was interesting. On the one hand, there was a reputation to uphold, an understood but unstated superiority to Julia, a need to show that she was somehow being granted undeserved favor, exalted over the normal run of humanity based on Tonio's selection of her as a wife, but now there was this additional difficulty, which was how to work Robbie into the equation, because if you were so superior, an appellate court judge like his father, aligned with all things intellectual and progressive, why did you have a screwed-up kid like this living in your house, part of your family, who was flunking chemistry and calculus and making everyone's life miserable? What a difficult tightrope to walk so early on such a fine day, birds chirping, sun shining, the scent of Mother Addison's roses floating on the breeze. Plus there was the whole issue of being nice, decent people, how you had to feel good about yourself when you went to bed at night. This was true, basically, Robbie knew—his parents were trying their best to do what they thought they were supposed to do on planet Earth. An admirable project, all things considered, but one that required a certain facility for lying to yourself in the dark at the end of the day, a way to smooth and finesse your prejudices and your shortcomings.

At any rate, there he was in the breakfast nook forcing the recalibration of the extended family dynamic, yawning, wiping away crusty stuff from his eyelashes. "Aaah," he said again. He seemed to be eating some sort of granola out of a bowl, the other family members staring at him.

"Julia made omelets," his mother said. "They're wonderful. Try one."

Robbie performed reconnaissance, sipping orange juice with one eye open over the glass rim. The night before, he'd been at a kegger at a campground and done four beer bongs in twenty minutes on a dare, after which he'd thrown up on himself and jumped in the Sammamish River with his clothes on.

"That's all right," Julia said. "He doesn't look like he's hungry." And she laughed.

It was the laugh that did it, that declared some secret alliance with Robbie and all his fucked-up-ness, that made them outlaws where the parental units were concerned. And there was another thing. When Julia laughed, she locked eyes with Robbie. "Are you okay?" she asked, and he said, "What, yeah, okay," but he wasn't okay, of course not, the whole fucking stream of human life and his participation in said stream bothered him and somehow Julia's question had tapped into this bothersome problem and somehow his answer had been an inadequate defense against it and suddenly everybody—even his parents—knew that there had been a moment when all these things escaped from under their usual cover. And ever since that moment there had been an awareness that Julia was her husband's brother's keeper.

It was that same voice he heard right now, from long ago, Julia that morning in the kitchen, but still repeating just that one word, *Robbie,* as if joining the two syllables often enough could convey some critical message—Julia's voice echoing, receding, faintly calling his name.

And then he was somewhere else, staring up at a dead plant hanging in a dirty window. It was the same dead plant he'd seen when he started his lonely sojourn. He sat on the stairs and watched his breath clouding out, dimly visible in the half-light of the snowy sky through the window. Had he been sitting here for hours? He must have been sitting here for hours. There had been footsteps at some point, the sound of a hand sliding on a banister. Julia had called his name. He had felt himself transported elsewhere. But here he was, still sitting, and he couldn't even be sure whether he'd slept, really. In some way it seemed that he'd been conscious of the dusty floor and the flat yellow light of the infinite hallways and the broken stairway the whole time. It took him a while even now to understand that he was shaking. He was *freezing* to death here. Somewhere out there on the verge of himself this almost made him laugh, the idea of freezing to death on a stairway in some shitkicker ghost town in Idaho. It wasn't all the drugs that had taken down Robbie Addison in the end—no, it was a snowstorm, like he was some old-timer who'd gotten lost on his way to the gold mine, some pioneer of fucking yesteryear. This was only humorous for a moment before it became kind of terrifying.

He had pissed his pants. That much seemed clear. Or whoever's pants these were. That had happened before, and it was generally a bad sign. He was all alone and he couldn't find his way out of this goddamn place and he hadn't had a drink or even so much as a beer for several hours now and there were no drugs readily available and, first and foremost, nobody seemed to care. He couldn't even quite believe, despite having heard her voice calling out to him, that Julia was searching for him or interested in his whereabouts. Or the Dooze Man. And who gave a fuck about Tonio. But Julia... Although he had thought at the time that he clearly heard her voice, he was now prepared to write it off as the front edge of hallucination, the shades of the various demons creeping up on him, into his imagination.

For a minute or two he watched the flakes fall in a lazy circular motion, appearing at the top of the window frame and drifting down and out of sight, and soon it looked to him as if the snow itself were stationary and the building, the one in which he was sitting, rocketed up into space. And he did have a feeling of being lifted, but he recognized it as the woozy drama of nerves and empty stomach and muscles asked to do work to which they were no longer accustomed. In short, he was fucked up here, and not in a good way.

He suspected that he was no longer in the hotel, though he knew that was where they had started out, Ruby and the others finding it hilarious that they had managed to lead him to the one place he didn't want to go, tricking him inside through some back entrance. Before he knew it, he was standing in the lobby. But then there had simply been too many corridors in too many directions and too many stairways and too many romps through cluttered attics and dark basements for one building to contain. He actually thought that he had at some point crossed *underneath the street,* and that he was now on the side with the bar and the diner. Everything in this town, apparently, was part of a giant labyrinth. And Robbie guessed he'd been ditched in it intentionally.

Well. Not much incentive to do much of anything. Feel the twitching cheeks, the buzzing teeth, the clamping jaw, the constricted chest and airways. In addition to frostbite, the joys of dependency.

It was funny that he'd dreamed about Julia, freezing to death here on the stairs. He supposed his subconscious was still caught up in the matter—how his brother had ever married her. As far as Robbie was concerned, every sexual relationship (and every friendship as far as that went) contained the possibility of a certain finite amount of pleasure, a prescription for which there was no refill, so that you had two choices, the same way you did with drugs—you could spread out the pleasure in very small doses over a long period of time, which as far as he could see was the only way it would ever be possible to make a marriage work, or you could go for it all in one big glorious bang. He and Tonio had an example of the first approach in their own parents, who had never used up any great portion of their allotted joy at any point in their forty-odd-year run.

It had always seemed to Robbie that Julia behaved as if she was in the second kind of relationship, while Tonio behaved as if he was in the first. That is, while what Julia seemed to feel for his brother might better be called warmth than passion, it definitely appeared to have an expiration date. Something about her suggested exhaustion, maybe as a result of neglect on Tonio's part, neglect of the myriad small attentions she paid him, the collection of the various articles of clothing Tonio carelessly laid around the house, the way she took his toast out of the toaster oven for him (because Tonio never remembered, the toast vanishing into thin air as far as he was concerned, resurrected only as a curious burned smell a few minutes later). Clearly there was something about Tonio that she admired, but her attentions toward him seemed like a means of getting to something else. And Robbie wasn't sure how he had intuited (although he often seemed to intuit this sort of thing, which sometimes made him suspect something that certainly no one else in his family had ever suspected, namely that, of the two brothers, he was actually the smarter one) that something deeper underlay Julia's attachments, that she saw her marriage and everything else in the world as the pieces of an intricately designed puzzle that she had only her allotted span of years to assemble. She was constantly alert, as if she sensed some disturbance within the visual or auditory or tactile dimension currently on display to everyone else, and never fully believed in what appeared on the surface, was always attuned to something else that might be occurring.

So this was another strange aspect of the partnership—why, if Julia was the kind of person who believed it was possible to solve life's deepest mysteries, had she tied herself to Tonio when the major thrust of Tonio's life, as far as Robbie could see, had been going about the intellectual and even physical business (the long bony hands busily fondling the bony skulls, the big hollow eyes examining the cast of a prehistoric femur) of demonstrating that people (at least people other than himself) had never solved *anything,* explaining to Robbie when he was age thirteen or so, as briefly as possible in response to Robbie's question on the subject, that cultural anthropology was the study of exactly where and when civilization had turned to shit?

A cat appeared. Right there. A *cat.* In the stairwell where he was sitting. It sashayed on up to him, a long-haired cat with multicolored markings, tan and black and white. It had a red collar with a silver tag that made a tinkling sound. This astonishing cat rubbed against Robbie's leg, but when his hand went out to it, it skittered away and approached a door—a *door,* not twenty feet away—and scratched to be let in. Amazingly, the door opened from the other side, soundlessly, and the cat disappeared.

It seemed like a good idea to try this door. His legs didn't want to work right away, but once he got his body tilted over to the side he was able to fold his legs up and get his feet under him a little bit and use the wall to help push up to a standing position. Then he staggered forward, arms outstretched, until he arrived at the door and commenced pounding.

Almost immediately the door swung open, and the closest thing Robbie had ever experienced to the feeling of the door opening was a dream he often had as a child of standing in some high place, in the sunshine, the background unfamiliar. Below him was a long valley, a river cutting across it, the valley green and meadow-like, fading away toward tall, purplish mountains in the distance—always some variation of this scene. He stepped forward and his stomach plunged when he found there was no ground under him.

Then the deathward dropping, the momentary panic, and it always seemed to him an act of sheer will on his part to avoid his fate and begin flying, soaring along the cliff wall, peering down into the valley where his shadow raced beneath him. How many different ways he had found to live out this childhood dream — they were almost beyond number.

19

The Dooze Man was back in his favorite booth, the same one he'd been in every day, eating pretty much the same food — French fries, always, and a burger or a sandwich, this time a sandwich, a steak sandwich to be precise. He liked this booth because it was where he'd sat with his dad before he disappeared forever, as Dewey was starting to see it, because if his dad was ever going to show up again why hadn't he already shown up again. When people were gone, Dewey decided, they were usually gone for good, like children on the news, taken away by strangers in cars or locked away in basements or closets, their bones found years later in the woods. Or criminals who had done something terribly wrong — was his father one of these? Changing their identities and wearing fake beards, flying to remote places like Borneo, every once in a while caught at the airport on the way out of town. Mom, Dad, and Uncle Robbie dressed up like tourists, wearing flowered shirts and floppy hats and sunglasses with the price tags still on the frames, lying on a beach somewhere drinking bright red drinks in tall glasses, discussing how soon it might be safe to send Dewey a postcard. *Sorry we left,* he could read in his mother's jagged handwriting (she had shockingly bad penmanship), *but Dad stole an old pile of bones that was worth a bazillion bucks, and we're living in a hut in Peru.*

More likely they were all dead in a ditch. The crazy hotel owner, the skinny evil dude with the big nose, had wasted them all one by one, first Uncle Robbie, then his dad, and then his mom, taken them in the back room and tortured them and cooked them in the massive oven. But that wasn't true. That sounded like a fairy tale, the early part of one, before the hero or the handsome prince came, when everything was horrible and wrong. The truth was going to be even scarier and more real. There was the illusion of his mother walking around that hotel room and sitting on the bed. There was the trail of dead souls, as Dewey had come to think of them, passing in the greenish light of the TV.

Lorraine came over to the table. She was a large, friendly person—not fat, just large—and one day she wore T-shirts and jeans and boots as if she were a man and the next day she would show up in a nice dress and lots of makeup. She said things like what she said right now: "Did you get enough to eat, babycakes? Are you doing okay, angel, you poor thing?"

They had taught him what to say, Hugh and Lorraine, so that he didn't have to pay any money. "Yes, thanks. Can you put it on my tab?" And Lorraine laughed real loud—"cackled" might be the exact word—and Hugh chuckled over at the grill. This thing about the tab really seemed to make their day. Actually, he seemed to make their day in general, if you judged by how happy they always were just to see him come in, how they practically fell all over themselves making sure he had everything he could possibly want or need. It made him wonder why, given the fact that they seemed to understand his situation more or less, they hadn't invited him home. Did they live in a trailer? Like one of those little ones you could hitch on the back of a truck? That would be perfectly fine. He had almost blurted it out a couple of times—*Get me out of here!*—but if there was one thing his mother hated, it was people who invited themselves. And even though these weren't exactly normal circumstances, he couldn't quite bring himself to do it. Besides, while it seemed more and more unlikely, what if his mom and dad came back for him at the hotel and he wasn't there?

He turned his gaze across the street. Out the window was the same thing he saw every time, the snow. The snow, the snow, the snow, the snow, the snow, the snow, the snow. And the hotel room on the third floor where every once in a while his mother's shadow passed behind the curtain, a thrilling, sad mirage. "Do you see her?" he'd asked Lorraine once.

"Who?" she said, looking up while she held his plate in her hand.

"The woman in the window," he said. "My mother."

Lorraine set the plate down, craning her neck. "There's nobody in the window, babycakes," she said. She shook her head and pursed her lips and glanced at Hugh, who stayed bent over the grill.

Sometimes Dewey could hear them talking about him in the kitchen, back through the rectangular window. It was like the dialogue in a movie.

Hugh: Well, what am *I* supposed to do?
Lorraine: Nothing. Don't do anything. Just flip a fucking burger.
Hugh: Come on, you can't—
Lorraine: Why not?
Hugh: Why *not*? What the fuck do you mean?
Lorraine: He can hear you.
Hugh: *You* just said it.
Lorraine: Said what?
Hugh: You know. The *f* word.
Lorraine: I did not.
Hugh: Yes, you *did*.

Lorraine: Well, if I did, I whispered it.

Hugh: Whatever. Anyway excuse my French, but you can't—

Lorraine: Why not?

Hugh: Here we go again.

It was like a *bad* movie where nothing ever happened.

He rose wearily from the booth and shuffled past the counter and Hugh gave him a quarter for a gumball, like he always did. What was the point of that? Dewey's whole family was missing. How was a gumball supposed to help? He went ahead anyway and put the quarter in, and yes, he noticed for the one millionth time now that the maze contained a reproduction of the stairway in the hotel, was in fact probably an exact replica of the whole layout of the town. But so what? What did that prove? And what did it matter if out the window now, past all the falling snow, he could see a man who resembled his father, only with a mustache, standing in the window of that very same room in which Dewey had encountered his mother? He'd seen the same thing before.

"How you doing, big guy?" Hugh said from behind the register.

His dad was the only adult he'd ever really understood how to talk to. Well, his mother, but he didn't even think of her as belonging to the world of adults, to a separate world from himself. And Dewey was the only kid his dad knew how to talk to. When his friends came to the house, for instance, his dad would make jokes and stray remarks that only Dewey could understand, so his friends thought his father was insane. And vice versa. Clearly, the Dooze Man wasn't what you'd think of as a normal ten-year-old, but his father thought so, so he made the mistake of thinking it was the *other* kids, Dewey's friends, who were freaks instead of Dewey. Example: Once, his dad walked into the living room and Dewey was in one of his moods, staring out the window for hours, and his dad said, "What are you thinking about, Doozer?"

And Dewey said, "Oh, I'm just sitting here thinking about how the universe is always expanding, and what it'll be like when everything stretches out too far and all the stars explode, and there won't be any more light or any life anywhere and everything will be just like a huge black hole."

And his dad kind of laughed to himself and came up behind Dewey and messed with his hair. "Kids," he said.

So obviously it was also true that his father wasn't normal in the things he thought and said, and Dewey would be making a mistake if he took his dad as any sort of indicator of how adults were supposed to interact with ten-year-olds. He doubted that Hugh, with his greasy apron and wool cap and guitar pick between his teeth, carried on a conversation in the same way his father did, and so he was a little unclear about how to proceed. But the time for proceeding had come. Things had gone on too long and become too weird.

"I don't think I'm doing very well," Dewey said, glancing sidelong at Hugh, who removed the pick from between his teeth and scratched it thoughtfully back and forth across the stubble on his chin.

"Unh," Hugh said. He squinted into the falling snow as if searching for something that could be obscured by it...an aardvark, a zeppelin. He took a peek toward the back of the dining area, where Lorraine was talking to the only other customer, some grizzled old guy who looked like he might have arrived on a burro. Then he walked over to where Dewey stood near the door. "It's hard, right?" he said, and he swallowed and glanced down at Dewey for a second. "I mean, right. You're in a tough spot for a kid."

"I think I'm in a tough spot for, like, anyone," Dewey said. "Like for any actual person. Irrespective of age."

"What'd you say?" Hugh said.

"I said, 'Irrespective of age.'"

Hugh didn't say anything. Across the street the woman, his mother, passed by the window. Just a shadow.

"You didn't see that," Dewey said, and gave Hugh a hard stare.

"I didn't see what," Hugh said.

Dewey sighed. "I mean I think I want to know what's going on around here if somebody can please tell me."

"Lorraine!" Hugh called out.

"Because I don't think this is normal," Dewey said. "What's wrong with this place? My dad's an anthropologist and so I know about the rules, okay? Like how things can happen. And this isn't how things can happen."

"Lorraine!" Hugh called again. "Like what?" he added.

"Like my uncle disappeared and my dad disappeared and my mom disappeared but then there's a lady who looks like my mom in that window over there only nobody else can see her and there's a weird guy who looks like my father in a disguise only he pretends he doesn't know me but he watches me from the window. One time he was out on the street, and I yelled at him, 'Dad!,' but all he did was run and disappear through a door." He was getting choked up now even though he had told himself not to. The old grizzled guy eyed him suspiciously in between drags on a cigarette, but Dewey didn't care. He started talking even louder. "And there's scary stuff on my TV," he said, "like dead people coming out of a hole and things like that. That's not supposed to happen, and I want someone to tell me."

The snow kept coming down, soft and quiet with no wind at all. He and Hugh stood there and watched it. In this town, you spent a lot of time looking at snow.

"Lorraine!" Hugh shouted.

"What?" she answered. "I'm talking to Jerome."

"You better come here," Hugh said to her. He guided Dewey over to the booth and made him sit down again. "Bring some Kleenex," he added, because the Dooze Man was crying now, yes, he most certainly was, the snow outside blurring till everything became a screen of gray. And he felt good about the crying, because the crying seemed normal, like something someone his age should do in a situation like this one, and he wondered why he hadn't let himself do it before. He started crying even harder and it felt even better. "And a piece of pie, maybe, while you're at it," Hugh said.

20

Ultimately, you lived and died entirely alone—that was at once the most satisfying and the most disturbing fact of life. He had his own body, his own mind, he moved through the world autonomously in both thought and action and experienced life on his own, in a way that no other creature on the earth presently or in what people called the past or the future experienced it exactly—that was what gave his life a kind of dignity. Despite all the people he knew, with whom he surrounded himself and occupied his time, life was ultimately finite and he would have to die alone, too—that was what made him sit up sometimes in the night, gasping, putting his hand to his chest to feel his heart beating there. There were two fears only—the fear of death, for which people had religion, and the fear of solitude, for which people had society. He wasn't religious and he didn't have much to do with society. But he also didn't have a misanthropic bone in his body, despite what Julia or Robbie might say; he knew that societies invented God to assuage the fear of death, but he also knew that people formed societies to increase the joy in life, that joy came from human companionship and human communication. He wasn't a robot. It was just that he had spent many years carefully, very carefully, learning how to bury his emotional life, covering it with the finest sediment, letting it sift under layer by layer, into a lower stratum, so that only the most practiced excavator would ever find anything there. Just the tiniest part of him poked through, like the eyes of a lizard that hides in desert sands. He had been happy that way.

Then his wife came along. And it wasn't that he was bowled over by her beauty (although she was very attractive, of course—any idiot could see that), or that he had experienced some version of love at first sight, or that he had gotten carried away in a romantic whirlwind. It was just that, within five minutes of meeting her, he had felt...comfortable. He had felt comfortable with her in a way that he rarely felt around people, even people he had known a long time—Robbie, for instance. Was that such a terrible thing? And yet if you listened to the popular ideas of what a marriage was supposed to be like, merely being comfortable wasn't enough. He had tried, at times, to do more—had tried buying flowers, tried going out to dinner, embarking on romantic getaways, had even made the occasional awkward confession of love. But with these things he was *not* comfortable, and, curiously, they had never seemed to be what his wife wanted from him anyway. And so while he had felt at ease in the relationship from the beginning, he had never been called completely out of his hole, and he had never tried to coax his wife out either. The effect was that he knew his wife now in the same way that he'd known her, say, after the first year they'd been married. There was a longer trail of shared experiences, but the track hadn't cut any deeper. He was still, to some degree, safe beneath the sand.

And then came Dewey. Game over. Defenses wiped out immediately, entirely, white flag waving in the breeze. Dewey was a different thing altogether, for which Tonio had no classification—his son was so much a part of his own internal world that it was hard to believe anything could happen to him that didn't also happen, simultaneously, to himself. It was almost incomprehensible that Dewey existed separately in the world, that he went to school and did who knew what all day long, talked to different people, had accidents on the playground, learned about geography. Tonio sometimes felt himself straining in the middle of one of his own lectures to imagine what Dewey might be doing that instant, how his hair was combed, the expression on his face. So much of his life was absorbed in Dewey that to be apart from his son was like having two separate experiences, one only half real and one entirely imagined. It was something that he could barely fathom, even though it was the state in which he now found himself. He was convinced, on some level, that this was all an elaborate trick, some cruel form of punishment for having, ten years ago, on the day he first held his son in his arms, allowed himself to love.

It was morning, and he sat in a chair staring hard out into a world of white and wrestling with what he thought he knew about his senses. "I was in this room yesterday," he said.

"That's possible," the owner, Tiffany, who was seated next to him, said.

"I looked out that same window," he said, "but it wasn't like this."

Tiffany rested his chin in the palm of his big hand. He was smoking a pipe, drawing in the tobacco with little sputtering sounds. It was cold in the room, room 306.

"It was nothing like this," Tonio continued. "The hotel was new and clean and my wife was here with me." He paused and turned his gaze from the window to the bed and he breathed in deep. "I can still smell my wife in this room," he said. "And there's something else. Something that happened."

"I'm not denying the possibility," Tiffany said.

Every time he talked to Tiffany he felt like killing him. He had never before felt the urge to strangle a man with his bare hands, but Tiffany brought forth this urge on every single occasion that the two of them were together in a room, forcibly and invariably. But Tiffany was all he had. There was no way to strangle him, at least not yet. It wouldn't be a good way to play the percentages.

"I was in this room," he said, staring out again at the snow, which continued to fall, floating silently into the heaps already on the ground, drifting into dunes that formed along the sidewalks. "But I don't think I was exactly myself."

At that he stopped talking for a long time and simply stared out the window until he felt that he had come unhooked from everything, as if his life were suspended in a world of quiet snow, not proceeding anywhere. This was a strange feeling he had come to have over and over since he'd been here, and when it settled on him he sometimes disappeared to himself, for how long or how short a time he couldn't say.

Tiffany's voice called him back on this occasion. "When you say that, what does it mean to you?"

Tonio ran his fingers slowly along the worn thread of the armchair. "When I say what?" he asked.

"When you say that you weren't...*exactly yourself.*"

He sat heavily in the chair with his eyes dully open, his fingers on the cool silk of the armrest, the light shifting subtly from gray to darker gray and back again, his mind foggily turning and drifting in contemplation of itself. He had come to this place, he knew, seeking shelter during a journey. He had arrived in the snow, in the evening, with his wife, Julia, and his son, Dewey, and his brother, Robbie, none of whom were with him any longer and all of whom seemed more difficult to conjure, to bring from nothingness into memory, as time passed. In the moments when he did feel exactly like himself, rooted in this present time and place as he had always been rooted before, it meant that he felt like the father of his son, the person in orbit around Dewey, that bright star burning on his life's horizon. He had been trying to find Dewey and he had been doing a very poor job of it, and the reason that he had done a very poor job had to do with exactly this—that as soon as he began to search for Dewey, he lost himself. The pattern was getting to be familiar—a period of growing frustration and then outright anger followed by yet another trek out into the snow followed by a sluggish feeling, a period of haziness, and then a complete loss of his senses followed by, yet again, his reappearance in a room with Tiffany.

He had by now spent so much time with Tiffany in rooms like this one, in fact, that he had learned a great many things he didn't really care to know about the hellhole he was stuck in: that the hotel had been built in response to the influx of mine workers and store proprietors and saloon denizens and travelers that descended on the town of Good Night as a result of the silver ore being dug from La Mine de Rêve ("The Dream Mine"); that the original claim had been filed in 1878 by a Frenchman, known to history only as Gardiener; that Gardiener's brush with history was brief, as he simply disappeared from all records of the Idaho Territory after 1880; that, according to local legend, the town got its name from the fact that it was the primary stopover after crossing the high pass of the Bitterroot Range to the east, tired travelers being greeted with a hot meal and sent to bed with a hearty "Good night"; that in its heyday the town boasted ten brothels frequented by the nearly one thousand miners who made up half the local citizenry; that prostitution remained legal in Good Night until well into the twentieth century; that, while they might be enduring quite a storm currently, it did not measure up—at least not yet—to the town's largest snowfall (seven feet, four inches exactly, according to Tiffany), which, oddly enough, occurred during the week of the hotel's opening, in 1886.

Tonio knew all these things, and even though some of the facts sounded familiar, as if he had encountered them in the article he'd read somewhere before, none of them were at all important to him. But he did know a few things that *were* important, for instance that time was passing and that it was imperative to find his family, right *now,* goddamn it, and yet as he rose from his chair and prepared once again to yell at Tiffany, to demand some explanations, a look of pity on Tiffany's face brought him to a stop. Tiffany, the despised Tiffany, felt sorry for *him*.

"You're beginning to understand that won't work, aren't you?" Tiffany said. Tonio said nothing. Tiffany reached over and placed his hand on the back of the armchair. "Relax and talk to me. That might help. It pains me to see you flailing around out there in the snow."

Tonio slumped in his seat and wondered what it would be like if the sun came out, just for a moment, whether that might make everything, all of it, clear. As it was, he couldn't really even be sure if it was day or night—it was a kind of perpetual half-light that couldn't be trusted to indicate morning or evening.

Tiffany leaned forward, his chair creaking under him. "I asked what it means to you when you say that you feel *exactly yourself*."

"Right," Tonio said. "Well, for the past ten years what it's meant to be exactly myself is to be my son Dewey's father."

"Hmm," Tiffany said. He settled his weight back, crossed his legs, and began waggling his foot. "Hmm. And have you *seen* your son in the past few days?"

Really, if he could crush this guy's skull in the palms of his hands. "What the fuck do you *mean* have I seen him? I've been looking for him the whole time I've *been* here. What do you think I've been asking you about?"

Tiffany's foot stopped and his head started to nod, as if the movement had passed all the way through his body by a series of shafts and gears and come out the other end. "I simply asked you," he said gently, "whether you had seen your son."

And something did come to mind. It was like a backward memory, the mental picture forming before the event that made the picture. There was a blond-haired boy out in the street—wasn't there?—fighting his way through the snow, his breath clouding above his head. It had hurt him in some way. But it was during the time when he wasn't exactly himself. He didn't know if he recognized himself or the boy in that moment, which had seemed like two imaginary people coming together in the confluence of different streams. He didn't tell Tiffany anything.

"It's all right," Tiffany said. "Go on."

"What I need is a policeman," Tonio said, more or less to himself. A raw energy crawled up his spine, as if he were a lizard awakening in the sun. He walked over and threw open the window so hard that the wood cracked. "I need a cop!" he shouted into the cold air. "Police!"

But outside there was no help and no police and in fact no one at all, not on the sidewalk, not in the windows across the street, not anywhere. He shoved the window back down into place and returned to his seat across from Tiffany. Tiffany tapped out his pipe into the cuff of his pants. He took out a tobacco pouch and pinched some leaves and stuffed them into the pipe and lit it with a match from a box of kitchen matches he pulled from his coat. He did not look at Tonio during the course of this procedure.

Tonio almost said "I'm sorry" but he didn't. "I don't know if you can help me or not," he said to Tiffany instead, "but I still hold you responsible." Tiffany sucked on the pipe, puffed smoke into the air. He opened a drawer on the end table next to his chair and dropped the spent match into it and closed the drawer. "I just want you to know that. I just want you to know, *mon ami,* old buddy old pal, that the shit will still hit the fan. Shit hits fan, fan is pointed at — Tiffany, are you listening to me?"

Tiffany held the pipe stem in one hand and placed the other on his belly. He blew smoke from his nostrils and rested the hand with the pipe on the chair arm. Then he opened his mouth a couple of times as if he were doing stretching exercises with his jaw and his eyes went toward the ceiling momentarily. "Not with any real degree of interest," he said.

Then they sat there that way without saying anything. Tiffany hummed a light tune to himself. Out the window, the snow fell so softly that it didn't appear to be falling at all.

"I feel exactly myself," Tonio said after a while, "when I'm talking to my son about things or I'm taking him places. Or sometimes when I'm just watching him. Or even just thinking about him — what I have to do, things I have to prepare for." He nodded for emphasis. "Being vigilant," he said.

"What else?"

"I don't know. I don't pay as much attention to things as I used to."

Tiffany made that sucking sound on his pipe. "But come now, Mr. Addison." He placed his pipe on the end table and held his hands together, the thumbs touching above his interlaced fingers. "What is it...and I mean really, here, the *essence* of it," he said, leaning forward and placing his elbows on his knees, "the thing that makes you *you?*"

"The thing that makes me me is that I have a son and he's my son and not someone else's. I have a wife who's mine and not someone else's. I have a house and a car and a cat. What do you want me to talk about — bipedalism, opposable thumbs, descended larynx, Broca's area? The things that make people people?" He waved his hand vaguely toward the window. "The solar system, the galaxy, the universe — here I am, right here in this one spot in the center of it, myself, conscious of being myself, who I am."

Tiffany picked up his pipe and puffed on it aggressively, smiling and nodding and shaking his index finger in Tonio's direction. "Very good, Mr. Addison, very good. Now we're getting to the bottom of it. You became who you are through an act of will. You're you because you made yourself you, correct? You made your own life."

This subject was, of course, one that Tonio studied all the time, or at least had studied for years, before he lost interest and began studying as little as possible. Insofar as he thought of these kinds of things anymore, he did in fact agree with Tiffany's statement. To the question of whether the self was more biologically or more socially constructed, it had always been Tonio's answer that the self was more *self*-constructed, a position that, even at the point at which he had ceased to concern himself with whether it was true, still rewarded him with the material for several well-placed articles and a number of conference presentations. He had borrowed from economics the term "collective autonomy" to describe his position—collective autonomy, anthropologically speaking, described the process by which a number of individuals acting independently chose the same course of action in response to the same set of stimuli, thereby creating, albeit unintentionally, new biological or social conditions. For instance, the evolution of a species or the establishment of a country—each was actually created by the individual will operating parallel to other individual wills. This was not unlike evolutionary theory in general, except it attempted to suggest that the result was due to an exercise of will rather than a biological imperative. And even though the strange events of the past few days suggested that Tonio's theory (and many, many others) didn't hold water, he still wanted, somewhere in that part of him that seemed like himself, in which the individual will that he postulated had to be rooted, to believe in the accuracy of Tiffany's statement. And so he said to Tiffany, as carefully as possible, because he was again having that unnerving feeling of floating away with the snowdrifts, "Correct."

"Mmm-hmm," Tiffany said. "And if this you that you think of as being yourself were whisked up from one place and plopped down in another, let's say transported from New York to Istanbul, this you would still be the same person."

"Correct," Tonio said after a second's consideration.

"What if the medium were time instead of space?" Tiffany asked. "If you somehow found yourself existing in a different time, say a hundred years or more in the past, would you still be you in that different time?"

Tonio had risen from his seat almost without being aware of having done so. There was a coldness in his hands and his fingers trembled slightly, as if he'd suddenly shifted to a position outside the window, observing himself through the window and seeing his own reflection in it at the same time, as well as the reflection of Tiffany in the chair behind him. He could tell where Tiffany was going with this, of course, and he rejected the notion flatly because it was ridiculous, but it caused him to feel something very cold inside nonetheless. "Not possible," he said, "and you know it. Time has no physical dimension. It's merely conceptual."

"Istanbul is merely conceptual," Tiffany said, his reflection casually examining something on his coat sleeve, "unless you happen to find yourself there."

Tonio shook his head and battled a kind of dizziness that seemed to be welling up. Anger, nerves—was he ill? "That's just dumb," he said. Tiffany grunted behind him. "I'm sorry, but it is. It's not the same thing at all."

"But why should everything be the same?" Tiffany said. "You keep talking about things being the same."

Across the street two figures emerged from the diner, huddled together, walking with their collars turned up along an icy trail where the sidewalk used to be. It reminded Tonio of something; he'd seen somebody else cross the street—the boy. There was this boy who kept coming back to him. "How else could they be?" he asked distractedly.

"Different," Tiffany said. "What if things were different?"

Tonio turned to face him. "What do you mean, different?"

Tiffany shook out his pants leg and ran his thumb and index finger along his mustache, pausing slightly when his fingers came together in the middle, as if he'd found what he wanted to say in the hairs on his upper lip and was now holding it up for Tonio's inspection. "Think of how many things have to come together perfectly to make it possible for you to be yourself, not just in the past—I mean the sequence of events that concluded with your birth, the circumstances of your childhood, the eventual meeting with your wife, all that sort of thing—but also in the present, the advance of every single day, every single new day which has to start off with all the celestial bodies maintaining their usual cosmic positions, all obeying the same laws of matter and space and physics and"—Tiffany waved his hand in the air—"and, well, I don't know what all, Mr. Addison. You're the scientist here." Tiffany chuckled.

Tonio wanted to say that he wasn't a scientist, that he was really more of a...but he couldn't recall what he was. He turned back to the window. There had been so much snow that he couldn't even see it anymore, as if there were nothing falling from the sky at all, and the world was just a silent, still tableau that included these suspended particles, tiny white absences of space, shimmering and light.

"I asked you this question before, but perhaps you'll understand better now." Tiffany talked from somewhere far away, almost as if he were behind a curtain of snow himself. "Is it easier to imagine a world in which everything always happens in exactly the same way over and over according to the same set of scientific principles—all the way down to the uniform behavior of the tiniest, most minute particles, mind you—or is it easier to imagine a world in which there exist places—maybe just *one* place, even, only *one*"—he paused dramatically, the word hanging in the air—"where *one* small piece of cosmic machinery, one tiny piece of the world's vast mechanical puzzle, would operate differently?"

Tonio felt almost as if he were lifting out of his shoes and floating, sailing up, and he recognized the feeling and the way his vision tunneled, the same way he'd felt when he went out into the snow, when he disappeared, and as he rose out of himself and everything narrowed he still saw, momentarily, the glowing sign of the diner across the street, and it was dark outside, as if the day had passed, and he thought of how he needed to go out there, cross the street to the diner and perhaps find Dewey, who had sat there with him eating French fries. That had been just days ago. And he had seen a boy in the street.

Tiffany's disembodied voice kept going on and on. "Why are we willing," it said, "to accept a wide range of divergence in human behavior, in the outcome of merely human events, while we admit no possibility of divergence whatsoever in the material operation of the rest of the universe? We don't even get upset about our lack of knowledge in this area. Two children are raised in the same environment in the same way by the same parents. One of them becomes an ax murderer while the other sells insurance in Cleveland. 'Just goes to show you never can tell,' we say. 'Anything can happen.' If anything can happen, why doesn't the principle extend beyond genetics into the other spheres?"

Tonio was drifting out there now, he was going away and away and away. He had been drifting for days, he knew, and he had been trying all that time—or during all the time that he could remember—to figure out what was wrong with him, to locate the problem *inside himself.* Was this what it felt like to become mentally ill? Was he experiencing an extreme version of one of Dewey's trances? How reassuring it would be to think, instead, that none of this had happened due to any fault of his own. "Or maybe I'm just dreaming," he said aloud, and for once, for just a second, he expected Tiffany not to say anything. He almost expected Tiffany not to be there at all.

"What if you are?" the familiar voice said. "How would that change things? Aren't dreams a part of our lives as well? Don't dreams *happen* just the same as anything else? What are they but the loose strands of our everyday experiences?" He could hear Tiffany puffing on his pipe, the slow draw of the spittle in the stem. Tonio held his own finger out in front of him and examined it carefully and then placed it to the cold glass of the window and drew it down through the film on the pane. "Maybe you *are* in a dream place, Mr. Addison. Maybe you're in that singular place, that different place."

He *was* in the different place, yes he was. The different place, the icy whiteness, the cold and the collapsing breath that fogged the windowpane, the vision of Dewey, the small, black outline of his beloved Dewey there in the street or in his mind's edge. He had either seen a boy who looked like Dewey or he had imagined seeing a boy who looked like Dewey, or, in some way, he had imagined another version of himself who saw a boy who looked like Dewey, or all this was an elaborate dream and Dewey was in fact right in front of him, right here if he just opened his eyes, which were closed now, but which still carried an impression, on the inside of the eyelid, of Dewey crossing the street as he had seen him do from this very window. He had rapped on the glass. The boy—Dewey or the one who looked like Dewey—had kept walking. There he walked right now, in the space behind Tonio's eyelids. If necessary, he could keep his eyes closed forever in order to keep seeing Dewey there.

"I want you to find your wife and your son and go on home," the unfailing voice of Tiffany said. "I sincerely do, Mr. Addison." And Tonio felt himself tip forward and fall, end over end, like the lightest flake of snow. "But I don't know anyone who ever has."

21

It was morning again, judging by the dull gray light slowly overtaking the room. Robbie sat up gingerly in bed—his feet hurt, his fingertips hurt, his eyes hurt, his skin hurt, his teeth hurt—and pulled back the window blind just slightly to glimpse, *again,* falling snow. He was in an upstairs room, and past the snow-laden bough of a big fir tree he could see a street, or what used to be a street, and on the other side of the street a boxy white house of the sort, he guessed, that he himself was in. A good three feet of snow covered the roof of the house and there were berms of snow where even more had slid from the roof or been shoveled off. A wall of snow rose on each side of the walkway leading to the front door. The walk had been shoveled very recently, as only a light coating with a fresh set of footprints kept it from being clean. Smoke rose in steady white puffs from the chimney. Clearly the place was inhabited, but the curtains were drawn, and up and down the street, at the other similar houses, there were signs of life but no actual people. And the street itself was impassable. No plow had touched it since the storm began, and now Robbie wondered if you could even get through it with a plow. Or a monster truck. Or a tank. The only moving thing in view, other than the chimney smoke, was the snow, of which the gray sky seemed to hold an endless supply.

The heartbeat of the world seemed almost to have stopped, the earth itself lulled into a state of hibernation by the silent, hypnotic whiteness all around, this invasion of the whole of visible space.

Grunting, he lay back down in the bed, and Stephanie, without appearing to wake up, curled herself against him. She reminded him of a large cat.

He'd been with her in this house for what...two days now? There had been another morning, yesterday, presumably, when he had woken up feeling like a half-thawed loaf of bread, his nerves and skin tingling and his insides frozen solid. He'd told Stephanie to take him to the hospital, and she'd laughed her soft laugh, like a cat's purr, and told him not to be ridiculous, there wasn't anything seriously wrong with him and there wasn't a hospital they could get to anyway. He fell back asleep and, sure enough, when he woke up again he felt much better, warm and buttery and soft all the way through. Stephanie made him eat some hot oatmeal and orange slices, and then they'd had a few shots of Jack Daniel's apiece and played several games of gin rummy sitting in bed. Stephanie gave him a guided tour of the house, sort of, without making him get up, explaining to him where the kitchen was downstairs and the TV and the shower and the closet with the towels in it and, here in the bedroom a drawer with clothes for him if he needed any. Then she was gone all day, most likely at work, and he slept for long stretches, getting up only to use the bathroom and find the bottle of Jack Daniel's, which, it turned out, was in plain view right next to the kitchen sink — she hadn't even tried to hide it, which he took to be a good sign. He carried the bottle back upstairs and finished off a fair portion of it before Stephanie returned from work, poured herself a glass, crawled in next to him, and sat reading by the light of a bedside lamp. He was mostly asleep, but he occasionally opened his eyes drowsily to see her there, her dark blonde hair tucked behind her ear, her black reading glasses perched on the end of her nose, her round arms and breasts, which she didn't bother to hide, above the covers.

And now here he was this morning feeling sore everywhere, and there Stephanie was still asleep beside him. She'd seemed like an angel, he could dimly recollect, when she'd opened the door for him and led him into the back room of the bar, half dead, dirty, piss-stained, to a table where he slept hunched over, shivering, until closing time. Then there had been a walk through the snowy streets, and again, here he was. He had no plans beyond the next thirty seconds (which he intended to spend studying Stephanie's closed eyes and the smooth skin of her cheeks and the downy blonde hair by her right ear, all of which made him feel calm for the moment and not so badly injured), but he knew what was *not* in the plan, and that was to set foot on any stairway or in any secret passage in this town ever again as long as he lived, or to go anywhere *near* that goddamn hotel.

So where did all this leave him? Here with Stephanie. This Stephanie, who was, insofar as it was possible these days, at this point in his life, a woman after his own heart. What wasn't to like? She had a pretty face and an even temperament. She kept a bottle of Jack Daniel's within reach, and she knew where to get pot and probably more if he pressed the issue. This house seemed to be hers alone, no roommates or, worse, a boyfriend. She appeared to be within a decade or so of his own age, in one direction or the other, and, as far as he could tell, she didn't behave as childishly as he did. He had no idea how much of Tonio's money he had left—come to think of it, he had no idea where his wallet was or when was the last time he'd seen it. Same with his cell phone. So the question was, how long would it be possible to string the current situation along before it became so ugly and painful that the long-term regret outweighed the short-term pleasures?

He'd gotten good at all the factoring. There had been a lot of

Stephanies. In this case, the Stephanie in question appeared to be particularly durable and even unusually enjoyable in certain ways. As best he could tell, she was prepared—he had no idea why—to stick with him, defend him, come hell or high water, against anybody and everybody, for as long as he cared to hang around. All offers of the sort became invalid after a certain point, but this one appeared to be good for quite a while.

What was there, then, to look forward to? A long stretch of drinking and hibernation in this snowbound ghost town? He could do worse. It didn't appear that he'd have to worry about Tonio either. Although he'd lost track, what with all the drinking and the near-death experiences, it must have been three or four days since they'd arrived in town, and there was no way Tonio would stick around that long, blizzard or no blizzard. He would have paid somebody to put on snow tires and chains, and off he would have gone. True, when Robbie was lost in the hotel (or wherever he was), he'd heard Julia calling his name—that was puzzling. But he was inclined now to consider it just another strange moment in the whole strange experience, probably just his imagination, whatever *that* meant anymore, and even if it had been Julia, it was two days ago. And if Tonio had gone hunting for him while he was holed up here in bed, how hard could it have been to find him? A couple questions here, a call to the police there...Was there any way you could escape notice for four days in a place as small as this? He felt pretty sure he could have tracked himself down in half an hour, and he'd been drunk or high most of the time.

So he was going to get to know this Stephanie better. Might as well get started. He moved in closer and she curled in tighter without opening her eyes, and soon, despite the prickling sensation he felt at her initial touch, they were working together under the heavy down comforter as smoothly and pleasantly as you could hope for. She made hardly any noise but she held on to him tight, as if she were falling from someplace, and he came hard, his mouth against a wisp of hair that had strayed across her cheek, and then they loosened and he stroked her leg lightly with his fingers and she finally opened her eyes and stared at him calmly while she ran her hand across the hair on his chest, as if she were inspecting him for ticks or fleas.

"What?" she said when he laughed at her.

"Nothing," he said. "Thank you."

"For what?" she said, and laughed herself. "Having sex with you?" She reached over his head with her breast up against his neck and plucked a hair band from the nightstand and sat up and wound her hair into a ponytail. She did it very prettily, and in fact the more you looked at her, the way she did things, easily and unself-consciously, the prettier she got in general. She had good, healthy, sturdy country girl looks and habits, a tribute to her solid Northwest roots. Robbie imagined that she voted for Tea Party candidates and spoke fondly of Randy Weaver and Ted Kaczynski. This didn't bother him a bit. "I didn't think you were desperate enough to have to thank people for it," she said. "And anyway, I had fun, too."

"I just mean thank you for taking such good care of me all around," he said. "I wasn't in very good shape when you found me."

She shrugged and pulled her legs up to her chest so that her breasts were covered. There was something a little troubled in her expression.

"Is it okay for me to be staying here?" he asked. He tried to make it sound like he was merely being polite, but what he really wanted to know was whether the look on her face had anything to do with a husband (unlikely) or a boyfriend (not unlikely at all) who might come barging in the door at any minute.

"Yes," she said with what seemed like real conviction. "Why shouldn't you? I want you to stay as long as you want to stay."

He smiled and turned back to the white square of windowpane. "Careful what you ask for," he said.

"Why?" she said. "I'm guessing you're not that dangerous."

That was slightly insulting, since Robbie had made a pretty long career of being a danger to himself and others, but he supposed that, in this town, only physical danger mattered, and he wasn't much for ass whippings or assault and battery, he would have to admit. The danger he represented was restricted to the realms of the emotional, psychological, petty criminal, and fiscal. "And when I get ready to leave, I just pack up and go on my merry way?" he asked her.

She squinted at him. "You didn't think we were going to get *married* or anything."

"Good," he said. "That's good to know. I'll just stay here awhile and hang out with you and all our buddies."

Again that look on her face, the drawing in around the corners of the eyes.

"You don't think that's a good idea?" he said.

She sat up and moved her feet over the side of the bed and reached down for a T-shirt she'd tossed on the floor. She glanced at him over her shoulder and pulled the shirt over one arm. "I just don't think I would call those guys my buddies if I were you," she said.

"You don't think their intentions are good?"

She was standing up now, pulling the T-shirt down over her hips. "I'm not trying to be funny," she said, tilting her head back as if she could inspect him better from a higher angle. "I am *telling* you that those people are not your friends. You have a grand total of one friend in this town. That's me."

Her tone depressed him and made him feel tired again, even though he'd slept most of the past two days. The tone suggested problems and arguments and deceptions practiced upon him rather than by him. It also suggested that his more or less friendless condition was something you could predict based solely on his appearance, and he didn't like to look like someone who had no friends. Robbie thought of the world as his friend and was genuinely surprised sometimes when the world didn't return the feeling. Although it was true that at other times it did not surprise him one bit.

She was in the bathroom now washing her face, the door partially closed. "This place really isn't all that bad," she called out. "But I can promise you it's different from anything you're imagining."

"I don't know," he said. "I've been to lots of places. I can imagine lots of things."

"Yeah," she said, "well," and left it at that.

He heard water splashing in the sink and then the door closed the rest of the way and he heard the curtain rod and then the shower started up. He lay there and closed his eyes for a few minutes, remembering all the stairs that had seemingly run everywhere, forever, and how he'd felt so desperate to get out, and then he fell asleep and he was having a dream in which he sat in a completely white space with stairways ascending all around him and a crowd of people talking to him in voices that sounded like Julia's, and all the people were confused about something that seemed obvious but that he couldn't find the words to explain. It made him feel uncomfortable and frustrated to understand something that no one else did.

Then Stephanie was standing over him, putting her hair back into a ponytail. She wore a sweatshirt, jeans, and heavy boots. Dressed that way, she seemed determined to get something done. "I'm walking to the grocery store," she said. "We need food." She leaned over the bed and kissed him on the forehead the way he guessed somebody's mother would. "Maybe you should get up and around before I get back," she said. "You'll probably feel better if you do."

She opened a closet door and took out a coat that appeared to be made at least partially from the skin of some animal. He lay there gazing at her, this big but still quite attractive girl who looked like she was dressed to go mountain climbing. He liked her, he really did. He closed his eyes and then he heard her boots on the stairs and he heard the door open and the whoosh of cold air come in. He figured he would wait awhile before he took her advice. Right now he felt better than he had in quite some time.

Eventually he got up and took a shower and then checked out the drawer Stephanie had pointed him toward. In it were his clothes—*his* clothes, his *own* clothes, the ones he'd left behind that night when he snuck out of the hotel.

22

By now Dewey had eaten not one but two pieces of chocolate cream pie, which was actually maybe half as many as he wanted, since he had what his mother called a terminal case of sweet tooth, and still Hugh and Lorraine hadn't gotten around to explaining anything. Oh, sure, they'd asked him *questions,* lots of *questions,* but what did asking *him* questions accomplish? *Nothing.* He had dutifully plowed through the story of how the massive snowstorm had forced his dad off the road and into this odd and scary town. Hugh made him go over all the details about the hotel slowly and carefully until Dewey finally said he was really tired right now so he really didn't know, but what he did know was that his degenerate uncle Robbie, who was always causing trouble, disappeared and then everyone disappeared, and then Hugh had a lot of questions about that, and still Hugh hadn't told him much of anything.

They were just sitting there across the Formica table from each other and there was no more pie to eat and nowhere to go, what with the snow and all, and it was pretty clear even to the Dooze Man that Lorraine was *not* going to let Hugh get up from the booth until he had told Dewey *something,* and yet they went on sitting there for what seemed like about forty-seven hours, until Dewey felt like the loneliest person in the world.

Last summer, they had gone on vacation to a place called Saint Simons Island, Georgia, and on the first morning, before Dewey even knew where he was at, before he'd even had a chance to get *acclimated,* as his father always used to say, they had gone to the beach down the block from the house they were renting and his mom and dad had pulled out their beach chairs and beach towels and lain there with their eyes closed, which was one of the few things they both enjoyed doing, Dewey had noticed, one of them usually being interested in one thing while the other was interested in something else. There they were, his mom in her beach chair and his dad on the towel, both of them wearing their sunglasses (which always bothered Dewey slightly because, ironically enough, when he couldn't see their eyes it was as if they had in some way vanished), and Dewey out in the water, where he had been told not to go above his waist. He waded in, and the little waves next to the shore rippled over his feet and the sun shot through the water so that there were little flashes of light everywhere, and the movement of the waves, when they were going out, made Dewey feel like he was walking sideways very fast, and conversely when they were coming in, so that overall it was such a puzzle of varying perceptions and shifting sensations that Dewey became quite fascinated and, he realized later, went into one of his spells where time disappeared. All he could remember was the bright sky and the pulsing sun and the quick silent passage of clouds, until at some point he became aware of himself and, turning back to find the beach in the distance, realized that he had walked out much farther than he was probably supposed to. But he was still not in over his waist.

Other than a few mottled clouds that passed swiftly overhead, the sky was a dazzling blue and the sun a white-hot bulb hung overhead and the light it cast down so sharp and bright that the waves popped like fireworks. The scene on the shore was laid out like a seaside painting by one of those impressionist guys his mother was fond of. To his left and right lay the other islands in the chain of islands off the Georgia coast, the dark green line of trees flat against the horizon, the thin strips of sand, the rows of hotels and condominiums. On the shore of Saint Simons, the brightly colored houses, three and four stories of balconies and windows facing the sea, shimmered in the light. Off to his left stretched a long bridge with tall cable towers that led to somewhere (Jekyll Island, he learned later) and in the nearer distance stood the Saint Simons lighthouse emerging from a green thicket of oak and palm trees. And far away to the east, very small against the horizon, a line of people appeared to be walking on the water, out to sea. Later he would hear of the sandbar that ran from the town's East Beach, but for the moment he thought that he was witnessing some strange miraculous happening, the exodus of some superrace of people in the process of leaving Georgia and walking across the ocean to an unseen shore, perhaps in another world.

His father, he knew, would be interested in this, and Dewey's plan was to rush back through the shallow water to alert him, but he stayed for a moment to savor a feeling that came over him, a feeling that he was experiencing this moment, this unusual moment, all by himself, as a person separate from every other person, and the things that he saw—the sparkling ocean, the towering lighthouse, the special people marching into the sea—were things that only he was seeing at this one certain time, and each sight, each individual second, was being stored in his own memory and would never exist anywhere else. And at the same time he felt achingly lonely, as if, in discovering this place inside himself that was in its own self a whole world separate from everyone else's world, he had also discovered his own isolation in that world, how all his specific memories and all his thoughts about the future and even—especially—what he was feeling right now could never be shared or acknowledged and in fact didn't exist as far as anyone else was concerned.

He knew in a distant way that for a long time he had been seeing his mother sitting back in her beach chair reading a book and his father lying on a towel, turning over and over like he was cooking himself on the grill, and that they had, maybe for the first time in his life, forgotten him entirely. This somehow, *paradoxically,* ballooned him with a sense of his own importance, reinforcing the notion of singularity he had just discovered, but at the same time making him nervous, as if his father was right and something bad really *would* happen to him if he wasn't under constant supervision. As he struggled with these mingled feelings of pride and anxiety he saw for the first time a group of older kids, probably high school or maybe even college age, carousing along the shore and out in the water, the boys yelling hoarsely, the girls screaming shrilly, everybody happy with everybody else and happy with themselves in the way Dewey imagined people mostly were in life, and the way he was himself, too, when he was, say, at basketball practice, but not the way he was, for instance, when he thought over and over of the polar ice caps melting, chunk by chunk, cracking and bending and snapping in the arctic waste, or the forests dying, being chopped and sawed and bulldozed, or, the worst, when he had the recurrent visions of the sun exploding. But he also saw that there was one kid apart from the others, standing sheepishly with his legs wide apart and his arms crossed over his chest, looking uncomfortable and going completely unnoticed for the moment. He was a fat kid, wearing nothing but a pair of gym shorts and a Georgia Bulldogs baseball cap. The other guys in the group were loud and active, splashing around in the water, shoving one another, performing for the girls in the group, who shrieked in feigned fear. But the fat boy just stood at the edge of the water in his gym shorts and his Bulldogs cap being fat. There wasn't anything else for him to do. No matter what he did, whether he ran out into the water and tackled one of the other guys, or splashed a lot of water around and pretended to be a whale, or attempted to drown himself by keeping his face down in the shallow water, or even caught a crab or a fish with his bare hands, he would still just be the fat kid doing whatever the fat kid did. *Hey,* someone would say, *did you see the fat kid catch that fish?* There was no way to get around it, being the fat kid. He would be the fat kid every second and every minute of every dog's-ass day (a favorite expression of Dewey's father when he was tired or when, like on the day every year that the students showed up after summer vacation, things were especially bad at work). The fat kid every dog's-ass day. What a life.

Dewey was the kid who could do anything. He won the Charleston County Spelling Bee last spring and he was the shortstop on the baseball all-stars and the point guard on the basketball all-stars and he finished third in the state ten-and-under tennis championships—and he hadn't even *tried.* He *hated* tennis. He had no clear idea of what it meant to be the fat kid, and he never would, and it made him sad for just a minute. It made him wonder about the various paths in life—how it would be very different, for instance, to be the fat kid than to belong to a superrace of people marching across the sea—and how you couldn't take all of them.

The fat kid walked slowly, without anyone noticing, back through the water and up onto the beach, apparently with some plan in mind, the execution of some action he had mulled over while he stood statue-like in the surf, something that, he had determined, might change the course of things forever, might make his life more like the lives of those iridescent figures skimming off across the cresting waves, oblivious to the force of gravity. He strode purposefully, Dewey thought, over to a towel where two tanned girls lay talking, and they didn't pay any attention to the fat kid either, even though it was clear that they were part of the same large group to which the fat kid belonged, and slowly, while Dewey held his breath in anticipation of what might occur (would the fat kid shout at the girls, accuse them of ignoring him? Would he declare his love for one of them? Would he do a giant belly flop onto the towels, crushing the girls underneath?), of what stupendous and monumental decision the fat kid had made and what the next crucial moments held in store, the fat kid raised one flabby arm and...took his Georgia Bulldogs cap off and tossed it onto the sand. Then he walked back to the water, waded in past his ankles, and resumed his position on the outskirts of the group, where he could quietly keep being the fat kid. It was depressing.

Then all hell broke loose, as his mother would describe it later to her friends on the phone. *All hell broke loose, Laura, you should have seen. All hell broke loose, Beth, all hell broke loose, Alicia.* What happened was that his dad, who, under the influence of the sun and the sand and several beers that Dewey had watched him down, uncharacteristically, the night before, out on the screened-in porch of their beach rental, and likely distracted by his mother's newly purchased and rather embarrassingly (for Dewey) revealing swimsuit, had relaxed his guard where Dewey was concerned, maybe for the first time in Dewey's whole young life. Dewey had gone—what—ten, fifteen minutes without being the object of his father's scrutiny? And then Dad, good old reliable, dependable Dad, had rolled over on his beach towel, tuned in the radar to discover Dewey's whereabouts, and had found that he was a rather distant figure across a long stretch of sunlit water, standing, as his father described it later when his mother was explaining how and why all hell broke loose to Laura, Beth, Alicia, etc., "like a dead man," or, more explicitly, on one memorable occasion when his father had grown really tired of the story being told over and over again to Beth, Laura, etc., and wanted once and for all to establish the level of potential danger as he had perceived it in the moment, like a dead man "who had been propped up with a stick, standing loosely in the waves, arms dangling lifelessly at his sides, soggy and inanimate." And so, Dewey's dad did what his dad always did, namely overreacted, namely panicked, and began to sprint across the sand into the shallow, surf-less, absolutely 100 percent undangerous water off the coast of Saint Simons Island toward Dewey, shouting his name as he came nearer. And Dewey, freshly awakened from his surreal experience with the superrace of water-treading people and his existential ruminations on the life and times of the fat kid, groggy with the wind and the dancing light on the waves and the philosophical headiness of it all, grew more than a bit alarmed due to his father's shouting and splashing and general haste, and came to the conclusion that there was something (shark? Pirate ship?) in the water right behind him, and that he was in imminent danger of an attack. So he began to thrash through the water, half swimming and half stumbling, toward his father, "shouting his little lungs right out of his mouth," according to his mother's subsequent eyewitness account.

The incident, which had by now drawn the attention of everyone for hundreds of yards along the beach, including, Dewey noticed, the fat kid, ended with father and son rushing awkwardly into each other's arms about shin-deep in the harmless waters of the Atlantic off this piece of the Georgia coast, Dewey shaking from head to toe, his dad frantically examining him for injuries, feeling no doubt that he had rescued his son from some terrible and as yet still unspecified disaster, Dewey himself feeling very much rescued from something, although he wasn't sure what at the moment, and soon enough determining that there was not now, nor had there ever been at any time during the adventure, anything wrong. This was the point of the story at which, once, talking on the phone to Aunt Josie, his mother had laughed so hard she almost peed her pants.

And right now, sitting across the table from silent and gloomy Hugh, in a town that seemed to be constructed about 90 percent from snow—mesmerizing, muffling, sleepy snow—he felt just as alone as he had that time out in the ocean when he saw those shimmering figures walking across the water in the distance, holding hands. And he realized that he had never told his father about those people, or about the fat kid whose life was, by comparison, so dull and sad.

Dewey stood up to leave. He felt very tired, and he wanted to go back to the only place he had to go, the creepy hotel, where he could fall asleep to the creepy images on the TV screen.

"Wait a sec, wait a sec," Hugh said.

Dewey wobbled on his feet. He rubbed his eyes and saw, briefly, two of Hugh, both exactly the same, both beckoning him back into his seat. He sat down. In fact he lay down, the cool orange Naugahyde of the booth against his cheek. He lay still, his eyes open just barely to a blurry vision of the green and pink gum stuck to the underside of the table. He could hear Hugh get up and shuffle over and sit down next to him and he could feel the weight of Hugh's thighs against his feet and then he felt Hugh's big hand, which smelled like French fries, descend upon his shoulder, where it rested with surprising lightness, and then the hand retreated and he heard the fingers drumming nervously on the tabletop, and then the hand returned and rested on his shoulder again, moving slightly, rhythmically, as if the movement were somehow connected to the beating of Dewey's heart.

"Look," Hugh said finally. "If it's any comfort, you're not the first."

Interesting. Not the first what? Not the first kid who'd been given free chocolate pie? Not the first kid who'd been abandoned and wound up lying in this booth? "What does that *mean*?" he asked.

"Well, let's put it this way," Hugh said. "This is a strange place."

Dewey sighed deeply. "That's what's called an understatement," he said.

This apparently "cracked Hugh up," as his dad would have said: lol, kml, ha ha ha very funny. After Hugh had finished coughing and his face wasn't so red, he began again by pointing out the obvious. "You make me laugh," he said. "I don't know where you get this stuff."

Of course this kind of thing was always pleasant, you couldn't deny it, and even though the Dooze Man was mindful of his mother's advice that he should "keep his head on straight," it was gratifying to have *somebody* in this frozen wilderness acknowledge his capabilities a tiny bit, and it made him a little less exasperated with Hugh for his plodding and incomplete explanations.

"Just how smart are you?" Hugh asked.

How was one to answer this? "I'm pretty smart," Dewey said, measuring the words carefully and trying not to let a bragging tone sneak in, because his mother hated bragging, even when it was his father bragging about him, which his mother said happened all too frequently. It was funny how much more readily he felt like doing what his mother or his father asked now that they weren't around to ask him. Thinking about it made his throat tighten so he concentrated hard on the old, dried-up gum for a few seconds. In one of the wads someone had used a pen or a toothpick to poke holes in the shape of a smiley face. The person probably never suspected that someone would actually notice it one day and feel better for a minute.

"Yeah," Hugh said, "so we're agreed. It's a pretty strange place." Then he was quiet for a while again and Dewey peeked up to see him staring across the street toward the hotel. "It probably wasn't a good idea to pull off the interstate here."

"Now we agree on two things," Dewey said.

Hugh chuckled and then did the thing where he acknowledged the chuckling. "Very funny," he said. "Touché."

Off to the side of where his head rested on the cool orange cushion, the Dooze Man saw Lorraine's legs approach, presumably attached to the rest of Lorraine. Her knees were red and chapped beneath the black skirt she wore. Like Dewey's mother, Lorraine did not seem to be a person who made concessions to the weather.

Lorraine's legs stood by the side of the table. Something about how they were positioned suggested frustration, or maybe impatience. "How's it going?" Lorraine's voice said.

Hugh patted Dewey's shoulder, as if maybe that would indicate the delicacy of the subject and keep Lorraine at bay awhile longer. "Uh," he said.

"We haven't gotten very far," Dewey said, "if that's what you're asking."

"Hugh," Lorraine said.

"All *right*," Hugh said.

"Dewey?" Lorraine said.

"Yes?"

"Can I get you anything?"

How could she help but remind him of his mother, especially when she could only be seen from the legs down, where people looked more or less the same? Dewey was quiet for a moment, thinking about his mother, about the apparition across the street in the hotel—maybe the delusion or the hallucination, if he had actually gone crazy like he thought sometimes during the night he might have—how the apparition would be there until you tried to cross the door to it. It was like going behind a mirror to search for yourself and thinking for a moment that you instead of your reflection had disappeared. He felt his mother's absence keenly. Still, there were small consolations for not having her around to tell him what to do. One had to take advantage.

"I could eat another piece of pie, I think," Dewey said.

A short argument ensued, in which Lorraine played the part of concerned mother and Hugh played the part of indulgent father, or at least a guy who didn't want to be bothered much with dietary issues. Dewey got his pie was the outcome of the argument, and he sat up and started to eat. Hugh moved to the other side of the booth and then changed his mind and came back again. He pulled his guitar pick out of his pocket and stuck it between his teeth and started flicking it. Dewey had yet to see a guitar in all his visits to the diner, but the pick was always there.

"This is the thing," Hugh said. "You probably ended up here because you had to."

"I *didn't* have to," Dewey said. "I could have stayed in Mount Pleasant at my friend Hunter's house." He dully forked up another bite of pie and eyed it for a long second before deciding to put it in his mouth. "They even offered," he said.

"I know it sounds weird," Hugh said, "but people get drawn here. It has a magnetic quality."

Dewey wondered what that meant. It sounded like something you'd read in a tourist brochure for Charleston or Saint Simons Island. "I'm not seeing it," he said.

"Seriously," Hugh said. "A magnetic quality. As in, like, a magnet. Like gravity."

"We ran into a blizzard," Dewey said.

"Blizzard, blown tire, sudden bout of fatigue," Hugh said. "They all end up here."

"Who?" Dewey said.

Hugh leaned in and started to say something and then thought about it and leaned back and flicked the guitar pick between his teeth and then removed it and looked out the window. He said quietly, "You." His mouth drew up in a tight line. "You, or someone like you."

When he was seven, Dewey had a black hamster that his dad insisted on calling Sparky, though its name was actually LeBron James. The hamster was pretty boring, mostly, but Dewey had loved to watch him run on his wheel, which Sparky-LeBron could do for hours—Dewey stopped watching only because, unfortunately, the wheel running became as habit-forming and trance-inducing for him as it was for SL. When SL's time came (which it did, two years later, from a big ugly tumor on his belly), it was his father's job, as his father had predicted it would be, to put SL out of his misery (with the Dooze Man secretly watching his father out in the backyard through the dining room window) by hitting him with a hammer. This conversation was turning out exactly the same as that—not the hammer part (no one was getting ready to hit anyone with a hammer) but the wheel-spinning part, the going on and on without getting anywhere, and also the overall predictability. And there was another, more unnerving similarity. Dewey often had a feeling, as he watched his hamster on the wheel, that there was something bigger going on, involving larger forces, and that Sparky-LeBron, behind his beady little black eye, knew it, too, that in running the wheel he was in fact marking time, that there would be only a certain number of times the tiny feet could scoot the metal wheel, propelling it backward and backward as if trying to reverse the process, until things reached their inevitable conclusion—the hammer to the head, the crushing of the tiny skull, the squeals and then the silence. This conversation was also like that, Dewey thought with unease. It was heading to some sort of ending that you couldn't come back from.

"Wow," Hugh said, and rubbed his hand over his stubbly scalp and pinched the beard on his chin. "This is *not* easy."

It didn't *look* easy for him, Dewey was surprised to find. It didn't look easy at all. "Just tell me," Dewey said softly, encouragingly, and he took his last bite of pie and he put his fork down on his plate and swallowed. He was pretty stuffed with pie. "It's okay," he said, and without knowing why he reached over and patted Hugh's big hairy arm.

And then Lorraine was standing at the table, too, with her arm on Hugh's shoulder, and Hugh covered his eyes, pausing for a second to pull himself together, Dewey realized, and right then he knew what Hugh was going to say, in that stupid infuriating way he had of always figuring things out too fast, too early, too completely, even when they were things he didn't want to know. He knew exactly positively without a shadow of a doubt what Hugh was going to tell him, and yes, it was going to change things.

"Twenty years ago, back when I was a kid," Hugh said, "the same thing happened to me."

23

Anthony Addison and his wife, Julia, were dressed for dinner, when Tiffany's celebration would begin in earnest. Tiffany had hired a French chef from a famous restaurant in San Francisco, and all week long the Harrington boy had been driving a wagon to and from the railroad depot, unloading crates of salmon on ice, sides of beef, the exotic secret ingredients of dishes no one in the town had ever heard of and would probably not appreciate sufficiently, at least from Tiffany's perspective. Addison found it all amusing, but there was no denying that Tiffany knew what he was doing when it came to this sort of thing. Addison had, maybe without admitting it to himself, been fashioning himself as a gentleman for the past few years, since he had become one of the principal owners of Le Rêve. It was an easy enough role to carry off during the course of the town's normal operations, but it became more difficult when he was faced with the likes of Tiffany, who knew the difference between being a real gentleman and simply putting on airs. Tiffany's aplomb was effortless, achieved, no doubt, as the result of a superior upbringing, although Tiffany was evasive concerning his origins, so much so that people who had spoken with him on the subject often whispered that he was either the descendant of a disgraced European aristocrat or a criminal of the more polite variety.

Addison himself was the son of immigrant farmers who had settled in the upper Midwest, Scotch-Irish Protestants among people who were not their kind, but hardworking and fertile to such a degree that he, the seventh of eight surviving children, had not much claim to any of the family holdings in Wisconsin, and had decided to take his chances out West, setting out with a modest sum that his father thought suitable, and which Addison considered more than fair. He was a rather tall and gangly man, with large hands and feet and long arms, but he had a lean strength and an inexhaustible store of energy and patience. He had found work in the Dream Mine (as it had come to be known locally) in its early days and applied himself to it steadily, living frugally and making friends easily enough. Before long, he became a pit boss (an unusually well-liked one), and after another year he approached one of the owners with a request to buy into the operation, which he did at first on a fairly small scale. Following a series of prudent investments in other business interests in the Northwest, he found himself in a position to enter into an agreement with the ownership. From that day until now, he had not gone back down into the mine. He had a home built, the finest structure in town until Tiffany came along with his hotel, and he traveled east to find a wife, making sure he found the right one. He believed, all things considered, that he had done quite well for someone who, as Tiffany, a Catholic, was always fond of reminding him, shared his name with the patron saint of swineherds.

But this day had unsettled him a bit. First, there was the hotel itself, which Tiffany had guarded jealously during construction, allowing only the workmen inside and threatening them as best he could to keep them from divulging details. It hadn't worked—the town buzzed with descriptions of the opulent interior taking shape, of the plans for the opening, and of course you couldn't hide the installation of pipes for the gas lighting, or the arrival of the chandeliers, or the veritable forest of oak cabinetry, or the glass tanks for exotic fish. It was as if, after having so often treated Tiffany as an amusing and somewhat absurd inferior, Addison's own nature had been exposed by Tiffany's triumph, by the revelation that Tiffany was indeed a man to be reckoned with, and that, in all likelihood, his knowledge and experience of the world not only far outstripped Addison's but also might be of the sort to result in a greater fortune for its possessor.

And there was the matter of the incident in the mine. It had been a mere six weeks since the first multiple fatality in Le Rêve. Addison had, as a kind of natural liaison between the miners and the ownership, been one of the first to speak with the only survivor of the accident, a man named Diamond, who had arrived in Good Night not long after Addison himself, and who had worked under him during his time as pit boss.

Diamond reported that he and four other members of his crew had struck a new vein in the lowest depths of the main shaft, the one that reached down into the earth like a throat. They were exhuming silver in nuggets as large as apples, so large that they had never seen the likes of it before, when, one by one, they had begun to sweat intensely. Addison knew what this meant, why Diamond paused significantly in the telling of the story at this point. The temperature that far down was not dependent on the weather, and only a little on the seasons, so that any change in the condition of the air that came about so rapidly was cause for alarm. The five of them, in considering the situation, had sat down to rest along the wall of the shaft when they felt the heat at their backs and a pressure building in their ears. Diamond moved quickly back toward the lift and away from the wall, while the others, he said, tried to investigate. As soon as they determined that they were all experiencing the same feeling—the heat, the pressure—a portion of the wall simply slid down, and there was a high shrieking or whistling that obliterated everything—Diamond's eardrums were in fact burst, according to the doctor in Spokane Falls—and, Diamond said, it was as if the explosion and the eruption of air, the swift wind about his head, filling his ears, had transported him to some strange place where everything was white, where it was as if he'd stepped through a door and come out beside himself, where he could see and hear the explosion that killed his companions but not be killed himself, and when it was all over he was surprised to find that he was still there in the mine shaft, amid the rubble and the bodies. He had thought he'd gone for good to the white place—and in fact he could still see it in the corner of his vision.

On the day Addison spoke to him, it had been only a week since the accident, a fact that Diamond, when reminded of it, found surprising but was ultimately willing to accept, given Addison's assurances; personally, he felt that he had been recollecting the incident for many, many years. It was Mr. Addison's turn to be surprised. Suddenly, he also seemed to remember the incident as if it belonged to his own distant past, as if he had carried the knowledge of it with him for a very long time. For a suspended moment, the two men looked at each other as if they had stumbled upon the answer to a question that neither of them had asked. But in the next moment both the answer and the question were forgotten, and Addison assured Diamond that he was mistaken, and suggested that he take a long rest, which Diamond admitted, with a smile, he was more than ready to do. That was the end of the matter, other than the completion of official reports and the notification of kin. But the interview had lingered in Addison's mind ever since, and today the memory of it felt particularly sharp. This was, he supposed, the result of his warm fellowship with the miners, the men who had been lost, and his feeling that, on this day of celebration, there was something slightly amiss in the general enthusiasm following so closely in the wake of such a tragedy. But that wasn't all—the accident itself seemed to loom very close for some reason just now, as if the heat of the mine shaft and the whistling sound that Diamond described had crept into his own consciousness. Probably this was due to his immediate situation—the discomfort of his starched shirt collar, the awkward position he had chosen in sitting on the bed.

"Mr. Addison?" his wife called from the lavatory, where she was making her final preparations for the evening. "Would you please ring for a needle and thread? The hem needs adjusting."

It was a little discouraging that, after having been married for nearly a year, his wife still referred to him, unfailingly, as "Mr. Addison." He did not expect, exactly, to be called by terms of endearment at this early stage—he did not expect "darling" or "dear"—but he didn't quite expect, or feel he deserved, "Mr. Addison" either.

He did not think that his wife referred to him this way out of obstinacy or spite. He did not think it was her way of punishing him for the position in which her father found himself, that of a formerly successful shipping agent in a river town of declining importance, so that the notion of sending his daughter across the country with a man of very new money and no family or education, which would have been unthinkable ten years before, was not so unthinkable now.

From what Addison could tell thus far, his wife was as fair-minded as any man, if not more so, and as capable a judge of character. He believed that she had a passable degree of respect for him, though this was not an opinion she would share with him, nor one that she would suspect he felt needed sharing. She was, Mr. Addison concluded with a measure of disappointment and even self-pity, deficient in feminine "softness," the enlarged sympathies one thought of in connection with women. But he could not fault her for anything else—she was perhaps a little vain about her looks.

He had been in the hotel room for some time now, and although the steam heat was marvelously efficient, the room did begin to feel a little close if you stayed shut up in it for too long. He decided he would get the needle and thread himself.

Truthfully, he could find no fault with Mrs. Addison whatsoever. It was only that something might be lacking, he felt, in the arrangement between the two of them, as perceived by a man like Tiffany, for instance, who, being a good bit older, likely knew more about marriage and the manner in which one should be properly conducted (although it was worth considering that Tiffany, to Addison's knowledge, had never been married himself). The suggestion of a smile on Tiffany's face when he had left them in the room together an hour ago said as much—there was the expectation of some intimacy that Addison knew did not exist. The several minutes following Tiffany's departure had been filled with a leaden silence, Mrs. Addison seated primly, hands clasped, at the foot of the bed, while he sat in the armchair attempting to smile pleasantly. He wanted to say something to her about the boy he had seen from the window, and about how he had been moved to tap the glass. He had noticed his wife's surprise at the urgency of the gesture. He had tapped hard on the glass but the boy had not turned toward him, and he'd grown conscious then of his wife's and Tiffany's stares, and he had straightened himself at the window and brushed a bit of moisture from the cuff of his shirtsleeve. "Young fellow out the window there," he said, grinning awkwardly. He had no other explanation to offer, and he reddened as Tiffany pointed out to Mrs. Addison the delicate design of the room's crown molding, which had been chosen and carved specially for the hotel by a company in Kansas City.

Once Tiffany had gone, he knew his wife wanted to ask him about it, the incident at the window, but there seemed to be no mechanism for broaching the subject. In a room with other people, the way it had been with Tiffany in the lobby earlier or how it would be in the dining room less than an hour from now, his wife conversed with him as lightly as if she had known him all her life. But when they were alone, the gleam left her eyes, the rosy color faded from her smooth cheeks, and the soft smile she presented to the outside world evaporated without a trace. The face she presented to him was a mask that seemed to mask nothing, a fixed advertisement of disinterest. This was, he supposed, a sort of intimacy in itself, but not one that offered much comfort. It would have to do for now.

Out in the hall, he shut the door behind him and proceeded down the corridor toward the stairs, hearing the sound of guests and activity from the lobby below and voices up ahead from one of the other rooms.

It might do sometime to ask Tiffany for a bit of advice—if Tiffany could be trusted. Addison had as little experience with women as he did with society. He had, with about equal parts guilt and fear, made his way to the local prostitutes, just like all the other young miners in the early days of the town. There were few other temptations and even fewer opportunities. These encounters had been interesting enough in their own way, but unfulfilling to the part of Addison that, even when he was as young as he was then, wished for a companionship that went beyond desire to a place he could not recognize or imagine. The only marriage at which he'd had a firsthand look was that of his own parents, who lived a hard life and had little time to devote to each other. In the small house his family occupied there was no room for privacy—five boys, three girls, Anthony the youngest of them all but one—and he had been aware all his life of the scuffling in the dark, the night-time noises, the grunting and puffing that interrupted his sleep on occasion. It was not until his oldest brother, Andrew, explained to him, much later, the true nature of the disturbance that Anthony had any idea of his parents' actions, and afterward he would listen hot with shame, imagining that his father was no different from a baboon in the nature of his attentions, and he felt an aching pity for his mother, whose voice he never heard. His partnership with Mrs. Addison so far had not been as horrible as that, but it had been awkward and quiet, and had not sufficiently put these painful memories to rest.

He moved down the corridor with his long-legged gait and thought for a moment of nothing more than the request for needle and thread—to whom should it be addressed, was there a certain color? His wife hadn't said. As he passed by an open door on his left, his movement was arrested momentarily by a strident voice, the flash of a hand...He looked round to see Tiffany and Miss Blanchard framed in the doorway, the snow falling in the window behind them, as if they were two characters posed in exaggerated form on a stage. Tiffany bent toward the actress and spoke to her urgently, his face red, the cords of his neck tight, extending his hand as if demanding something. Miss Blanchard's eyes flashed at him angrily, her mouth was set in a perfectly straight line, but she held out her closed hand and Tiffany grabbed it. For a moment the two of them were frozen there, and Addison himself had halted almost midstep. Slowly, though, Tiffany's head turned toward the door, and as he saw Addison a frown took shape on his face. Miss Blanchard, however, lifted her head and turned to Addison directly, so that he noticed the perfect shape of her white throat and rounded shoulders. Her eyes glowed in the lamplight, brimming with some sort of mischief, and the smile that turned up the corners of her mouth spoke to Mr. Addison, and only Mr. Addison, of secrets she would soon reveal.

24

There was the door and there was the key. And when she used the key, when she opened the door, there was a sensation of doing the same thing over and over, as if she opened the door in some cascading dream that tumbled down upon itself, repeating and repeating. She tried not to open the door often, because the door opening seemed important and not to be taken lightly, but sometimes she felt as though she was constantly using the key and opening the door. She would suddenly find herself standing with the key in her hand, the door in front of her, and she would think to herself, *Why do I open the door?,* and she would answer herself, *Because you have the key.* So she would open the door, whether she was dreaming or she was awake, it was often difficult to tell, and on the other side she would find narrow stairways stretching up and down, rising on the one hand as if they would extend beyond the clouds that dropped the snow so incessantly, descending on the other into a place that seemed infinitely cold and black, a tunnel without end. Or she would open the door and find herself on a snowy street at nighttime, the shops closed, the smell of smoke in the air. Sometimes she would turn the key and open the door and step into a room exactly like the one she was leaving, a mirror image of itself, and she would be staring at her own face, a face that belonged to a woman who was, like her, standing in the doorway and holding open the door. And sometimes when she looked into the actual mirror, on the front of the armoire, she would glance away and think that, out of the corner of her eye, she had seen the mirror image performing some different operation from the one she was performing, maybe a moment ahead or a moment behind. And sometimes when she used the key to open the door, or stood outside on the snowy street and looked up at the window, as she had that first time, she would see a woman much like herself standing in the room and preparing to use the key, or turning a snow globe slowly in her hands, or lying there asleep. When she saw these women, she imagined herself doing the same things they were doing, or even *remembered* herself doing the same things they were doing, and sometimes even remembered herself *remembering* having done these same things.

The reason it was so important to keep using the key to open the door, at least periodically, just to check, was that soon now she would open the door and find something completely different. She didn't know what this different thing would be, except that it would be something she hadn't yet encountered in life, but it would somehow be familiar, in the same way that a scent in an entirely new place could suddenly draw you back to sometime long ago, when you had entered a place that smelled that same way. The hotel, from the moment she'd arrived, had been full of these sensory impressions, these things that wanted, somehow, to be memories. And soon, using the key to open the door, she would come upon the final one of these impressions, the one that unlocked the meaning of everything in the same way that, yes, a key unlocked a door.

Meanwhile she seemed to be in such a constant state of activity, or at least her mind was, what with the stream of thoughts, dreams, recollections, whatever they were, of doors, and keys, and rooms, and windows, that she hadn't had much time to consider what might be going on beyond her room, beyond the door, outside the hotel, past the ever-falling snow. She knew the real world was out there somewhere, and there were times when she thought she was in it—always, interestingly, when she was locked in the room, and never when she used the key and opened the door and found herself elsewhere. Much of the time she felt like more than one person, a set of multiplied selves, living on several planes. Maybe that was because she was starving.

She had not forgotten about Dewey or Tonio or Robbie. Far from it. What had happened, clearly, was that *they* had forgotten about *her*. This wasn't anything to worry about overmuch—she was having far too good a time here in her small, quiet room with her door and her key and all these thoughts that she was able to keep to herself.

When she wasn't preoccupied with the door, usually when she was lying in bed and hovering close to sleep, she had taken to thinking back on her life, which was something she normally didn't have time for. But now, in the room, as time continued to move ahead (or at least she assumed it did, though she had no way of knowing, and it was true that time didn't seem to pass at all, the only way to measure it being the screen of snow outside the window, which was so constant and uniform that it didn't seem to move in either space or time), she felt it stretching back as well, the way the Ashley River in Charleston flowed back and forth with the incoming tide.

She hadn't realized how constricted her life had become, how tightly wound into the present moment, or at least the day or week—what night was Dewey's basketball game, was she going to have to get a babysitter if she wanted to go to her book club or was it one of the nights Tonio would be home early, how many days could she wait to go grocery shopping, did she have stuff in the fridge to whip up something for dinner, whose turn was it in the car pool to pick up the kids from school, had she agreed to volunteer at Helping Hands this week, were they really almost out of toilet paper again, why was there a clunking noise in the undercarriage of the Nissan, how long could she wait before calling someone about the problem with the gutters, why had all Dewey's socks disappeared, was it time for the cat's flea medicine, when would the interim report cards come home and had Dewey left his in his backpack again, was it a good idea to refinance the house, when was Dewey's last dentist appointment, was it too late to cut back the azaleas, who loaded the dishwasher wrong, was it too hard for Tonio to take thirty minutes out of his schedule to mow the overgrown patch of lawn that looked so shitty out the window, or was she going to have to do that herself? She was constantly busy, and yet she never felt like she was really *doing* anything, as if she'd never figured out, in her whole life, what exactly to do with or for herself, the only thing she'd ever fully committed to, really, being to marry this man and raise this child. That in itself had been enough to keep her so occupied that she never had time to think.

But now her thoughts swelled like a great expanded breath, gathering in all the moments from her past that had lingered just outside her memory. When she was eight or nine years old she and her mother and her two older sisters had lived for a while in Mammoth Lakes, California, and she had gone to a school run by a guru who had taken a vow of silence. Every day the guru would arrive in a chauffeur-driven Mercedes, emerge in his flowing robes when the door was opened for him, and approach the school, smiling his closemouthed smile, shuffling his sandaled feet, the tiny fingers on his tiny hands gently tapping together in front of him. Instead of speaking, he wrote messages on a chalkboard hung from a string around his neck, and what she remembered now was the way the chalk sounded when he wrote, the way the students all grew quiet, and how her eyes would drift to the bright morning sunlight coming through the window.

It must have been just a little later—she was still too young, she knew, to be wearing a bra or starting her period—that they moved to Gold Point, Nevada, a ghost town inhabited by only a few diehards trying to cash in with tourists on the run-down mining camp and wood-planked stores, convincing parents to let their kids pan for gold in the ice-cold river. Her mother had moved them there with her current boyfriend, who operated the only bar left in town. She remembered the walk home from the small school (maybe twenty kids, total, grades K through twelve, in a converted barn) and a boy named Griffin Turbin, who, she suspected at the time and still did to this day, had a crush on her and followed her down the dusty main street with the collapsing storefronts and the vacant lots strewn with broken glass and rusted hubcaps and plastic bags blowing like tumbleweed, shouting her name and laughing and making fun of her clothes, which, actually, took her a lot of time to pick out and coordinate, since all she had were other people's castoffs or things her mother had picked up from Goodwill or J. C. Penney. She'd felt, from the very start, a strong need to present herself well, especially since her mother and her friends, with their shapeless dresses and patched-up jeans and patchouli and excessive body hair, obviously didn't care. So, if Griffin Turbin was trying to tease her into liking him, he was picking the wrong way to go about it by ridiculing her skirt, which was a cute corduroy that had maybe gotten a little worn in the seat but was the best she had, and her paisley blouse and maroon scarf, the combination of which she'd spent half an hour debating in front of the foggy bathroom mirror.

She decided to ignore Griffin Turbin and walk on, imagining that there were actually people watching from inside the empty stores with the broken windows. They would see, if they were looking out, a girl who could take care of herself, who could rise above circumstances. As she thought this she realized she no longer heard anything from Griffin Turbin behind her, and she took this as a sign of victory, began imagining how her icy treatment of this crude boy, who was so unlike the boys she had grown up around in California, who were always either too cool or too indifferent to stoop to Griffin Turbin's level, would play out at school from now on ("now on" meaning, probably, considering the typical length of her mother's infatuations, another month or two), how it would earn her a much-desired *solitude,* when suddenly a cracking sound made everything else stop and disappear. Here in the room, all these years later, she remembered it as a sound more than a feeling, although certainly she must have felt it, too, the rock hitting her right at the base of her skull, but she remembered it as a reverberation, something almost echoing, and then what she remembered next was not turning to see Griffin Turbin—she never looked back to see if he was running away, if he was standing there defiantly, jeering at her—but looking down at the ground to see the rock lying at her feet. She remembered the slow trickle of blood down the back of her neck as she walked on, refusing to give Griffin Turbin the satisfaction. That was really her last memory of Gold Point, since the rock incident proved to be the catalyst for her mother's decision to get out of town. She never saw Griffin Turbin again.

She remembered a particular day in some beach town along the California coast, in wintertime. This would have been sometime before either Mammoth Lakes or Gold Point, back when she was maybe six or seven, when the rush of cities and towns and houses and apartments and neighborhoods and schools was so confusing that she had to count on her sisters to tell her where she was, a geography of transience that could be recaptured only if she was to actually *call* her mother, who probably, maddeningly, wouldn't remember any of it anyway. On the day she remembered, there was a hard, white quality to the air, like bone, and a coldish sun cast long shadows down the sidewalk where her mother browsed through clothes on racks—peasant skirts and silk bandannas and muslin blouses. She was cold inside her mother's beat-up Datsun wagon. Her sisters weren't there that day—they were considerably older, after all, could do their own thing and usually did, which maybe explained why they had seemed such a small part of her childhood—so she was able to sit quietly in the car and watch her mother on the sidewalk, a little bit of fog creeping up the passenger window whenever she exhaled. Through the windshield was a view of an almost empty beach, a few people walking their dogs, hugging themselves in coats and sweaters, their hair tossed by the wind. The waves arrived on shore rough and angry.

And then for a second she froze right through. She had turned her attention back to her mother, who was trying on a big turquoise necklace she could never actually afford and talking to a blonde salesgirl whose hands were tucked inside a heavy wool sweater, and it occurred to her suddenly that her mother had completely forgotten about her in the car, that she didn't exist, in that moment, for anyone in the world other than herself. She couldn't have named the feeling at the time, but she remembered it vividly, and now, here in the room, thinking back, it seemed like the defining feeling of her childhood, the feeling that only her mother connected her to the world, that without her mother she would be off in some airy, unmoored place all alone. It was because of this feeling that she both loved her mother and resented her, both now and then. But that day at the beach must have been the first time she had ever felt it, and the freezing came right up her legs into her chest, and she couldn't breathe, her breath trapped somewhere inside her and the window unfogging inch by inch, and because she was scared her hand lurched up from her lap and her fingers stretched out to tap the window and get her mother's attention...and then her fingers stopped moving, her hand hovered in the air motionless, and she sat examining the back of her hand and her skinny wrist and the lining of her coat sleeve. The fog returned to the window. The ice ran out of her the same way it had come in and she felt wonderfully warm, a little bit sleepy, and, most of all, utterly alone. It felt good to her. The moments stretched one into another slowly and smoothly and she could see time's passing by her mother's movements, the smile on the salesgirl's face, or, if she turned her head, by the steady push of the steel-blue waves and the scurrying of the sand birds. But alone there in the car, time didn't seem to pass at all, as if the moment were suspended or widening, almost as if it were giving birth to something, and her hand never moved, never completed its tapping. She was waiting for something, something that was *bound* to happen. She'd had that feeling all her life.

And now, here in the room, what she remembered best was how in that moment when she had felt so alone, so *only,* but also at the same time so connected to the whole causal process of everything else that moved outside the window, so subject in some way to destiny or fate, she had seen the dirty white cuff of her cheap nylon jacket above her elbow, how the coat was dingy and too small, and she had determined right then that when she was a grown woman she was going to have nice, clean clothes that fit her right, and her children were going to have them, too. She remembered that thought and that dirty coat sleeve as if they were happening right now, in this new solitude, as if that solitary moment and this one had bypassed time and slipped alongside each other.

And later things, too, from beyond her childhood. She kept seeing over and over something from when she first met Tonio. She had wound up in Santa Barbara at the same time Tonio happened to be there on his first fellowship. Actually, she had lucked out pretty incredibly and found a friend whose parents had a two-bedroom apartment near the beach, and this friend had even gotten her a job, with her father's influence, working as a bank teller. The only bad part was that the bank was way out in Isla Vista, and she didn't have a car at the time, which meant she had to ride the bus at 8 a.m.

She'd always liked crossword puzzles, and that morning she was doing the one from the *San Diego Union-Tribune*. It was maybe ten minutes before her stop when Tonio got on the bus and took the seat next to her. She didn't look up and would probably never have noticed him if not for his hands. He had the longest fingers she'd ever seen. His hands didn't appear especially big or clumsy, it was just that the fingers were preternaturally long, as if they were specially made instruments of some kind, designed to pry things open or probe things, maybe with adhesive pads on the tips for increased grip. But they were also nice hands, with a look of elegant strength to them, and they weren't ever quite at rest, the palms always adjusting slightly on his pants legs, the fingers lightly bobbing up and down, as if they were humming with a light charge of electricity. She was certain he had something to do with the college — her stop was the one right after UC Santa Barbara, so there were a lot of college types on the bus, and Tonio, with the John Lennon glasses and the plaid shirt and the slightly dirty jeans and the scuffed-up leather sandals, was obviously one of them. She had him figured for a graduate student, a designation that, even at twenty-three years old, she didn't quite understand — she just knew that graduate students were typically a little older than she was. It surprised her to learn later that he was almost thirty and on his way to becoming a professor. At that time, he had a serious but also boyish face that made him seem younger than he was, the thought line at the bridge of his nose where his eyebrows furrowed not quite able to offset the chubby cheeks and slightly pug nose.

A guy she dated once, whom she remembered only as having long hair and driving a restored Triumph Spitfire, had described her as "punch bowl pretty"—heads didn't turn automatically when she walked into a room, but five minutes later, when she was standing by the punch bowl and talking to a friend, every guy at the party would ask himself, "Who's *that?*" And while she didn't exactly feel indebted to Spitfire guy for this semiflattering assessment, she did come to recognize its accuracy over time. So while she didn't expect to be hit on constantly, she also wasn't used to being ignored, and she wasn't used to making advances or being forward herself. But there was something about Tonio when she first saw him on the bus that made her feel two things—1) she became aware that she was thinking about the time remaining until her stop in terms of a potential missed opportunity, and 2) it was going to be up to her to say something, because this guy wasn't going to say anything, didn't even know she was there, wouldn't notice her if she stood beside the punch bowl for *years*.

So their relationship had begun with her asking him if he knew a seven-letter word meaning "brackish waterway." He did. She had always found it amusing that the first word her future husband ever said to her was "estuary"—and that was all he'd said. Then she had to prompt him by asking about a coffee shop she'd seen near campus. He knew the place but couldn't say much about it. After question number four or five, he squinted behind the glasses and finally took a good look at her, his mouth open slightly, the long tensile fingers of one hand playing at his chin. And what she remembered about this moment now, sitting alone in room 306 and probably starving to death, was not that there had been any kind of *spark* between them, nothing as romantic or clichéd as that, but that there had been some mutual acknowledgment of each other, a loosening of the body's tension, as if something had been recognized and admitted and agreed upon already, so that Tonio's hands rested more quietly in his lap, and his leg slackened and inched closer to hers, and she put away her newspaper. It was as if they were married by the time he got off the bus, standing on the sidewalk and smiling at her there in the window, waving exaggeratedly to show where he had written her phone number on his hand.

With Dewey, it was curious the moment she thought of most. Neither she nor Tonio really understood the sports thing, the whole competitive business with the screaming in the stands and complaining about the coaches, the money spent to get the newest basketball shoes, the most expensive tennis bag. Tonio seemed okay with it, enjoyed the games for the most part. She found it disgusting, honestly. But she had learned it all, out of necessity, what an RBI was, why you got two free throws sometimes and only one some others, how many points it took to win a set tiebreak. None of it meant anything to her, but these past few days she kept thinking of a single moment during one of Dewey's basketball games. His team was in the Youth League County Championship or whatever it was called, and there was a lot of excitement and commotion because the other team made a basket and took the lead with less than a minute to go, but when they passed the ball inbounds to Dewey, like they always did, and he started dribbling the ball down the court, she could see in his eyes exactly what he was going to do. He went straight to the three-point line, just like she knew he would, stopped, shot, and made it. She didn't even cheer. The rest of the parents, even Tonio, went nuts, jumping up and down and screaming, but it had seemed so obvious to her what was going to happen that she didn't even think to react. Of course that's what happened. That was *her son* out there, and she knew him. She'd given *birth* to him, for God's sake.

The other team threw the ball away, the game was over, Dewey was the hero, the moment was past. But Julia had seen it in those few seconds while Dewey brought the ball up the floor, while everyone else was going crazy—she had caught a glimpse of the grown man Dewey would become, *was* becoming. It was the adult

Dewey looking out of her child's face—serious, determined, calm, confident, a person who could do important things. And it thrilled her, and she would never forget. She was prepared, from that time forward, to forgive all his lapses—his odd anxieties, his weird fugue states, the sometimes startling depths of his absentmindedness. They were the wavering of the line but not the line itself, the heat wave—the illusion of wavering—but not the heat. She had seen the man, David (Dewey) Addison, exposed within the image of the boy, the future standing out with the present in relief.

All this was very interesting, the way these moments stretched out through all different times of her life and came together in such a tactile, visceral way for this current Julia, the one here in this room, like lily pads upon still water, stepping-stones along a path. Interesting, interesting—it was almost as if she could see herself, for the first time, in the same way she had seen Dewey then.

But there was this starving problem. She hadn't eaten since before they pulled off the interstate. She recalled that last meal—a chicken sandwich at a Denny's off an exit ramp somewhere in eastern Washington—with great wistfulness. What she wouldn't do for a chicken sandwich now. She walked into the bathroom and turned on the cold water and cupped her hand under it and drank. She turned off the water and went back out and sat on the bed. Water did nothing to whet her appetite. Why hadn't she eaten? It was a good question. She had used the key, hadn't she, over and over, venturing up the stairs or down the hall or out into the street? But there were never any people. She had found the letter in the window, but she had never encountered another person. And there had never been anything to eat.

Had she ever been out of the room, really? When she used the key, did it actually unlock or open anything? There was always a moment during the passage—a held breath, an icy instant, a sense of separation. It was as if some other version of herself embarked upon the journey, went out into the other rooms of the hotel, out into the snow. Someone else was remembering these things, not her—they were borrowed memories. She had the distinct impression sometimes that she had become trapped inside not a room but a dream.

Out the window the snowflakes were like an army of small, light creatures descending on the earth in some form of quiet destruction. She pushed up the window and scooped snow off the ledge and squeezed her hand tight, letting the ice numb her fingers. Then she slung the rest of the snow away and leaned her head out. She had tried a few times calling out for someone but no one answered or came. She was as alone all the time now as she had been in those few vivid moments of her life she remembered so well. Something was bound to happen. She had thought of jumping from the window. She was on the third floor. If the snow got much deeper, she thought she might have a good chance of surviving the fall without serious injury. But she hadn't given up on the door and the key yet. The letter in the window had promised her.

And so she moved across the room to the door, her hand on the key inside the pocket of her dress, prepared to open it and find again one of those mirror images on the other side, peering hopefully and curiously back at her. The key turned. There was that rush of cold air, maybe from the hallway, maybe from something else. She opened the door. There stood Robbie, with his back to her, in the hall. When she touched his shoulder, he didn't disappear. Instead he turned and looked at her strangely, as if he was finding, simultaneously, exactly what he had been searching for but also what he most feared. She took his hand and led him across the threshold.

25

Hugh and the Dooze Man trudged through the house-high snow, destination unknown, at least so far, at least to the Doozer. Hugh, presumably, knew where he was going. It seemed to Dewey that they had been walking a long time without covering much ground, but that was likely due to the agonizingly slow pace of the proceedings, which were hampered a lot by the fact that Dewey kept sinking in the snow up to his waist and Hugh kept having to turn around and help pull him out. It wasn't the kind of thing he'd had in mind on all the winter days in Mount Pleasant when he sat looking out the window and wishing for snow instead of rain. Right now, he'd go for rain any day. Little harmless drops of rain.

"You hanging in there all right?" Hugh called over his shoulder. He was walking in front of Dewey and when he took his wool cap off a burst of steam rose into the cold air from his sweaty bald head. Nice as Hugh was, he was not the sort of person Dewey would be hanging around with if his father was here.

"I'm okay," Dewey said, but then thought better of it. "Actually, I'm soaking wet all the way past my waist," he said. He wanted Hugh to know that he was potentially going to freeze to death if they didn't head back to the diner soon. He had no gloves, but at least he'd remembered to wear his hat, so his ears were pretty warm, but the bottom half of him felt like it could be chipped away with an ice pick.

Hugh stopped and turned to him, his breath wafting up in a huge cloud, almost purple in the fading light. "Do you want to ride on my shoulders?"

It would be nice to ride on someone's shoulders right now, thought the Dooze Man, but not Hugh's. If you rode on Hugh's shoulders, where would you have to put your hands if you didn't want to fall off? Answer: On his sweaty bald head. "No, thank you," Dewey said. "Where are we going again?"

"It's just up here," Hugh said, forging ahead. From behind, he resembled a large troll. "You'll see."

Dewey's left foot sank deep into the snow with his next step and he grabbed the back of Hugh's coat to haul himself forward. "Why did your mom and dad come here?"

Hugh barely even lifted his legs to go through the snow. He just plowed through it like a horse. You could hang on to the back of his coat like reins. "It was only my mom and my sister and me," Hugh said. "I never knew my dad. He never came around."

"Oh," Dewey said, because he didn't know what else to say.

"Yeah," Hugh said, which somehow made sense.

"What was your sister's name?" Dewey asked.

"What *is* my sister's name, do you mean?" Hugh said. "She's still here, same as me. Her name's Stephanie. The two of us are souvenirs. That's what they call the kids who get left behind."

"Why would they call them that?" Dewey said. "Why would you call a person a souvenir?"

Hugh plowed ahead faster, forgetting he had to wait for Dewey to catch up. "That's just how these people are," he said. "It's just their way of letting you know you're not like them, that you don't belong. Like you're some trinket that got left behind when the people at Travelers Rest disappeared." Hugh's knees jerked up and down and his legs drove ahead. He was getting almost out of earshot. "It's just because they don't want to admit they're afraid."

"Hold up," Dewey shouted.

Hugh turned around. "*Jeez,* buddy, come on," he said. "I don't have all day." Dewey plodded up and got behind him again. "Grab on to my coat and let me pull you," Hugh said.

They went along for a while without saying anything, and while Dewey stared at Hugh's wide back and big shoulders he tried to imagine him as a kid, at the time he would have first come here.

Hugh's story, most of which he'd told Dewey before they left the diner, would have made no sense at all if pretty much the same thing wasn't happening to Dewey. The story went like this. Hugh and his younger sister and his mother had stayed at the hotel and the next morning his mother disappeared. This was in the summer, and the temperature in the town had stayed at well over a hundred degrees every day. Even in the morning there was almost no relief from the heat, which was so dry, Hugh said, that it made your eyes feel like sandpaper. He was afraid of the hotel, so he slept in a park by the creek. He saw his mother walking through the park, more than once, and then on the third day the weather turned cooler and the air rushed upward like a lid had been taken off the sky, and there was a popping sound, like your ears popping, almost, and then he never saw his mother again. And now here he was, a grown man who owned a diner. It seemed like a magical transformation.

They had turned off the main street and onto a short road that led to some snow-covered steps and a handrail that resembled a long, white caterpillar. So much snow had swept across the steps that you couldn't really tell where to put your feet, and Hugh had to pull himself up by the handrail while Dewey held on to his waist from behind. Hugh was breathing so hard that Dewey thought he might explode. He should probably get some more exercise, Hugh, and maybe eat something besides the food at the diner, which was tasty but probably not what Dewey's mother would refer to as "heart smart."

"I don't really know why my mother came here," Hugh said, catching his breath after they'd reached the top of the stairs. "The only thing I remember her saying before she pulled off the highway was that she wanted to take pictures. It was like she already decided she wanted to take pictures before she even saw any of the things she could take pictures of." He leaned over and grabbed his knees and groaned once and then started walking again. "Anything else you'd have to ask my sister," he said.

They were up on a hill and there were a lot of snowy bushes and evergreens and you could hear the snow hiss into them and you could look back to Main Street and see the snow sweep across the streetlights. There were the top floors of the hotel, not as far away as you might think, considering all the walking. The town was actually kind of pretty when you stood here and viewed it this way, from this angle, if you didn't think about it being evil and creepy and how if you ever found your mom and dad you were going to get the hell out of here and never come back to the state of Idaho again—if you didn't think about any of that, then the view was sort of peaceful. But Hugh pulled on Dewey's coat sleeve and pointed him toward a huge rock wall that was closed off, for some reason, by a heavy iron door or gate cut into the cliff face. Cold as he was, Dewey found this wall and this door fascinating, and he felt himself creeping dangerously toward that place in his head where he went to be all alone, where he wouldn't hear Hugh anymore or know that time was passing. To keep himself from going there he reached out and grabbed Hugh's arm, squeezed the rough material of his coat sleeve.

"It's the entrance to the mine," Hugh said. Very gently he took

Dewey's hand off his arm and he stepped forward and brushed away the snow from an inscription above the entrance.

"Is that where you're taking me?" Dewey asked. He could see himself following Hugh into the pitch-dark hole, no flashlight or anything, feeling his way along the rocks, the noises echoing everywhere, water dripping down from the cave ceiling. Still dangerously close to zoning out here. When you'd done nothing for four days but sit in a lonely, cold hotel room missing your parents, Dewey thought, your brain probably got overstimulated easily.

"Shit," Hugh said, and then apologized. "There's not enough money in the world. You couldn't pay me enough to go in there." He reached out and pulled on the door. "Anyway, see? It's locked." He wiped the last of the snow from the inscription above the doorframe. "There's a reason they closed this up, bud. Here, look at this."

Dewey waded forward through the snow. His face felt hot and cold at the same time from all the walking, and his nose was running. The engraving was like something he would have done in kindergarten—the uneven lettering, the simple phrase—except that it was carved in stone: "All Our Dreams Are True," it said.

Dewey wiped his nose on his sleeve, which he knew was pretty gross, but who was there that cared. "That's stupid," he said.

"I guess," Hugh said. "Sort of."

"It doesn't even say it right," Dewey said. "It's *come* true."

Hugh wrapped his arms across his chest. "I don't think the guy who owned the mine knew English very good," he said. He unwrapped his arms and took off his gloves and put his hands up to his face and then put the gloves on again. "But that's not exactly the point I was trying to make."

Yes, Dewey thought, it would be nice, after all the walking and the sweating and the freezing, after being soaked from head to toe with the snow that fell from overhead, constantly, and the snow that kept piling up on the ground, constantly, if there was a *point*. That would be nice. Regardless, the idea of that mine was like an itch inside his skin. It was hard to think about anything else, especially now that it dawned on him — "like a light breaking through the clouds," as it would say in a book — that he had seen this place before, on the weird TV. It was this place, this dark, open mouth, that the lights moved in and out of. Scary close, really scary close now to getting sucked in, so he bent down and cupped his hands in the snow and packed a snowball as quick as he could because it *stung*, a *good* sting that did what he wanted it to do, which was get his mind back inside his body — but wow, he could sure use some gloves about now. He could sure use *Hugh's* gloves about now, but apparently Hugh wasn't used to thinking about what kids needed, and Dewey didn't think it was his place to tell him. He took good aim and, with the same fluid motion he used to throw out runners on ground balls to short, pegged the snowball at Hugh and hit him square in the ass.

"Ow, man!" Hugh said. "What the hey?" He turned to Dewey with a momentary expression of outrage. "That *hurt*, little dude." He rubbed his butt. "You got an arm on you."

"I play shortstop," Dewey said. He put his hands back in his coat pockets, which didn't help much because the pockets were wet. Next time he left the hotel, he'd have to substitute the sweater for the coat, so it could dry.

"Do you want to know about your parents or not?" Hugh said, looking at him earnestly.

Yes and no. Yes and no. There stood this big guy with the stubbly hair and the oversized jacket with grease stains. It was pretty ridiculous that he had to listen to this guy, who he'd only known for like *four days,* tell him *anything* about his parents, with whom he'd spent his entire life. It wasn't right. It wasn't fair. He looked up at the sky, where it was getting dark again, another day gone, and he felt the snowflakes on his face but he couldn't see them.

"Hey, Dewey, I'm sorry," Hugh said. "Come here."

He shuffled over to Hugh and his shoulders drooped and Hugh picked him up around the waist, and together they examined the inscription.

"All our dreams are true," Hugh said, almost under his breath. In some little corner of Dewey's brain the concept was already taking hold—dreams are true, dreams are true. In this strange place, what did that mean?

"The reason I brought you here," Hugh said, "was to show you this is where the first event occurred."

Then there was a story about an explosion in the mine and a guy named Diamond and while Hugh continued to talk Dewey's thoughts went, finally, where they wanted to go, which was down into that hole where Hugh was telling him the first disaster had occurred. He could imagine it, the hole pulling him in while he felt dreamier and dreamier, farther and farther away, in a cold and unreachable place. He could feel the hole throbbing in time with his breath, and in the darkening sky he saw the same pulse in the snow clouds overhead.

Then he looked back at the gate, barely visible now. A terrible thought had occurred to him. "Are my mom and dad in there?" he said, and took a step toward the entrance, but Hugh put a firm grip on his arm.

"No," Hugh said. "No." He let go of Dewey's arm and patted him on the shoulder. "This place has been closed off since before you and I were born. It's the hotel where things happen now. But this was the first place."

"I don't get it," Dewey said. "What does the mine have to do with the hotel? Why'd you bring me out here?"

Hugh laughed. "Have you been down the stairs underneath the hotel?"

"No," Dewey said. "Why would I go underneath the hotel?"

"Exactly," Hugh said. "I wouldn't either. Smart man. But if you did, you'd see pretty quick how things are around here. Everything in this entire town is connected. There are shafts in this mine that run right down under the streets." He nodded his head toward the mine entrance. "Something went wrong in there and it ruined the whole place."

None of it made any sense, of course, but Dewey had noticed how sometimes things that didn't make any sense turned out to be true. And while his father would certainly make that little snorting laugh under his breath at what Hugh was suggesting, and call it superstition, and remind Dewey of the myriad ways in which cultures from the most primitive to the most modern assuaged their fears of death and cosmic aloneness, his father wasn't here now and in fact had seemed to disappear in the very way that Hugh was suggesting, and so if Dewey wanted to get his mom and his dad back he might have to deviate somewhat from his dad's way of thinking, because while it was always logical, maybe it wasn't always right.

"So what *is* it? The thing that happens to people," Dewey said. "You bring me out here in the snow to some mine shaft I can't even go into and you tell me some story and then you expect me to stop believing in the laws of physics, like all the things I learned in third grade science class." Right away he regretted saying this because, as his mother was always pointing out to people, he was a very nice kid with an enviable disposition, and he really didn't like hurting people's feelings. "Can we maybe just go back to the diner and get some hot chocolate? It's really cold," he said. "Can't you tell me the rest on the way?"

"Sure," Hugh said. "Let's go back." But he stood there gazing at something down the other side of the hill, and Dewey all of a sudden sensed, once again, what Hugh was thinking—he was thinking about his mother. He nodded toward something in the near distance that Dewey couldn't see. "That's where I saw my mother," he said, and pointed. "The creek is right through those trees." He reached into his pocket and pulled out his wool hat and put it back on his head. "Let's go," he said. Dewey took one last look at the heavy gate that hid the opening. Then they went back to the steps and down the hill.

When they reached the edge of town, Hugh stopped under the first streetlight and pointed toward the hotel, which was still a ways away, a lot farther than Dewey wanted it to be.

"You see your mother in the window, right? You *see* her there."

Dewey nodded glumly.

"And you see your father. But when you go to them, they're not there."

Dewey nodded again.

"The way I feel about it, that means they have to be here somewhere," Hugh said. "They have to be." He started walking again, kind of agitated, it seemed, and Dewey followed a step or two behind. "I've always thought that, no matter what anyone says," Hugh said, as if he were arguing with someone who wasn't there. They got to the next streetlight and Hugh stopped again. Dewey wished he would quit doing that. "Have you ever sat in the bathtub and checked out your feet underwater?" Hugh said.

Dewey sighed, somewhat inaudibly, he hoped. Of course he had looked at his feet underwater in the bathtub. Hugh wanted to tell him something about perception. "I take showers," Dewey said.

"All right," Hugh said. "But you know what I mean."

"Your feet look bigger or they look smaller or they look like they're bent in the middle. Yeah." Dewey started to walk again, just to hurry Hugh along. "It depends on the angle of perception."

"Yes," Hugh said, *"perception."* He sounded like he'd made an extraordinary scientific discovery, like when Dewey's dad used to go *"Eureka,"* only it was a joke, because he would have discovered

something like, for instance, that Dewey had remembered to put down the toilet seat. "So which perception is real, then?" Hugh persisted. "The one where you see your mom right there in front of you? The one where she disappears? The one where you try to follow your dad but he can't hear you all of a sudden? Or what about the perceptions *they* have when you can't see them but you know they're still there?"

Dewey took a deep breath. "That would be, like, *anyone* when you weren't with them. They wouldn't have to be vanished to go on having perceptions when you're not there."

Hugh didn't say anything for a while. They passed beneath two streetlights before he stopped again. They were about halfway between the end of town and the hotel. The snow was blowing down in huge sheets now, the wind whipping down the street about twice as hard as when they left the diner, like the blizzard was *gaining* in intensity instead of slowing down. Dewey couldn't feel anything below his knees. "Can we *please* just go inside?" he asked.

"Sorry, sorry," Hugh said, and started walking again, pushing through the snow briskly this time.

The diner came into sight up ahead across the street from the hotel. Dewey took his hands out of his coat pockets and blew on them and put them back in his pockets.

"Here," Hugh said, "take these." He took off his gloves and tried to hand them to Dewey.

Dewey glanced up the street. The diner was about half a block away. They'd be there in two minutes. They'd left over an hour ago. "No, thanks," he said.

Hugh shrugged. "Suit yourself," he said. "I'd think you'd be cold by now."

They walked the rest of the way in silence, but right when they got outside the door, right when Dewey could almost *feel* the heat coming from inside the building, something made him stop. "I still don't get it, though," he said. "*Who* gets drawn here?" He could see Lorraine serving a plate of roast beef and mashed potatoes to an old guy wearing suspenders. She'd be upset they were gone so long. The teenager who cooked with Hugh in the kitchen wasn't all that great, even when they hardly had any orders to fill. "We didn't even know about this place. We just ended up here on accident."

Hugh was fixated on the window, his eyes not moving, and Dewey knew he was thinking about his mother again. "I'm not exactly sure," Hugh said, "but I think it's people who are trying to remember something, or maybe they want to change something they regret."

Dewey wondered if this was what he looked like when he had one of his episodes. Hugh was like a blind man who was also drunk and standing there with his eyes open. He wobbled back and forth like he was going to fall asleep. Then he raised his eyebrows slightly, just the tiniest amount. "Or maybe there's just a certain type of person who's more susceptible," he said, and he breathed quietly in and out, so that the words seemed to go up into the air like the thinnest trail of smoke. "My mother was always dreamy."

"And you really never saw her again?"

"I saw her the same way you've been seeing your mother. Does that count?" Hugh nodded in little tiny jerks and chewed on his bottom lip. Dewey realized something kind of scary, which was that Hugh was about to cry himself, a big guy like that.

"I *hope* it does," Dewey said.

"Right," Hugh said. "Hope it does. That's good." Dewey made a move to go inside but Hugh held him back gently by the shoulder and looked at him real hard. Dewey could feel the cold all over him for a second, rushing from his head down into his legs, and he started to shake. Hugh took hold of both his shoulders. "Listen to me now, Dewey." Dewey shook so hard he thought he would shake right out of his clothes, but he did his best to pay attention. "You've been a really big boy about this, a real tough little guy. But this is going to get hard. If there's a way to find your mother and your father and your uncle, we've got to do it fast. Because it usually only takes a day or two before people disappear for good. It's been four days already."

"Good!" Dewey said. He was crying now. It was hopeless to try to hide it. His nose was running all over the place. "Whatever happens, let's just go ahead and get it over with. I don't want to be in this creepy town. I don't want to be a stupid 'souvenir.'"

"Don't say that," Hugh said. "Don't say that."

"Why?" Dewey said. "What difference does it make?"

"It's not always just the grown-ups," Hugh said, and he pulled Dewey close to him. Dewey could feel Hugh shaking inside his coat and hear his voice tremble. "Sometimes the little kids disappear."

26

When he woke from a deep sleep the first thing he thought was, *I'm lying in bed with my brother's wife.* His eyes were still closed as his consciousness crept forward, and he steeled himself for the slap of this new wave against the fortress of his wellbeing. The shitty things he'd done in his life had a way of coming at him wave by wave, and he beat them back relentlessly, but this was a big one, tsunami-size—this one would hit the shore hard and keep pushing its way in. What he dreaded most at the moment was opening his eyes to see Julia, at which point he would have to think of that first thing to say, which would be the hardest part, at least until he had to say the second thing.

But when he did open his eyes he was greeted by the sort of dull, leaden pain he associated with a long bout of hard drinking, and he was adjusting to what felt like the new and somewhat squashed shape of his head when he realized that the wall he faced looked very much like the wall he'd woken up to the past few mornings, and when he had taken that impression far enough to make him curious, he turned to find that the woman he lay next to was that very same Stephanie he'd woken up next to the past few mornings as well.

She was awake, with her head propped against a pillow, reading a book as she usually was. Her preference seemed to be either crime fiction or bulky European novels of the nineteenth century, which she read alternately, sometimes switching back and forth several times within an hour. Just to make sure of her and of himself, he reached over and touched the birthmark on her arm, and she lifted her eyes from the page and smiled at him briefly. It was Stephanie all right. Relief shot through him, with just a twinge of regret.

"Do we have any of those cigarettes left?" he asked her.

She grimaced at him as if to say, *Really, right now, you just woke up,* but she nodded to her coat hanging off the back of a chair, and he got a cigarette and a lighter and pulled on a pair of sweats and a T-shirt and made his way downstairs and out onto the covered porch, where he lit up and managed to puff away for a few seconds without thinking much of anything, his head still soft and damaged, one eye open to the view of his breath clouding out and the snow continuing to fall. It seemed impossible both that the snow could still be falling and that it could ever stop.

Soon he started to shiver in his T-shirt and his bare feet grew numb on the thin ice of the porch step. He was an infrequent smoker, generally used cigarettes just as a way to shake things up with a high or change the rhythm of what was going on, or, like now, as a way to help him slow down for a minute and think, and what he had come outside to think about was what he had done last night, or what he thought he had done, which was go back to the hotel, possibly feeling contrite, possibly to issue an apology (although he couldn't imagine why he suddenly would have felt like apologizing), where he had found Julia alone (why? Where was everyone else?) and, as he thought he remembered it, wound up in bed with her. Of course it was a possibility he had thought about before, sometimes for weeks on end, subtly shifting the fantasies around in his head as if they were a rare and expensive drug he intended to savor, erotic bouts that would be followed by something nearly resembling a hangover. But this was not at all the same. He had *been there with her*. He had been lost again, in one of the never-ending twists and turns of the stairways and hallways, and a door had opened and a hand had taken his, Julia's hand, he had seen her face, she was smiling at him in what he would have described as a weary way, as if she were dealing with a stubborn child, and he had been led into a room. There was an unusual smell in the air, like incense, almost, but more like he imagined it would smell if you actually burned flowers, and the air was hazy and thick, and whatever light there'd been when he stood in the doorway disappeared. Julia moved to him, close enough that he could feel her warmth...but now he couldn't see her face. Then there were the familiar motions of two bodies coming together, although the process was complicated by all sorts of strange clothing that he couldn't make out in the darkness—a dress that seemed to go on for miles, bulky undergarments like petticoats or corsets or who knew what it all was. He could remember the feel of her long hair, which he'd had to unpin, sifting through his fingers as he lay down on the bed. None of it felt even remotely like a dream—here on the porch step he could still smell that strange burning sweetness that had been in the air, and he remembered in some detail how, even while it was happening, he had run the whole gallery of Robbie personas through his head for inspection and censure—Robbie the sleazebag, Robbie the traitor, the asshole, the ingrate, the fool. He had even managed to feel bad about Stephanie for a minute or two. He felt more certain, all in all, about what had happened than he usually did in the morning.

On the other hand. Even aside from the obvious, that he'd woken up next to Stephanie instead of Julia, there were problems with the whole thing. He and Julia hadn't ever spoken, not once. That made no sense, because there were a lot of things to talk about. He hadn't asked her, and she hadn't told him, where Tonio was or where Dewey was or what they had all been doing in town for the last few days while he cavorted with the local female citizenry. And he didn't remember going to the hotel, which was something he'd sworn he would never do again for any reason, although neither of those facts eliminated the possibility that he had indeed gone there. But he also didn't remember anything he'd been doing that would cause him to black out or to go back on such a staunch resolution. But again, on the *other* hand, he now had in his head what distinctly seemed like a memory and not a product of his imagination—that when Julia first led him through the doorway, she had pulled him toward her quickly and impulsively kissed his forehead, just above his left eyebrow. Which made it really difficult to explain or understand why, the next thing he knew, he was waking up in bed with Stephanie, and also why he would remember the kiss on the forehead but have no recollection, or not much, of the more intimate details.

Overall, it seemed to Robbie like one of those sad and sordid tales from a long evening that got told to him bit by bit over a period of days and weeks as he ran one by one into the various spectators and participants, and that usually ended with another trip to detox. But maybe he only thought that because the other possibility—that he was beginning to understand what Stephanie meant when she said he had no idea what he was getting into with this town—was even more disturbing. He could see, for instance, that he had seriously underestimated this place's capacity to mess up a person in a big and frightening way over a very short period of time. It was, very likely, the most fucked-up place in the world. Why, he wondered, tilting his head up toward the mountains and the snowy pines, were the prettiest places always the most horrible?

His cigarette was down to the last drag and he tossed it out into the snow, where its flight ended in a little hiss. Everything was so quiet that you could literally hear not just the cigarette but the *snowflakes* landing. A row of giant icicles hung from the porch awning and he broke one off with both hands and smashed it on the porch steps just to hear some noise, then he went inside and back upstairs. Stephanie was right where he'd left her, wearing her black reading glasses, the detective novel propped on her knees. He could tell she was about to get in the shower because the digital clock on the end table was turned to face her. When she was trying to sleep, the blue light of the display bothered her, and she turned the clock to face out into the room. In the morning, when she started to think about getting up, she turned the clock toward her to check the time. It was amazing how fast you could learn people's habits. He'd probably learned a hundred different habits of a few dozen different women in exactly the same way and forgotten them all just as quickly. Right now, this was the only one he could recall, this one of Stephanie's.

"So, if I were going to quiz you on the subject," he said to her, standing in the middle of the bedroom. She glanced up from her book but made sure not to lose her place. "What would you say we did last night?"

She laid the book down flat in her lap and gave him a look. "You don't know what we did last night," she said.

He shrugged apologetically. "I mean, at one point I *thought* I knew what we were doing."

She stared at him as if to say go on.

"I thought we drank beer and smoked a bowl and played rummy. But then when I woke up, I thought maybe something else had happened."

"Like what?"

Honestly he had no idea how to explain about Julia, so he just shook his head and raised one hand in a helpless gesture.

"Did you think you were in the hotel?" Stephanie asked him.

That was an easy way to put it. "Yes," he said. "Yeah. I did."

She folded the corner of the page she was on and put the book away. "There's a lot you're not telling me about why you're here," she said.

What he'd told her, as best he could remember, was that Tonio was an asshole and he'd left him at the hotel. He'd been ashamed to say anything about Julia and Dewey because he knew who would look like the asshole then, and afterward, when she pressed him a little further, he changed his story to make it sound like *Tonio* had gone on home without *him*. That seemed like the most convenient way to get what he wanted out of the situation, which was Robbie's rule of thumb in terms of conduct. When you'd done the things he'd done, when you'd gotten into dangerous situations with unstable people as a matter of course, when you'd formed alliances and made enemies on the fly, in very short and very intense bursts of time and energy, when there was always money involved, either way too much or way too little, when things crashed and burned and blew themselves up completely and irrevocably sometimes in a matter of minutes, sometimes with nasty consequences for what seemed like small transgressions and only negligible damage for what seemed like catastrophic personal failures, what Robbie had learned was that ultimately everyone was going to act in his or her own self-interest anyway, and the person who acknowledged that the soonest, behaved the most selfishly from the outset, would usually come out ahead. But the longer he stayed in this town (or was stuck in this town, because it was starting to feel that way), the more it seemed in his best interest to trust Stephanie. He stood there thinking of these things and staring at the snow swirling against the windowpane.

"Where's the closest bus station?" was what he ended up saying.

Stephanie rolled her eyes at him behind her glasses.

"Let me guess," he said. "Nowhere near."

"Thanks," she said. "Thank you."

"Hey," he said, and he went over and sat on the edge of the bed and put his hand on the place where her feet stuck up under the covers. "Look, I'm having fun, I really am, but I *am* starting to get freaked out a little, you know?" He pointed out the window. "I mean, this is a *weird fucking place*. Just for starters—seriously, this is just the tip of the iceberg—where the fuck does it snow like this? Have you seen anything like this before?"

Stephanie didn't answer.

So then he told her the actual story, hiding maybe one or two things, such as stealing Tonio's money and sleeping with his wife. He ended with how he had absolutely thought he was at the hotel the night before.

She took off her glasses and put them on the nightstand. "You probably were," she said.

"You said I was here the whole time."

"You were kind of in both places at once," she said. "It takes some getting used to."

He was, at this point, almost prepared to accept that explanation. It had the unfortunate quality of feeling true to him. It was as if he had two different memories of the same time, and each was as real as the other. He was not as baffled by this development, the possibility that his brain contained two separate memories of the same evening, as, say, Tonio would have been. In fact, having the ability to be in two different places at one time was something he'd often wished for, especially when it involved two different women, although one of them was Julia, which created a whole lot of complications, and also there was the hotel, which he would never be able to think about with anything approaching pleasure. Really, he'd had a nagging sense of being stuck in that fucking hotel ever since he'd left it, some part of him constantly plodding up the rickety steps, huddled shivering in the cold and airless passageways. It lingered beneath his skin.

Stephanie flopped back onto the pillow. "Wow," she said. "You really should have told me about this before, Robbie. You *really really should* have told me."

Here was another occasion on which he was going to have to feel guilty, then. That much seemed clear. He hated these situations, this feeling, and he bristled instinctively, or by long habit, whenever anyone or anything made him feel this way. As far as relationships went, this was, generally, the beginning of the end. It made him so *tired* to be arriving at this point, he'd been here too often, and you'd think by now people would realize that he wasn't going to bend, he wasn't going to act better or do anything different or—especially—apologize. The one person who understood this (well, Tonio *understood* it, but he also hated Robbie for it, for his capacity to get away over and over again with his self-destructive behavior and never accept responsibility, etc.) was Julia, who, whenever Robbie fucked up, simply looked at him in a way that said she understood his silence was in essence his acknowledgment of guilt and even an expression of remorse, and that his failure to mend his ways or apologize for them was an example of both his weakness and his strength. But now he had gone off and complicated his relationship with Julia, too—or he hadn't. He could go to the hotel and talk to her—or not, because she might not actually be there. The front edge of panic was setting in: the prickling in the skin, the tightness in the chest, the cramping in the fingers—this was what it felt like, finally, to go nuts. It was something he had worried about in the past, and now it was here.

He tried to get himself together by taking a deep breath and sitting up ramrod straight on the bed, raising his arms above his head as if he were suddenly overcome with a violent need to stretch. "I'm sure it's no big deal," he said. "I'm sure they're long gone by now."

"No," she said, and laughed in a quiet, incredulous way that meant there was nothing funny. "I guarantee you they haven't gone anywhere."

He tried to bite his tongue but he wasn't good at it. "How the fuck would you know that?" he said. "You don't know anything about my family. You don't even know much about me, but I can tell you one thing — I don't like to be criticized."

This time she laughed a little louder and sat up and pulled the covers away and got up and put on her robe. "And I don't like to be threatened," she said. She had a hard gleam in her eye that he hadn't expected. Things might get interesting here in a minute. She said very coolly, "You should probably stop speaking to me in that tone of voice."

This was the kind of thing that made him boil, and he hated her right at the moment, whoever she was or thought she was or thought she should or could be, but this was the side that his bread was being buttered on currently, and there was no practical alternative he could see other than to head back to the hotel, which he wasn't going to do. It was the hour of compromise, which he also hated. The morning wasn't going the way he'd hoped it would. He flashed her a grim little smile. "You're right," he said. "Probably."

Then she told him a story. In the story, a little girl named Stephanie, only seven years old at the time, was in the car with her mother and her older brother, driving to Spokane. As the little girl remembered it, they were simply going to shop at the stores downtown, which were the best and most numerous this side of Seattle. The older brother remembered it differently. He thought there was something more complicated and sinister, something that had to do with a man their mother knew — maybe their father, who had been mysteriously absent all their lives, never seen, never spoken of. The boy and the girl agreed, though, that the stated reason for the mother turning off the interstate into the small town of Good Night was that she wanted to take pictures of the old buildings and the mountains surrounding town. The weather was hot, unusually hot for North Idaho even in the middle of the summer, a dry heat that almost puckered your skin, as if you were being browned slowly in an oven. The afternoon had gotten longer and the sunshine had turned hard and long shadows stretched from the buildings across the silent street. The mother decided to stay overnight, and while she checked them into the hotel, the little girl and her brother waited in the car, not saying anything, and in the little girl's memory everything was absolutely still. Two men walked across the street and into a tavern. A girl rode a bicycle down the sidewalk. An empty logging truck rattled its way home. There was cottonwood in the air, floating lazily through the harsh sunshine.

The mother came out and got the boy and the girl and they went inside. The girl remembered that they didn't have any bags. The hotel was old and empty and their room felt like it belonged to a different century. While the light was still good, the mother used her Nikon to take pictures of the old furniture, the steam radiators, the bathroom fixtures. Then she positioned the boy and the girl on the antique sofa and took a picture. The girl remembered that. The TV in the room didn't work, so that night they played cards. The girl was too young to play games like poker and spades so they humored her by playing Old Maid and Go Fish. In the night, the girl heard a noise. Her brother was on the other side of the bed from her, but the mother's bed was empty. The girl turned to the door in time to see her mother moving toward it, dressed in nothing but a long T-shirt. She remembered that her mother looked very pretty that way, with her sturdy tan legs and her long blonde hair loose on her shoulders. The mother's attention, the girl could tell, was being called to something outside the room. She seemed to be listening to something far away. Quickly then she stepped outside the room, and, at the last moment, she turned back toward the girl, smiled, and put one finger to her lips. To this day, the daughter didn't know whether the mother was saying to be quiet or blowing a kiss. Then the mother heard the faraway noise, and walked away down the corridor. The girl watched the open doorway for a few minutes and then fell back asleep. When she awoke in the morning, the door to the room was still open and the mother's bed still empty.

She and her brother spent the morning wandering around the deserted hotel and waiting for their mother to return. There were no people in the hotel and the people on the street didn't pay any attention to them. The boy unlocked the car and the two of them sat in there for a while. The boy honked the horn. They went back up to the room and waited some more. The mother still didn't come back. Her clothes were there, her purse was there, just not her. Finally the sun dropped level with the windows and it was evening again. The sunlight poured onto the old dusty furniture and the boy, not the girl, started to cry. Something about the hotel scared him and it scared the girl too but for some reason she wouldn't say so. The boy said he wouldn't spend another night in the hotel and when the girl wouldn't agree to leave with him he left by himself and, like the mother, didn't return. She was seven years old and she stayed there alone in the dark hotel. There was nothing to eat but she didn't feel like eating anyway. She was thirsty, though, so she finally took a pencil out of her mother's purse and wrote a note on a piece of paper saying that she had gone to get a glass of water and then she took a piece of gum from her mother's purse and chewed it for a minute and used the gum to stick the note to the mirror on the armoire. She was sure her mother would see it there because her mother had a curious habit of never passing a mirror without inspecting her face in it, even though she never seemed to like what she saw.

At the diner across the street a woman gave the girl a glass of water but she glared at the girl as if she hated her and wanted her to leave, so the girl left as soon as she finished the water.

That night the girl saw her mother walking down the hall and somehow it made her scream, and the mother paused in the corridor but then she went on, and when the girl got to the doorway her mother was gone again. The girl spent all night searching the hotel for the mother and she found a lot of interesting things but not what she was looking for.

She was still sleeping the next day when she heard someone calling her name out in the street. It was her brother. He had brought her a sandwich and a Sunkist orange soda but he refused to come inside the hotel. She went out to him and they sat on the curb and ate their lunch and talked while the people on the street tried to pretend they weren't there, the two of them, just two small kids sitting there eating by themselves. The girl said all these years later that no matter how long she lived in the town she would never forget the way those people had ignored her.

The boy said he'd seen their mother in the park, walking beneath the cottonwood trees. She appeared there in the afternoon, walking slowly in a long dress, bending her head to one side as if she was listening to something. In the sunlight, the brother said, she appeared to be slightly transparent, and if he approached too close she disappeared.

The girl refused to leave the hotel so the boy gave her ten dollars he had taken from the mother's purse and told her to get something to eat. Then he went back to the park to sleep.

But instead of getting something to eat that night, the girl wandered through the strange hotel, going up and down the stairways in the moonlight, peeking into the empty rooms, sitting on the old furniture in the lobby and staring out the window at the street. Finally she fell asleep there, but she was awakened by the uncomfortable feeling of something pulling on her, pulling her up and out of herself, and she woke up startled, out of breath, to find the lights of the lobby blazing and her mother not twenty feet away, her back turned, walking through the lobby as if she were carrying on a conversation with someone, though she never made a sound.

All that night the girl followed her mother around the rooms, barely feeling herself move, afraid that it was just a dream. Her mother sat at a long table moving her lips silently, an endless pantomime that she seemed to perform for no one. Finally she danced alone in a big empty room while a hot breeze from an open window blew around and around. The girl remembered later that if she stayed perfectly still sitting in a corner, she could half hear voices and music. She fell asleep that way, for the second time that night, and she woke up to a cold room with sheets of rain coming in the window. She walked across the street and spent her ten dollars at the diner and she never saw her mother again.

That was it, the girl said. End of story. Then she got out of bed and went into the bathroom and closed the door behind her and turned on the shower. Robbie went downstairs to the kitchen and started to make a pot of coffee but it was too much trouble so he got a beer and sat at the kitchen table drinking it. He didn't think that Stephanie was crazy or delusional, but maybe she was one of those garden-variety spiritual nuts, the kind the Northwest seemed to sprout like toadstools. He had a way of attracting these women: Wiccans, Pentecostals, Sierra Club whack jobs — various self-appointed spiritual advisors and do-gooders from all ends of the spectrum. Sometimes Robbie wished he'd grown up in, say, an old Polish neighborhood in Chicago, someplace that was maybe less scenic but where the people had more common sense. He tilted his head back and closed his eyes. This Stephanie had seemed so normal.

For a minute or two, sitting there with his head tilted back and the inside of his skull filled with the same uniform gray light of the sky, he simply felt himself drifting, the only sensations the soft sound of the shower overhead in the bathroom and the cold bottle against the fingertips of his right hand, but then even these sensations faded and everything was white and cold, like snow, and he was no place at all, everything was gone. Another sound started to establish itself, as if it were hammering its way up out of a great void. Robbie knew the sound, or at least knew that it was familiar, but it took a long time before he could tell himself what it was—it was the sound of the stairs in the hotel. As soon as he realized this he was in fact running up them, up the numberless stairs in the white light of the snow outside, his heart and head pounding. He was running toward something or he was running away from something, he didn't know which, but there was no doubt about the urgency of the situation, it was of the utmost importance that he get up the stairs quickly. He was running from those assholes, who were shouting behind him, intent on doing him harm, or he was running to help Julia, or someone, the shouts were from up ahead now. He pulled himself up as fast as he could by the banister, slivers stinging his hands, and there was a knocking sound, a weird light, an acrid smell, and heat.

He exhaled sharply and lurched up in the kitchen chair and the beer spilled across the table. Before he could make up his mind to do anything about it, Stephanie was there with a towel wiping it up. He watched her as if from a great distance, everything muffled. His hands shook where they rested on his legs and it felt like a heavy belt was tied tightly across his forehead and his chest, making it almost impossible for him to move or breathe. Stephanie had almost finished with the mess.

"I think I might be having a heart attack," he said to her.

At which she laughed—not in a mean way, actually in a very nice, soothing way, but it was laughing, just the same. It helped him, though, the laughing, to get hold of himself a little bit, and he managed to lean forward and prop his elbows on his knees and place his head in his hands. "What the *hell*," he said.

Her hand touched his wrist. "You were in the hotel again, right?" she said. He nodded, not looking at anything but a sliver of light between his hands. "Does that mean you're ready to listen now?"

"Okay."

She took her hand from his wrist and he glanced up to see that she had a coffee cup in front of her. He'd been out of it at least long enough for her to finish her shower, comb her hair, put on the robe she was wearing, and make a pot of coffee. These mundane events were transpiring while he thought he was dying.

"Take a deep breath," she said, and he did, and he felt better. She got up for a second and then came back and sat down across from him. "Beer for breakfast?" she said, and placed another bottle on the table.

"Thanks," he managed to say, and he opened the bottle and took a drink and the world began to right itself. Stephanie began to look quite attractive there in her blue robe, for instance, and he imagined immediately several things he'd like to do to her right now if she let him. It was amazing, if he really thought about it, that he didn't disgust himself more. But at least he didn't feel like he was having a heart attack.

"*So,*" she said, reaching across to pick at the label on the beer bottle, "what did you think of my story?"

"It was very interesting," he said. "I enjoyed it immensely."

She didn't laugh, but almost, which meant he hadn't screwed things up too badly, at least not yet. "Any questions?"

"Yes," he said. He leaned forward and tried to appear both mature and considerate, the way he'd seen attorneys do when following a delicate line of questioning. "Let's agree on one thing beforehand, though, okay?"

"What?" she said, moving a strand of damp blonde hair behind her ear. What a find, really, in a place like this. He could have done a lot, lot worse.

"Let's not get angry."

Right away he could tell this request wasn't going over the way he'd hoped it would. Stephanie leaned back in her chair and crossed one leg over the other, a nice little gap opening in the robe, but it was clear she wasn't trying to be seductive. He didn't like the expression on her face.

"Why would I get angry, Robbie?"

He shook his head innocently to say he didn't know.

"Because I'm unstable? Because I'm psycho?" She said this in a relaxed voice that had, he noted, no hint of anger in it. "Do you feel the need to be *careful* with me now that I've told you my story?" She laughed and stared at the ceiling.

"I just thought it would be good if we didn't get angry with each other."

"This is nothing," she said, and she waved her hand out to indicate everything in the room—him, his beer, this morning, the constant snow falling outside the window. "*Nothing*. You have no idea what I've been through."

"Okay," he said. "Still—"

"What makes you so funny," she went on, still speaking pleasantly, as if she was making sure to take Robbie up on his suggestion, "is that you actually think *you're* the one in control here, that *you're* in charge of everything. That's hilarious." She creased her eyebrows and made a little movement with her shoulders that had a military air to it. "Robbie Addison. So hard, so cold, so distant. Bulletproof. Able to leap tall buildings in a single bound." She sipped her coffee and put down the cup and stared at him and shook her head, like she was seeing something sad.

So this was how it was going to be. Things were going to end badly, and there didn't seem to be a good way to avert the outcome, and he really *wanted* to avert the outcome suddenly—whether that was because he honestly liked Stephanie or because he was currently in a precarious situation, more vulnerable than usual, he couldn't say. "Thanks," he said quietly, and put both hands around his beer bottle.

"You're a sweet guy at heart," she said, with some genuine feeling, and she leaned in and put one hand on top of his. "You may not even think that yourself, but you are." She rubbed her thumb on the knuckle of his index finger, and a crazy thing happened—the pressure of her hand on his aroused no thoughts of sex, but made him feel grateful and slightly melancholy instead. It was a day of marvels, no doubt. "I could fall for you in two seconds if I let myself." Then she pulled back her hand and took up the strand of unruly hair again, holding it out in front of her eyes as if she were chastising it. "But you're in way over your head here. You have *no idea*." She laughed lightly in the back of her throat. Then she did something surprising, which was to get up and rummage in a drawer until she found a cigarette pack, from which she pulled a cigarette, which she then lit right there in the house, in the kitchen, which was completely against the rules as they'd been laid out to him. She smoked with her back against the sink, turning around occasionally to tap her ash over the drain.

"There are some things I'm confused about, for sure," he said after a couple of minutes. "Maybe that means I'm in over my head, I don't know. I'm fairly good at getting myself out of bad situations."

"Not this time," she said.

"Okay, whatever," he said. "But tell me, seriously—you seem certain that my brother and his family are still here, but where?" She started to say something but he cut her off. "Because I...

dreamed, I guess, last night, that I saw my sister-in-law at the hotel, but no one else was there."

"You dreamed it," she said. "Yeah, I know those dreams." She turned on the tap and doused her cigarette in the running water and shut the water off and leaned over the counter to put the butt in the trash. Her left breast hung out of the robe invitingly, but she straightened up and pulled the sides of the robe closer together at the neck and tightened the belt at her waist.

Then she told him in what sounded like a reasonable voice (as long as you didn't actually listen to what she was saying) that she was pretty sure the rest of his family was still "here." Being here, she said, meant being in a kind of limbo, or not really in a kind of limbo but more of a multiple set of "presences" that made each particular presence difficult to navigate—witness, for example, Robbie's insistence that he had been in the hotel last night when he had really been with her the whole time (on hearing this assessment of the situation, that sense of relief threaded with regret again). As a veteran of this sort of thing, she herself had learned to deal with it pretty well, even to the point that she could go into the hotel itself without suffering any additional damage, at least that anyone could see. "But it's with me all the time," she said, "inside me. Sometimes it's personal, like it's related to me. I can see my mother sometimes inside my head. Sometimes if I wander around the hotel late at night I can see her for real, like right there in front of me, but I can't be sure that that's not just inside my head, too. Sometimes I even find things." She walked over by the refrigerator and slid open a drawer and took something out and brought it to him. "I found this that night when I went to get your clothes out of your room. This was in the bottom of the drawer where your socks were." She handed him a photograph. It was of a little girl with blonde hair and a boy a couple of years older, both seated on an old sofa, smiling somewhat reluctantly at the camera. Robbie looked back and forth from the girl in the photo to Stephanie, who glanced away from him.

"The really hard part for me," she said, "is you take on other people's memories, other people who've been there. You're remembering what other people remember or remembered—sometimes good, sometimes bad. They're like memories of things that never happened, not to you. They get stuck in your head."

He had been sitting there nodding in an intent but puzzled way for quite a while now, and he wasn't sure how long he could keep on doing it. He kept wanting something, he didn't know what, or not really wanting something but being aware of the absence of something, and he figured it out now, with Stephanie talking about memories of things that never happened. When he was little, not as old as Dewey even, he would imagine what his older brother—his mysterious, almost supernatural older brother, out there in the world pursuing a special kind of knowledge, a knowledge of the past and people of the past, lost civilizations—might be up to, and he would store up these imagined events almost as if they'd really happened. He was missing Tonio right now. For one of the few times in his adult life, he really wished Tonio were here. He would like to know what Tonio thought about *this* whole thing.

Of course he didn't believe any of it, not really, but he believed that Stephanie believed it, and he had experienced enough of the disconcerting effects of the place to know there was something unusual going on, something that at least needed explaining. There had to be (as some character always insisted in movies of the supernatural, he realized, usually the first one to die as a result of not believing in the phenomenon) a logical explanation. It was only because the town's collective IQ fell somewhat short of triple digits that no one had figured it out yet. But he *trusted* Stephanie—she was no idiot, by any means.

He drank the last of his beer. Stephanie got another one and handed it to him and sat down on the chair next to him again. He'd been sitting in the same position too long and his knee hurt, the old basketball injury. Basketball—the only thing he'd ever been any good at, which he quit in eleventh grade because he wanted to drink beer and smoke pot instead of practice. If he had it to do over again, he'd make the same decision. Who was he kidding here.

He put his hand on Stephanie's knee, as if he were trying to be gentle in acknowledging the difficult things she was telling him, but really he just wanted to feel her leg. The smooth skin of her knee, slightly red from where she'd had her legs crossed before, was infinitely soothing to him at the moment, in a way that only serious narcotics usually made him feel. "Once," he said, "when we were on vacation, my dad decided it would be fun to take me to this haunted house. We were in the Black Hills, South Dakota, billboards for this place all along the side of the road, obviously a tourist trap." She was only halfway paying attention, but talking about it made him feel better, so he went ahead. "Freaked me out at the time. A bunch of weird shit, chairs balancing on one leg, rubber balls that rolled uphill. There was a totally level place on the floor where if you stood two people side by side, one would be taller, but if they switched places the other one suddenly would be. It scared the crap out of me. My dad thought it was funny."

She sighed—a long sigh that seemed to go on forever, as if she were in the process of sighing her entire body inside out.

"Not the same thing?" he volunteered.

She didn't even bother to answer. She got up and went to the fridge and grabbed the last beer and sat back down. "I'll finish this one off," she said. "Then no more today. We've got stuff to do."

This was, naturally, exactly what he didn't want to hear, never liked to hear, exactly what he'd hoped to avoid when he snuck out that first night from the hotel room. It was one of the only things someone could say that got him right in the gut: There's stuff you have to do. It's all your fault. Be patient. That's enough. Stop. Don't. No.

"Let me ask you something," Stephanie said, "and then I'm going to finish getting ready."

"What?" he said.

"Who was it that insisted on pulling off the interstate? Who was adamant about it?"

Adamant. Huh. "No one, really," he said. "My sister-in-law got interested in the town."

"What about at the hotel? Did anyone act like they really *liked* the place? Like, found it fascinating?"

"Julia. Definitely."

"What about your brother?"

"What about him?"

"What was he doing?"

"I don't know. Being a dick."

She sighed that long sigh again. "It's your sister-in-law, then," she said. "She's the one it's happening to. The rest of you are just stuck here with her." And with that she went off up the stairs.

He didn't want to think about Julia, but he couldn't help it. He didn't want to admit that some part of him wished he were in that hotel room right now. He wished, above all, that he could have seen her face.

He sat in the chair finishing what Stephanie promised would be his last beer of the day, and after a while someone knocked on the back door, where he'd gone outside to smoke earlier. It surprised him to find that there was another human being in the world. He went to the door and opened it and there stood a guy in a stocking cap flicking a guitar pick against his teeth. "You must be Uncle Robbie," the guy said.

27

W hy she felt compelled to follow Miss Blanchard back through the kitchen in the aftermath of Tiffany's lavish feast she couldn't have said. Miss Blanchard was a famous actress. She had visited with the president and she had taken the stage in all the major cities, and yet here she was, through some old association of Mr. Tiffany's, sleeping under the same roof, in the same hotel, as herself, Julia Addison. Mrs. Anthony Addison. Especially in this new role, this new garment, almost, that she felt she wore night and day, she didn't want to be so easily swayed by the attentions of someone like Miss Blanchard, but there the fact was—she found herself leaving her husband in the lobby with the other gentlemen and following Rose Blanchard, who carried two unlit cigars and a bottle of Armagnac in her left hand, back through the kitchen to the pantry.

She had at first resisted being impressed by Miss Blanchard. As predicted, she had arrived on the back of the Harrington boy, all loose and aflutter, laughing and chattering, her skirts above her knees as she was whisked in through the hotel doors. Her blonde hair was piled on her head and fastened with a stunning diamond brooch and on her feet were sparkling silver slippers. She was a pretty woman, certainly, if not a beautiful one, her features perhaps a bit too perfect and regular (the smoothly arching eyebrows over the pale blue eyes, the almost perfectly straight and average-size nose, the thin lips that opened smiling to reveal the small, even teeth, the high cheekbones set in the perfectly oval face, the complete absence of freckles or pockmarks or scars of any kind, the skin as smooth as the surface of a mask) to achieve the uniqueness of beauty, unless it could be said that perfect regularity itself was a form of beauty. Privately, in her own heart, which she had kept closed off to others (including her new husband, whom she often felt she barely knew) since she left her mother and father and sisters in Virginia, Mrs. Addison felt that she was at least Miss Blanchard's equal in terms of looks. And indeed it was a little disconcerting to find herself, so used to being fussed over by men, particularly in this new place, Good Night, Idaho, which seemed like an outpost at the edge of the world, connected like a bead on a long, loose string to the other outposts of "progress"—Helena, Boise, Salt Lake, Spokane Falls, she had learned all the names—so thoroughly ignored in the excitement of Miss Blanchard's arrival.

There was nothing much to be impressed with in Miss Blanchard's background, which Mrs. Addison had learned from the newspapers. In some sense, her story had the same slight flaw as her pretty face, in that it was the perfect story in a very usual way: orphaned at birth, parentage unknown, raised in the charity ward of a Lutheran church in Saint Paul, Minnesota, a bright, eager child who excelled in her studies and had very early shown signs of great imagination, as well as a penchant for attracting the attention of visitors to the orphanage, who inevitably chose her from among all the children to single out for praise. Even her stage name had the quality of perfect artifice—the last name, Blanchard, had been adopted in appreciation of the director of the home, Miss Greta Blanchard, who reported that Rose had been "the most darling of so many, many darling girls," while the first name had been chosen to remind its bearer of the flowers that erupted in a blaze of color each spring below the orphanage's dormitory windows.

Mrs. Addison's own maiden name was Joseph, and her father, Samuel, was a successful shipping agent in Richmond. She had no reason to feel either charitable or condescending toward Miss Blanchard based on her life's story—while the Josephs were not snobbish in their views of class, they were also not overly swayed by the popular sympathies. Mrs. Addison had been taught, above all, to maintain a high regard for propriety and reserve. In light of this regard, she found Miss Blanchard more than a bit disappointing when she caroused with the hotel staff and teased Mr. Tiffany. It came as a surprise that Miss Blanchard treated even her own husband, Anthony, with signs of affection and familiarity. Miss Blanchard had gone so far as to ask that Anthony introduce the two of them, as if she knew him already. Mrs. Addison had half expected an explanation, had imagined for a moment that Anthony would say, apologies, he had neglected to tell her about his old and dear friend Miss Blanchard, whom he had known for so many years. But Anthony had registered surprise at the request, and had in fact introduced himself along with his wife, which seemed to amuse Miss Blanchard.

What finally impressed her about Miss Blanchard was something happening below the surface of the evening, in some place beneath the stylish table settings that Tiffany had purchased and the ostentatious swell of the dining room and the aromas wafting from the hotel's kitchen and the lilting melodies of the chamber orchestra Tiffany had hired—beneath all these things, which Miss Blanchard responded to with the appropriate degree of surprise and pleasure and gratitude, as if she were made to play the part of famous actress to perfection, something flashed out from her eyes from time to time and shaped an underlying impression. In short, Miss Blanchard knew what she was about. While she did not fail to attend to her admirers or to heap praise on the establishment, she seemed to be living inwardly on some plane of investigation that had nothing to do with any of these externalities, as if her body and her voice were unconnected to her thoughts in the usual way.

Mrs. Addison often thought of herself in this same fashion, as a person who negotiated the shallow waters effortlessly, moving through life's evident and visible social dimensions in a way that always left her better off than before—more comfortable, more secure, with increasingly better prospects—while at the same time attempting to plunge beneath the surface without attracting attention.

And so after the dinner was over and after the dancing was done and after everyone had congratulated Tiffany on his fine hotel and his great success, on how he had brought a new and very necessary air of civilization, a harbinger of progress, to the mining town, and after all the dignitaries, all the finest of the fine people to be found for hundreds of miles around, had shuffled happily off to the lobby or the drawing room or in some cases off to bed, when Miss Blanchard tugged lightly on her sleeve and, with a mischievous smile and a nod of her head and that look in her eye that Mrs. Addison had found attractive and somewhat conspiratorial earlier in the evening, invited her away from the others, Mrs. Addison followed. There was a moment in which the light touch of Rose Blanchard's hand on her sleeve, the slight but insistent pull, made her feel as though she was leaving something behind or moving on to something, that when she came back into this room perhaps no more than a quarter of an hour from now there would be some real difference. The gas lamps cast a dull yellow light across the space of the lobby, making her feel as she walked away that she was suspended in the warm stillness of a summer dusk, as if she moved through space while time stood still and dust motes hung forever in midair. At the door she paused to take in the lobby with its fine carpets and its fine chandelier and its graceful ebony furniture, the height of the new Aestheticism, an assertion on the part of its proud owner that here, too, in the barely tamed wilderness of the western territories, one could find the evidence of refined natures and sensibilities.

"Hurry," Rose Blanchard said to her, laughing softly. "Before they cut off our means of escape." And then they were darting through the kitchen while the staff looked on with surprise and vague good humor, Rose guiding her past crates of live hens and towering piles of gleaming fruit and the greasy mess of discarded napkins and silverware, the detritus of the feast. In the rear of the immense space, she came upon a latched door and threw it open to expose shelves and shelves of various foodstuffs, bins of rice and beans, sacks of flour and meal.

Rose shut the door partway, leaving just a shaft of light to see by, and plopped down on a sack of flour, pulling Mrs. Addison with her. "Perfect," she said. She slipped a box of matches from the sleeve of her dress and lit one of the cigars, then handed over the other.

Mrs. Addison was not unfamiliar with cigars. Her father, a devoted smoker, had delighted in allowing his daughters to have a puff on an imported cigar in the presence of their mother, who objected to the practice strenuously. Liquor, on the other hand, was new to her. After only a few sips of the brandy, things became loose in her head, objects drifting from side to side, possible outcomes of this evening spreading out in her thoughts like waves.

"Christ almighty," Rose Blanchard said, "I could see after five minutes that you were the only person here worth speaking to."

Mrs. Addison, somewhat taken aback, said nothing.

"You and your husband," Rose said. "Your husband is an interesting and capable man. And handsome." She leaned forward, patted Mrs. Addison's leg, and winked.

"Thank you," Mrs. Addison said, not knowing what else to say. She wondered if Rose Blanchard had confused her husband with someone else.

28

After they'd warmed up back at the diner over cups of hot chocolate, and while Hugh and Lorraine were feeling good about having gotten everything out in the open, which from Dewey's perspective seemed to have taken maybe a little too long for them to be congratulating themselves about, since it seemed important to tell someone who was in imminent danger of disappearing (according to Hugh) that fact *immediately,* the two of them had finally invited Dewey to leave the hotel and come to their house to stay. It was important not to waste any more time, they said, if they were going to try to figure out a way to help Dewey and his mom and dad—*which they were committed to doing, right?* (At this point they had looked very seriously into each other's eyes and their hands had shot out almost by magic and clasped at the center of the table, like a really dramatic scene in a movie, one performed quite effectively, Dewey had to admit.) When they said these things it was like they were making a secret pact that no one else in the diner (three people, including the teenage cook) could know about, which was really confusing and frustrating and not very confidence-inspiring, because even a ten-year-old kid knew that this type of situation, one that involved disappearing persons and violation of the laws of the entire physical universe, if Hugh was to be believed, didn't require secrecy so much as it required a buttload of scientists and federal law enforcement officials and search dogs and possibly a SWAT team. Again Dewey was left with the question: What was wrong with these people? But who else was he going to trust? Uncle Robbie was gone for good, apparently, and of course he might not have been much help anyway, so who was there? Hugh and Lorraine. It was like a movie called *The Two Stooges*.

So Dewey had been dispatched to the hotel to round up his things and come back in a half hour. As he walked across the street, he looked back at Lorraine waving happily in the window, and then turned to face the hotel and wondered what it might feel like to vanish. He suspected it would be a lot like one of his "states" or "episodes," as his parents referred to them when they talked to his therapist or school counselor (or as his mom referred to them, really, because his dad just kind of sat there in a bored way during these sessions and winked at Dewey every once in a while). You would just fade off into someplace and not know you'd gone there, only you wouldn't come back. Or maybe when "the little kids disappeared," as Hugh so delicately put it to one of these little kids who was, supposedly, on the verge of disappearing himself, they simply went to wherever it was that their parents had gone to, and everyone was reunited. Maybe he, his mom, and his dad would magically reappear in the living room in Mount Pleasant, watching a basketball game on TV and eating popcorn—they had never actually done this, since Dewey was the only one who liked (a) basketball and (b) popcorn, but it was nice to think about, anyway—and this whole thing would have been like a long, bad, awful dream, or maybe even one of his "states" for real. This was a possibility almost too good to start considering, and Dewey resisted the urge to lose himself in the idea because, as Hugh and Lorraine said, there was no time to waste.

He opened the heavy door to the hotel and fought his way successfully past the snow that had built up around the doorway, then made his way up the creaky old stairs and into his musty old room and looked around at all the clothes and stuff. His father's things were still packed, so it was mostly a matter of packing his mother's clothes and the items of his own that he had scattered around the room, which was going to take some time when all he had to work with was the streetlight outside the window. This was going to be a lot like the tedious task of cleaning his room at home.

He changed out of his wet pants and his coat and he managed to pick up some clothes for a while and then he sat on the bed to think about how he was going to get the heavy suitcases out of the hotel and ended up deciding he would just wheel them out and shove them down the stairs. The image of the suitcases smashing their way to the lobby got him back up and packing again for a minute, but then he sat back down because the phrase "a boy on the point of vanishing" started going through his head and he couldn't make it quit. *A boy on the point of vanishing.* He could hear it as a voice-over narration by that guy who played the part of the snowman in *Rudolph the Red-Nosed Reindeer,* which Dewey had watched on TV a few weeks before: *Ten-year-old David "Dewey" Addison, a boy on the point of vanishing, had a very shiny nose.* He sat on the edge of the bed marveling at this voice and at the story that it told him about himself: that he was in danger of not being Dewey anymore, that he could vanish, cease to exist, that he could—say it—*die* here. It seemed totally unfair to Dewey that all this could have happened as the result of one tiny decision like getting off the interstate during a snowstorm, which after all was the responsible thing to do. He didn't even have a driver's license and he knew that much.

A lot of what Hugh said seemed pretty hard to believe. He didn't think that Hugh and Lorraine had any kind of bad intentions—they had been too nice to him and were obviously too concerned for his well-being for him to doubt their sincerity—but maybe they were just stupid. Maybe everyone around here was stupid, like it was a whole town that had gotten cut off from the modern world (where were the cell phones? The iPads? The flat-screen TVs?) and kept reproducing out of the same gene pool—Dewey knew from his father that a situation like that could, over time, produce truly mind-boggling results, such as all the weird animals of Madagascar. And in fact that creepy hotel owner with his big crooked nose had looked a lot like a proboscis monkey, which might actually *be* from Madagascar.

The hotel owner. Dewey had forgotten about him entirely. Where *was* that guy when you needed him? Or not even when you needed him—just where *was* he?

It was dark and wet-looking outside. The snow came down in fluffy clumps that stuck to the windowpane almost like big rain-drops, and the wind had died down to a sigh. For the first time it seemed that the storm might be letting up. Maybe if it really stopped snowing for, like, five minutes, his parents would emerge from some shelter they'd been hiding in, possibly, and come back to get him.

It had been over half an hour. The Dooze Man didn't care. Either Hugh or Lorraine would be at the diner till ten o'clock, so he wasn't really in a hurry, and it wasn't like they could punish him or anything. Plus he knew neither one of them would dare set foot in the hotel. They might stand down on the street and shout up at the windows, but that was about it.

He was going deep into a particular line of thinking, yes he was, and he wasn't about to let anything interrupt it this time—day-dreaming was bad for him, or so everyone said, but this was differ-ent, this was *thinking*. He had been here by himself for four days and he had been scared by a lot of things during that time but he wasn't scared now of disappearing—why not? Because he wasn't.

Disappearing. Everything was just the same as always—here he was, he was Dewey, the same curly hair on his head, wearing the same ugly sweater. He didn't feel at all like a person in danger of vanishing. Hugh and Lorraine weren't responsible for their superstitions—they were just like members of some primitive culture that worshipped the sun or believed in human sacrifices or thought that Jesus would come back soon. Hugh's mother had disappeared and he had seen a mirage of her walking through the park, so he believed that the town was a "magnet" that sucked people in and turned them into ghosts. Dewey's mother and father had disappeared, and he had seen mirages of them in the hotel or on the street, so he believed what Hugh said. But what if none of that was true at all? What if the whole thing had a much more regular, human explanation? His dad would be disappointed in him for not having thought of this before, for having been tricked by all the stuff about vanishing people and black holes disguised as mine shafts.

Hugh himself even said that all the bad stuff happened now at the hotel and not the mine. And nobody in the town, except the Dooze Man himself and one other person, was brave enough to even set foot in the hotel—and that one other person was the creepy owner, who had been there to check them in. So what was the greater probability, as his dad would say—that the physical laws of the universe would somehow be different in some little town called Good Night, Idaho, or that the creepy owner was messing with people's heads? How hard would it be to create some sort of hologram out of a digital image you'd taken of Dewey's mother, for instance? And how hard would it be to make up some tall guy to look like his dad and send him out to lurch around in the snow like a freak? It reminded him of an episode of *Scooby-Doo*. He couldn't believe people had fallen for it all these years. The real thing that must be going on, it seemed to the Dooze Man, was that the adults were all being kidnapped, and sometimes the kids, too, unless the owner decided he didn't want them for some reason, in which case, like Hugh, they were left to fend for themselves. (It wouldn't be fair to speculate, Dewey thought, about why Hugh hadn't been an enticing kidnap victim, though he did recall, for a moment, Hugh's smoldering bald head once he'd taken off his hat.)

Obviously, there had to be a logical explanation. Obviously, his mother and father had not actually vanished, nor had they left him on purpose, and chances were heavily in favor of their still being here somewhere and trying to reach him but being kept from it by someone, the hotel owner, most likely. Obviously, Dewey was not about to "disappear." The thing to do now was…

That was a problem. In fact, after just a minute or two of confronting this problem, sitting in the dark and staring out the window, Dewey became more frightened of the hotel than he had ever been before, because if all these things he'd thought of were true, it meant the creepy owner *was still in here somewhere* and would no doubt like to get his hands on Dewey, who had so far managed to avoid attracting his attention somehow.

The whole place was so absolutely quiet and still that Dewey could hear only three things—the wind, the buzzing streetlight, and his own breath. He sat like that for a long time listening for some fourth noise, something that might tell him where his parents were or where the owner was, but he didn't hear anything. He thought about turning on the TV, but that wouldn't help. He knew that facts came with obligations—once you recognized something was true, you were bound in some way to act on it. So there was only one thing to do, which was to get on with the business of searching the hotel from top to bottom for his parents, or at least some clues—but he was held back because, for the first time, he was really afraid to leave the room.

Then he started thinking of his father again and what his father would tell him to do: *Doozer, a good rule of thumb in a situation like this would be...* what? If you're going to begin an investigation, you have to start with clues — that seemed logical enough. And where had he found the most clues so far? Room 306, which also had the advantage of being the only other place in the hotel where he felt marginally at ease, since he'd been in there several times.

The door to 306 was open like it always was. He peered nervously into the room but his mother wasn't there. When his mother wasn't there, the room was bare and dark and dusty and old. When his mother was seated there on the bed, the room looked entirely different, lit by the flickering wall lamps, all the colors bright, a nice smell in the air. Did the creepy owner have some way of lighting the room when someone peeked in? Of magically cleaning and straightening everything? There was no doubt that the room was, in fact, neat, clean, and well lit when his mother was in it, whether day or night. The only thing he could deduce from this was that the creepy owner must be pretty smart. He also might be crazy, because it was still unclear to Dewey what any of this was supposed to accomplish. Who but a crazy person would torture a little kid by making him think his mother was there when she wasn't?

It was definitely *not* his mother. He needed to decide that once and for all, so that he could stop being fooled by the same illusion over and over again. His mother was okay, she was fine, but she was somewhere else, probably trying to get back to him right now. The mother who appeared in this room, room 306, could not be his actual mother because she did not behave like his mother at all. If you tried talking to this mother, you got no response. If you tried yelling, crying, screaming, even possibly raging and breaking things, Dewey suspected, you would still get no response from this mother. When you stepped into the room, you got the icy feeling under your skin, like cold water trickling along your nerves, and your vision went white and you felt like you were going to faint, and then your eyes opened and you were standing there in an empty, old, crappy, cold, musty, nasty room, and you got no response from this mother, who was no longer there. It had happened more times than he could count.

Right now the room was empty and especially gray and dreary-looking what with the snow continuing to fall there out the window and the night getting fully dark as the earth spun away from another day here in the middle of nowhere. It made Dewey think of the life he had on the other side of the country, or the one he had had just a couple of weeks ago, where he could do things like spend the day at the gym while his mom worked out in the fitness center, or decide which invitation to spend the night at which friend's house he should accept, or ride his bike to the soccer field, or go eat barbecue with his dad. It was possible that none of those things would ever happen again, not in this lifetime, that he wouldn't go to Folly Beach or gaze out the car window at the Intracoastal Waterway and the palmetto trees. But he couldn't believe that, not really. The entire time since they'd pulled off the road in the snowstorm had the quality of being one long, bad dream, and even though Dewey knew he was wide awake, he still believed there had to be a point at which all this would end suddenly, in a flash of recognition, the way dreams ended, and everything would go back to the way it was before.

It was too dark to search for clues, but he walked over to the window and looked out, and when he turned back something flashed under the bed. He got down on his hands and knees and wiggled his way under the bed frame and after coughing twice from all the dust he emerged with the object in his hand. By the time he reached the thin light from the window, he already knew that it was the snow globe he'd seen his mother holding when he'd watched her from the street. He shook it and lifted it now in the light from the streetlamp, the way he'd seen his mother do.

It didn't surprise him that the snow inside the globe fell on what appeared to be a miniature version of the hotel—he'd seen the gumball machine, after all, and there was the crazy television. But there *was* a surprise. Dewey held the snow globe up closer to the light and watched the tiny pieces of fake snow settle to the bottom and, behind them, the real snow pass down as if through the glass, and his breath came in short, heavy bursts, as if he were trying to breathe from inside the globe itself, but he kept turning it in the light. Right there—fingerprints. He'd seen what he thought was a mirage of his mother holding this snow globe in the window, but she was real, she had been here, she had held this globe in her hands. He had found his mother's fingerprints.

It seemed strange that this discovery should be accompanied by a thumping noise, but there it was, an arrhythmic series of faint *thump-thump-thumps* that he took to be the blood rushing in his brain until he was startled by something smashing against the window with a loud *whup!* He lurched back, hit his foot against the bedpost, and fell backward over the corner of the bed. The snow globe got loose from his outstretched hand, and he heard it shatter on the floor. He was being attacked from somewhere. *Whup!*—there it came again, against the window. Dewey crouched down and scooted behind the bed. He peeked around the bedpost to check out the windowpane, trying hard to quiet his breathing. *Whup!* This time he saw clearly what it was.

"Dewey!" a voice shouted.

He rarely cursed, but on this occasion Dewey tried out a few choice words under his breath, and then he crawled to the wall and relaxed against it, and he listened, while his heartbeat returned to normal, to Hugh calling his name and throwing snowballs against the window.

No way would Dewey answer him. He had no intention of leaving this hotel now until he found his mother and father. If the snow globe had real fingerprints on it, then his mother was somewhere in this hotel. In the darkness he could barely make out the broken pieces of the snow globe on the floor. There would be no way to put it back together, but it didn't matter—he knew what he'd seen. Something had been set in motion, things were happening now, and in the same way that the snow globe was gone for good, so were the times when he would sit lazily around the hotel room doing nothing or playing jacks, the hours when he would hang out at the diner stuffing his face with pie and falling under the spell of Hugh and Lorraine. He sat quietly next to the bed and listened until Hugh quit calling his name and the snowballs stopped thumping against the window, and then he got to his feet and began, in earnest, his search.

About a half hour later, he was tiptoeing around the far back end of the fourth floor, an area he hadn't explored up to now, when he passed an open doorway and thought he saw something move. He stopped in the hall and stood very still. There was almost no light except up ahead where snowflakes twirled down past a large rectangular window above a stairway landing. The air was colder here than it was on the floors below, and he started to shiver. Ahead of him were the stairs—he could run down to the lobby and escape if he needed to. But then he might never know what the thing was, the thing that moved. What would it feel like to be grabbed from behind, he wondered, in the dark, by someone you didn't know? The instant the hand touched your neck, the moment you knew there was no escaping—that would have to be the scariest moment ever. He didn't want anything behind him, so he turned and walked the few steps back to the doorway as quickly and bravely as possible, faced squarely into the room, and was met with a burst of light.

"Who's there?" a voice said.

It was someone with a flashlight, that much Dewey could figure out, and once he'd gotten his back against the wall of the corridor and a hand up to shade his eyes, he saw that the figure behind the light was nowhere near the size of the hotel owner. Then the flashlight beam lurched up and illuminated the face of a boy about Dewey's age with a sharp nose and a thick head of jet-black hair. This was a surprising development, but a welcome one, at least from Dewey's perspective.

"Are you real?" Dewey said.

The boy pointed the flashlight at the floor. He pulled his head back sort of like a chicken. "Why wouldn't I be?" he asked. Then he put the light back on Dewey. "Are you?"

"Sure," Dewey said.

"You don't look so good," the boy said.

Dewey glanced up and down the corridor, wondering if all the noise might attract the attention of the owner. He lowered his voice a little. "What are you doing here?"

The kid started to take a step toward Dewey but then seemed to think better of it and stayed where he was. "What do you mean?" he said.

"I don't know," Dewey said. "I was just asking." The conversation wasn't off to a very promising start.

"My name's Hector Jones," the boy said. "I'm half Nez Perce Indian."

"I'm Dewey," Dewey said.

"Cool," Hector Jones said. He seemed to want to talk to Dewey the way he would talk to someone in a lower grade, but he was actually smaller than Dewey. "My dad's full-blood Nez Perce," Hector Jones said. "My mom's not anything."

Dewey looked back up the hall again and Hector pointed the flashlight up that way out of curiosity, but there was nothing there. "Well," Dewey said, "technically, she has to be *something*."

"She's not anything," Hector said.

"Oh," said Dewey. He tried to think of what he knew about the Native American tribe of the Nez Perce. If his father were here, he could and almost certainly would tell Dewey in his monotonous professor voice the history of the Nez Perce and where they were located and which tribes they were allied with or opposed to and what their mode of living was and what they were mostly doing nowadays. As it was, he remembered only one thing. "Chief Joseph," he said.

"Yeah, so?" Hector said. "*Everyone* knows *that*."

"Not where I come from," Dewey said.

"Where's that?"

"South Carolina."

Hector pointed his index finger at Dewey's chest. "You started the Civil War," he said.

Dewey acknowledged that his home state had, unfortunately, played a major role in the outbreak of hostilities but denied any personal involvement in the matter. "Anyway, that was a long time ago," he said.

"Nothing is a long time ago to a Nez Perce," Hector said. "To answer your question," he continued, walking back into his room and plopping down on the only bed, "we had to stop here 'cause my dad ran his truck in the ditch."

"When was that?" Dewey asked.

"Last night."

"And where's your dad now?"

"He went to see if he could find someone to pull us out." Hector narrowed his eyes and cocked his head as if he suspected that Dewey might have some information.

Dewey swallowed hard. His mouth was really dry. He could use a Coke over at the diner about now. "How long ago did he leave?" he asked.

Hector turned off the flashlight and dropped it on the bed and walked over to the window and looked outside. "It was a pretty long time ago," he said.

It was extra dark in the room now with the flashlight off, so Dewey didn't so much see as simply understand that Hector was trying to get control of himself, to keep from crying.

"That's a pretty good flashlight," Dewey said.

"It's my dad's," Hector said. "He's a builder, so he only uses good tools."

"It's warmer down in my room," Dewey said.

"My dad told me to wait here," Hector said.

Dewey was so glad that he'd found Hector Jones, another smart kid, someone who knew something about history and was a Nez Perce Indian, someone who could be his friend. He didn't want to scare Hector any more than necessary or make him feel sad. But Hugh was probably right about one thing—there was no time to waste. A short while ago, he had been wishing that someone had been honest with him sooner, and now he had his own chance. "Yeah," Dewey told Hector. "That's what my dad said, too."

Hector turned from the window, silhouetted against the snow clouds. "Is your dad missing?" he asked, and he sounded a lot younger all of a sudden, as if Dewey had a younger brother, which he'd always wished he had.

"My mom and my dad," Dewey said. "And my uncle, too, sort of."

Hector just kind of stood at the window. "Oh," he said.

Dewey grabbed the flashlight off the bed and figured out how to turn it on and shined the light out into the hall. It didn't seem nearly as scary now that he'd found Hector, but he knew the dangers were just as real. "Come on," he said.

Hector fell in behind him as they left the room and moved toward the stairs. "What are we doing?" he asked.

Dewey thought hard about the snow globe, tried to see, in his mind, his mother's fingerprints. "We're going to make a plan to find everybody," he said. He turned around and looked at Hector. His eyes were dark and shining in the glow of the flashlight. He held his hand out to Dewey, fist closed. Dewey gave him a fist bump.

"Let's do it," Hector Jones said.

PART III

THE PERMANENCE OF MEMORY

Will it ultimately reach the clear surface of my consciousness, this memory, this old, dead moment which the magnetism of an identical moment has traveled so far to importune, to disturb, to raise up out of the very depths of my being? I cannot tell. Now that I feel nothing, it has stopped, has perhaps gone down again into its darkness, from which who can say whether it will ever rise?

—Marcel Proust, *Remembrance of Things Past*

29

She dreamed that she had a dream about something she should remember. In the dream that she was dreaming she had, she was opening the door to a room, and something important was happening on the other side of the door. She could feel herself leaning into the truth concealed by the door, but she couldn't fit the key into the lock fast enough before the dream she dreamed she was having ended because she dreamed of waking up, outside in the snow, standing in front of a window reading the letter about the key. This dream made her impatient, because after all she'd already read the letter in a different dream, or what she had thought was a dream before she seemed, at times, to be in possession of an actual key which actually did open the door to room 306. But in this dream, anyway, she was impatient to get back inside the hotel. She hurried through the falling snow as best she could, taking small steps in an unwieldy pair of shoes, ankle boots, really, which she didn't recognize as her own but liked immensely just the same, holding up her long skirt in the snow, a skirt she didn't recognize either.

And then she suddenly found herself standing outside the door to her own room, and she pressed her ear close to the wood, listening for noises. It was in her very own room that the important thing was happening, the thing that had been in the other dream. She was spying on someone, she realized, but she didn't know if it was herself or someone else. What did she think was going on behind there? She heard a man's voice, and then the low, muffled voice of a woman and recognized in a hot wave of embarrassment that she was listening to two people having intercourse, but she didn't know if it was herself she was listening to. She was mostly curious to know who the man was, so she began very quietly to fit the key to the lock, and it was the fear of finding out something about herself, something she didn't want to know, that woke her from the dream of turning the key in her own door to watch the couple, whoever they were, and when she jerked awake in bed, sitting straight upright, naked, she quickly looked down to find out if she was with anyone, if she could still catch herself in the dream.

No one was there. There was the impression of a head on the other pillow. The sheets were tangled on that side of the bed. When she put her hand to the mattress, on the other side from where she slept, it was warm to the touch.

But she was confused about who might have been there. She was alone in the room, and everything was white. All she could see was snow, everywhere she looked, as if she were flying through a whole world of snow where nothing was solid, where she was weightless and suspended. She knew she hadn't eaten in a long time and she felt so light in both her body and her mind that it was as if she didn't exist at all. She had been dreaming, hadn't she? Of what? She couldn't remember. But she was awake now, or she thought she was awake, if that word meant anything anymore. She rose and stood naked in front of the mirror. Julia. Julia was the woman in the mirror. And as had been the case lately, when she stood in front of the mirror, there were other Julias—each just a little fainter, each just a little further removed—reflected behind the first Julia, but there was no mirror behind her to create the reflections. And as always, when she stepped away, the women in the mirror followed her, one by one, each just a fraction of a second behind the one before her.

Slipping on her nightgown, she found that the key was in her hand, and she moved to the door and used the key and passed into the hallway. She was hungry, that was all she knew, and not necessarily for food, though food would do. She floated down corridors and through rooms and up and down stairways and narrow passages, cold and light, like a faraway star. She did not find what she was looking for. She never did. She had been in this corridor for years.

Once, as she was moving weightlessly, almost invisibly (was there anyone to see her?), she felt something clutching at her, pulling her, and she turned around to see a black upright telephone on a small gilt table. The telephone emitted a faint crackling, or possibly she felt it under her skin.

She picked up the phone by its stem and held the mouthpiece in front of her. Staring into the air of the hallway, focusing on nothing but the empty space there, she raised the receiver to her ear. She could hear someone breathing, and she could hear herself breathing, too, into the mouthpiece.

"Is it you?" a voice finally said.

It was the voice of a child. Or it was the voice of a man with a child's voice contained inside it. Again she felt something pulling her, as if she were being held back from a place or a time that she was going toward. For a moment she was confused, and her breath came up tight in her throat, and she held her hand over her mouth. She was listening to the breathing, which seemed to come from somewhere deep inside herself.

"Is it you?" the voice said again.

She could not remember how she knew the voice, but it tugged at her, it stole her breath, it carried her heart away, and she knew, somehow, the answer to the question. "Yes," she said. "It's me."

30

For a while now (he didn't know how long, he seemed to have lost the ability to track time altogether, and could tell that days were going by only because he had a pretty good beginning to a beard and it was itching mightily), he had been not doing much of anything but sitting around with Tiffany, "waiting out the storm," as Tiffany put it, a strategy that, if you trusted Tiffany's word on the matter, showed infinite good sense. But he didn't trust Tiffany. Or Rose Blanchard. The two were in cahoots about something. You could see it in the way they looked at each other.

Tiffany was decent company, it turned out, if you could quit being angry and more or less accept the situation as inevitable—but he didn't want to accept the situation or believe it was inevitable. In his better, more alert moments, he reprimanded himself for his own weakness, his inability to make something happen that would shake him out of this, return him to the place where he could find Dewey and Julia and be the man, the father, the husband, even the brother he was before, or possibly a better version of all these things. But whenever this strong desire and fear gripped him, the only thing he knew to do was leave the hotel, try to notify someone, get some help, and it always turned out the same—the freezing cold, the panic, the onset of the whiteness, and then, inevitably, the return inside the hotel, where he would, inevitably, find himself sitting with Tiffany and, lately, Rose Blanchard, more drained, more scared, more confused and dazed and humbled than before...more accustomed to defeat. In his most lucid moments he imagined that he must be a lot like a drugged-up patient in an insane asylum, slow and listless in thought and action, muttering and shuffling, a speck of drool at the corner of his mouth.

It seemed to Tonio—and this was certainly part of why he didn't trust his host—that Tiffany wanted him to stay shut up in the hotel forever, chatting with him and Rose and drinking tea. After a certain period of time, after talking to Tiffany about what the fossil record suggested regarding the development of bipedalism in the great apes, or Etruscan pottery, or the rise of the great European industrial centers in the nineteenth century (Tiffany had a wide-ranging if superficial knowledge of virtually any subject Tonio could bring up, and he seemed interested in all of them to one degree or another), and to Rose about contemporary cinema and "the cult of instant celebrity," both of which she held in disdain but wanted to know more about, as if, strangely, she was some sort of expatriate receiving word from home (Tiffany said of Rose's past only that she had been "on the stage"), his feelings of desperation, anger, impatience, outrage would resurface, and after shouting obscenities at Tiffany and apologizing to Rose, he would do, again, the only thing he could think to do, which was set off in the snow, raging and fuming, to find some help, after which he would wake up staring groggily at Rose's silver shoe and Tiffany's pipe tobacco on the marble table and enjoying the comforts of a warm, crackling fire in the fireplace, and the whole cycle would begin again. They were very good at casting their spell, making you feel as though nothing existed outside this room and their cups of tea and their conversation and Tiffany's occasional "nips" or "fingers" of brandy, which he offered to Tonio and Rose as if he were up to something naughty.

But he had lately hatched a plan. The solution, he believed now, was to be disciplined enough to hold back, to wait until his strength had been completely restored and his will absolutely cemented to the completion of the task, which was this—to go resolutely out into the snow, to continue down the alley that seemed to want to lead him somewhere, to keep from surrendering to the panic that seized him when he thought he was lost and freezing, to resist, most of all, the door that offered him reentry and the long, white funnel it led to. He would have to keep going, stay on the path until he arrived at a destination where he could get help, or, if his instincts were wrong, be prepared to freeze to death curled up somewhere all alone like any other animal. He would not be the first creature to suffer such a fate, and he had decided firmly that he would rather die that way than live without Dewey (or, more accurately, live a life in which he knew that he had failed to save Dewey), and maybe, he had begun to think, without his wife, although he had never thought of giving up his life for her before. It had always been part of his basic understanding of himself that he would instinctively, if the moment ever arose, suffer any physical injury no matter how severe in order to save his son, and in fact he had dreams in which this occurred—the snake about to strike, the bus plowing heedlessly down the city street close to the curb, the tornado bearing down upon them in the open field. For some reason, though, it had never occurred to him that this same obligation should extend to Julia, and yet in the past few days he had found himself imagining scenarios—crazed kidnapper, roaring conflagration, avalanche of snow—in which he would rush to Julia's aid without considering his own safety.

Currently, the discussion with Tiffany and Rose had drifted into the area of animism, or "life force," and Tonio grew bored, having listened to Julia cover this ground too often. But the subject seemed to excite Tiffany immensely. On certain topics, Tiffany seemed merely to be making polite conversation, while others roused in him a passionate intensity. You could gauge his level of excitement, Tonio had figured out, by how hard he puffed on his pipe, the bowl glowing bright orange whenever he got really worked up, as if the color of his emotions appeared in the pipe instead of on his cheeks. Tiffany had suggested that maybe Tonio couldn't appreciate the concept of said "life force" because "scientists" (as he insisted on referring to Tonio) lacked the requisite imagination, to which Tonio replied that in fact animism was *invented* by an anthropologist, or at least the term was.

"A smart man, then," Tiffany said.

"He didn't *believe* in animism, Tiffany," Tonio said. He tried, in general, to mask his irritation, but at times Tiffany's smug layman's views, well-informed as they often were, got too much under his skin. "He wasn't an animist *himself*. He used it as a term to describe the religious beliefs of primitive cultures. *Primitive*. He saw all religions as the persistence of earlier, survivalist beliefs."

Tiffany puffed away like a bellows, exhausting the orange glow in the bowl. He tapped out the pipe and immediately refilled it from his small leather pouch, sneaking a quick peek at Rose, who sat across from Tonio in a velvet armchair, her teacup in one hand, her saucer in the other. Clearly she was as bored with the proceedings as Tonio, and she wouldn't hesitate to let Tiffany know this in a minute—she was almost always prickly with Tiffany and invariably deferential and flattering toward Tonio, which Tonio assumed was a contrivance on the part of them both. He didn't believe in Rose Blanchard's admiration for him any more than he believed in Tiffany's desire to help him find his family again. The only thing that was hard to figure out was whether Tiffany had designs on Rose himself, whether his sneaky glances were an actual attempt to gauge her reactions to what he was saying, or whether they were merely a part of the surreptitious communication they seemed to carry on all the time, obviously trying to signal each other regarding Tonio's current mental state, whether he seemed adequately pacified.

Tiffany lit his pipe and shook out the match and took two big puffs. "Perhaps I should bring out the brandy and the playing cards," he said.

"Perhaps you should," Rose said. She smiled knowingly at Tonio, as if they were in perfect agreement on the subject of Tiffany's long-windedness. As if they were in perfect agreement on everything under the sun and moon.

"Very well," Tiffany said, with obvious irritation. He made it halfway to the drawer behind the front desk where he kept the brandy but then came back and sat down again. "But I don't understand why people find it so strange," he said. "It's been a mystery to me all these years. Why shouldn't the earth be alive in its own way? How can a living thing come from a dead thing? As I've acknowledged, I'm not a scientist, and I am prepared to bow humbly before another man's expert opinion, if he can demonstrate the truth of it to me. But there are many things the scientists do not know. And one of the questions I have not heard answered to my satisfaction is how something stagnant, inert, fixed, dead, should give birth to so many living and moving things. The earth gives us life, and the natural end of life is death, and death is nothing more than an extended kind of sleep, and sleep is the gateway to dreaming, and dreams are nothing more than disguised memories, and memories, finally, are all that we have left in the world. All these things are in essence the same thing. And why shouldn't there be a nexus, a place where they all come together as one?"

The room was quiet for a moment while no one attempted to answer. The fire crackled in the fireplace. Rose yawned.

"My apologies," Tiffany said, and he tapped out his pipe in a silver ashtray on the table and went to get the brandy and the playing cards.

Rose put down her teacup and saucer and leaned across the table toward Tonio. "He really is brilliant, you know?" She turned halfway to watch Tiffany going about his business. "He drives me crazy, but he really does have a wonderful mind. So chock-full of"—she shook her head back and forth dramatically, as if searching desperately for the right word—"things."

Yeah, his mind was full of "things," all right, they could agree on that much. Tonio sat quietly and observed the same scene it felt like he'd been observing for a good portion of his life now: the period furniture, the crackling fire, the snow outside the window. He did not look at Rose Blanchard, because he found her unsettling. The reason wasn't that she was attractive—she *was* attractive, beautiful, even, according to most men's standards, probably, but attractive women didn't usually unsettle him, and there was no good reason that Rose should. He was still capable of hiding behind his academic disinterest and his intellectual superiority and his emotional grayness the same way he always had been. He still knew the routine, even if he hadn't been himself much lately. No, there was something else, and it must have something to do with the way she treated him so familiarly and the fact that he too had thought at first that he'd known her elsewhere. He kept looking, for instance, at those silver shoes, which were embedded in his memory someplace.

He hazarded a glance at her now. It was strange that he perceived something indecent about her, almost, when she would have been considered downright demure by any contemporary standard. She was elegant and charming, her attentions were discreet, she dressed modestly and tastefully as far as Tonio could tell. But there was something that made him feel indecent when he looked at her. There she was now in her white dress, her blonde hair pinned up, no plunging neckline, no skin showing, it wasn't like she was wearing a bikini, for God's sake, but still...she was getting to him in a way he wasn't used to. And the smile on her face proved it. She knew what she was doing.

She reached across the table and touched his hand where it rested on the arm of the sofa. "Can I speak to you later, alone?" she asked him.

Right then Tiffany sat down, placing three snifters and a bottle on the table. The wind blew outside and the snowdrifts sifted up against the windowpane. The fire guttered as the wind reached down the chimney and the open flue. A clock sounded the time from the corner of the room.

"It *has* been quite snowy," Tiffany said. "I don't know when I've seen the like." He unstoppered the bottle and filled the glasses and held up his own to the firelight. "Cheers," he said. "To us."

31

The dinner had proved as wondrous as advertised and then some, with a host of servers (some of whom Addison recognized from the mine, their beards trimmed and hair carefully managed, in most cases not too badly, for the occasion) and a great deal of clattering and shouting emerging from the large and rather festive kitchen, so that the quartet that played throughout the feast had a good bit to do to be heard over the noise and the conversation. Addison and his wife were seated near the middle of the long table with a territorial senator, Mr. Faiser, and his wife, whose name Addison forgot as soon as he heard it, so nervous was he about the proper employment of the various utensils set before him, the likelihood of getting crumbs in his mustache. He was certain to come off as a rube, but he hoped to avoid seeming downright vulgar. Some others at the table appeared as perturbed and bewildered as he did, newly minted gentlemen like himself uncomfortable in their coats and tails, their foreheads shining brilliantly from the slight misapplication of Macassar oil. But there were also those who felt perfectly at home, as Tiffany obviously did, grateful for the opportunity to demonstrate their superior breeding, the social refinements learned in Boston, New York, London, Paris, and transported here by historical accident or economic necessity.

To Julia's right sat an actual French marquis, the Marquis de Mores, who, fascinated by tales of the American West, had crossed the Atlantic, laid claim to nearly fifty thousand acres of Dakota grazing land, and built a château along the banks of the Little Missouri River. Throughout dinner, the marquis kept up a lively conversation with Julia—his own wife, to whom Addison himself sometimes found it difficult to speak a dozen words—on a variety of subjects including French poetry and Virginia colonial architecture and possibly several others that Addison couldn't pick up because they *began speaking French*. It was both galling and humbling to realize that he had not even known his wife spoke French, a language of which he did not know the first words himself. And so he kept quiet almost throughout dinner.

Then the dancing began. The dance program, which was printed on ornamental cards for all the guests and distributed at table, contained just one dance, a kind of quadrille, that Addison knew, and when the first waltzes began he realized upon seeing the skill of some of the dancers that he would not even attempt the quadrille, much less any of the others, and he hoped his wife would not ask him to. She did not. She danced more than once with both Tiffany and the Marquis de Mores, and he watched her with mingled pride and embarrassment. She was easily the most elegant of the dancers on the floor, and he felt ashamed that he was not able to offer her this sort of pleasure, but he saw at the same time that her attentions to the marquis, who was more forward and probably more drunk than Addison would have liked, were utterly correct and merely formal. Her dark hair curled over her forehead very prettily, and with her petite figure she glided through the room like a windup ballerina. The eyes of everyone in the room would have been trained on his wife, he felt, had it not been for the presence of Rose Blanchard.

His experience had been so slight, and of such a different order than he would have preferred, that it was hard for him to judge Miss Blanchard the way, perhaps, another man would—the Marquis de Mores, for instance. To Mr. Addison's way of seeing things, his wife was every bit Miss Blanchard's equal, but to the senator, to the banker from Spokane Falls, to the newspaper editor from Portland, to the waiters who were still busy bringing out silver trays of champagne and sweets, to the musicians who tracked her movements from behind their instruments, to, above all, the Harrington boy, who had managed to get quite drunk somehow while sitting on a chair in the corner, and who blushed and squirmed each time she raised her two little fingers to wave at him as she twirled around the room, Rose Blanchard was clearly the main attraction.

Yes, one could easily see that Miss Blanchard's looks were more superficially appealing, but Addison found the stage makeup and the bountiful blonde curls and the puffed-up bustle of her dress garish and even tawdry in comparison with his wife's smart, trim ballroom dress, which was alluring without being salacious. Were even these wealthy, important men so easily fooled by that kind of artifice? By the same darkened eyes and powdered cheeks and swelling bodices that you could find in the town's whorehouses? Or was it Miss Blanchard's face that had such a strong influence? She was pretty, undoubtedly, but she lacked the refinement he prized so much in his wife. He was proud of Julia now, watching her and the marquis execute the intricate steps of a dance he'd never seen before, and which the majority of the guests were not even attempting. At least the marquis seemed to share his appreciation for her.

The expansive room was warm with life, and Addison leaned back in his chair with his legs and arms crossed in front of him, and he watched his wife move in slow, precise circles around the room while the snow flew by the windows in a dark world that seemed to have nothing to do with this lighted place. A feeling of tranquility and assurance descended on him, clearing his mind of the usual doubts and worries. Under the influence of Tiffany's champagne it was easy to contemplate a future in which he and his wife would achieve a desirable harmony, in which they could regularly attend fine parties like this one—finer, in the bigger, finer cities of the world for which this current life in this half-formed town was but a simple preparation—and afterward gaze together at snow out the window, snow in Boston, snow in Paris, snow in Vienna, and smile at something absurd that had been said by an acquaintance at dinner, while he helped unpin her dress and brush her hair, and they would fall eagerly into each other's arms with the city dark and restless beneath them.

This reverie was interrupted by a hand on his coat sleeve, and he turned to see Rose Blanchard seated next to him, smiling at him with her bright eyes, in the same way he had just imagined his wife doing. It was rather disconcerting.

"You look lost," she said to him, and patted his arm with her small white hand, the perfectly curved fingernails like smoothed claws, softened until they were no longer dangerous. He was irritated to feel heat rush up under his shirt collar, the back of his neck turn moist, a blush no doubt coloring his cheeks. Was it a sort of magic that made men respond to her this way? He had thought he was immune.

"Not at all," he said with a pinched smile.

She smiled gently back at him. Her hand still rested lightly on his arm, and he became conscious of the gaze of other men and women around the room, and he saw a few turn toward their companions, lean in with a hand on an arm, whisper confidentially—*To whom is Miss Blanchard speaking?* or *Why is she speaking to Mr. Addison?* And something expanded in his chest, as if he were gaining power and strength while the famed actress sat next to him.

It disturbed him how quickly he could forget to look for his wife across the room.

"Lonely, then," Rose Blanchard said. "I meant no offense."

"Not at all," he said cautiously, and then realized those were the same words with which he had responded to her first statement. He shifted his legs uncomfortably. Her smile showed just a hint of amusement. "I'm not at all lonely, thank you," he said stiffly. "I'm afraid I'm not much of a dancer, but I enjoy watching. Mr. Tiffany has created quite a spectacle here in our modest town. We are still very rough and very new, and Mr. Tiffany's hotel and his grand opening will undoubtedly apply a little polish."

He had almost no time to congratulate himself on this little speech. Right then, as if on cue, the main doors to the ballroom burst open, and five men in boots and rough wool coats strode into the room, shouting and weaving somewhat dangerously through the dancers and onlookers, the tables set with candelabras and silver serving trays. It was bound to happen, and Addison was secretly pleased as he watched Tiffany's rapid advance on the invaders. It was a situation Addison hoped to avoid becoming involved in directly, but he would involve himself if necessary. He recognized at least two of the miners at this distance, and probably had a passing acquaintance with all of them. No matter Tiffany's thoughts on the subject or his lofty intentions, the mine still ran this town and not the other way around. He would go point that out to Tiffany if he had to. As long as they behaved themselves, the miners were staying. Addison would see to that.

He was surprised to hear Miss Blanchard laughing heartily behind him. When he turned, her face was alight with pleasure. It was the same glow of mischief he'd spied earlier when he found her in the upstairs room with Tiffany. She seemed to greatly enjoy watching Tiffany's attempts to handle his predicament. With one raised hand he tried to slow the miners' advance, while with the other he waved encouragement to the musicians to continue, all the while glancing over his shoulder with strained geniality at his guests, who were by now aware of the interruption. And listening to Miss Blanchard's low and somehow musical laugh, Addison felt an undeniable attraction now, not to her made-up image and her fame, but to that part of her that he could tell ran much deeper, an earthier element akin to his own leanings toward the unpolished and unrefined. He recognized something in Miss Blanchard that he missed in his relations with Julia, and he turned his gaze sadly toward the windows and the snow. It was as if he had become aware of a high wall he would never breach.

"I'm sorry," Rose Blanchard said. "Alfred plans everything so scrupulously. I shouldn't be laughing at his expense."

"It *is* marvelous," Addison said. "He deserves credit. No one else could have done this."

Across the room, Tiffany had managed to forge a compromise with the miners, who were now seated along the wall near the kitchen entrance drinking tentatively from champagne flutes. One of them accepted a bottle passed to him surreptitiously by young Harrington.

"Alfred has always demonstrated a certain fondness for the dramatic gesture," Miss Blanchard said.

She seemed perched quite comfortably on the edge of her seat, the long train of her skirt spread out behind her. Guiltily, Addison scanned the room for his wife, whom he spotted near the musicians, talking to the senator's wife. Just then, her eyes happened to meet his, and he felt for one fleeting moment the thrill of being caught doing something of which a jealous spouse would not approve—but then she offered him the same polite smile as always, as if it would never occur to her to find Rose Blanchard threatening, or to care.

Miss Blanchard's eyes flashed attentively at this silent exchange, with what feeling behind them he couldn't tell. She said nothing, but continued to sit next to him in a kind of relaxed intimacy, as if it were she who was his wife instead of Julia. And for a moment he allowed himself to imagine that that was the case, that he shared with this woman the long familiarity and easy companionship he had dreamed, a short while ago, of having with his wife.

But it did not help him much in the present moment. He was still casting about for something to say, and his eyes settled on Tiffany, who seemed, oddly, to be taking a break from the proceedings, standing idly by a window, his hand on the windowsill, in an attitude of apparent boredom. "And how are you acquainted with Mr. Tiffany?" he heard himself ask Miss Blanchard. At the window Tiffany brushed his hair back with one hand, surveyed the room briefly, took out his pocket watch and consulted it, wound the watch and put it back in his pocket again. Miss Blanchard had not spoken but she sighed softly and he looked over to see on her face an undeniable expression of sadness.

"It's me, Anthony," she said. "This is me you're speaking to. Pretend we're in the lobby drinking tea."

In some dreamlike way he found himself staring at the snow. The noises in the room—the slow waltz the musicians played and the spiral of the dance, the way the ladies' skirts bloomed outward like the opening of flowers, the nervous buzz of conversation in the ballroom, the bustling clatter in the kitchen and the loud talk of the miners, who could no longer contain their excitement at finding themselves in such a grand place in the middle of so much wilderness—whirlpooled down and down and his vision of the lights and the colors slipped to the edges of the sensate world, as if all of it were merely hovering somewhere slightly below and behind him, and all that remained was the light gravitational pull of the earth on the frozen atmosphere above it, the silent progress of the white flakes toward the ground.

"I don't know what you mean," he said as evenly as he could, looking straight ahead at nothing, feeling weightless and adrift.

Again he felt her hand on his arm. "We have an appointment later this evening, you and me," she said. "It's the same appointment as always." Her soft fingers reached inside the cuff of his shirtsleeve and rested lightly on his pulse. "I'm afraid you'll never miss it no matter how hard you try."

He had never learned to swim, but once his father had taken him on a boat ride in the Wisconsin Dells, and he remembered now how it felt to be carried along rapidly on the stream, floating free above the water, a tiny rippling beneath the boat's surface. The night was turning out like that, just something underneath him, something he skimmed along on top of, his wife, Julia, there on the other side of the room, just someone he passed by on the way to something or somewhere else, and Rose Blanchard's hand on his wrist, connected to him at the point where his blood flowed, was all that was real or that mattered, and he tried to bring himself into the moment with her, understand what she was saying.

"I want to help you this time if I can," she said, and she squeezed his arm tight and leaned in close. "You tried to help me."

Now the people around the room stared at him in earnest, but it didn't matter. His eyes were trained on some spot on the ballroom floor, but his head stirred with images: the boy he'd seen from the window, the same boy but in a different place, by the ocean, looking out at the water, his hand resting lightly on the boy's hair; his wife, Julia, but somewhere else, across a table drinking steaming tea or coffee from an unusual cup; himself facing a roomful of young people, speaking to them in a lecture hall; Rose Blanchard, again and again, more familiar to him suddenly than anyone he'd ever known. The images lay on top of one another like thin transparencies, all in his mind at once as if he could see from multiple sets of eyes, or from the eyes of many people. He felt that if he fixed his concentration on any one of these images it would lead him to still more images, to things recollected in the dim caverns of his mind, faint shadows of his former self or other selves. He was a man who had managed his life carefully, taking chances only when necessary, only calculated risks, and he was scared of what was happening to him now, and because he was scared he paid no attention to the shocked gaze of the people in the room when he turned toward Miss Blanchard and nervously held her hand. "When I saw you in the snow," he said to her.

She smiled at him reassuringly. "Yes," she said. "That was when." She squeezed his hand. "It didn't work, did it? I'm still here."

"I talked you into going out there. I was trying to help you leave."

"Yes," she said, "but by the time you saw me in the snow, you had already forgotten me, forgotten where we were."

There was a kind of terror in discovery, in the word itself, something discovered, uncovered, like a beam of light thrown across a darkness in which a creature made for darkness knew nothing at all of light. He was learning, now, that he did not know who he was, really, and this was something he had never thought of in his life except in dreams.

Rose stroked the back of his hand, and the room they sat in, along with the collection of images, faded to a whiteness, a nothingness, a tiny hiss at the edge of his consciousness like the hiss of falling snow. Her voice came to him soothingly, softer and softer, like a lullaby. It was the only thing he knew in the world and it was the only thing he wanted to know.

"There are so many different worlds," she said. "It's fascinating to think of. They're being created all the time, every second, right here." She nodded, presumably at the other people, whom he could no longer see or even imagine. "Most of us are only aware of one world, or one 'presence,' if you want to call it that—that's Alfred's word—but some of us live in more than one, only with limitations. I understand that now. I will always be here, for instance, and I can't change anything—not anything important, anyway. Not by myself, at least. But some others of us"—she gazed out into the vast space of the world that included more than the two of them, and he knew somehow that with a tilt of her head she meant to indicate Julia, his wife—"some other very, very lucky ones get to *choose*."

32

He must have dozed off, because he dreamed he was at home, having one of his better moments with his wife, and when he came to he was slumped forward on the sofa, holding Rose's hand, which rested loosely on his knee. He wondered how long he had been there like that, and he could see by the look on her face that she was curious about something, and he felt compelled to answer some question that he had unfortunately not heard. He unfolded his hand from hers, trying not to seem startled at himself, but he jerked awkwardly back into the couch, and a trace of disappointment passed over her features. Her eyes fluttered and her fingers fumbled together in her lap.

"I'm sorry," he said.

She swallowed hard, shook her head firmly, once, and, much to his surprise, reached inside a small purse she had next to her, pulled out a Kleenex, and wiped tears from her eyes. "It's okay," she said. "It doesn't matter."

"Really," he said. "I'm sorry. I didn't mean—"

But she waved the Kleenex at him to be quiet and gestured across the table. He looked over to see Tiffany fast asleep, his head against the chair back and his mouth open, a rhythmic snore escaping slowly from his throat, as if he were being strangled gradually.

He and Rose laughed together quietly. "You know how they always say babies look cute when they're sleeping," she said.

"Right," Tonio said. "Babies. Not this guy." He jerked his thumb toward Tiffany, whose tongue now appeared prominently in his mouth, muffling the snoring to some degree. "Not him."

"No," Rose said, and she laughed and wiped her eyes again.

He had not really liked or trusted her up until now, and it was strange to feel close to her for a moment. In fact, he felt almost sorry for her. The prettiness that had bothered him earlier now made her seem delicate and fragile.

"Were we..." he said, and he waved his hand back and forth between the two of them. "Were we in the middle of talking about something?"

She smiled. "We were, but never mind."

"I'm sorry I fell asleep," he said. "That was rude."

She didn't say anything. Instead she sat looking at Tiffany, and he was surprised by what he would have described as a look of hatred on her face. She pursed her lips and squinted her eyes tight and leaned forward, putting her elbows on her knees, her hands held together in midair. "I think he's crazy," she said, as though talking to herself. "I think he'll try something reckless this time." She rose from her seat, crept over to Tiffany, put her small hand inside the pocket of his coat, and withdrew a skeleton key. She tiptoed over and sat close to Tonio on the couch. "This is what you saw him take from me when you passed by the room earlier," she whispered.

It was another of these strange things that kept happening. He hadn't seen her earlier in a room, had he? Had he seen her with Tiffany? They had been here in the lobby all afternoon...but he *did* recall something like that...Tiffany and Rose facing each other, angry, Tiffany squeezing her hand, Rose looking up and seeing him in a doorway. "I can't—" He sighed and took off his glasses and rubbed his eyes. "I don't know. I don't remember."

She waved away his words. "I forgot," she said. "Of course you didn't see me." Then she grabbed his wrist, turned his hand over, placed the key in his open palm, and shut his fingers tight over it. "You'll want this," she said.

So she knew, then, that he planned to make an escape. Had he told her this? Before he fell asleep? Had they drunk that much brandy? There were three empty glasses on the table, but the bottle was more than half full. "What's it for?" he asked her.

"It's the master key," she told him. "It opens everything."

There was a noise from the armchair. Tiffany rolled his head from one side to the other, and his eyes opened momentarily, but they didn't focus on anything. Tonio and Rose kept still. The snoring didn't start again, but Tiffany seemed to be asleep.

"He always wanted me to have it," Rose whispered. "He said it was safer with me." She patted Tonio's arm. "But he sensed something this time. He was afraid I was going to give it to you, so he wanted it back."

"He was right," Tonio said.

Rose turned for a moment to the pale light sifting through the windows. "It's almost dark," she said. "That will make it harder. You'd better go now if you're going to."

His head throbbed at the thought of venturing out into the snow again, the misery of it, the bone-chilling cold, the scary descent into the white space that pulled him and brought him back, always somehow less than himself, into this room again. He hadn't tried it for days. He'd been conditioned not to. "Should I?" he asked her.

"Yes," she said. "I think you have to."

"But isn't the idea that the two of you want to keep me here forever? Isn't that what this has been all about?"

"That's not something we really have any control over." She studied Tiffany anxiously, as if to tell Tonio to hurry.

"Of course you do. We all do."

Rose offered him a grave stare. "I'm afraid something will happen to Dewey," she said. Her eyes were a cold cobalt blue, and their color heightened the icy feeling that came over him at the mention of some potential harm to his son.

"What could happen to Dewey?"

"I don't know."

Tonio was up from his seat now, stumbling over a chair leg. "Where do I go?" he said a little too loudly. He was on the verge of waking Tiffany, he knew, but the thought of Dewey pressed him down, smothered him—some unknown thing in a dark place.

"When you were outside, did you feel like something was leading you?"

"Yes," he said.

"Then go there."

Which was exactly what he had planned to do. He hurried toward the entrance.

"Anthony?" she said. He looked back at her. She stood there primly dressed, still wearing the same little silver shoes. "Let me say this. You can make mistakes. There are blunders. There are moments of stupidity. We all know that." She folded her arms across her waist and pressed her lips together, the way Julia always did when she applied lipstick.

"I've got to go," he said. "What is it?"

"But you can't screw up the one or two really big things," she said. "That's what matters, isn't it?"

"I don't know," he answered. So why did he feel, as he opened the door and narrowed his eyes at the sky filled with snow and winter light, that he'd ruined something already?

33

Hector Jones came armed with a variety of useful tools. In addition to the flashlight, he had a Swiss Army knife that featured a bottle opener and scissors, and, best of all, a pellet gun that his father had allowed him to bring into the hotel if he promised not to shoot it. At first the pellet gun had seemed too good to be true, one of the kind of wild stories that other kids his age often made up, even though, Dewey had noticed, they seldom held up to even the most preliminary rounds of questioning. *Our Yorkshire terrier killed a python. My dad beat Kobe Bryant at one on one when he was in high school. Ashley Bostic told Kaneesha Green that when we got to ninth grade she would have sex with me.*

Dewey had become proficient at defusing these stories gently, like time bombs in the movies, snipping each wire very carefully one at a time so that there was no explosion, so that the tellers of the stories weren't embarrassed by them or too disappointed to find out they weren't true (it was interesting to Dewey that, most of the time, they actually seemed to believe them). In this case, when Hector claimed to be in possession of a, quote, "Winchester Model 1028 break-barrel pellet rifle with mounted scope that shoots the distance of three football fields," unquote, Dewey had suggested to him that it probably wasn't a *real* pellet gun but more likely an airsoft rifle, which his friend Hunter had and which his own parents had refused to buy him this very Christmas—at which point Hector, without a word, picked up the flashlight and, with Dewey in tow, marched back down the hall and up the stairs to the room on the fourth floor and produced the gun proudly from where he'd stashed it under the bed. "If I would've heard you coming at first, I would've shot you with this," Hector told Dewey impressively.

Back in Dewey's room, Dewey convinced Hector, by pointing out to him that his father had told him only that he shouldn't shoot the gun *inside* the hotel, to take some target practice out the window. This produced an exhilarating five minutes of fun and forgetfulness until Dewey shot the metal No Parking sign outside the diner and it clanked loud enough to bring Lorraine out the door and into the street, where she looked left and right and then up to the second-floor window, which fortunately was dark because Hector had been smart enough to turn off the flashlight. Seeing Lorraine had the unfortunate effect, though, of bringing Dewey back to reality, and there were a depressing few minutes in which he and Hector sat on the floor under the window and thought, without speaking, about their missing parents, if Hector was thinking the same thing, which Dewey guessed he might be.

But Hector Jones was more of a doer than a thinker, it turned out, or, maybe more accurately, a *planner* instead of a *worrier,* so that it wasn't long until he had laid out, with a great deal of energy, several ideas for finding their parents and/or getting help. The first of these was a highly proactive proposal that involved going door-to-door in the town and using the pellet gun to threaten homeowners into revealing the whereabouts of Hector's father and Dewey's mom and dad. Dewey was skeptical of this plan because (a) the pellet gun didn't look enough like a real rifle to scare anyone all that much (an argument that Hector disputed vigorously, insisting that the stock and the barrel were made of, respectively, "real hardwood" and "real gunmetal") and (b) the people in the town were very weird, distrustful of and downright hostile toward outsiders, children, even, much less children who showed up at their doors brandishing imitation firearms. Dewey predicted that this proposed course of action would only get them killed.

The second plan was much simpler, and under normal circumstances would probably have been quite effective. It involved using a cell phone to make a video of themselves stranded in the hotel and posting it to YouTube, but under questioning from Dewey, Hector had to admit he lacked the cell phone required to conduct the procedure.

The last of Hector's plans was to snowshoe back to his dad's truck at the interstate, use a large rock to bust open the storage box in the truck bed, take out the flares his dad kept there, then come back to the hotel and fire them from the roof. Certain parts of this plan made sense to Dewey and certain parts did not. He began by questioning the part about the snowshoes, which he figured would be hard to obtain, but Hector swore that he could make them out of sticks and shoelaces, and that this was a common skill possessed by Nez Perce Indians. And while Dewey did not doubt Hector's ability to "bust the box lid open with a big ass rock," he did have some questions about the flares.

Actually, Dewey was surprised and a little bit ashamed of himself that he hadn't thought on his own about walking back to the interstate. That seemed like a pretty smart plan. The problem would be getting through the snow, which by now was so deep that it had made even the comparatively short hike to the mine entrance almost impossible without Hugh's help. How far was it to the interstate? The best that Dewey could remember, it was maybe three miles, but Hector insisted that he and his father had walked at least ten. This seemed unlikely to the Dooze Man. But it was no doubt a long way, and the snow was very high, and it was only getting higher, and it would be pretty tough, he supposed, if you were relying on snowshoes made out of sticks and shoelaces. And if you got stuck out there, you could freeze to death. Still, of all Hector's plans, this one struck him as the most viable, especially when you considered that if you actually did get the flares from the locked box in the pickup bed, you wouldn't necessarily have to bring them back to the hotel to fire from the roof (even though it would definitely be pretty awesome, you could agree with Hector on that much)—you could just fire them off right there by the interstate. And if you made it all the way to the interstate, wouldn't there be signs of life anyway? Wouldn't there be cars? Or was this blizzard so massive that it had wiped out the entire American transportation system? It was hard to say, although Hector did report the presence of other vehicles as of the previous evening. It was all pretty exhausting to think about, so they decided to table the discussion till tomorrow.

There were two things that Hector was absolutely adamant about; one was that they should not go ask Hugh and Lorraine for help, and the other was that they needed to search the entire hotel right away in an attempt to rescue the prisoners. The fact that Hector kept talking about the situation in those terms gave Dewey the uneasy sense that his new friend still wasn't taking the whole thing seriously, that he hadn't reached the point at which he really believed his father was no longer around.

That had been a difficult thing for Dewey as well, but he felt he had, in a way his mom and dad would be proud of, grown up some in the past few days. Definitely he would rather not have had to go about it this particular way. Definitely he would be happy to go back to being a regular ten-year-old at any point his mom and dad decided to show up. But even though, as it turned out, Hector Jones was twelve years old and in middle school, Dewey could see that it was going to be up to him, at least for the first couple of days, to keep Hector thinking clearly. This business of searching the hotel at night was kind of scary, but now that someone was with him it wouldn't be as hard or as nerve-racking. He did like the fact that he now had in his possession, or at least in the possession of his companion, a Winchester Model 1028 break-barrel pellet rifle with mounted scope that shot the distance of three football fields, but he wondered if the gun would impress the creepy hotel owner much if it was pointed at him. And even though he too had just a couple of hours ago been thinking of his mother and father as prisoners and the hotel owner as the one who was keeping them captive, he felt that he and Hector were understanding these words on two entirely different levels. This wasn't a game of capture the flag. It wasn't a mission on Call of Duty where you got to start over when your dude got killed. Hector still thought his father was going to come walking in the door any minute, and that this would all end up being an adventure. Dewey felt sorry for him for that reason.

And then there was the deal with Hugh and Lorraine. Dewey had made the mistake of saying he had some doubts about Hugh and Lorraine, which was the wrong thing to say to a twelve-year-old, apparently, because you could see the idea kind of take off like a rocket in the mind of Hector Jones, soaring out into the atmosphere a million miles an hour and bursting into flame. Hugh and Lorraine were evil, they were probably zombies or vampires, he would lie in ambush for them waiting quietly and patiently as only Nez Perce Indians could, and when they appeared he would shoot them between the eyes with his Winchester Model 1028 break-barrel etc., etc., etc. Dewey didn't like to hear Hugh and Lorraine talked about that way, but it was his own fault for bringing it up in the first place. It really did bother him, though—how they'd held hands across the table at the diner and asked each other if they were *committed* to this thing. What the heck sort of question was that? Of *course* they should be committed—Dewey was freaking *ten years old* for crying out loud. Who wasn't committed to helping a ten-year-old whose mother and father were missing? Yet they acted like it was a really big deal, like they needed to be congratulated for making an effort, needed a pat on the back for offering him a place to sleep other than the freezing, piece-of-dog-crap hotel. Again Dewey wanted to ask himself: What was wrong with the people in this town? Where were the police, the investigators, the news teams, that Nancy Grace woman his mom claimed to hate but kept on watching? In the past few days, he had felt tragically uninformed regarding the adult world, but he still felt pretty sure this kind of shit just wasn't supposed to happen.

And he didn't want to say it out loud or even think it to himself...but wasn't Hugh kind of a chicken? Here was this big, presumably pretty strong guy three times as old as Dewey who was totally, absolutely, never under any circumstances in the history of the world going to set even one foot inside this hotel. He, Dewey, had slept in here for *four straight nights.* It gave one pause.

While the Dooze Man was thinking through all this, Hector had been readying for the expedition. "Do we have some rope?" he asked Dewey.

"What for?" Dewey said.

Hector gave him a look that said what kind of idiot doesn't know what you need rope for.

"I don't think so," Dewey said.

"That sucks," Hector said. He searched around casually with the flashlight beam. "Can I have your shoelaces?"

"For what?" Dewey said.

Hector sighed elaborately. "Dude," he said, "you're tripping."

Dewey offered no response.

"Instead of the *rope,* dude," Hector said in a tone that suggested he had lost all hope for Dewey both now and in the foreseeable future. " 'Cause we don't have no *rope*."

Dewey thought about this for a second. "I'm not taking out my shoelaces," he said.

Then there was a rapid-fire series of requests: Did they have extra batteries for the flashlight? No. Backup food supply? No. Not even, like, some potato chips? No. What had Dewey been living on? Food from the diner. From the zombies? Zombie food? Yes. Shit. Cell phone? They didn't work here. Dewey had already told him that. Fuck. Water? You could scrape snow off the windowsill and drink it. What were you supposed to do about flushing the toilets, by the way? Keep using different toilets on each floor or better yet go to the diner. Wow. Crazy. Toothbrush? Why? In case it turned out to be an overnight trip. Oh, yes, and toothpaste, and Dewey didn't mind sharing. How did you rinse your mouth, though? You could scrape snow—yeah, right, off the windowsill.

Hector stood there with the Winchester Model 1028 break-barrel pellet gun in one hand and Dewey's toothbrush and toothpaste in the other, Dewey shining the flashlight on him. "Are you ready?" Hector said.

"Sure."

They headed up to the fourth floor first, Hector leading the way, Dewey behind him with the light. Ghostly Hector, climbing the creaky stairs in the jerky motion of the flashlight beam, like the doomed character in a horror film. It was spookier than Dewey had thought it would be, and for a minute he wished he were alone again.

They didn't find much. Everything was dark, and it was cold from holes in the roof, and there were cobwebs everywhere, and in the stairwell the dried-up remains of a plant in a swinging pot scared the crap out of them when Dewey accidentally hit it with his head. Only as they were walking down the long fourth-floor corridor did Dewey feel something like a shushing in his blood, a little thrum of particles, and from somewhere in his vision he conjured a dim image of his mother, so lightly imprinted that he couldn't be sure it wasn't a strange shadow from the flashlight or a moment in which he had drifted into dream. A dim outline of her there in the hallway, but then it was like he'd rubbed his eyes and opened them and nothing was there except for a phone, an old black phone of the kind with the separate receiver and mouthpiece. It was the same kind they used in *It's a Wonderful Life*. This was another one of the few things his parents agreed on: they would search the TV listings every Christmas to find out when it was showing. His mother knew practically every line in the entire movie, and his father claimed to watch it mostly to humor her, but once, at the part where George Bailey hugs his son real hard after he thinks they've lost all their money and he won't be able to take care of his family anymore, Dewey saw his father take off his glasses and wipe his eyes with the back of his hand and real quick put the glasses on again. He thought of *It's a Wonderful Life* now, the snowstorm that hits Bedford Falls, and he imagined how easy it would be if you had your own guardian angel to tell you what the hell was going on and what important lessons you were supposed to learn from it. It turned out real life wasn't like a movie.

The fourth floor produced nothing of any particular value, and it was colder than the rest of the hotel, and Hector worried that bats might fly in through the holes in the roof, and even though Dewey pointed out that such a thing was unlikely to occur during a snowstorm, they agreed that the fourth floor was not a good place to be. They went back down to the third floor, which Dewey said he had already investigated recently, so they went to the second floor, which of course was Dewey's own floor and for that reason pretty familiar, so they were headed down the stairs to the lobby when Dewey shined the flashlight beam toward the old fireplace at the far end of the room and there stood a large man with long black hair, his back turned to Dewey and Hector.

Dewey came to a dead stop, gripping the banister hard with his free hand, still directing the flashlight steadily at the man, who paid no attention to the flashlight beam, or to Dewey and Hector. Hector stumbled against Dewey and let out a yelp and both of them fell, the flashlight beam careening around the walls until Dewey got hold of the banister again and steadied himself, Hector now on the stairs just below him.

The man, who was now walking slowly across the room toward the long desk where Dewey's father had talked to the owner, wore a dull-looking brown coat, old jeans rolled up at the cuffs, and a pair of heavy boots that made no sound as he moved across the floor. His long black hair spilled out from beneath a wide-brimmed hat with a leather band around the middle. He held, Dewey saw now, a long pistol in his right hand. This should have been terrifying, Dewey realized, but he felt that he had seen it before—the man's total unawareness of any outside presence, his quiet, ghostly movements, the way all his energy seemed to be directed toward something inside his own head—it was the same way his mother looked when he saw her in room 306. Grimly determined, composed and slow and calm, the man advanced a few more steps toward the desk, the muscles along his jaw twitching, and raised the pistol as if he were pointing the barrel straight at someone's head—but there was no one there. Dewey tensed, preparing for the blast.

"That's my dad," Hector said, seemingly out of nowhere. Dewey had forgotten Hector was even there with him on the stairs. "Dad!" Hector shouted, his voice loud and hoarse in the whispery quiet of the lobby, the strange eerie scene playing out in the flashlight, and before Dewey could grab hold of his arm, Hector was bounding down the stairs toward his father, who still held the gun outstretched in his hand, the tip of the barrel waving back and forth, like the menacing head of a snake about to strike.

Later, Dewey would have a hard time piecing together exactly what happened next, because it happened very fast. Hector's father stepped backward suddenly, his head and shoulders drooping, and lowered the gun to his side. He swiveled and walked toward the front entrance, and just as he did so, with Dewey shouting at him to stop, Hector barreled across the room toward his father, who, of course, paid no attention. Then, right when Hector seemed about to intercept his father at the door, all the lights of the lobby—the huge old chandelier and the lamps along the walls—erupted in a blinding whiteness all at once, like a giant sunburst, so that Dewey became dizzy there on the stairs, his eyes open but not seeing anything, and there was a rush of air as if someone had thrown open all the doors and windows to the blizzard outside, and then Dewey found himself sitting on the stairs in the pitch dark, a dark so intense and full that at first he couldn't even find the switch on the flashlight with his shaking hand.

When he did, and the switch flicked and the beam flashed, what he saw in the pool of light was Hector curled up on the dusty floor in the space where his father had been, lying completely still. He wasn't dead. Dewey knew that. But when he knelt to help Hector up and placed his hand under his arm, the word that crossed Dewey's mind was "corpse-like."

But Hector was fine. He was all right. He sat up and put his elbows on his knees and his head in his hands. "What happened?" he moaned.

Dewey shined the flashlight around the room, searching for any sign of Hector's father. Everything looked the same as it usually did in the lobby, or the way it had ever since his mother and father disappeared—the dilapidated furniture, the peeling walls, the sagging ceiling.

"I'm not sure," Dewey said. There was no sign that anything had happened except for a faint smell of smoke in the air.

"I don't feel real good," Hector said.

Dewey picked up the pellet gun and helped Hector to his feet and they stumbled up the stairs. They returned to Dewey's room and he was straightening up Uncle Robbie's bed for his friend when Hector brought up the subject Dewey had been dreading.

"Where's my dad?" he asked.

And Dewey had to explain to Hector all over again, because, just as Dewey had suspected, he hadn't been listening before, that his dad probably hadn't really been there at all, which made Hector start to cry. Hector thanked him for making up the bed, and then he got under the blankets with his pellet gun, and Dewey went to his bed in the other room and lay there trying to go to sleep but he couldn't because he could hear Hector crying. And then after a while he heard Hector's footsteps and he looked up and saw him shivering there in the glow from the streetlight.

"I'm really cold," Hector said.

Dewey told him to get the blankets from the other room and they could pile all of them up together and both sleep in the same bed.

"I'm really, really cold," Hector said again when he lay down on the other side of the bed and started pulling the blankets around him.

Dewey remembered the corpse-like feel of that arm, which was not like anything he had felt before. "It'll be okay," he said, which was something his mother used to tell him a lot.

They lay there for a long time and Dewey watched the snow fly by out the window and the bed shook just slightly from Hector's shivering. Earlier, it had looked like the storm might be ending, but now it didn't look that way at all.

It seemed like a long time later when Hector said, "Do you think so?"

Dewey was almost asleep. "Yes," he said, and he reached over and patted the blanket where it was pulled up over Hector's shoulder. He could feel him shivering under there.

"Okay," Hector said.

Then Dewey listened in the dark for a while, and Hector's breathing grew quiet and he wasn't crying anymore, and Dewey knew that he was asleep.

And he fell asleep himself. He dreamed that he and Hector Jones were walking along the highway. It was out in the huge open area of South Dakota or Montana, one of the long, empty stretches he and his parents had passed through on the way west, Dewey sitting in the backseat with his head against the window, amazed at the distance he could see, the earth stretching out so far you could almost imagine its curvature, how it dipped slightly out there on the horizon, turning over into tomorrow, traveling through cold, lifeless space, the stars like little pricks of fire too far away to warm anything. Hector carried his pellet gun as they walked, and Dewey's shoes scuffed through the rocks, and the wind blew, and it wasn't snowing but it was going to snow. He and Hector didn't say anything to each other but it was okay, they knew what they were walking toward. And then a car slowed down on the highway and the window rolled down and Dewey's mother was sitting in the passenger seat and staring hard out the window, searching for something, and his father, who was driving the car, asked his mother urgently what she saw. But she didn't see anything. Dewey waved and waved, he shouted till he couldn't shout anymore, and Hector shouted, too, their voices rang like bells in the air, but his mother didn't hear, and as the car passed slowly, slowly, slowly, she rolled up the window and the car went on. Dewey and Hector walked along the highway and the day was growing dark, and up ahead there was a cold, purple sky above the mountains.

When he woke in the morning, Dewey peeked out from under the covers to see the ice on the window and the snow flying down. He was in the usual place. When he turned over to see how Hector was doing, Hector wasn't there.

34

Mrs. Addison had never been drunk before. Even when she accepted Miss Blanchard's invitation to run off to the pantry with a bottle of brandy, she had not really believed that this would be the outcome. But this must be what it was like—for a long time she had felt pleasantly warm inside, but now the pantry was growing stifling, and when she looked down, the floor had begun to turn slowly, in a counterclockwise direction.

Miss Blanchard had talked about so many things that Mrs. Addison could no longer remember them all. She had retained, however, two prevailing impressions: first, that Rose Blanchard, for all her fame and her stable of male and even female admirers, was a lonely person, perhaps the loneliest that Mrs. Addison had ever met, and second, that she had a very high regard for Mr. Addison.

This latter being, her husband, had never seemed so immaterial and far away as he did now. To think that he was out there somewhere, that he sat on a stuffed chair surrounded by other men, talking and smoking cigars, and that he had some right to claim influence over her behavior, that he would, for instance, be entitled to sit in judgment of her present occupation, seemed as unlikely and foreign to her as the idea of men on the moon. Who was this man Rose Blanchard praised so eagerly and incessantly? Usually, he was a somewhat suffocating presence in her life, but for the moment she felt herself free of him entirely and could summon him to the mind's eye in a way that took no account of the control he had exerted over her from the time she agreed to marry him. She could see the way he stood, his long loose frame, the rather large head with the smallish eyes that looked as if they were constantly peering into something, weighing things and measuring, his large hands always in motion. He was not a graceful man, but she could see that he had a kind of smooth, loping energy that other women might admire. If she compared him to an animal, she thought, it would be a giraffe. On a trip to Philadelphia with her family, before she came out West, she had seen a giraffe at the zoo, and now she pictured it standing there squarely on its long legs, its head up in the sky, but with her husband's face on it, nibbling leaves. This made her laugh in the middle of something her companion was saying, and Rose Blanchard pressed her lips together and waited impatiently.

"I'm sorry," Mrs. Addison said, and fanned at herself with one hand, her face feeling flushed. "Please go on."

Rose raised the brandy bottle to her lips and took another sip and offered it to Mrs. Addison, who declined. "I was only reminding you of how fortunate you are," Rose said, as if in conclusion to something, though Mrs. Addison had long since lost track of what. It was becoming positively overheated in the pantry.

Mrs. Addison's thoughts drifted lazily while she looked at a flour sack propped in a corner of the room, its letters blurring so that she had trouble keeping the name straight—Delaporte Flour. She was remembering an expression she had seen on her husband's face earlier...when Mr. Tiffany was showing her the room, and her husband had tapped on the window and looked out into the street. He said he had seen a boy out there, and then it was as if she too had seen this boy, though she was nowhere near the window—he was wearing a bright sweater and funny boots. She had seen her husband's expression, how his eyebrows pinched together, how his lips twitched as if he wanted to smile. And then he turned to her from the window—it was as if they knew something they weren't saying. Now she had the strange sensation that she had known her husband for years. But that of course wasn't true. Most of the time she felt that she didn't know him at all. Maybe it was hearing Rose talk about him now. Why did she talk about him so much? In what way was he so remarkable as to draw her attention? How did she seem to know him so well? She wanted to ask Rose this question, but then it was too late, because she was being asked something herself.

"Do you have any idea what it feels like to be an orphan?" Rose said.

She examined this woman sitting next to her, the legs drawn up in front with the skirts pushed around behind, holding a bottle of brandy in her lap. The white throat, the flushed cheeks, the manner in which she held her head back so proudly, the blonde hair woven up on her head. She was famous across America. In every city and every town, in every out-of-the-way place where there was a newspaper, a dance hall, a saloon, her name was known and passed around. How was it that this woman seemed so intimately connected to her own life? Why did it feel as if the two of them had been sitting and talking in the pantry almost eternally?

She giggled under her breath, grabbed the bottle of brandy from between Rose's legs, and took another sip. She immediately wished she hadn't, and handed the bottle back.

Rose fixed her with an icy stare. "I asked if you knew what it was like to be an orphan," she said. "It is a serious question. I ask you in all seriousness. I was under the impression that you were a serious person, not a giggling fool."

Maybe because she had not expected to be spoken to in that manner, Miss Blanchard having been solicitous of her attention in only a friendly way up to that point, this statement made the floor stop spinning briefly, and Mrs. Addison attended to the question, which was not a thing she had ever considered. What did it matter that Miss Blanchard was an orphan? What *could* it matter, now that she was celebrated universally for her talent and her beauty? Why should it concern Miss Blanchard that she had been—long ago in her infancy, a time she could not even remember—abandoned by her mother, or that her childhood had been spent in the coldness of the institutions for the poor, that she had had to invent herself from her own dreams of glory, finding her name in the colorful flowers that grew outside the dormitory windows? She was Rose Blanchard now, and there she sat with those icy eyes that seemed to absorb everything, pull everything in, her blonde hair gloriously piled on her head, her head tilted back so that everything she drew to herself, all the attention she commanded, seemed to be balanced there on her chin. Surely being an orphan meant nothing to Rose Blanchard.

And yet to satisfy Rose's desire that she be a serious person, for it seemed impossible not to give Rose what she asked, Mrs. Addison tried to think of the question seriously, and was surprised to find how strongly affected she was by the sudden memory of her mother and father, by a picture she conjured of them seated near the hearth at home in Virginia on a rainy winter day, her father busy with the morning newspaper while her mother stared out the window into the gray world thinking of her daughter far away. She could not be having a "vision," as it were, because, first, she did not believe in such nonsense, and also because it would be past midnight in Virginia, and her mother and father would certainly have long since retired for the evening. No, it was just that for a moment her imagination afflicted her strongly, but there was also something more, a strange feeling like an internal echo, a memory being created like a tiny sound inside her, and she listened to its hollow, mournful progress, and found that it brought tears to her eyes. She tried hard to straighten herself, to bring her swirling vision and her thoughts into stern focus, so that she could answer properly for what she was feeling. "I would expect that to be an orphan means that one experiences a terrible longing," she finally said.

Rose, who was leaning forward, gripping the bottle of brandy in her smooth white hands as if poised to attack, softened her expression, her clenched pose receding so that she seemed to be melting into herself, becoming rounder and less angled. "There is nothing worse," she said, apparently satisfied, and tipped back the brandy, taking a long drink. A man's voice sounded sharply from the kitchen. It was the first voice other than Miss Blanchard's that she had heard in some time, Mrs. Addison realized. It had apparently gotten very late, and the kitchen had been cleaned and vacated, leaving only the two of them. The man's voice rang out once more, from farther away, and then a door swung to. She felt a sudden rushing in her head, and she tried to steady her gaze on a box of dried apricots residing somewhere above Rose's head. It occurred to her that she needed to find her husband. He would know what to do about this, how to get rid of this awful fuzziness. The bottle of brandy was placed in her hand, and without thinking she drank from it again, but it only made her mouth drier.

"There is nothing worse," she heard Rose say, "than to know—every day, every hour of every day—as a child, that you are an unwanted person, that the most simple, basic impulse guiding the continuance of the species, that of a mother's love for a child, is somehow absent in your case. And to be surrounded, every day, by other wretched children, who know the same thing about themselves."

The room was now spinning hard, and Mrs. Addison was overcome with a desire to lie down, if only for a moment, and, as if she understood this perfectly, Rose set aside the brandy and motioned for Mrs. Addison to rest her head in her lap. The room then tilted to the side, and her cheek met the cool satin of Rose's dress.

"Don't close your eyes," Rose said from somewhere above and outside her, and fingers brushed lightly through her hair. It was an effort to keep her eyes open, but she did as she was told. "This is the sort of game we would play at the orphanage," Rose said. "Soothe each other, comfort one another—each of us taking turns being the child and then the mother." The light touch of the fingers continued in her hair, and she began to feel as if she were somewhere else, no longer in the pantry at all, no longer in this place a whole continent away from her home. "You can't imagine the loneliness," Rose said. "It never leaves you. It's there in every part of your being, it's there in every breath." The fingers running through her hair, everything so soft and still, even the light in the pantry fading. "I suppose my compensation is that I developed an unusual strength, that I had to develop it or perish. But even such strength is a poor substitute for the love a child receives from its mother and father. Without that love, I don't think a child can ever learn how to truly love anything." The fingers went motionless in her hair, everything was completely quiet. Her eyes were closed, and the room was turning again. "There's not a thing I love in this world." She could feel Rose's breathing, how her heartbeat quickened. "So as I say, you're fortunate. You have enjoyed the love of a caring mother and father, and now, as a mother yourself, you have the experience of loving your own child."

With her head pressed against Rose's stomach, she could feel the emptiness and the loneliness, as if it were coming from inside Rose, and she could feel too the opposite of that inside herself, a warmth, a fullness...then she knew. Rose Blanchard had just called her a mother. How Rose knew was a mystery, as was so much else about her, but Mrs. Addison felt the truth of it inside her: she was carrying a child. She was pregnant with Mr. Addison's child.

She gasped and sat up. Everything was dark, and Rose appeared as a shadow in the thin light seeping through the tall windows. "I'm having a son," she said.

"Yes."

And then everything began to spin around her and she felt her stomach churn. "I'm afraid I'm ill," she said. "Help me. Please, I need air."

Rose lifted her to her feet and guided her by the arm out of the pantry and down some steps and into a long corridor that seemed to lead toward the back of the hotel. There were no windows, and it grew darker and darker as they moved farther down the passageway, and soon she had been swallowed by a smooth black space that was like nothing on earth, and she felt that she would suffocate if she could not get outside. Up ahead, a dim rectangle of light materialized around the borders of a doorway that seemed to float in midair. She could see absolutely nothing between herself and the light, and she had to trust completely in Rose, who moved along the passageway as easily and swiftly as a cat.

The only thing she wanted now was to find her husband. He was the only one she trusted. This would have been a shocking thing to realize if not for the fact that, in the near-total blackness, as she struggled to breathe, she could now picture her husband perfectly, but he was not the same as she knew him. She could see him as if they were in a different time and place, he was transformed into someone wholly different and new and yet he was the same, his face with no sideburns or mustache, a pair of spectacles on the bridge of his nose, looking out a window. She was nearing the light from the doorway but she came to an abrupt halt and felt with her hands to brace herself against the wall. Her husband was looking out the window—she knew now, she *knew*—at the same boy he had seen earlier from the hotel room. She could see the boy herself as if through her husband's eyes, she could see him there herself, had seen him hundreds, thousands of times—he was her own *son*, he was Dewey. She had lost him she didn't know where and she hadn't remembered him because something had happened to her but now she *knew*, and yet she also knew that she carried a child inside her, a child that belonged to her and her husband, who was the same as but different from Dewey's father. Where was Dewey? She was being rushed along by Rose Blanchard, who now pulled her toward the door, tugging on her rather than guiding her, and then the door was thrown open into cloud light and night air and she stumbled outside into the snow and fell to her knees.

"Wait," she said. "Wait, I have to find my son and my husband."

There was no answer. She looked up to see Rose framed in the doorway. She could just make out her features in the white light of the falling snow and the clouds overhead, and it was the same face she'd seen in the pantry—the cold, refined beauty of someone horribly alone.

"I'm sorry," Rose Blanchard said, and she stepped back inside and closed the door.

35

Things were even worse than he would have guessed. If this guy Hugh, who turned out to be the very brother recently introduced in Stephanie's story, so that it was as if he had sprung to life suddenly from the pages of a fairy tale (he would be the troll or ogre), could be believed, and Robbie didn't know why he couldn't be, his one and only nephew, Dewey, had been mysteriously abandoned at the hotel, where he had spent several days sleeping in a cold room by himself and eating cheeseburgers, French fries, and chocolate pie in the diner across the street.

Officially, on behalf of his absent brother and semi-absent sister-in-law (in what way did this news explain or not explain their hazy nocturnal encounter?), he was angry beyond words at the poor judgment reportedly exercised by Hugh and one Lorraine, two adults of roughly the same age as Robbie himself who had done such a shockingly poor job of attending to the needs of a lost and frightened child that he felt somewhat justified in thinking that he might have done better himself. At the same time, he could very well have done a lot worse, and if he decided to let his frustrations boil over into a self-righteous diatribe directed at Hugh, he would no doubt open himself up to a lot of questions, such as where the fuck were you while all this was going on and why don't you take care of your goddamn nephew yourself. Besides, Hugh seemed like a nice guy, though surprisingly timid and nervous for a man of his size. Stephanie was clearly the dominant sibling.

They were sitting at the kitchen table. Stephanie was dressed now and ready to go. She seemed prepared to tackle large problems. Hugh looked more like Robbie himself did, probably—tired and overwhelmed.

"Well, where the hell is he now, Hugh?" Stephanie was asking. This seemed to be the most pertinent question of the session thus far.

Hugh took off his hat and revealed a sweaty, matted-down mess of stubbly, thinning hair. His mouth was open in the manner of confused people or large animals masticating something. "That's the thing," he said. "We don't know. He's got me and Lorraine scared shitless. We told him to come stay with us and he went to get his things, and I saw him once through the window, and then he disappeared."

Everything was quiet in the kitchen. Robbie leaned his chair back and forth on two legs and listened to it squeak. He was feeling shittier by the minute.

"So," Stephanie said to Hugh, coaxing him along. "You *heard* something, *saw* something?"

Hugh stared down at his hands and one of them rose as if it had been summoned. He ran it over his mostly bald head and then wiped it on his pants leg. "Yeah," he said, not looking up at Stephanie. His chin trembled. For the first time, Robbie felt that something really bad might have happened. His nephew, his only brother's son. Dewey. The Dooze Man, who loved card games and magic tricks.

Stephanie stood up and walked, shoulders slumped, to the sink. Definitely not nice to see her that way, definitely not a good sensation. Robbie really liked the vigorous, peppy Stephanie a lot all of a sudden.

"I told him what could happen," Hugh said. "I told him about souvenirs."

Stephanie stood there looking into the sink. "There probably wasn't anything you could do," she said. She glanced over at Robbie. "Anything you *can* do," she added in a softer, apologetic tone.

"We've got to try, though, Steph," Hugh said. "We *have* to. If you—" He dug his top teeth into his bottom lip. "I mean if you could see this kid," he said, and he rubbed his knees with his big hands.

All right, that was enough. Enough already. "Let's just back up a second here," Robbie said. "Let's just back the fuck up."

Hugh and Stephanie were quiet.

"First off," he said, and he was breathing harder than he liked to, feeling that tightness in his chest that never augured good things, "what do you mean did he *hear* things, did he *see* things... *What* things?"

Stephanie pulled her arms tight across herself and looked up at the ceiling. "When someone"—she nodded, as if she was assuring herself that she was getting things right, saying the right thing—"disappears, there's a certain noise. It's kind of like your ears popping. And you sometimes see a flash. Sometimes it's big, like an explosion, sometimes not so much. It's like letting the pressure off."

Keeping his cool here, not going ballistic. "And this 'souvenir' thing?" Robbie asked. Neither of them looked at him. "What the fuck is this 'souvenir' thing?"

"The 'souvenir thing,'" Hugh said in a soft voice, "is us. We're the 'souvenir thing.'"

In Stephanie's story, the little girl and the little boy had been left in the fucked-up little town. They had lived there forever after. Robbie was at a loss to put his feelings about this into words, the deeply backward way of this place, the level to which people had sunk here. It was as if he'd been admitted into a circle of the damned where the people were all like him.

Stephanie came over closer to Robbie but she didn't touch him or try to console him. "I've been trying to explain to you," she said.

He looked at Hugh sitting there pathetically and then he looked out at the world of snow—the snowy sky, the snowy streets—with a feeling that it would never, ever end. "Fuck everybody in this place," he said.

You would have thought that might get a rise out of Hugh, but it didn't. The guy just seemed too hurt and beat down.

Stephanie stood over him, though, and he could see her hands shaking. "You asshole," she said. "Who the fuck are you? Souvenirs or no souvenirs, people who were born here or not—we're all the same, none of us have anything, really. We're all jealous of people like you. That's why all of those guys hate you. We've got no connection to the world. We're just some shitty little forgotten place off the interstate."

Much of this speech was lost on Robbie. It had occurred to him that he didn't know where his brother was, that his brother was actually gone. More than anything that had happened, this seemed impossible. Where was Tonio to fix this mess? Did he, *Robbie,* really have to do this himself? Somehow rescue Julia and Dewey, do it in his brother's name? Had these local fuckers kidnapped his brother, killed his brother? The only thing he knew anymore was that he believed Stephanie, believed whatever she told him, or at least believed in his own interpretation of it. It was probably not a good thing, was it, how much he depended on other people—always some other person to keep things straight, tell him when to go to work, what was his court date.

He made Stephanie sit down in one of the kitchen chairs, drew her up next to him. "Tell me," he said. "I'll listen."

She looked like she wanted to slap him. It was a look he'd seen plenty of times before, and it was sometimes followed by an actual slap, sometimes not. He braced himself. But then the tightness around her eyes faded, and she stared down into her lap and frowned and picked at a stray thread on her sweater sleeve.

Then she looked back up at him. "Really?" she said. She glanced over at Hugh. "You really want to hear about this place? Because I've thought about how to describe it for a long time."

"Yeah," he said, and nodded. "Please."

Hugh fidgeted in his seat. "Is this going to be the mirror thing?" he said.

Stephanie leaned forward and propped her elbows on her knees, then leaned back and put a strand of hair behind one ear, then leaned in again. Hugh scraped his chair across the floor and got up and went over to the refrigerator.

"Okay," Stephanie said, "first of all, think of a place where everything is opposite. Everything that's alive is dead, and everything that's dead is alive. The past is the future, and the future is the past. Dreams are reality, and— "

"Okay," Robbie said, "I get it."

"All right," Stephanie said, "now think of a place where everything is its opposite but also still itself at the same time. Both things at once."

"Not getting that one," Robbie said.

"The best way I can describe this place: if you took two mirrors and placed them, like, one centimeter apart, facing each other." She held her hands out in front of her, fingertips vibrating, not quite touching. Hugh rummaged in the refrigerator door and pulled out a bag of shredded cheese. "The mirrors would be exactly the same. They would both be themselves, but the image in them would be the image of the opposite mirror. Which would also be each mirror's own image. If you could *see* into them, you wouldn't be able to tell the difference one from the other, right? They would show what was opposite but they would be the same thing—but you can't see into them because they're too close."

"Okay," Robbie said.

Stephanie leaned in further, still holding her hands close together but not touching. "Now think if the space between the mirrors, that one centimeter of light, was the line between the two opposite things that were also exactly the same—the present between the past and the future, or the moment just between waking and dreaming, or whatever. And if you shove them just a *little bit* closer, so that they touch, everything disappears. There's nothing at all." She clapped her hands softly together in front of her, palm to palm, fingertips to fingertips.

Hugh dug his fingers into the bag and put a few shreds of cheese in his mouth and put the bag back in the refrigerator door. "You should sell tickets," he said.

"Shut up," Stephanie said. "Now imagine that you're in between the mirrors when the space starts to close." Her hair had fallen into her eyes and she shook her head trying to get it back in place, still not moving her fingers. "Everything is its opposite but everything is the same, no matter which way you turn, all around you." Her voice lowered to an emphatic whisper. "Then the mirrors press together—it feels like there's no air—there's a sound of pressure building and releasing—and *poof!* You're gone."

The people who were drawn here, Stephanie went on, were people who lived in the space between the mirrors—not alive or dead, not awake and not dreaming, not in the past or in the future, but in this little sliver of light between all these things.

"News flash," Hugh said, sitting back down in his chair. "It's called the present. The space between the future and the past."

"I *know* that." Stephanie stared at Hugh reproachfully. "But with the people I'm talking about the present is razor thin. That's exactly my *point*."

She thought it was something deep inside a person's consciousness, she said, something that could only be reached by going into the past, or even someone else's past. Maybe some of the people drawn here were the descendants of other people who came here or they were the same people thrown back in time or they were people who somehow lived the same lives over and over again, drifting in and out of memories. But they came here because there was something they had to see, something they had to do, and this was the only place it could happen. She felt it herself, this deep pull, because she'd gone into the hotel so often that she'd begun to collect her mother's dreams and memories. And in turn, she might pass it along to a daughter, a son, she might unintentionally be planting the seeds, which was why she had never wanted to have children, which was why almost none of the souvenirs did. Because where did people go when the space between the mirrors closed?

On the table in front of Robbie lay the picture Stephanie had found in his sock drawer at the hotel, the little girl and the little boy seated on the sofa, smiling hopefully into their mother's camera. Their mother had disappeared that very day. Now the boy and girl sat across from him, and the girl was trying to tell him that his own family, as much as they could be called his family, as much as anyone could be called his family, had disappeared the same way. All this talk about noises and vanishings and mirrors and souvenirs—the people here were like a strange cult, a stunted, cut-off remnant of some primitive tribe existing in this lost pocket in the mountains. But this was where he was—these were the people he had to deal with. And, taking Stephanie's hand in his, looking down at her chipped fingernail polish, he could say in all honesty that she was one of the few people he'd had actual feelings for in years.

"All right," he said to her. "So what do I do?"

Stephanie and Hugh looked at each other but didn't say anything.

"Call the police, right?" Robbie suggested rather helpfully, he thought. "Hand me the phone," he said to Stephanie. "I'll call the police."

Stephanie and Hugh still didn't say anything.

"You're kidding, right? You're fucking with me."

Hugh cleared his throat. "Have you seen a phone since you've been here? You heard a phone ring?"

"Wow," Robbie said. He went over to the kitchen window. The weather report today seemed to call for snow. Snow in drifts, snow in blankets, snow in swirling clouds. An infinite supply of snow falling from the sky, snow, snow, and snow. A beautiful, mesmerizing, numbing white trap, a straitjacket fitted on him from the sky. And now Stephanie was saying it was all just a dream? Was he going to have to convince himself that he never actually saw Julia in the hotel? Could you seriously think about it—Julia was dead somehow, and he had been visited by her ghost? Where was all this leading? Tonio had never left the hotel? Or he had left the hotel, but nobody knew where he was? How was that possible when Tonio hovered over Dewey so incessantly? And now, after having been there all alone, Dewey was gone, too? That was the one that hurt the most—that Dewey would have relied on two strangers because he thought his worthless uncle Robbie skipped town. That was a tough one. The Doozer. If there was one thing he *had* to do here, it was find the Dooze Man.

It had been quiet for a long time. "There *is* a phone at the diner," Hugh said at last. "I don't use it, but you can if you think you have to."

"If I *think* I have to?" Robbie asked him. "What do *you* think? My brother's gone, my sister-in-law…Now you tell me that my nephew went in that…that fucking *nightmare* of a hotel last night and hasn't come back out and you *heard* something…" He tried hard to stop himself, to corral his anger. He stood there at the window and put his hands behind his back and tried to stay calm and watch the snow. Across the backyard there was a half-caved-in shed, and a magpie sat on the ridge of the tin roof where some of the snow had slid off. It was the first bird he could remember seeing since he'd been here.

"Yes," he said after a minute, and turned to Hugh. "I would like to use your phone, thank you."

Hugh's big hands were spread out on his legs. He was sweating a lot, it seemed to Robbie. Maybe it wasn't a good idea to make Hugh angry, but he'd made a lot of people angry that it wasn't a good idea to make angry, and there wasn't any good reason to change course now. "The reason we don't use phones," Hugh said, "is that phones don't work the way they're supposed to here."

Robbie looked at Stephanie. "Meaning…?"

"Meaning with phones," she said, "satellite things, stuff with batteries, radio waves, computers…anything more than a simple electrical current—"

"How many cars do you see around here?" Hugh interjected.

"Can you let me talk?" Stephanie said. Hugh shrugged. "Basically, you use them, you don't always know what you'll get."

"Would you like to go back in the hotel?" Hugh said.

"No, thank you," he said. "I don't feel very good about my experiences so far in the hotel."

"Then I don't think you'll like using the phone, either."

So that was that. If there was one thing he knew he didn't want, it was something that was anything like the hotel. But there was Dewey. He had to get Dewey out of there. Suddenly he and Hugh were both watching Stephanie.

She frowned and shook her head and then closed her eyes for a moment. "Yes," she said. "I'll go in there and try to find him."

"Thank you," Robbie said. "Seriously, I mean thank you. I'm being an asshole to both of you, I know."

"You are," Stephanie said.

"Yep," Hugh said.

"I don't mean it," Robbie said. He tried to catch Stephanie's eye, so he could express some kind of proper feeling, if only with a glance, but she wasn't having any of it. "I just...got into a little more than I was thinking at first."

"I tried to tell you," Stephanie said.

"Yeah," he said, and then she looked up at him and he could tell everything was all right. It was funny how he seemed to know her that way.

"But Robbie," she said, "I don't want you to get your hopes up."

Hugh fidgeted in his seat. He probably hadn't changed much, Robbie thought, since he first came to this town when he was ten. He could see how Hugh and the Dooze Man would get along, although he guessed Hugh had some work to do to keep up.

"I don't think anything happened to him," Hugh said. "I think he's all right. He just got scared by something and didn't want to leave. That noise could have been anything."

"All right," Stephanie said, "but you know as well as I do that I've been in that hotel more than anybody in this town, and I've never found one person who vanished and then came back."

"You said you saw your mother," Robbie said.

"I *see* her," Stephanie said. "That doesn't mean she's there."

He thought of Julia. "Can you touch her?" he asked.

Stephanie eyed him suspiciously. "No," she said. "I've tried to. The air gets really cold and I can't see anything and then she's...just not there."

"When I was in the hotel," Robbie said, "right? In the dream or whatever it was. I told you I thought I saw my sister-in-law, but I didn't tell you this." He looked out the window. The magpie was gone. Maybe it had never been there at all. He could feel Stephanie examining him. "She grabbed me and pulled me right through a doorway."

"See?" Hugh said, almost lurching out of his chair. "They're still there."

"I guess you kind of skipped over that part, huh?" Stephanie said. Robbie didn't turn from the window. "Hey, I want to believe this as much as you two do. And maybe there *is* some way you can say that people go on"—she paused, and Robbie turned to see her wave her arm in a circle—"*living.* Some way that you could say they're alive in some sense. But they're not *here.* They're not here in *this* world."

Hugh was absorbed in the picture on the table. He held it down with his thumbs on either side, lost in this image of him and his sister on the sofa all those years ago.

"We have to try," Robbie said. "Or *I* have to." He walked over to Stephanie and put his arm on her shoulder, not, he hoped, in a way that suggested he was trying to seduce her into doing something dangerous. "You'll go in there and look for him?" he asked her, and she nodded. "And then if you don't find anything, I'm going to have to try calling the police."

There was a loud pop, and he grabbed Stephanie's arm. But her eyes were on Hugh, who had just slapped his palm on the table, apparently.

Hugh pointed vigorously at the picture with his index finger. "You don't know as much as you think you know about all this," he said, presumably to Stephanie.

"I'm just saying," Stephanie said. "I've been there, you haven't."

"You said you found this in a drawer when you went in there to get his clothes." He was like a detective hot on a lead.

"Yes."

"And this"—he held up the picture like a piece of evidence—"is the picture Mom took of you and me sitting on the couch on the day she disappeared."

"Right," Stephanie said, stepping toward him now to examine the picture herself.

"Mom took the picture with her camera," Hugh said. He sat back in his chair and folded his arms across his broad chest triumphantly. "So tell me this," he said. "Who developed the film?"

36

Once, when he was much younger and much better suited to that sort of endeavor, he had traveled in western Alaska in the spring. There was still a great deal of snow and everything was wintry and wet and there was a musty smell he could still remember of vegetation that was almost constantly covered in water and ice. One day he sat in the cold sun in a hooded parka that offered little warmth or protection from the wind and talked for an hour to a young Inuit man selling trinkets illegally by the side of a mostly deserted road—key rings and bracelets made of polar bear claws, polar bear teeth. The man had gone to college for two years at the University of Alaska Fairbanks and had come home to take care of his mother after his father fell in the Nushagak River and drowned. He was an interesting young man, not much younger than Tonio himself at the time, and he had taken an anthropology class in college. He asked a lot of questions about how he might be able to travel to somewhere warmer and get an education at the same time. Tonio of course asked numerous questions in turn about the habits of the people in the area and how they had changed over time, and he had eventually used some of what the young man said as source material for one of his first published articles, "Conversion and Aversion: Adaptation of Western Alaskan Residents to

U.S. Government Encroachment on Traditional Subsistence Zones."

One story the young man told him was about his grandfather, the tribe's greatest seal hunter. In the winter months, when the bay was so solidly frozen that the ice could not be hacked away, the seal hunters had to find the seals' blowholes in the ice and harpoon them through the narrow openings when the seals surfaced for air. His grandfather's special ability was knowing when the seals would surface at particular holes, but one day he miscalculated and had to sit alert, silent, motionless, by the hole for many hours, long past the time when the sun went down on the brief arctic day, stubborn in his insistence that he would return with a seal. But when he saw, finally, the surface of the seal's head glisten in the moonlight, rising quietly and smoothly above the water for only a moment, he could not move—he was frozen in place, and could not raise the harpoon or straighten to an upright stance. Fortunately, his son found him there soon after and helped him home. The grandfather referred to being frozen as the "cold passage," combining the Inuit root for "feels cold" (*ikkiertok*) with the root for "passing beyond" (*ingiarsiwok*). What his grandfather meant by that, the young man said, was that he had become so cold that he passed through death to the other side, which was why his son had been able to unfreeze him.

Tonio had written this story into his article, paying close attention to the correct names for things, and he had highlighted it as an example of the Inuits' startling innate capacity for withstanding the elements. Now he found himself trying to use the grandfather's story as inspiration.

He had wanted to upgrade his clothing a little bit in preparation, but the moment of his departure was so sudden that he had not taken the overcoat he stole from Tiffany, for instance, or tied the flour sacks over his shoes as he had planned to do, to give him an additional layer against the wet snow. So it was the running shoes and the Patagonia jacket again, neither of which had been packed at the outset of the trip with the idea that he would be forging his way through several feet of snow in near-zero temperatures.

But he seemed to himself to be particularly lucid this time, which gave him hope. If the Inuit fisherman could go through the process of freezing and thawing, pass through death and beyond it, then he could, too, at least metaphorically.

It was the same as the other times. Once he had left the hotel, nothing looked the same on the outside as it had from the inside, through the windows. No diner, no bar, no cars parked along the street, just the brick walls and the long alleyway. He tucked his chin into the collar of his jacket and headed up it, but now he'd walked a long way without anything changing, except that it kept getting colder. If he could think about things like the story of the Inuit man and forget the actual sensation of freezing that the Inuit man's story was really about, then maybe he could get through this. He had known what to expect—there would be the increasing cold, the feeling of his bones being charred from the inside while his skin went numb, the shortness of breath, the tightness in his chest, the sensation that as he walked up the alley it was only getting longer, that the snow fell harder and harder until it became a screen that altered his vision, skewed his consciousness, induced the panic that would make him forget the things he had to remember in order to save himself, save his family, namely Dewey, and Julia, and Robbie, each of whom he tried to think of in turn as he passed down the increasingly long and narrow alleyway and his breath came out in huge white swirls that drifted back and smothered him.

Dewey Dewey Dewey, he said to himself, closing his eyes and stumbling blindly against an icy gust of wind. *Dewey Dewey.* He was approaching the moment of all-out panic, and he told himself to resist the whiteness, the passage, maybe the same passage that the

Inuit grandfather had named, to resist it and refuse to be whirled into the easy clockwise revolution, like a moon being drawn into the orbit of a planet, or a planet locked onto a star. The entrance of the whiteness would be signaled by the appearance of the door. And there it was. It achieved the shimmering, luminous quality of a mirage—against the relentless cold that pushed beneath his skin, the door appeared like a saving oasis rising above waves of desert heat. But he could not go to the door, because the door was a false promise, not the thing he was being led toward, which, he became more and more certain, was a memory, and had nothing to do with any journal article, which he suspected he had never read at all. He would not go to the door, he would not go to it, he would not go to it, he would march on past. For the first time, he did. The alleyway went on. Tears froze to his eyelashes, and he pried his eyes open with stiff fingers.

While he fought his way along he couldn't help, because it was his nature, thinking in abstract terms. His own struggle was an illustrative example of larger problems—*no creature wanted to die, species exceeded their carrying capacities, humans couldn't rise above their animal tendencies.* He tried hard to shut down that part of his brain. Because what he wanted now was for the struggle to be a small one. He wanted it to be about his own life, his own family. He wished the rest of the world well, but, goddamn it, he wanted his own family to be all right. He wanted only to do what it was in his power to do. Let us go back to what we were. Let us go back there. He had loved that life. He had loved it.

He reached what appeared to be a stairway. There was a metal railing, at least, and a hill of snow that perhaps hid a series of steps. He tried to remind himself of what he was doing, of why he was out here. His failure to do this had been a problem before. He was out here because staying in the hotel, where it was warm and sleepy and comfortable but deadly in a slowly strangling way, would never get him back to the life he'd had before, would never help him find his son or his wife. He could only get back to the life he had before by venturing out, by trying to break the spell that had been placed on him by Tiffany, by this place, by, maybe, in some strange way, intrusions from the past, memories of some former time and place that had begun to encroach upon him.

There was the white space, the white tunnel at the edge of his consciousness, but he had gone into a place where he was able to resist—the cold passage.

Ascend the stairway. Pull yourself up by the metal rail. Take a deep breath. Look around you. Here is someplace new.

He had made mistakes. Above all, there had been some essential disconnection within him. But as Rose had said, you were permitted certain errors as long as you didn't screw up the one or two important things. Had he screwed up the important things thus far? He had loved his son as well as anyone could love a child, and yet maybe he had tried too hard to make Dewey just like him. Maybe he had clung too much, hovered too often, fed his own obsession, not allowed Dewey to grow up in his own way and at his own pace, as Julia often lamented. He had loved his wife but, out of some deeply rooted fear, maybe, he had directed the feelings he should have shared with her toward Dewey instead, and with her he had kept himself detached, unavailable, *safe*. He had, on occasion, ventured to take some responsibility for the guidance of his brother, but he had never done it in the right spirit, had always used it as a kind of weapon, a way to elevate himself in his own estimation, and in Julia's, and it had never worked, not for anyone concerned. It was interesting that, when you were utterly frozen and had made it through the passageway, everything became focused on the internal rather than the external—it was on the internal level that all the difference could be made, where you could accomplish whatever mattered. He had screwed up some things, maybe even some important things—but there was still time to correct past mistakes. He would be different from now on.

In front of him, at the top of the railing, was an iron door. He didn't know why he was here or what he was facing. There was a lock and a keyhole. Magically, it seemed to him, he had a key. Above the iron door was an engraving in the hard granite of the hillside: "All Our Dreams Are True." He put the key into the keyhole and turned it and the lock gave way. When he shoved the heavy door aside, he was greeted by a rush of warm air from the depths of the earth.

37

Standing there in the room Hector Jones had occupied with his father, he tried to think of the things he knew about his friend—he was a Nez Perce Indian and proud of that fact, he went to Marcus Whitman Middle School, he very much enjoyed snowmobiling, and he insisted vehemently on the superiority of the Seattle Seahawks to Dewey's own favorite football team, the New Orleans Saints. Having gone over as solemnly and completely as possible these memories of his brief friendship with Hector Jones, he took the Winchester Model 1028 break-barrel pellet rifle with mounted scope that shot the distance of three football fields and, as a tribute, laid it on the pillow of the saggy bed. He sighed hard. He wiped his nose with the sleeve of his sweater.

It was difficult to admit that Hector had disappeared. It was real, like Hugh said. It wasn't like Hector had gotten sick and died there in bed—he was just gone, vanished, no trace of him anywhere. That was the only explanation. There was no way Hector was messing with him, hiding behind doors and following him around, quiet as only a Nez Perce Indian could be. It had been way too long for him to jump out now from behind a doorway and scare Dewey or anything like that. It had been all day. It was dark outside again.

And even though Dewey was more than familiar with the strange logic sometimes practiced by other children his own age, he could in no way believe that Hector Jones would have simply left him, that, for instance, his father had returned and said, "Come on, Hector, let's go," and Hector had jumped out of bed and said, "Okay, see ya, bro," and left Dewey behind without even bothering to see if he was awake. He *wished* that had happened, he truly did. It was far better to believe that Hector had ditched him than to believe the alternative, but it was the alternative that was the truth, and Dewey's father had taught him about the inescapability of the truth, how the record would always bear it out eventually, even if it took millions of years.

And since he had spent pretty much all day scouring the hotel, he didn't think it was likely that he had missed Hector. He had set out with the flashlight and the pellet gun to investigate every possible means of Hector's disappearance, using the flashlight only sparingly to inspect dark closets and other places where the gray light coming through the dirty windows wasn't enough. He had investigated every floor, wandering through rooms of all different kinds and guessing what they might have been long ago, in another century, when the hotel was a place where you might have actually wanted to stay. There was a room filled with high metal chairs like the ones where his mom got her hair cut, and there was a room that contained an *enormous* pool table larger than any Dewey had ever seen. There was one room with an old piano with keys that didn't work, and another that looked like it might at one time have contained a small, shallow pool, with wide steps leading down into it, almost like a gigantic bathtub. He had walked through what he thought was the ballroom and the kitchen, and then, back behind an area with lots of shelves and cabinets, he found a narrow door shut with a rusted latch, and when he pulled up the hook on the latch and opened the door, he decided immediately that this was the one place not to go into. This was, he knew, the passage under the hotel that Hugh had mentioned.

A long, rickety wooden staircase descended into a hole that the flashlight would barely illuminate. Dewey could see a dirt floor far below but nothing else, only the place where the stairs came to an end and the bare earth spread away from them. The stairs looked like they might collapse if you tried to step on them, and there would be a long drop if they did. But it was more than the condition of the stairs that made him hesitate. A strange warmth was coming from down in the basement, and even though he was only ten years old, the Dooze Man knew enough about physical science to make him wonder what exactly was up with that. He could see how maybe since it was below the ground and…what was the word…*insulated* from the wind and the snow it could be not quite as cold as the air in the big open rooms on the upper floors, but it felt like it might be *hot* if you went down there, which there was not, at least in Dewey's mind, a good explanation for. Maybe there was a big furnace down there that was supposed to heat the hotel, but it certainly wasn't heating room 202, where he resided. There was something funny about it.

And another thing—if you stood there very quiet, as quiet as Hector Jones said he could be, you could hear something that sounded a lot like breathing. Dewey kept still and held his breath but he couldn't tell if he was right, if something really was breathing down there, or if it was just his own blood throbbing, or maybe just his overactive imagination. But he was not in a million years going to go down those stairs, and he felt pretty sure that Hector Jones would have made the same decision. Just to be certain, he prepared himself for the worst and took a deep breath and shouted into the darkness, "Hector!"—and instead of the sound echoing dizzily around the cavern the way he had expected it to, it was more like his shout was swallowed, as if the air in this dark hole smothered and contained it. His heart beating way faster than he thought was probably healthy, Dewey real quick shut the wooden door, fumbled with the latch, and finally fastened it. And then he got the heck out of there. But that was the only place he hadn't thoroughly checked.

He eventually made his way wearily back up the stairs to the second floor, where he lay down on the bed feeling lonely and cold and thinking about how it would be really good to go to Hugh and Lorraine's house and take a hot shower. That was the only thing left to do, really, so he started gathering up his things, the same process he had begun the night before, and then the tribute to Hector occurred to him, and that was why he stood here now, in Hector's old room, saying goodbye to the friend he'd had for just a short time but liked very much.

Hector Jones was gone. All the things he talked about and said he was going to do no longer meant anything. Nobody in the world except Dewey even knew that Hector Jones had said those things. And the same thing could happen to Dewey. It could happen to him at any second—like, literally it could happen five seconds from now, before he moved from this very spot. Or it could happen in fifty years. Who knew? But it could happen. *Would* happen. The grades he made in school that his dad was so proud of, the way he had learned under his mother's supervision how to take out the garbage and wash a load of his own clothes, all the tennis trophies lining his dresser—none of it would matter at all once he disappeared. Your whole life was just sucked away, and it only made a difference to a few people you left behind who remembered you, and then when they were gone you weren't anything at all. Hector hadn't even had a chance to become a souvenir, really, since Dewey was the only person in the whole awful town who knew he'd even been here. But that was important, Dewey told himself, the fact that someone had been here to acknowledge

Hector Jones's presence and be his friend. And it made him think of something else: during the weeks before he won the Charleston County Spelling Bee, he had obsessively studied lists of thousands of words that might be used for fourth grade contests—roots, alternate spellings, pronunciations, etymologies. *Souvenir,* he knew, was a French word meaning "to remember." Hector Jones was not a souvenir but a memory. That made it sound not quite so bad.

Well, it was time to go to Hugh and Lorraine and ask if they could please think of a way to help him. He was only ten years old and he had tried hard and he had done everything he could. He wanted some grown-ups to figure out how to fix things now. Hugh and Lorraine would have to do.

He was getting set to return to his room and grab the rest of his things when he heard, he was sure of it, someone moving in the hallway. His immediate impulse was to shout for help, but something made him stop the noise before it left his throat, and he stood quietly in the dark where he could see what little light filtered into the corridor. Maybe it was Hector…but maybe it was the scary hotel owner instead. Maybe it was his father come to rescue him…or maybe it was something even worse than anything or anybody he'd seen so far. You never knew what was going to happen next in this crazy place. It was best to wait and see.

And then there was the yellow beam of a flashlight, advancing slowly, surely, bobbing up and down. A voice was connected to it, singsongy, the notes of it rising up and down just like the flashlight beam, as if the person coming down the hallway was…what, jumping rope and singing at the same time? It was a female voice, certainly not the hotel owner's, certainly not Hector's, and it made a familiar sound as it went along, until, in a few seconds, it arrived at the very doorway to the room in which Dewey stood motionless. The familiar sound, Dewey realized, was his own name. This surprising development, the fact that this as yet disembodied human voice bouncing down the hallway not only knew but was actually vocalizing his very own name, almost made the Dooze Man pee his pants. It was like the scariest moment in the scariest movie ever made in the history of scary movies, and it was happening to him. Right now. This thought was actually a major help, because it caused him to react instinctually in the manner of a horror movie main character, the one pursued relentlessly throughout the film by the killer, which meant that he backed up very slowly, taking great care not to make the old floorboards creak, into a small space behind a closet door. It was a good thing, because right at that moment the flashlight beam bobbed into the doorway and shined across the snow-swept windowpanes and the old, moldy furniture and the sad, curled-up wallpaper. Dewey inched his way back as far as he could into the space against the wall and held his breath as the intruder came forward into the doorway. It was a woman, not particularly scary-looking by the standards of casual observation—what his mother, so tiny herself, would have called a "full-figured girl," with long blondish hair and round features—but extremely weird in the current situation, mainly because it appeared that, when she wasn't calling out Dewey's name, she was talking to herself in a steady, high whisper that sounded like a nursery rhyme. The manner in which she bounced the flashlight beam up and down on the curtains, the dresser, was very curious, and Dewey wanted to find a name for it but couldn't quite until she had turned and glided from the doorway and down the hall, and he had come out from his hiding place to approach the doorway and find the woman skipping— *skipping*—toward the stairs. The name he would give to the woman's movements was "childish." She moved like a child, the way Dewey would expect one of his female classmates at Sumter Elementary School to do.

He followed her cautiously down the stairs to the second floor, where she walked down the hall and disappeared into his very own room. For a minute he stayed close to the stairs in case he needed to make a quick escape, but eventually he was drawn out into the hall and partway down the corridor by the odd show the woman was performing, seemingly for the benefit of no one other than herself—she spoke in a high childish voice and then answered, apparently, in more soothing, rounded tones, and then her voice boomed out like a man's, and she laughed strangely and shouted as if she was afraid, and then made bizarre noises, cluckings and squallings, and spoke to herself in what sounded like other languages. It was as if she were enacting an elaborate drama, or some kind of insane puppet show without the puppets, in which all the parts were hers and she was her own audience as well.

Then the noises stopped, and a dim, shifting light seeped from the room—she had turned on the television. Dewey tiptoed forward until, through the half-open doorway, he could see the woman sitting on the sofa, leaning forward and smiling widely at the TV screen. If he tilted his head far to the left, he could see the TV at a slant, but he couldn't quite make out the picture well enough to see what the woman smiled at. It appeared to be the face of a woman on the screen, large and shifting, but it was hard to get a good look at it from this angle. But the woman sat there forever just looking at the screen, one arm draped across her knees, one hand holding up her chin. At one point she shot up from the sofa, and with a squeal approached the TV and held out her hand toward it, although she stopped short of actually touching the screen. Then she returned to the sofa and resumed staring at the TV. Eventually she lay down and curled into a ball with her arms tucked in tight to her body, and every once in a while she dabbed at her eyes or moved a strand of hair out of her face.

Dewey felt sorry for the woman (he was softhearted, his mother always said), but he was still afraid of her, and he wished she would go somewhere else so he could have his own room back. She didn't seem to be interested in finding him anymore—she'd stopped calling out his name a long time ago—and he was getting tired of standing in the hallway. Finally he gave up and went back to Hector Jones's room. He pulled the pellet gun out from under the covers and he went and sat against the wall with the gun across his lap. He thought about how if he were in Mount Pleasant now he would be doing homework for his world history class—he knew they were supposed to start a group project making a 3-D map of the Roman Empire, which he had been very much looking forward to—and his mom would be nagging him to start getting ready for bed and his dad would be saying, Oh, come on, Julia, let him stay up a little longer and watch TV. He had missed his team's first basketball game after Christmas break, and they had probably lost because Devonte Price would have had to play point guard, and Devonte Price, despite possessing admirable dribbling skills, always got overly excited and put up crazy, impossible shots or threw the ball away. Probably his friend Hunter had used his absence as a chance to move in on Emily Ott, even though he knew Dewey had liked her for at least six weeks. Outside the wind would be warm and salty and the air would smell like pluff mud from the marshes. In the sky there would be stars. He closed his eyes and he could hear his father pointing out the constellations to him—Orion, Gemini, Cassiopeia. Aries, his birth sign, though only his mother paid any attention to astral signs or starry predictions.

It was much later, he knew, when he opened his eyes again. He stretched out his legs, which were stiff more from the cold air in the room than from the position he'd slept in, and he pushed himself up against the wall. He rubbed his eyes and focused out the window. Snow.

He went back downstairs and the woman was gone. The greenish light of the TV drifted out into the corridor, but she was no longer on the sofa. Dewey called out tentatively—"Hello?"—flinching at the possibility of a response, but no one was there. He was too tired and dejected to think about anything so he got a blanket from the bed and lay down on the sofa where the strange woman had been and watched the TV to see if he could figure out what she'd seen.

A curious thing—there appeared to be an actual show on the TV, one with actors and a director and a script. Definitely it wasn't what the woman was watching before. There wasn't any sound but you could see the picture really clear. The show looked like it cost maybe five dollars to make—it had this totally fake tropical island with a bunch of people who had been shipwrecked, apparently, only everyone had clean clothes and the women were pretty and wore lots of makeup. There was a fat man in a blue shirt who chased a skinny guy in a red shirt and hit him with his hat. Dewey guessed it was supposed to be funny. If you were an actual castaway, though, not so much. He'd learned that in the last week. He fell asleep again.

When he woke up, the TV had gone back to its usual greenish-gray light. It was like it was diseased or something, a sick TV that needed a visit to the emergency room. He squinted and focused the best he could on the grainy image the TV presented to him. A hole, a cavity. It was the opening to the mine shaft—a throat trying to swallow him, and he was ready to go down, down, down. Why not? Everything was hopeless. He would die. He, the Dooze Man, would die. This was what it looked like, on the TV. The mouth like a breathing tube that sucked you into the earth. Everything in the whole world was just a dream anyway, or at least to people like him, Dewey, who thought too much. Hugh had said his own mother was "dreamy," but Dewey's mother wasn't. Whose fault was it, then? Who was to blame for all this? He, Dewey, who lived his life in a dream.

The greenish light of the TV screen, the yawning chasm attempting to pull him under—he could feel himself entering the zone he couldn't escape from, the place where he went and stayed gone, and everything was worn down to elements, the cold, the dark, the *snow,* which right now, in his mind, fell so softly and peacefully. Everything was like an icy, burning dream, and he was in it now, on the inside and all alone. Time passed.

The next thing he became aware of was a figure on the TV screen, orbiting the edges of his consciousness. It was a human being, tired and cold, limping a little, hunched over, lost. A tall figure, strong but weakened by circumstance, shuffling into the mine entrance. The green light made the character weirdly fluid, as if it were moving underwater, but Dewey began to make it out now, see something familiar. A tall man wearing glasses, urgently searching, seeking someone he loved, someone he was desperately missing.

38

You didn't see many kids in this town, but here one was, at the diner, with what was probably his grandpa, feeding a quarter into the gumball machine. The kid had some kind of fucked-up haircut that looked like it had been done with a lawn mower, and snot pumped out of his nose in copious streams. Robbie was glad he hadn't ordered anything to eat. His stomach felt even worse when he realized what the gumball machine was — an actual replica of the maze of stairways and passages connecting all the buildings in the goddamn town, a miniature version of the torture chamber he'd been trapped in.

"For fuck's sake," he said.

The grandfather paid up and gave Robbie the evil eye for no reason he could figure or at least admit and he and the kid shuffled over to the door and headed out into the snow, the grandfather pulling his old coat tight around his neck and the kid hacking and coughing and swallowing snot. Robbie walked on over and had a look. There it was, inside the transparent plastic shell, the whole network of stairways and doors and tunnels, like a game of Chutes and Ladders for the eternally damned. There was the biggest building, the hotel, dead center, with its mass of stairways and passages. A long stairway descended below the ground and then tunneled across the street and came up a set of stairs and branched out in several different directions, and he could see the way he'd gone and the stairs that led to the door at the back room of the bar where Stephanie worked. That's where he'd been stuck, *right there.*

"Where the hell did you get this?" he asked Hugh, who had walked over to stand next to him. He was flicking the guitar pick between his teeth. Robbie recognized him now as the guitar player of the crappy band that was playing the night they'd arrived.

"I made it," Hugh said.

"You *made* it?"

"Yeah," Hugh said. "I found it in a novelty shop up in Cranbrook. It had these metal tracks that the gumball traveled down. I thought it would be cool to have this instead so I cut the top off and made the model out of balsa wood and cardboard and toothpicks and Popsicle sticks. Then I painted it and put the top back on with a hinge." He stood there breathing in and out like a horse and regarding the gumball machine in a proprietary way. "It's folk art, I guess you'd call it."

"Yeah," Robbie said. "That's what I was thinking of calling it."

Hugh looked at him unfondly. "A lot of people around here make stuff like this. It's kind of a local hobby."

"Commemorate the fucked-up nature of your town with toothpicks and balsa wood and model airplane glue. Why not." He stood there studying the model, which was actually pretty astonishing. He wondered how much time it would take to craft such a thing.

"Do you get the shit beat out of you a lot?" Hugh asked him.

"Surprisingly rarely," Robbie said.

"Here," Hugh said, and handed him a quarter.

Robbie put it in the coin slot and turned the handle. An orange gumball rose up in a little bucket that dumped it over the top of the diner, where it bounced off the roof and rolled down the stairway to the bar, where it plunged down into the basement and rolled under the street to the hotel and dropped down a hole and landed in the tray. Robbie took it out and put it in his shirt pocket to give to Dewey later, when they found him.

"It had a deal where you could use these levers to guide the gumball along and if you got it in a certain slot it would give you an extra gumball," Hugh said. "But I couldn't figure out how to make it work."

"That's okay," Robbie said. "It's pretty impressive just how it is." Hugh eyed him with mistrust. "Seriously."

"Thanks," Hugh said. "You'd be surprised to see how many of us here make stuff like this. You just take something old about the town and turn it into something new." He gazed out at the street and craned his neck to see up to the windows in the hotel. Stephanie had gone in there over an hour ago. Robbie and Hugh had been trying not to mention it for a good half hour now. "I know exactly how things look to you here. I'm not an idiot. And believe me, I've tried to leave. I went to Seattle for a while."

"Really," Robbie said. His old home in Seattle seemed about a million miles away. It was almost incomprehensible that, theoretically, you could drive there from here in less than six hours.

"I worked at a restaurant on Capitol Hill," Hugh said. "But there didn't seem to be any reason to live there, so one day I just left and came back here."

"Did Stephanie ever move away?"

Hugh shook his head. "She's hardly ever been anywhere since our mother disappeared. Once a souvenir, always a souvenir. So they say." He went on to tell Robbie about all the times you'd see somebody, could be a person of any age, old, young, male, female, black, white, staring at the hotel, snapping pictures, hanging around the street—people who had left, moved on, sometimes started whole different lives, but finally couldn't stay away. "You always think you can find the person you lost somehow, bring them back, that there must be some way…and maybe there is. I'm still looking. Why do you think we bought this diner? So I could be right across the street. So I could keep some kind of connection between this world and that world." His gaze drifted around the walls of the diner, as if he were surprised to find himself in the same place after all these years, and then out the window to the hotel sign—Travelers Rest—the letters partly obscured by snow. "When my mother went to develop that film, I could have been standing right here watching the street. There's always a chance."

Robbie inspected the interior of the diner: rather nondescript, clean enough, serviceable, old prints of the mining town decorating the walls. It could be a diner just about anywhere. The kid in the kitchen dinged the bell and Lorraine took the order from the window and set it in front of an old man with sunken gums and eyes who sat quietly at a back table.

"What about her?" Robbie asked. "Your wife—is she a…souvenir?"

Hugh shook his head. "It was her family that took in me and Stephanie after we got left here. You kind of get stuck with whoever the town picks out for you. They were nice enough till Lorraine decided to marry me. Now not so much." Hugh stood there stolidly, his hands in the front pockets of his jeans, utterly unperturbed. He looked like he might start whistling in a minute.

"Amazing," Robbie said. He scanned the place once more—the kid washing dishes in the kitchen, two old ladies in a booth, Lorraine scratching down an order on a pad, everything as normal as it could be—and then turned back and faced the street and the hotel windows. "Why doesn't anybody say anything? Why aren't the cops crawling all over this place?"

"People make reports sometimes," Hugh said. "It's not unheard of. But most of the time they don't say anything." He looked at

Robbie. "I mean, what would the police find? How exactly would you explain what happens here?"

Two people fucking disappeared—that's how he would explain it. And he intended to, as soon as Stephanie found Dewey. Or at least that was what he'd been telling himself, although it was becoming a less effective story the longer Stephanie stayed in that hotel. Because what the deeper part of him suspected was this: that Tonio and Julia had gotten lost in the labyrinth the same way he had. That would explain a lot of things—why he remembered hearing Julia's voice when he was lost in one of the passageways, for instance. Why the thing had happened between him and Julia—maybe they'd both just been confused. He had been lost in the maze for what he guessed was a period of several hours. How disoriented would you be if you'd been wandering around that hotel for several *days*?

And while he knew that Stephanie was looking for Dewey, he also knew that on some level what Stephanie was always doing when she set foot in the hotel was looking for her mother, and that in some very strange ways —like the picture—she kept on finding her, or pieces of her, or evidence of her, at least. And if Hugh had gotten her hopes up with the picture this time, who knew how long the journey could take? There was an even deeper fear that assailed him now while he stood by the gumball machine and stared silently with Hugh out the window, waiting for something, anything to move: what if, this time, Stephanie went so far into her own memories and fantasies and desires that *she* got lost in there? What if Tonio, Julia, Dewey, and Stephanie were all lost in there? Almost his whole life at this point, in other words, because what else did he have right now? His parents? The people he'd met this last time in rehab? A bunch of fucked-up loser friends in his hometown who would only get him in more trouble as soon as he returned? Everything he had was now in the hands of Stephanie, who, with every passing second, had been in there too long even longer. And way, way down at the bottom of himself, in the nether regions where he harbored any sense of obligation, there was something he also knew.

"I can tell you this," he said to Hugh, both of them standing there with their arms crossed, staring at nothing, the only sound the scraping knife and fork of the old man and the subdued chatter of the old ladies in the booth. "As soon as I find somebody to talk to, I'm going to do a lot of talking. I'm going to tell somebody *everything*."

Hugh unfolded one arm and put the guitar pick, which he'd been twirling with his fingers, in the pocket of his shirt. "Well," he said, "I don't mind that. I really don't." He checked out the tables, peeked back toward the kitchen. "I wouldn't say that too loud, though. There are some people who would be upset to hear you say that, but not me." He appraised Robbie one last time and shuffled back toward the kitchen. "But you haven't been through the whole thing yet. We'll see."

There it was again, that rock at the pit of his stomach, that little voice that told him what he didn't want to hear, what he didn't want to do. He knew what would make it go away: a drink. He started to feel that electric pull in his feet, and while Lorraine was asking the old guy if he needed anything else and Hugh was telling the kid in the kitchen that he could go home now, Robbie escaped the diner and made his way to the Miner's Hat, a few doors down the street.

It was cozy in the bar and he didn't mind that people stared at him. The only window onto the street was the small square one in the front door, so he didn't have to feel compelled to look out the windows every second in hopes of seeing Dewey and Stephanie. The rock in his gut—the dry, nagging voice—was beginning to disappear already, and he hadn't even had a drink. This had been a good decision. Still, there were plenty of things happening, the evening promised to be eventful, so he decided it was best to order a beer instead of whiskey. One problem that he had forgotten — he didn't have a dime to his name. He didn't even have ID.

The bartender stood in front of him. Robbie ordered a beer and looked at him pleasantly. "Stephanie said to put it on her tab," he said.

It worked. He drank one beer and ordered another and he even found that there were ten unused selections on the ancient jukebox in the corner and he chose seventies rock songs with all of them and he ordered a third beer and sat on a barstool contentedly listening to the Eagles. The world was just fine. He could forget there was anything unusual going on at all.

Then a swift blast of cold air came through the door and Robbie turned to see some of his buddies walking in — there was Ray, and there was Ruby, and there were a couple of other guys he didn't think he knew.

"Hey, Ray. Hey, Ruby," he said, but they said nothing in return. "Good to see you again." Robbie saluted them with his beer can. The four of them kind of ranged themselves around him at the bar in a none too neighborly way.

He considered whether it would be a good idea to bring up his newly formed friendship with Hugh at this point, but he decided that probably wouldn't accomplish much. He turned to ask for another beer but the bartender had mysteriously disappeared. There were two old codgers at the bar and a middle-aged couple smoking cigarettes and nursing drinks in a booth near the back — no one that was going to be of any help. The one thing that could help would be if Stephanie walked in the door right about now — she'd set these assholes straight in less than a minute.

Robbie nodded at the new guys. "Who's your friends?" he said.

Ruby looked down at the guy nearest the front entrance, to Robbie's right. "There on the end, that's Rusty," he said. "You met him before."

"Rusty, Ruby, Ray," Robbie said. "Readin', writin', 'rithmetic."

Nobody even tried to smile. It was possible, he supposed, that they didn't get the reference.

"Next to him," Ruby said, "is Miles."

Miles offered him a slight head bob but nothing verbal in the way of a response.

Ruby stepped a little closer to Robbie's barstool. "You may be interested to know that Miles"—Ruby nodded in Miles's direction, as if Robbie might have forgotten who he was in the past two seconds—"was going out with your friend Stephanie until about a week ago."

Robbie checked out Miles briefly—on the tall side, sandy blond hair, a bit listless, shoulders a tad slumped. Not much to speak of in any respect. "That *is* interesting," Robbie said, getting up from his stool. Before Miles had a chance to react, Robbie snuck up and shook his hand. "That's great," he said. "Good to meet you."

Miles peeked sideways at Ruby and the others, as if seeking direction. Possibly he was a halfway decent guy—it didn't seem like this whole thing had been his idea.

"Come on, Miles," Ruby said, and nudged him toward Robbie.

Right then the bartender reappeared. He walked out from behind the bar to the front door and locked it. Son of a bitch. The two old guys had swiveled on their barstools to face Robbie. One of them was missing his right eye. Both of them looked like they were willing to give this whole thing a go. The couple in the booth leered grotesquely. The Eagles sang "Life in the Fast Lane."

"We tried to be nice to you when you came here," Ruby said.

"You sure did," Robbie said. "You guys were solid. You were aces. I enjoyed that night we went up and down the stairs." Ruby and Rusty and Ray and Miles looked at one another. "I've actually got a question for you," Robbie said. "There's something I'm concerned about with Stephanie. Hang on just a second. I've gotta take a leak."

He turned as quickly as he could without seeming hurried and walked past Ruby. He counted in his head—thousand one, thousand two, thousand three. There was the men's room door to his right. To his left was another familiar door. Next to it lay the cat he'd seen when he was stuck in the stairwell.

This was exactly what he'd been afraid of, what the rock in his gut and the annoying voice had been telling him lay in his future. Calmly, he opened the door on the left, stepped through, and shut the door behind him. Then he ran like hell down the rickety stairs, back into the nightmare labyrinth, hoping to find his way across the street.

39

It was stupid, of course, to try to go down a mine shaft without a light. You would think an anthropology professor had enough sense to procure a flashlight, no matter how difficult that might have proved to be under the circumstances, before attempting to crawl down a black hole. But no. Here he was.

The gray light from the clouds extended just a few feet into the shaft, and after that it was all black. But he continued. This was where he believed he was being led. As long as the slope was gradual, he could take it slowly, step by step, feeling his way amid the rocks and clutter. In a sense, there was no point to it. What was he, a grown man, doing groping his way down an abandoned mine shaft, an empty hole, in the middle of nowhere? He was looking for his son. He was also, he knew, looking for himself. And in that respect, he had already achieved something—he felt more lucid than he had in days, maybe in weeks, perhaps ever.

Nothing existed in the world but him and this darkness. It was as if he were sprouting, as if he had been planted in this very spot where his feet searched for purchase on the hard, damp ground. For most of his life he had maintained a rigid certainty regarding objective reality that even now he steadfastly clung to...but maybe he was starting to grant reality some wiggle room. Or maybe it was just that objective reality encompassed more than he had bargained for. Here in the total blackness where, if he stood completely still, he could imagine that he existed only as a form of consciousness, he could see how life stretched out in space and time to encompass everything. The individual was the universal and the universal was the individual, no difference between the two, each wrapping itself inside out with the other—a black hole could be right here in this small town in Idaho, it could form inside a human heart, and the farthest galaxies in space existed only because people had discovered them.

The problem with this wealth of lucidity was that it didn't accomplish much. It wasn't getting him his life back. It wasn't helping to find Dewey or Julia. He was just standing here, in a hole in the ground, in the dark. Or was it dark? His eyes were confused, no two ways about it. In the absence of any light, the synapses were apt to play tricks on you, but he could see a red glow far off in his vision. He shut his eyes and the red scar cut through the space behind his sight, growing sharper the tighter his eyes were closed. When he opened his eyes again, the light was brighter, closer, as if he had coaxed it into coming near. He held out his hand and could begin to see his fingers. The light widened like an iris, and soon he clearly saw a figure, a bearded man wearing a miner's cap, bent somewhat at the waist, clambering up the incline with an oil lamp in his hand. In what seemed to be mere seconds, the man was positioned in front of him, breathing heavily, wiping his forehead with his free hand.

"You're Diamond," Tonio said.

The man chuckled, then wiped his face, then chuckled again. "Yes, Mr. Addison, I'm Diamond. I'm still Diamond."

The man stood there looking at him in the lamplight. Tonio wasn't sure whether it was an effect of the lamp, or the sharpness of the light in contrast with the utter blackness of the mine shaft, but Diamond's blue eyes appeared almost glacial in their depths, as if the lenses were layered inward.

"Come, Mr. Addison," Diamond said. "It's the middle of the night. This is no place to be. Come with me." And he started shuffling back toward the entrance.

"But I came here for a reason," Tonio told him. "And it's warm. I haven't been warm..." And he shook his head trying to remember for how long.

"I know," Diamond said. "Believe me, I know it's easy to get confused." He was still moving back toward the mine entrance. Tonio reached out and grabbed his shirtsleeve, which was oily and cold to the touch. Diamond turned on him reproachfully, his icy eyes forming hard crystals in the orange lamplight.

"I understand who you are," Tonio said, even though he wasn't sure how. "But I came here because I believe something has been leading me to this place. I came here because I believe I'll see my son."

Diamond's eyes softened. The pupils narrowed and the irises flattened out, adjusting to the light like those of a nocturnal animal. "Mr. Addison," he said, "I appreciate the sentiment. You're a fine man. I'd sooner work for you than any pit boss I ever had. But I'm telling you that you're mistaken here."

"I'm not mistaken," Tonio said. "I'm more certain right now than I've ever been in my life."

Diamond blinked his strange eyes, pulled a handkerchief from his pants pocket, and wiped the back of his neck. It was warmer here than it had any reason to be.

"Of what?" Diamond asked him.

"That I'm supposed to be here."

Diamond lowered the lamp to his side and his face was lit weirdly from below, one eye glistening in the light, the other dull and dark. "It's my job to keep people from passing through."

"Your *job*?" Tonio said. "You *work* here?"

"I've worked here a long time," Diamond said. "You know that. It's dangerous here. It's my job to protect people, to keep them from passing through. This place is too close to things."

"*This* place," Tonio said. His sense of well-being had evaporated. He felt suddenly as if he'd been confronting obstacles like Diamond all his life. "What about that crazy hotel?" he said. "What about *that* place?"

"The hotel is Mr. Tiffany's affair. It belongs to him."

"Well, who does this place belong to? It's an abandoned mine shaft. Who says I can't come in here?"

The suggestion of a smile took shape in a corner of Diamond's mouth, but his eyes, or at least the one Tonio could see, looked tired. He pulled off his cap and ran his fingers back through his hair. "'All our dreams are true'?" He put his cap back on and held up the lamp and peered into Tonio's face.

"Right," Tonio said. "I saw the sign."

Diamond shook his head and lowered the oil lamp again. "I'd say the sign is about equal parts promise and warning. If you…" His cheeks, which had been drawn up tightly, suddenly loosened and fell, and his mouth opened. His eyes were trained over Tonio's shoulder. "It's too late now," he said. "You won't be able to leave, Mr. Addison."

Tonio turned to find another light meandering down from the entrance, this one obviously a flashlight beam, steady and strong and white against the walls. The shaft was now lit from two directions, Tonio situated in the middle, so that he was almost blinded no matter which way he turned. He held up a hand against the flashlight beam, and he discerned the shadowy form of the intruder, a smallish person who appeared to be carrying a rifle in his left hand. He was being tricked in some way, cornered, trapped—but Diamond's expression indicated that he was just as confused as Tonio.

Together they watched the figure assume a certain size, take on a certain shape, and Tonio's breath left him so fast that he could barely stay on his feet. He managed to set himself in motion, his legs like an old man's, uncooperative and shaky, but still he stumbled ahead. For just a moment he saw clearly the curly head of hair and the familiar gait before the flashlight struck the ground and threw a wobbly light on the rocky wall. And then he was grasping him tight, his own son, Dewey.

These strange few days dissolved and faded, and he knew that in this moment he had reached his objective, that he had found both Dewey and himself, because the only self he knew anymore lived inside this boy, was sparked to life by their connection. When you wanted something, when you waited for it and wouldn't let it go, when you fought so hard in your own mind that the absence of the desired object became impossible, then the desired object returned to you, or you forced your way to it, because it contained a true part of yourself. The best part of him was in this boy. With this boy he had shot baskets in the driveway, with this boy he had collected shells. This boy he had pulled in the wagon, and when the wagon tipped, and the boy scraped his chin, and he could see in those eyes the look of pain and betrayal, it was he, Tonio, who had soothed the wound and made it better.

He had thought just minutes earlier that he was making discoveries about the world, but, it turned out, there were only a few things he really knew in it, and one of them was the feel of this child in his arms. He lowered himself to his knees, and Dewey's hand patted his hair.

"Is Mom with you?" Dewey said.

He could feel his son's heartbeat, how it fluttered with hope. "No," he said. "We'll find her. I thought maybe she was with you."

They stayed like that for a while in the warm cave with the

flashlight shining against the wall. He breathed in and out against Dewey's wool sweater and he could feel Dewey breathing back. It was some time before he realized that Diamond was gone.

It didn't matter. There was no reason that Diamond should be there. But the shaft seemed darker than before, and peering over Dewey's shoulder in the dim light he saw that the iron gate was closed. He stood and grasped Dewey's shoulder for a moment and walked resolutely to the cave entrance, stumbling a little over the rocks, and then Dewey was behind him with the light. The gate was shut all the way and there was no handle and no lock on the inside of the door.

He pushed and shoved and prodded for all he was worth. He banged until his fists were sore and he shouted until he was hoarse, until his lungs ached with the pressure of shouting, until the mine shaft seemed to burst with the accumulated noise. He shouted until Dewey grew alarmed at all the shouting, and then he shouted some more, but no one came.

Finally he sat down, exhausted, and Dewey sat down with him. Now that, for the first time since they'd arrived here, he couldn't get at the snow, he was very thirsty.

He thought to turn off the flashlight. It was dark and quiet and beyond the iron door no doubt the snow still fell outside. Someone was chopping wood somewhere, a steady *thock, thock, thock*. People still existed in the outside world, even if they paid no attention.

"It's a big mine," Dewey said. "There's another entrance somewhere."

"We'll find it," he said. "I hope this flashlight has good batteries."

"It does," Dewey said. "It belonged to Hector Jones's dad. He made sure it had good batteries."

"Who?"

"I'll tell you later," Dewey said, and with that he took the flashlight from his father's hand and turned on the beam and stood up and wiped off his pants. "Let's go, Dad," he said.

Tonio stood up and brushed himself off. "All right," he said. "Let's go find Mom. Let's get out of here."

They made their way down the shaft. Dewey stopped to pick up the gun where he'd dropped it. He handed Tonio the flashlight.

"It's just a pellet gun," Dewey said.

The shaft followed a gentle curve downward and to the right, and the ground was drier and the footing better the farther along they went. Tonio asked Dewey questions: Yes, he had been staying in the hotel. Yes, by himself. There wasn't any food or running water, so he had been eating and using the restroom at the diner. Hugh and Lorraine were very nice and looked after him. They made sure he washed up in the kitchen sink and brushed his teeth. Yes, he'd seen his father watching him from a window. He'd seen his mother, too. He'd seen his father in the street. He'd seen a lot of strange things. No, one of the strange things was not Uncle Robbie, whom he hadn't seen at all. He was fine, really, he was fine. He just wanted to find his mother and go home.

While Tonio listened, he thought about how this was exactly the thing that he'd wanted, to find his son, and how he had almost everything he wanted now, except that he, too, wanted to find his wife and go home, and he also wished he could hold his son's hand, the way he used to do when they crossed the busy streets in downtown Charleston. But Dewey had recently warned him against that, saying he was too old for it now. So they walked along with Dewey holding the pellet gun and Tonio holding the flashlight. He could see Dewey in the flashlight beam. His face was dirty and his hair was a mess and the sweater drooped from him comically and he had to constantly push up the sleeves, but his face and eyes looked sharper, with a new kind of calm and determination. Julia would be proud. Tonio had always been interested in Dewey thinking like a grown man, but it was Julia who had wanted him to conduct himself like one.

Soon they reached a place where the shaft forked, the path to the left angling off in a level track while the one to the right descended sharply.

"It's this way," Tonio said.

"How do you know?" Dewey said.

"I just do."

"Like you just know it," Dewey said. "Like for no reason."

"Right," he said, and shrugged.

"I feel that way sometimes, too," Dewey said. "Like I know things here. This is a weird place."

Tonio nodded. "It is a very weird place."

They had come upon a cave-in or an excavation, a pile of rocks knee-high and halfway across the path. They stopped and sat for a moment. Tonio set the flashlight carefully on the rocks. They had never had a language for their emotions. People remarked on the way they talked with each other, how each understood what the other meant, how each knew what the other would say. He had taught his son all he knew to teach, but he regretted now that one of the things he'd taught him might have been his own reticence. He wanted to talk now not about what he knew but what he felt.

"I'm sorry, Dewey," he said. "I didn't know what was going to happen when I left the hotel."

"I know," Dewey said.

With a trembling hand, Tonio balanced the flashlight so it angled up toward Dewey's face.

Dewey drew back and held his hand in front of his eyes. "Stop, Dad," he said. "What are you doing?"

"I just want to see you for a second," he said.

Dewey relaxed. He was used to his father's eccentricities. He inspected the ceiling of the shaft, and Tonio knew, because it was the kind of thing he always knew about his son, that Dewey was wondering how the ceiling had been cut so square with the wall. Normally, he would have attempted to say something about nineteenth-century hard-rock mining techniques.

"I love you, Dewey," he said instead.

"I love you, too, Dad," Dewey answered him. And when they began to walk again, his son reached out and took his hand.

Tonio shined the light on the tunnel walls. There was nothing to see and nothing to hear, except that somewhere deep beneath the sound of water dripping there was at this level of the mine a steady movement of air, a wafting in and out, a suspiration. Dewey stared back and forth at the path ahead and the path behind, as if listening to the sound.

The air had been getting steadily warmer, but Dewey's shoulders shook, as if he had a chill. "I see her sometimes. I found her fingerprints."

And he too could see Julia then, standing in the driveway of their house in Mount Pleasant, a pair of hedge clippers in her gloved hand, assessing the status of her azaleas. How had they never understood each other better? Why had they wasted so much time?

"I see her in the hotel, but she's not there," Dewey said. He sucked in a couple of hard breaths. "I see you sometimes, too, but you're not the same."

"I'm here," he said. "Look at us. Both of us. We're here."

"Sometimes I don't even know if I'm alive," Dewey said. Tonio shined the flashlight on Dewey's face, which was streaked with tears or sweat. "*Don't,* Dad," Dewey said, and he shined the light away. "How do you even know you're alive in this weird place?"

"I know I'm alive because I'm with you," he said.

They walked on in silence, keeping to the right when the path forked once more, and soon it became more level though it still didn't seem that they were getting nearer an entrance.

"What about Mom?" Dewey said after a while. "How do we know she's okay?"

He didn't know how to answer this question himself, but he thought hard about it while they walked. He tried his best to corner his own feeling and make it speak, make it give his son, make it give both of them, something to hope for when logic failed. "Did you see the sign at the mine entrance?" he said.

"Hugh showed it to me. It's a stupid sign."

"Maybe not if you think of it the right way."

"How do you know what's the right way?" Dewey asked.

He wanted to say, *Because it's my sign, I made it with my own hands,* but it sounded too strange, and he wasn't sure he could explain to Dewey what he meant. "I'm just saying what I think," he said. "What I think it means is that if you dream something, or you wish for something, that thing is already real."

Dewey didn't say anything in response and they walked along with the sound of their footsteps echoing. From somewhere below the passageway, farther down in the mine, there came a noise that sounded like an engine laboring.

"Let me tell you a story," Tonio said. "When I was about your age, maybe a little bit younger, my mother and father planned a surprise for me on Halloween."

"Halloween is fun," Dewey said. "This is starting off to be a good story."

"You have to understand, though, that your grandparents weren't very good with surprises. They didn't understand children." He thought about Robbie, and how Robbie had to grow up there with them, too, when they were much older and probably understood children even less. "My father was a judge, you know."

"I know," Dewey said.

"Very proper, very stern."

"I know," Dewey said. "He's pretty stern *now.*"

"But he loves you," Tonio said. "He loved me, too, but he wouldn't show it. I didn't know he loved me when I was a child."

"I always knew you loved me," Dewey said.

Tonio stopped walking for a moment, and he put his hand on his son's head, felt the matted hair, and then he started walking again. "Good," he said, and he took a deep breath, the musty air making him cough a little. "So it was Halloween, and it was before school, and I was at the table eating breakfast."

"What did you eat?" Dewey said.

"I don't remember."

"But *generally* what did you eat? I mean, what *in general* did you like to eat for breakfast as a kid?"

"That's a good question, Doozer," he said. "I don't really remember. I don't think it matters now."

"Everything matters now," Dewey said.

He looked down at his son, who seemed to have grown taller in the last week. "Let's say cereal, then. I think I liked to eat cereal as a kid."

"Okay," Dewey said. He reached out his hand and ran it along the tunnel wall. "Ew," he said, and wiped his hand on his sweater.

"I wouldn't touch that," Tonio said. "Dripstone formation. Bacteria. It's what happens where water gets in. It also might mean we're getting closer."

They walked along hearing their footsteps and that sound like the hollow whistle of a distant machine beneath them. "I know what that is," Dewey said.

"Dripstone," he asked, "or that sound in the air?"

"Both," Dewey said. He was looking at his feet.

Tonio knew the sound, too. He'd heard it before somewhere.

It wasn't a good sound and it didn't foretell good things. "So," he said, "Halloween. I'd had a dream…Don't you have a coat to wear?"

"It's wet," Dewey said, and wiped his nose on his sweater sleeve. "It's hard to keep things dry here." He kept walking without looking up.

"I'd had a dream the night before, probably because I watched a scary movie."

"Because it was the night before Halloween," Dewey said.

"Right," Tonio said. "It was the first time I'd had the dream, but I've had it many times since. I was walking in the dark, and there was something burning somewhere, and no matter which way I went the fire kept getting closer. Soon I had walked into the middle of the fire, but before it burned me, everything went black and the fire suddenly went out and there in its place was the biggest diamond I'd ever seen."

"So it turned out to be a good dream."

"Sort of. The next morning I was eating breakfast, and my mother and father rushed into the kitchen. They were both smiling for some reason, which was unusual. Normally only one of them would smile at a time. My mother said, 'Come quick, Anthony, we found treasure in the hall closet!' So I ran to the hall closet and I opened the door and there it was, glowing in the dark, the biggest diamond I'd ever seen."

"Really?"

Tonio pointed the light back the way they had come but there was nothing to see. It seemed as though the noise kept getting closer. "No, not really. It was a glass candle my mother had lit to try to set the mood. The treasure turned out to be two tickets to an Egyptian exhibition at the museum."

"That's it?" Dewey said. He pulled his hand away from Tonio's and wiped it on his pants and then held Tonio's hand again.

"But when I opened the closet door, I *saw* the diamond. It was like an illusion that disappeared when I stared at it too long."

Dewey stopped walking. Tonio pulled up beside him and shined the light ahead in the tunnel. The shaft felt hollow like a mouth and you could hear steady dripping from the ceiling now and behind it there was that humming or rasping noise from down below. Dewey stared straight ahead but his face was blank.

"What?" Tonio said. "What's wrong?"

"Nothing. I'm just listening."

"To what?" he asked. "My story or that noise?"

"Both," Dewey said. "Go on telling it."

Something in his son's voice made him pause for a moment. "You sure?"

"Yes," Dewey said mechanically. "Finish telling me about the diamond."

"Well," he said, a little uncertainly, searching his son's face, which was pale and glistening in the oblique beam of the flashlight. "There's not that much more to tell. At the same time, my mother and father shouted 'Happy Halloween!,' and then my mother picked up an envelope from behind the candle and gave it to me. The envelope had the tickets in it. I was just mad about the diamond."

They had started walking again and Dewey seemed to have gotten back into the rhythm of the story. "Your parents were really weird," he said.

"Right," Tonio said, "but my point has nothing to do with that."

They had reached another fork and to the left was a rubble-strewn path and an old lift going down to even lower subterranean levels. The rasping noise had grown louder, and Tonio had to stop talking while they veered away and into a tunnel that rose slightly upward.

"The point is this," he said, and he stopped, and he knelt down so that he was looking directly into Dewey's eyes, at his dirty face and greasy hair. "Have you not been able to take a shower?"

"Like I said, Hugh and Lorraine make me wash up in the kitchen."

"Who are Hugh and Lorraine again? Never mind for now." He put his hand on Dewey's shoulder. "The point is this. What I remember after all these years is that, when I opened the closet door, I saw a sparkling diamond, the biggest one in the world. Do you understand?"

"Yes," Dewey said. "I think so."

"I can still see the diamond as if it were actually there, and I've dreamed about it ever since. It doesn't matter that it didn't actually happen. What matters now is that I stored it that way in my memory. It's in my memory the same way as...I don't know, the time when we surprised you with the hamster."

"So what are you saying?" Dewey said. A note of panic had crept into his voice. "That I should just be happy *remembering* Mom?"

He pulled Dewey in closer, as if he were afraid he might fly away. "No, what I'm saying is that I *believe* Mom is okay someplace and that she's trying to find us." Unexpectedly, a vision of Julia in the hotel alone, seated on the edge of the bed, surrounded by suitcases, troubled him. He adjusted his glasses on his nose and continued. "And we have to keep trying to find her. We have to keep on believing that we'll find her for however long it takes. I know that's not logical, and I'm not saying that all the things I tried to teach you before were wrong—I'm just saying that maybe I haven't paid enough attention to my subjective experience of the world." He thought about that, everything he'd stored up inside him, all this time, all these years. He had been afraid of it, how strongly he felt about the life he'd made, how every little event, every time Julia had ever kissed him lightly on the lips to say goodbye, every time she'd touched his hand in passing, added something to a foundation, an edifice of accrued memories. He had wanted it not to be dangerous. He had thought you could hide yourself away. "What's true is what I make true. That's what the sign means. That's how I know Mom is okay somewhere. Does that make sense?"

"Maybe to someone else," Dewey said, "but not to me. I'm only *ten years old*."

His son stood there sniffling. Tonio pulled his shirtsleeve down over his hand and wiped Dewey's nose with it. "You *know* Mom. You can picture her right now." Dewey looked down at the ground and nodded. "*Keep* that picture. Keep it in your head and Mom will come back to you."

Dewey leaned in and rested his forehead against Tonio's cheek. For the few moments that they stayed there that way, Tonio formed his own picture of his wife, a picture of her lying in their bed in Mount Pleasant in the morning with the sun coming through the windows, the cat, Cleopatra, sitting on her stomach and kneading her paws on the blanket while Julia talked to her in the way she had a habit of doing—*How is Cleo this morning?*

He pulled Dewey in closer. "I kept picturing you, and you kept picturing me. That's why we found each other in this place."

"I know about Sparky," Dewey said. "I saw. I was watching from the window." Tonio could feel his son's breath catch, and he ran his hand through Dewey's sweaty hair, and kissed him lightly on his forehead. He had killed Sparky with a hammer and buried him out behind the trees, and then he had stood there by the small grave trying to compose himself before he went back to the house. He wasn't upset because of Sparky—Sparky was better off—but because he remembered the day they had brought Sparky home, how his son had looked at him with such joy, and how he had known it couldn't last.

"Sparky was suffering."

"I know, Dad. I'm not blaming you." Dewey turned his head so that his face was buried in Tonio's chest. "I'm saying I understand."

"You do?"

"Yes," Dewey said. "I understand everything."

In a minute they went on. The passage was cut squarely out of the rock and it rose more and more and he knew they were close to the surface now. Dewey walked along beside him and they switched off holding the flashlight and the pellet gun. Tonio sensed that there was a door up ahead in the passageway before he actually saw it. It was a plain steel door at the top of a flight of wooden stairs, a door that looked less like the opening to a mine than to his faculty office building back home in Charleston.

As they moved toward the door the wind picked up, whistling from down in the mine shaft. Tonio pulled Dewey close and walked faster, the door looming in the near distance, flickering in the yellow light like a flame. The wind stopped, everything went still, and the heat rushed in and there was no air to breathe. Tonio gasped but drew in nothing, and Dewey bent over next to him, and Tonio had to straighten him up and keep him moving toward the door.

They could see well enough to get up the stairs, and he pushed Dewey up ahead of him. But then there was nothing left in the world except heat, and the ground convulsed beneath Tonio's feet like a live thing shaking itself from slumber, and he hurried Dewey on as he heard the sound from below again, stronger this time, an extended moan. He fumbled the key from his pocket to open the door but there was Diamond on the stairs, as if he had been forged in the flashlight beam.

"Hurry, hurry, boy," Diamond said, and boosted Dewey up with a hand to the back. The door opened to a rush of cold air and the sound of it went screaming down the shaft, and from far below came a rumble of expanding air, as if the cold air were being taken in, and then the rumble grew and the wind roared back up, burning hot.

Tonio clung to Dewey's sweater and peeked carefully out the doorway. Outside was the snow and the cloudy night sky and one streetlight and, just across the alleyway, the side door leading into the hotel, the door that he had so often disappeared through. He pushed Dewey ahead of him out into the alley and handed him the flashlight and then mounted the top step, preparing to go out himself, still feeling the heat at his back and the earsplitting noise, but then an arm crossed his chest and barred his way, Diamond grappling with him there on the top step so that he almost lost his balance and tumbled down.

"No," Diamond shouted. "No, sir, you can't now, you can't! Just the boy! Just the boy!"

He wrenched Diamond's hand away and surveyed the street and right there, behind Dewey, fitting a key into the lock of the door across the alleyway, was Julia.

They were going to be all right. They would be all right after all, just as he had said. Within an hour they would be gone from here, even if they had to walk all the way to the interstate. They could do it together, they could make it. Things would be different, there would not be so much distance between him and his wife, there never should have been, they had known they would be together since the day they met on that bus, they had known it even before then, it had been in the air forever. Dewey saw her, too, his mother, and he slipped and scrambled through the snow calling her name but she seemed not to hear. She opened the door, and she stepped inside, and at the last moment she turned. Tonio saw her clearly in the streetlight. She wore a puzzled expression, as if she was trying hard to remember something that barely eluded her, like peering through a curtain at a light, and for a moment he thought their eyes locked, and he wanted to convey something to her, he wanted to let her know something important, but he didn't know the words, it was only a feeling—he smiled at her. He smiled, he hoped, in the same way he had smiled that day when they met on the bus, when he held out his hand to show where he'd written her number. He smiled for all he was worth, but he didn't know if she smiled back at him, because his eyes were clouded with tears.

The door across the street slammed shut and Dewey called out and ran to his mother and Tonio stepped out into the street himself, and he had the strangest feeling. He saw Diamond standing there to the side of the door, Diamond with that tragic look on his face, *Please stop, Mr. Addison, you can't,* and he called out to Dewey and Dewey turned, and now he was coming out the door to his son and he could see him there in his sweater standing forlornly in the street, but he felt the crystal in his veins, the ice contracting. He was being pulled, harder this time than ever, through the cold passage. He could feel himself shattering like ice—his bones, his skin—and with what was left of him, of Tonio, of Mr. Addison, of Julia's husband and Dewey's father, he reached out his arm, and he opened his hand, and he tossed Dewey the key.

40

Outside in the snow it was cold but it was also quiet, the party long since ended, the guests all gone to bed, only she out here alone. Gradually her thoughts began to come around her and the brandy haze cleared some and she knew where she was and what she was doing there. She had arrived once again where she knew she would be arriving, and she was aware that she had been arriving there over and over, it was the same place she always arrived, and yet as many times as she had arrived there she could never see it in her head beforehand, couldn't make the discovery until after the scene had played itself out, as if she were facing a mirror and wearing a mask, but each time the mask was removed to reveal her secret identity the mirror went dark.

The first thing to do was get back inside, and for that she had the key, she always had the key. It seemed the simplest, most obvious thing now to turn it in the lock. As she did, and as the snow blew down a white screen against the world, she thought for a moment that she saw Dewey in the snow, but the ground shook beneath her and the vision faded to nothing and she stepped inside the door. There was nothing out there but the snow.

Inside, the wooden steps dropped down into the dark cavern Rose Blanchard had led her through. The cavern was warm and there was an orange glow in the air and from somewhere she heard movement. All this felt natural, as if it were part of a story that she had been told before. Cautiously she made her way down the steps, enough light there in the underground passage to spot rotted boards, broken railings—it had been entirely black when she and Rose Blanchard passed through earlier.

She reached the bottom and the underground room widened, and she could see at what seemed like a vast distance the small figure of a man working by lantern light, bent over a space where the light disappeared. Her feet carried her forward over the uneven earth floor as if she already knew the way, and she held the man steady in her gaze. She could see now that it was Mr. Tiffany, dressed in jeans and a work shirt, and at first, by the stertorous rasp she could hear coming from his direction, and the movement of the air against her face, she guessed he was pumping a giant bellows. And indeed the space near him was uncomfortably warm as she drew near, and she felt now as if she were being pulled in by a great vacuum. Mr. Tiffany's face ran with sweat, and his shirtsleeves were rolled up to reveal arms streaked with dirt. He appeared to be turning the crank of a long iron door or hatchway that extended almost across the expanse of the cavern floor, yanking on the handle as he tried to pry the hatch all the way back, and with each turn of the handle, the hole beneath widened, the heat and the orange glow became more intense, the rush and suck of air more unbearable, and the noise more like a vast groan or snore.

Mr. Tiffany turned toward her, unsurprised, as if he'd known all along that she was there above the noise and the heat. He continued at his task, but he acknowledged her with a nod of his head. She remained perfectly still, watching the orange light from below dance in Tiffany's eyes as he turned the handle with all his might, drops of sweat falling from his chin.

He paused for a moment in his labors. "This is where the earth breathes in and out," he said, and forced his weight onto the handle again. The maw opened wider, and the light seemed to be approaching full intensity far below. "I apologize for all of this, Mrs. Addison," Mr. Tiffany gasped in between turns. "If it were left up to me, it wouldn't necessarily turn out this way."

"What do you mean?" Sweat broke out on her face and under her collar, and she breathed hard and shielded her eyes from the light with one arm.

"Things need tending to, so I tend them," Mr. Tiffany said. "I don't judge or make decisions."

"Who does make decisions?" she asked him.

He turned his gaze toward her but kept at the handle, his muscles tight beneath the rolled-up shirtsleeves. "You do, Mrs. Addison," he told her.

Grunting loudly, he gave the handle one final hard turn and the door locked into place. He stepped aside and shook out his arms and surveyed the results of his labor. He took a pipe and a packet of tobacco from his jeans pocket and struck a match.

"You'll want to move along now," he said. He bent his head to the flame and puffed once and raised his head. "Quickly. The stairs you're looking for are over there." He nodded toward a passageway that she knew led toward the pantry, the same passageway she had come down with Rose Blanchard. She glided toward the stairs, felt as if she were dreaming. Mr. Tiffany stood below, a figure in the depths of the earth, his face glowing red, his cheeks puffing in and out. "I always felt a great deal of admiration for you and your husband. What happened never changed my mind, at least not in your case." Her face was burning now, the air almost crackling. She saw Mr. Tiffany's face through waves of heat. "Now you'd best move along." In the weird light, rippling black and orange, she saw his shirt catch fire, and she watched the flames spread upward to his face. He stepped back calmly and disappeared into the shadows.

She had almost reached the stairs when from behind her the air shuddered in a long roar and she was yanked backward—the hair pulling back on her head, the skin pulling back against her cheeks—and then propelled forward to the foot of the stairs, and there was a simultaneous explosion and implosion, a sucking in and out, so that everything popped but she could not tell whether it was in the air or in her ears, the entire atmosphere at once cracking open and simply disappearing.

Without turning back, she hurried up the stairs and opened the door and found herself in the small pantry as she knew she would. As she stepped through, her shoe hit the brandy bottle and sent it skittering across the floor. On through the kitchen and the ballroom and the lobby, seeing everything as she had on the night when she and Tonio and Robbie and Dewey checked in, the ladders and the sawhorses and the faded wallpaper, and also on the night when she had first seen the hotel, in 1886, in all its opulence and self-conscious glory. Two sets of stairs, a palimpsest, layered over each other so that she could see them both, the fresh woodwork and the new gas lamps, the faded wallpaper and the broken banister, knowing that above her in the rooms lay all the people fast asleep on the night the hotel opened, sleepy and satisfied with the sumptuous meal and the drinking and dancing, as well as her son, Dewey, all alone, and her husband, Tonio, all alone, and Robbie out there somewhere, all alone, all of them, in the cold, in the night, everyone alone. She thought of Dewey, and inside her she felt the new child, or the child from long ago, the one she would bear for Mr. Addison way back across time. She climbed the last of the stairs, headed down the corridor to room 306, where she knew that, as if she were an actress preparing for her time to come on stage, she would wait outside the door.

As she took her place along the wall, listening to the voices of her husband and Rose Blanchard in the room, the smell of smoke hung, quite distinctly, in the air. The photographs in the lobby—there had been no mistake at all.

41

H e had known what would happen from the time his father said the word "illusion." He had known it, he had seen it coming, he had understood that it wasn't real, or at least not in the way he had conceived of that word in his lifetime prior to his arrival in Good Night, Idaho. And yet for Dewey, that short time he had been able to spend with his dad, even in a nasty dark mine shaft deeper and more evil than the deepest pit in hell if there had been a hell, which his father had assured him there wasn't, had been so peaceful, so safe and secure in a dreamlike way, that he had allowed himself to go along with it until the bitter end, and he couldn't say he regretted it, illusion or no illusion. He understood, he thought, what his father was trying to tell him about the sign. He meant that any time you imagined something, that imagined thing took its place in the world, in the mind of the person who imagined it, which was as real a place as Kalamazoo, Michigan, or Schenectady, New York, or maybe even more real, maybe the *only* real place. What had happened was that the two of them, Dewey and his dad, wanted to find each other so much that they had dreamed of seeing each other in the mine, and when both of them dreamed it together it was real. Out of their best imaginings, they had constructed each other and brought each other to the same place. But then the ground had started to rumble and he couldn't get his breath and he had been thrust through a door and out into the snow, in a dark alleyway, where he had seen the strange old man from the mine shaft and then once again his mother, and then the old man disappeared and of course his mother, too, although this time through the doorway like a "normal" person, whatever that meant anymore.

So here he was, alone again in the snow. There was one thing he wished he had thought to tell his father—he wished he had told his father that, even though he was only ten years old, and even though it had been less than a week, he had learned to take care of himself. His father would have liked to hear him say that.

And what it meant to take care of himself right now was to go through that door and follow his mother. He knew well enough by this time that opening the door in the alleyway and going inside wouldn't necessarily lead him to her—doors could lead to a lot of different things—but this door at this moment was the best hope he had, so he tried the door, he shoved and pulled and turned and twisted, but it was locked. He slumped down with his back against the brick wall of the hotel and considered his surroundings. The alley stretched forever in either direction, and he was tired. This had been the longest night of his life. In fact, it might be getting close to morning. And it was as cold outside as always. If there was one thing he was really tired of, it was being cold.

He would have to walk out of the long alley to the hotel entrance. It seemed like a monumental endeavor. Wouldn't it be nice to just wait right here. When Hugh and Lorraine came in the morning to open the diner, he could get them to bring him to their house so he could take a shower. He would be so cold by then. He could just lie around and wait to disappear like Hector Jones. He was, he realized, on the verge of giving up. His father wasn't there and his mother wasn't there and none of the coaches he ever had were there to tell him he had to keep trying. How easy it was to sit in the snow, his pants and sweater getting wet again, the pellet gun propped against his shoulder, simply fading away. Easiest thing ever. He was about to fall asleep.

Drifting off, he thought of his mother floating through the hallways like a ghost, how she sat on the bed in room 306, composed and calm, as if trying to impart to him this peaceful feeling he felt right now, and he thought of his father and how they had walked together through the mine, and how his father had clung to him even then, in a dream, in the same hard way he had clung to him during his whole life, so that he felt himself raveling and unraveling, his mother setting him loose, smiling at him in that way she had, telling him Dewey, you're all right, I love you and you're all right, and his father keeping him close, always watching, always saying there's danger, Dewey, there's danger, and then he saw his father in those final moments as they came out of the mine shaft and into the alley, his father behind him, and he, Dewey, had turned, and it was as if his father were evaporating, as if the snow had been too hot instead of cold, but at the last second he had raised his hand and... he had raised his hand. He had opened it and let go of something. At the edge of sleep, Dewey had the physical memory of reaching out, of trying to catch something his father had thrown to him.

His arm jerked. He opened his eyes and turned on the flashlight. The beam was sluggish but still strong enough to cast some light on the snow of the alleyway. He got to his feet and moved step-by-step toward the doorway on the other side of the alley, the one they had come out of, and he inspected the freshly fallen snow. There... right there. A little oblong cavity, the slightest residue of disturbance. He put his hand into the snow and felt around until it settled on an actual object, which he removed with his numb fingers — a key. It was a real key, a key his father had thrown to him. His father had, after all, really been there. He had hugged Dewey and told him he loved him. In some way it was not a dream. Dewey squeezed the key, cold and tight in his palm. There had to be a reason his father had thrown it to him—it meant something, his father wanted him to do something with it. But there were so many levels to things. You could never know what was actually happening. He was reminded of Cleo, his cat, back in South Carolina, how Cleo would sometimes twitch in her sleep, imagining enemies, coyotes chasing her, snakes in tall grass, while the actual Cleo lay safely on the rug. Who knew what the truth was? How could you say? Right now, he had a key.

Sure enough, it turned in the lock. Dewey balanced the pellet gun and flashlight across his knees and pushed the door open and placed the key back in his pocket. He looked up at the falling snow, the flakes settling on his cheeks. He went through the doorway, and a warm wind hit him full in the face, and there was a loud pop and a flash of light, and he tumbled partway down the stairs and stopped himself by clinging to the rickety banister.

The strange air came at him in waves, puffing him up and then suffocating him. He pulled himself to his feet, stood on the stairs, and looked down to see a fire pouring from the earth. Out of the fire strode the dark figure of the creepy hotel owner, face covered in soot, thin hair singed and smoking around his head. "This is not where you belong," the hotel owner said. And he started up the stairway toward Dewey.

Dewey's aim wasn't good—no doubt Hector Jones, who'd had training from his dad, would have done better—but he squinted through one eye and raised the Winchester etc. etc. to his shoulder, pulled the trigger, and hit his target in the left ear.

"Goddamn," the hotel owner said, reeling back down the stairs and holding his blistered hand against his head. "Goddamn it."

Dewey bolted back up the stairs and out into the cold again, making sure the door was closed behind him, and he staggered as fast as he could through the snow. Surprisingly, in such a short time, the sky had begun to lighten, and as Dewey neared the corner of the alleyway, he hoped to God that Hugh and Lorraine would be opening the diner soon. But when he turned the corner and stood before the hotel in the faint morning light, he saw that the building was burning, and he felt his skin begin to crackle—not like fire, but like electricity, like ice, like the last moment before something shatters.

42

He thought they had come down behind him from the bar, chasing him, and he had lost them or thought he had by going through one of the side doors that led into the basement of another establishment, but there had been, embarrassingly enough, an old man standing in a corner in the dark, talking to an imaginary woman he called Margaret, and he had apologized for intruding on someone else's fantasy, and he had gone back out into the maze to find that no one was there, no one was after him.

There were passages everywhere underground, doors everywhere, doors connecting buildings to other buildings and doors that opened onto empty rooms and doors that opened only onto other doors, and very soon he was lost again, and he began to hear the voices talking to him, a stream of whispers flowing by in the air, the owners of the voices so close it seemed that they might have been behind a curtain, just out of reach. *I'm not happy anymore,* one voice said, *I try to be happy but the day passes by and then it's over and there's not one moment when I was happy.* And another voice spoke over the top of it in the same low whisper: *I'll kill you I swear I will, don't you ever touch her again I'll kill you* and then *Yesterday was sunny isn't it pretty when the sun shines why can't the sun shine you fucking whore my God your heartbeat I can hear your heartbeat no more tomorrow I loved you I always loved you I swear if you say* *that one more time at night we could see fireflies high in the trees,* the voices merging into a chorus, some plaint etched for eternity in the ether. And then the dreams started to go behind his eyes, the memories *in the dusty light there in the lobby with the gun at his head got* *to stop it if you want to stop it you have to stop him it's him that causes* *everything pull the trigger, his hands up in the air with blood on them* *asking why and listening to a sound outside a room, raising his finger to* *his lips—Shhh! Goodbye—going silently down a hall and in a chair* *watching TV but so much pain the roses out the window and the hospi-* *tal where his wife who looked like Julia just like Julia held a baby in her* *arms, mother baby both asleep while he stood there breathing watch-* *ing the baby breathe its hard jerky breaths its tiny red fist on his wife's* *skin at her throat the narrow pathway down through the sycamores the* *rainbow in the lane the wet cobblestones the church bells in the late af-* *ternoon jumping from the bridge, so high the bridge in the moonlight* *watching the water come the dark water there in the hotel room with* *the smoke seeping through the floorboards where the woman slipped off* *her silver shoe.*

When he came around enough to remember who he was, and he found himself lying on the cold ground in a damp place that felt far away from everything, staring up at a network of dripping pipes, it occurred to him that by coming down here he'd done exactly what they wanted him to do—the bartender giving him beers on Stephanie's tab, waiting for those guys to show up so he could lock the door. What a bunch of bullshit. He was lost now for good. He would never get out of here, at least not with his sanity intact.

He rolled over and got to his knees and saw a pair of blue-jeaned legs standing at the bottom of a stairway. He raised himself up to see a dark-skinned kid with dark hair, about Dewey's age, standing there silently with no expression on his face. There was something wrong with him, something other than the vacant look, something Robbie couldn't quite put his finger on until he realized that he could see the stairs behind the kid, *through* the kid, and then the kid turned—was he motioning to Robbie, waving his hand?—and went up the stairs.

Then there was a rush of air like a window suddenly thrown open, followed by a sound so shockingly loud that it filled the air entirely, to the exclusion of everything else, or there was the inverse, all the sound sucked away into a vacuum so that you couldn't hear anything at all. Then everything rumbled around him and the pipes clanked overhead and he moved in the direction the boy had gone, up the stairs.

The air had grown hot and damp and the sweat poured from him almost as if he were in the process of drying out, coming down after a binge, and his hands shook the same way. He found himself climbing a rickety set of steps and he emerged into what appeared to be the hotel kitchen. There was a sharp sulfur smell and the air was filled with smoke.

He would think for a long time afterward of his strange passage from the kitchen to room 306, and though he could never adequately explain it to himself he could never quite dismiss it from his memory either. He made his way through a giant ballroom with floor-to-ceiling windows, the glass still perfectly intact, the floors polished to a high shine, and on to a lobby that was utterly different from the one he had seen before, this one perfectly restored, the huge chandelier throwing spears of light to the far reaches of the room. The smoke grew thicker as he went, a strange yellowish smoke seeping up through the heating ducts and the floorboards, and he heard the sound of fire but could not yet see any flames, though it continued to get hotter. All the while as his heart raced and his hands tingled and he told himself he was an idiot for returning to this place, the parade of dreams or memories continued, though now they were his own memories and not someone else's—the voices of his mother and father, an argument he actually recalled them having when he was little, about a play at the theater, his mother wanted to go but his father refused, and he remembered thinking, at the time, that it was the stupidest argument in the history of the world. Now it was pleasing to hear those familiar voices and remember himself as a child. Middle school basketball practice, field trip to the Space Needle, he and his friends at Volunteer Park throwing pinecones at cars, sneaking shots of bourbon from the bottle his mother kept under the sink, a dirty Pioneer Square bar where he used to hang out, sitting on a barstool with a guy named Corey who would sell him meth and Darvocets—that was how he had spent his time, how he had spent his life.

And then, as happened often in his dreams, he was flying. He was flying up the stairs, knowing where he was going, where the room was, the one where he'd found Julia, weird motes floating in his vision, and from somewhere behind his sight came an exodus of people, the hotel guests, men with bushy beards racing down the stairs in nightshirts, holding the hands of women with braided hair and long white gowns, making frantic gestures, silently fleeing, and then he was up the stairs and rushing down the hallway toward the flames, the smoke almost thick enough to obscure Julia, whose eyes met his in a way that said she knew what he knew, or wondered what he wondered, but the only thing that mattered now was that she believed in him and could rely on him to do what she needed him to do. Then she backed against the wall opposite the room, staring at the door, and he could see right through her, as if she were only a thin transparency. Someone banged on the door from inside the room, coughing and shouting, the voices of a man and a woman, and still somewhere behind it all this memory: five or six years old and amped up for the arrival of his beloved older brother home from college on some holiday, his body almost vibrating with anticipation, so that he could do nothing besides what he always did, run from room to room shouting, to his father's consternation, *Tony, oh Tony, oh Tony, oh Tony, oh Tony.* The name stuck. His brother, Tonio. This was the best memory of all.

43

I thought I might find you here," Miss Blanchard said.

The drawing room had emptied out and he was left alone smoking a cigar and wondering where his wife had gone off to. He had seen her more than an hour earlier walking away with Miss Blanchard, and he had thought of little else since, though a senator from Boise had engaged him in an endless conversation on the question of statehood and the realignment of territorial boundaries.

"Were you looking for me?" he asked her.

"As a matter of fact, I was," she said, and sat down close to him on the divan. "I have news of your wife."

"Yes?" he asked, a familiar unease setting in.

Miss Blanchard smiled demurely. "She was feeling faint." Mr. Addison raised an arm as if this motion somehow implied his intention to stand. He was feeling rather faint and weary himself by now. It had been a long evening. "She is apparently not used to strong drink, even in small amounts."

"That's probably true," he said. He couldn't work up much interest in the subject suddenly.

"I put her to bed in my room," Miss Blanchard said, as if that ended all possible discussion of the matter. "She'll be fine there until morning, but she did ask me to procure certain…*feminine* items from among her toiletries."

"Tell me what they are, then, and I'll bring them to you."

Miss Blanchard said nothing but continued to smile politely, perhaps with a trace of mischief, it was hard for Mr. Addison to tell at this advanced stage of the game. He might have been intrigued by Miss Blanchard's attentions earlier, but now he simply wanted to lie down under the fresh linen sheets Tiffany had supplied in all the bedrooms.

"Come with me," he said. "And thank you for your interest in my wife's welfare." He thought he saw Miss Blanchard's eyes flash.

Up the green-carpeted stairway they went, Miss Blanchard leading the way. He glanced around the elegant lobby, the chandelier still blazing away even in the absence of guests or staff or owner, throwing its gaudy light into the surrounding darkness, a sign of all the things to come in this rugged place he had made his home. This hotel, this emblem of progress, would still be here in a hundred, in two hundred years. He took a measure of pride in it, as if it were his own accomplishment. He had a vision of himself as a man who inhabited a particular moment, who performed his work, whether big or small, while the world moved on. Local industry was already expanding. Not everything was mining anymore. There were already logging operations tearing down the timber on the hills.

When they reached the door to room 306, he realized that he did not have a key. He had given it to his wife to keep in the pocket of her dress. But the door opened at the light touch of Miss Blanchard's fingers, swinging inward with the slightest creak. She entered the room smoothly in her long gown, pulling up the train behind her with her soft white hand. She was, he realized, the perfect complement to the surroundings—impressive but not quite real. He stepped through the doorway into the room, and Miss

Blanchard backed against the door until he heard it shut with a tiny click.

There was no mention of the items they were sent to retrieve. As Miss Blanchard came toward him, he stared into her eyes, those beautiful cold blue eyes that were partly responsible for her stature in the world, haunted now with a kind of solemnity or regret, and he felt a corresponding regret in himself. This was not his wife. And yet she came into his arms in a way that seemed old and familiar, so old that he felt himself sagging on his own frame, a shored up collection of skin and bones and nothing more, and there was nothing to think about and nothing to feel as she kissed him lightly on the lips and they closed their eyes. From somewhere far below, there came a rush of warm air and a distant rumble, but it was not worth mentioning here in this room, here with his old friend Rose, his fellow captive to the same ancient mistake, the one they had made together so long ago. He opened his eyes for a moment and, looking down at the floor, noticed the broken, scattered pieces of the snow globe he'd turned in his hand earlier, just before he saw the boy out the window.

"Here we are again," Rose whispered, close to his ear, her voice thick with sorrow but also tenderness, and yes, he told her, they were here, and he loosened the dress from her shoulders, taking up once more the rhythm of this slow, sad dance, the only one he knew.

44

She had been a young wife, vulnerable, prey to so many misunderstandings. Married out of a perceived necessity, and not even her own, separated somewhat cruelly from parents who, perhaps, hadn't loved her as much as she thought they did, she had been whisked out of her old life into a new one far away, a coarser life with coarser people. However accommodating, however friendly, her new surroundings were still much different and less · polite than she had supposed they might be. And her husband was a man she barely knew — on some deep level that expressed her resentment or wounded pride, she hadn't wanted to know him, or, more precisely, maybe, to let him know her.

All these things she understood now, standing with her back against the wall across from room 306, listening to the sounds of lovemaking coming through the door (thinking at first that she was listening to herself, then clearly hearing Rose Blanchard's silvery voice), followed by the sounds of her husband's and Rose Blanchard's growing alarm — at the heat, at the smoke, at the flames that curled through the walls now at the far end of the corridor. She understood all these things and much more. She and her family had been blown off course by a snowstorm, seemingly, and they had come to this little out-of-the-way town in a seemingly innocent fashion, but it hadn't been innocent, and it hadn't been any sort of accident. She had, in a sense, she and Tonio, been here the whole time, ever since that bus ride long ago in California, during which they thought—each of them, supposedly alone in their own worlds, unaware, when really their lives were connected from a long, long time before, from the very beginning—that they were strangers, that they were two people who shared a "spark" of some sort, maybe, mistaking their ages-old familiarity for the early seed of a physical attraction. It had been much more than that, she knew now.

And so here she was in the midst of the fire and smoke but not experiencing it at all, not in the way those poor people behind the door were experiencing it—the coughing, the onset of fear, now the first tentative poundings on the door, almost as if their cries for help were a source of embarrassment, or, more likely, given the circumstances, an admission of guilt—removed from this particular moment in time and space and somehow hovering beyond time and space, in some separate realm of consciousness that allowed for the coexistence of direct experience and memory, reality and dream, where everything came together and broke apart, where everything was a thing and its own shadow, passing silently down a hall. Everything came to this point, everyone would—it was just that it was *her* time now, not someone else's.

Mr. Tiffany had told her that she was the one who made decisions. And she could see what her decision entailed, and she thought she knew the terms. She had been a young wife, there had been a party, the opening of the new hotel. She had enjoyed herself, she had made a friend in Miss Blanchard, she had let her habitual defenses down, and she had been betrayed, not so much by Miss Blanchard, who, it turned out, was never really a friend to begin with, but by this new husband of hers, a man whom, if she had not loved him, not yet, she had most certainly trusted. She had been pregnant with his child. She had awoken in a strange place and come back to her room in the hotel, wanting only to go to sleep, maybe wanting, for the first time in her young and awkward marriage, to take some comfort in her husband's company, to trust herself, at the end of this strange evening, to his care, and instead she had found this—her husband and Rose Blanchard. And now, having observed her own story through this lens of lifetimes, of moments that existed simultaneously, she could even understand and forgive his part in it—he was as lonely as she was, as confused, as disappointed in the unfulfilled possibilities of his love and his passion. He was, after all, still a young man.

But the decision—her decision *now*, not the one she had made the first time, back then—had nothing to do with forgiveness or redemption. It had to do with whether she would stay true to the past—even the horrible memories, the awful mistakes, the terribly regrettable decisions—or replace it with a softer version of itself, the smoothed-over past rearranged by hindsight, by what a better version of herself should have done or might have said. She had come all this way in space and time so that she would have the capacity to reverse this moment if she chose, remake the present out of the past or the past out of the present.

Robbie—who seemed magically to have arrived on the scene now, looking at her for a moment with bewilderment and guilt and even a touching measure of trust before he commenced pounding on the door, calling out his brother's name, trying to crack the doorframe or knock down the door with his shoulder, all the while choking with the smoke and the heat and his effort—lacked the one piece of information that would have saved him the trouble of putting himself in peril, that would have let him know that this was *her* decision: in her pocket she had the key.

She had always had the key. She had it before, on the night of the hotel's opening, when Tiffany and the Harrington boy (sobbing uncontrollably the whole time) and a few other brave men tried to break down the door to save her husband and Rose Blanchard. She had stood there feeling a burning anger and jealousy, and she had pinched the key so hard in her pocket that it cramped her fingers, but she would not relent, and in the crucial moment when the men's bravery turned to fear, when their thoughts turned to self-preservation, she closed her fist tight around that key and allowed herself to be hurried down the stairs, and she stood outside in the dizzying snow flurries and watched the hotel burn. Many months later she had given birth to her child, but she had lived a solitary and bitter life.

Now she listened to her husband pleading behind that same door, listened to him beg for help, and she loved him, her husband, Anthony, Tonio, the father of Dewey, their child, and she squeezed the key in her hand. There was Robbie trying with all his might to knock down the door, no trace left of the rebellious, cynical younger brother, the wounded act he had put on all these years, and in this moment she saw what it was that she and Robbie had always sensed they shared between them—*he* was the one who would continue, on whom everything would depend from this day forward, and she had somehow known this from the first time she laid eyes on him, there out the window past his mother's rosebushes. He could never have come between her and Tonio, even though she had never quite been able to reach her husband, or to allow him to reach her, despite the love they had shared for their son, for the nucleus of their little family.

She squeezed the key and squeezed it, and at one point, finally, hearing her husband call her name in a thick voice full of emotion, she almost stepped forward—but she couldn't. She could use the key, she could change what had happened, the decision she had made so long ago, but she knew that, then, she would go on living that life, the life she could have lived with Mr. Addison in that far distant past but chose not to. She would be *in* that past with her husband and her unborn child, her life back then fully restored. And then what would happen to the life she carried in her mind now, the one that contained all these memories? What would happen to Tonio and Dewey and their home and their life in another place, so different and so far away in time that she would be incapable of even imagining it, of dreaming it in her sleep? Would Dewey even live if she, in this other time and this other place and this altered past in which she had used the key, opened the door, saved her husband, saved herself, couldn't even conceive of his existence? Could a child live if he had never been a thought, a dream, in his own mother's head? There was the fact of him, Dewey, there was the fact of him in her heart and in her mind, and she would not give up that fact, not for anything. And there was her husband, calling out from behind the door, and she could open the door, she could go to him, she could lead him down the stairs and outside into the snow, and they could see where that future, that long-ago future, might take them. But neither of them would know Dewey, love Dewey, *this* Dewey, the one they had, the one they had made and loved together. She knew her husband in this moment as well as she knew herself, and she knew that he, Tonio, would make the same decision. In this moment when she refused to save him, she was more loyal to his wishes than she ever had been.

She could barely see Robbie now through the smoke, even though he was right in front of her, but she could hear him gasping for breath and talking as best he could to his brother behind the door, telling him it was all right, telling him help was on the way, acknowledging his brother's feeble attempts to pound on the door, telling him, yes, keep trying, and she could hear him trying himself, rattling at the lock, pushing at the doorframe. She stepped forward and put her hand to Robbie's shoulder, but his shoulder wasn't there, or her hand wasn't there, and she sensed that he didn't need her anyway for what he had to do. He turned halfway, sweat dripping from his mop of hair, and he saw her, she knew he did, and she saw that he understood. He returned to his task, renewing his efforts more vigorously, ramming the door with whatever remained of his strength. Flames burst from a doorway farther down the hall, and the floorboards cracked and splintered. As she had done before, except alone this time, she made her way to the stairs and descended them, and as she faced the closed door at the hotel entrance, she knew this would not be the last time, that in some way she and Tonio would always be here, locked in the struggle with this memory.

And then she had opened the door, and after the smoke-filled corridors the snowy early-morning air was brilliantly light. There was a cold, crisp feeling to the world, and she stepped out into it, gingerly, careful of her footing, and when her eyes adjusted to the light she saw a crowd of people gathered round, and there in front, in the center, was Dewey. He was here, he was well, he looked so grown-up standing there in the snow, wearing the sweater she had always tried to get him to wear, and it made her smile to see him that way, the love of her life, her little man. She recognized the same thing she had seen before, the outlines of the man he would become in the features of the boy, the strength of character in the eyes that looked back at her. She had once believed in a kind of world spirit that guided and controlled things, that eventually would guide her path to the place where she was destined to arrive, but now she knew that there was no such thing, that it was only her, that she had always guided herself only by her own desire and that she had arrived here only by her own choices, and she could see in the square set of her son's stance all those future choices, that future life, resting on his shoulders, and she wanted to tell him. She started forward, but at that moment she felt a crushing brittleness inside her, the feel of ice compressing, and she knew what was happening then, with everything so cold, and she reached out her hand toward her son and saw, as she did so, that same hand disappearing, and with the last of her breath, seeing her voice come out in a cloud of white, she said to him even though she knew she shouldn't have, her heart in this last moment not able to let go of him, "You'll know I'm here. You'll dream of me."

45

He had fought through the mountainous snowdrifts to the front of the hotel, hoping to find Hugh and Lorraine and the warm light of the diner, but instead there was this cold, crackling feeling inside him, as if he had been frozen all the way through and was on the point of breaking apart, and now there were the smoke and the flames. His mother was in the hotel, he had seen her go in the door, and he would go in after her but he was frozen in place, this was the moment he had been afraid of, when he would drift into one of his states and never come back, where his own mind, the thing that made him who he was, Dewey, would be sucked back into the infinite and the universal, to be found somehow only at the center of the universe, part of the dark mass of the world, billions of years from now, millions of miles away, before everything exploded and died.

In some distant place in his consciousness he knew that the hotel was burning. It was like a movie that you barely paid attention to while you thought of something else, and it was surprising that the heat emanating from the building did nothing to warm him at his core, where he seemed to go on freezing, where his blood slowed and gelled, and if he breathed at all it was the light respiration of a hibernating animal. Even simple dreams of childhood things would not come to him and never would. He was beyond almost everything and the only thing in his mind, at the edge of his awareness, was a picture of Hector Jones as he had lain in the bed asleep, cold and vanishing.

And then, as if a curtain had been pushed aside to reveal a grand prize, or a priceless work of art, or something as simple as sunshine, his mother appeared in front of him, walking calmly from the hotel entrance as the flames roared behind her and the smoke poured into the sky. It was his mother the way he had always known her, not the ghostly presence of the past several days, but his real live mother coming to him, smiling at him in a way that only she could smile at him, in a way that only he could understand, because it was something that they had shared between them always, this special feeling, and he knew she was thinking what a treasure he was to her, how much she loved him, she didn't have to say a word and he would still know it forever. He wanted to go to her but still there was the feeling of ice inside him and cold shards prickled his face and his hands and he felt that he was dying, that he was right now going to disappear, but then his mother reached out to him, and in that same sad way it had happened before, his vision of her grew dim, and as she faded into the air he came back into himself, life returned to him, and he started toward her but she was gone, only those words she spoke to him—*Know I'm here, dream of me*—vibrating, rising into the cold winter sky and the falling snow.

He did not cry. He felt that he was done with crying for good. His mother, who liked to half believe horoscopes and fortunes, signs and projections, once told him that he was an "old soul," and he thought he knew what that meant now, if not why she had said it about him. He was only ten years old, but it seemed like he had lived a long, long time.

He stood in the snowy street and stared blankly at the space in front of him where his mother had been, and gradually he became